The Lion of Khum Jung

The Lion of Khum Jung

Ronald Bagliere

For my beautiful lady — Linda

Acknowledgments

I would like to thank those who have endured listening to my brainstorming over the last year. You were all my alter egos, keeping me pointed in the right direction. Special thanks go to my friend, Carolyn, who spent countless hours helping me see things from Sarah's point of view. I could not have done it without you! Also, to Martin who looks at the world from the inside out, and made me think of things I would not have imagined. To my Monday night critique group, The Syracuse Writer's Roundtable, who kept the pedal to the metal on me by demanding a new chapter every week. To my graphic designer, Kim, who keeps surprising me with images I hadn't considered, and last of all to my publisher, Next Chapter Publishing, who took a chance on me. I am forever grateful.

Prologue

Everest Base Camp – 1985

Frank ran into the Frontier Expedition Command tent and found Jack Trammel talking on the radio while the rest of his team crowded around him. When Frank stepped beside him, Jack glanced up from where he sat. The alarm in the expedition leader's deep brown eyes told all as the crackled voice came back over the two-way radio.

"We on way down, but he locking up. Can you radio Camp 4? See if Tar-Chin there? Over," the faint voice said.

"Will do, over," Jack replied. "Keep moving, over."

"Trying. Wind picking up, snow too, over."

Frank's eyes widened when he glanced at the large bulky laptop sitting amongst the strewn weather reports on the table. The data glaring back on the screen wasn't good: FL270, 290/80, MS48, valid at 10:15 GMT. That meant Jack's Sirdar Sherpa and his client were walking right into a goddamned blizzard. He tapped Jack's arm, pointed to the laptop and whispered, "When did these numbers come in?"

Jack nodded, put his hand over the microphone. "Fifteen minutes ago."

"Jesus," Frank muttered. The mountain had once again decided to have its own party while the rest of the world obeyed the weather forecasts. "What's their elevation?"

"8,400 meters," Jack replied, and gave Frank a knowing look. There was no way Pasang and the American with him were going to make it back to Camp 4 before the storm roared in. They were trapped. In fact, for those who had already made it back, it was going to be a hell of a ride.

Again, the Sherpa's voice came through the static. "Has Tar-chin made Camp 4 yet? Over."

Jack bit his lip and rubbed his grizzled face. Frank knew the expedition leader was in a tight spot. If Jack told Sherpa Tar-chin that Sherpa Pasang was in trouble and asking for him, the man would go without question. But how could he ask Tar-chin knowing there was barely a chance of success, let alone that it would likely cost the Sherpa his life?

Finally, Jack radioed back. "No response yet. How's your O2? Over."

A long silence passed and Frank worried for the worst. Finally, Pasang's voice came crackling back. "One hour on Steve's tank, maybe little more if I crank it back to one. But doubt he could stand it. I have four on mine. I could switch if need be. Over."

"Up to you Pasang, over," Jack said, as the crowd behind them in the Command Tent whispered back and forth.

Frank turned to look at those who'd gotten news of the unfolding drama on the mountain. Word always traveled quickly in the climbing community when lives were at stake. It was the one time when the guarded members of Base Camp came together; working tirelessly to figure out a way to bring men back alive. But the stone-cold fact was that there was little anyone could do when the mountain decided to roar, and that was what it was doing right now.

Jack Trammel's job was keeping Pasang's spirits alive and strong, and he was trying every trick in the book. Whether Pasang knew his expedition leader was lying to him about Tar-chin being at Camp 4 was anyone's guess, but it was a fair bet Pasang knew Jack wasn't being straight with him. Every climber knew it was whatever kept you going that mattered, and if you had to be lied to, then so be it. As long as you kept moving, that was the only thing that mattered. Freeze up and stop thinking and you die, simple as that.

The minutes turned into an hour and the hour turned into two then three, and as the minutes slid by, Pasang's voice came back less and less over the radio. The end had come for Pasang and the American, or it was looming close and it was crushing Frank's hopes. The last time he'd heard Pasang's reedy voice, it was obvious they weren't going to make it down to Camp 4 where the wind was barreling across the slopes and creating wind-chills of minus sixty-five and lower.

Frank plopped down in the corner of the command tent brooding and checked in with Camp 4 at Jack's request to keep track of their situation. He knew Jack had given him the task to take his mind off the tragedy going on high above. But it wasn't working. All Frank could think about was Pasang lying in the snow and fighting for his last breath. He closed his eyes, saw the short, stout, round face of the Sherpa smiling back at him, and felt his lip quiver.

Someone came around with mugs of warm Mango juice and Masala tea. Frank waved them off when they came to him. He couldn't eat or drink knowing Pasang was dying in a futile attempt to drag a man off the mountain who hadn't listened to reason.

Moreover, Frank was angry Pasang had let the American manipulate him and doubly frustrated that he couldn't do a damn thing about it.

As he sat listening to the wind lash the Command tent's nylon skin beside him, he thought of Pasang's mother, Nuri. It would fall on him to tell her Pasang wasn't coming back. The thought of it was more than he could handle. His throat knotted as he balled his hand into a fist. *If I ever lead an expedition, I'll make sure this never happens again. Any asshole that disobeys my Sirdar's advice is on his own!*

* * *

Los Angeles, California – 1985

Sarah popped a bagel in her toaster and turned to the portable TV sitting on the kitchen countertop to listen to the morning news. As she watched the tall, suited man give his report, she thought about her husband over in Nepal. He should have been back at Everest Base Camp from the climb two days ago, but as of yet, she had heard nothing from him. She tried to put the growing ominous concern out of her mind as her son, Gregory, blew raspberries in his high chair. Turning to him, she scooped a mouthful of cereal into his Bugs Bunny spoon and steered it toward his open mouth. At eighteen months old, he already had his father's deep blue eyes.

"Daddy should be on back down from the top of the world right now," Sarah said as he kicked his pudgy legs back and forth. She wiped his chin and forced a smile. "How exciting is that?"

Gregory gummed his cereal, bunched his little round face into a smile and pounded his hands on the highchair tray. Sarah smiled at her happy and animated child. He was the one constant in her life since Steven left for the mountain two months ago, and he got her through each day. But she also discovered, quite unexpectedly, that being on her own gave her a strength she'd never experienced and she liked it. Now, if she could only balance it with Steven's sure-mindedness and quick decision-making.

Today, she had a field trip lined up for her sixth grade students at Lincoln Elementary. Steven had suggested the idea of taking her class to the zoo before he left for Nepal. Said it would be a nice way to say good-bye to the kids she had watched grow into intelligent, curious, and pretentious youngsters. But behind his suggestion was another motive; to give her something to plan and thus distract her from worrying about him.

She looked up at the kitchen clock over the window. It was going on 6:00 AM. Her girlfriend and classroom aide, Roxanne, would be over to pick Gregory and her up in fifteen minutes. After dropping Gregory off at day care, they'd abandon their usual morning walk and head straight to work. Thirty minutes later, she was tapping her fingers on the kitchen counter while peering out the window. "Where are you, Rox? Of all days to be late, this isn't one of them." She debated if she should pick up the phone and call her. As she went for the receiver, it rang out.

"Hey, where are you?"

"Excuse me," said a man's voice.

Sarah took a deep breath and stared up at the ceiling, feeling embarrassed. "Oh, I'm sorry. I was thinking you were someone else."

"No problem Ma'am. My name is Jack Trammel. Is Sarah Madden there?"

"This is she."

There was a slight pause on the other end and Sarah wondered if he had hung up. "Sarah, I'm the Everest Expedition leader from Frontier Expeditions."

Finally! Sarah thought, feeling relieved. She pushed a lock of her dark brown hair over her ear. "Oh, yes, I've been waiting for your call. Is my husband there? Can I speak to him?"

"Mrs. Madden ... um, there's been an accident on the mountain. I ... I wish there was an easier way to say this, but your husband, he's ... well ... he didn't make it."

Sarah blinked, trying to comprehend what the man had just told her. Suddenly, the room grew very small around her and she couldn't feel the floor beneath her feet.

"Mrs. Madden? You there?"

Sarah switched hands holding the receiver and cleared her throat. "Um …Yes."

There was another pause on the other end. "I'm so very sorry."

"Ummm, can you repeat what you just said, please? I'm afraid I didn't hear you."

Jack's shaky voice came back. "There was a sudden storm no one could predict. Your husband … he got caught in it. I'm so, so sorry. I waited to call you until I was absolutely sure there was no chance he was —. Ummm, is there anything —"

Sarah dropped the receiver and felt her body slide down the cabinet and onto the floor. This was not happening. Steven told her he was going to be just fine. People climbed the mountain all the time. He was with the best expedition company in the world, with all the safety precautions money could buy. But he was — she couldn't say the word.

A car pulled into her driveway as Gregory started to fuss in his carrier. A horn blew, the TV babbled and the world went dark.

Chapter 1

Present Day — Kathmandu International Airport, Nepal

Sarah glanced at her son, Greg, sitting next to her reading his mountaineering magazine. He hadn't said but a dozen words to her since leaving Hong Kong. At length, she thought about the heated exchange they'd had just before boarding the plane. She had tried to see it his way and had agreed reluctantly to stay in Kathmandu while he was on the mountain, but in the long run, she just couldn't do it. Why couldn't he understand how she felt? She bit her lip as her gaze drifted to the window overlooking the darkened hills passing below.

The airliner banked left and started its descent to Kathmandu International Airport. As it did, she wondered what it was that drew men to risk their lives on such nonsense. Did they have some sort of death wish? Her husband had said it was the challenge of testing himself to find out what he was made of. Well, he found out all right. It had cost him his life. And more than that, it had left her alone to raise a son who deserved a father.

She took a deep breath, unable to endure her son's silence another minute. "I'm sorry. Are you going to be mad at me forever?"

"I'm not mad," he said, but his tone was brittle and sharp.

Sarah felt her body tighten. "Then what? You've been prickly since we left Hong Kong," she said, eyeing him pointedly.

Greg set his magazine down and looked up. "I just can't understand why you called Kincaid. We agreed you'd stay in Kathmandu!" he shot back, raising his voice.

"I know, but I can't do it," Sarah said, glancing at a man staring back at them.

Greg gritted his teeth and lowered his voice. "You're gonna cost me my shot at this, you know," he replied, holding her with a chilly gaze.

Sarah stared back into her son's piercing blue eyes. "I don't see how my being there is going to cost you your one shot."

"You'll be a distraction I don't need. Why can't you understand that?"

"A distraction? I'm coming to support you," Sarah said, though in truth she rather discourage him and be done with this whole insane odyssey.

"Support me from Kathmandu then," Greg replied. "I'm sure Kincaid will refund your money."

"Money has nothing to do with it and you know it," Sarah said. "I've lost too much to this damned mountain, and I'll be damned if I'm going to sit in some hotel room waiting to —"

"Nothing's going to happen," Greg interjected. "Look, mountaineering has come a long way since Dad's accident."

"You sound just like your father," Sarah volleyed back louder than she intended. Greg stiffened his jaw. "Is that so?"

"Yes." She paused, looking for a verbal weapon to arrest him with. But she knew there was no weapon capable of piercing his Teflon resolve to go forward with the climb. Finally, she sighed and lowered her voice. "This isn't just any mountain. This mountain kills people."

"It does if you don't know what you're doing," Greg said. "It's why I've been training for over a year."

"You can't train for the weather."

"It was a freak storm that killed Dad," Greg countered emphatically. "They have better equipment now. Hell, they can predict a dusting of snow three days out with ninety-five percent accuracy."

"Right, but it's that five percent that scares the hell out of me," Sarah said, looking away toward the cabin window.

Greg was quiet for a long time. Finally, he said, "You worry too much. Kincaid's the best. He's never lost anyone on the mountain. The guy doesn't take chances."

"Worry too much?" Sarah fired back. It was a standard comment Steven had used more than once with her. She didn't like being patronized then, and she didn't like it now, especially coming from her son. "Excuse me if I care about what happens to you!"

Greg pressed his lips together and softened his furrowed brow. "I'm sorry. I know you care."

"Then why are you fighting me on this? The least you can do is accept my decision. I haven't asked for much," Sarah said pointedly. When Greg looked away, she shook her head. How could she get through to him? Part of it had to do with his fragile male ego. At length, she cleared her throat. "I won't embarrass you."

She heard him laugh. "I'm not worried about that. I worry about you getting sick, and like I keep telling you, I don't need that kind of distraction." He was quiet a moment, then said, "I know you want to be there, but this is personal to me. I need … to do this … alone."

"I understand that," Sarah answered, turning back to him. "But —"

"No, you don't," Greg said. He tightened his jaw. "If you did, you wouldn't have booked yourself with the expedition without talking to me first. That was wrong and you know it."

The reply stung and Sarah felt her throat tighten. Why couldn't he understand how his quest to conquer the monster was killing her? She bit her lip. "Yes, I know. I'm sorry. That was wrong."

"Yes, it was," Greg answered.

Sarah was quiet a long time. Finally, she said, "I did it because I love you."

"If you love me then stay in Kathmandu," Greg muttered.

Sarah studied his imploring expression, loving him so much she could barely breathe. But staying in Kathmandu was not an option. She turned toward the window, unable to bear his forthcoming frown, and said, "I'm sorry, I can't."

* * *

Thirty minutes later, they walked out of the old two-story masonry terminal into the warm night air. Across the two-lane service drive, a mob of eager men were waiting to help anyone emerging through the doors for a hefty tip. Sarah took a deep breath, tightened her grip on her luggage, and followed Greg across the broken macadam drive to a tall Nepalese man holding a cardboard sign scribbled with the words, 'Khum Jung Mountaineering'.

Well, so much for professional marketing, Sarah thought as Greg pushed the cart carrying their mountain of gear. When they came to him, the man smiled.

"Namaste! You are Mr. Madden?" he said, offering a toothy smile.

"Yes," Greg said. "Where to?"

The man directed them to a break in the long, roped off line between the emerging travelers and the crowd. Parked a hundred feet ahead was a Ford mini-van with the Khum Jung Mountaineering logo on it. As they strode toward it, several men in the crowd gathered behind them trying to vie for an opportunity to be of assistance.

The hopeful contingent was cut short though when a tall, broad-shouldered man hopped out of the mini-van's side door. "We'll take it from here, gentlemen," the man said, shooing them off.

Sarah casually glanced at the man's shoulder length salt and pepper hair that was tied back into a ponytail. Was he just another cog in the Khum Jung Mountaineering machine or was he was one of the guides? He appeared to be the latter.

He broke into a broad smile. "Namaste! Frank Kincaid here. Let me get that for you," he said, taking her bag.

"Thank you," Sarah replied, surprised. She never expected the renowned Mr. Kincaid, whom her son bragged about so much, to meet them personally.

The man turned to her son. "You must be Greg. And you would be Sarah, I assume?" he said, glancing back at her.

"That would be correct," Sarah answered. Though his glance had been fleeting, she felt judgment in it.

"Well then, welcome to Nepal," Frank replied, opening the hatchback and tossing her bag in. "How was your flight?"

"Long," Greg said.

"I bet," Frank replied, closing the van door. "Why don't you both get inside while I get your gear stowed away up top?"

* * *

As they drove through a maze of narrow, dark streets, Sarah listened to Greg pepper Frank with questions about the mountain, and the prognosis of the Ice Fall region. Last year, the warm weather in the perilous pass had shut down all of the expeditions from attempting a summit. It had been the first time since the commercial climbing of the mountain began, and it had cost those who'd ponied up enormous amounts of their own money dearly. Others, who were sponsored, suffered losses as well.

Sarah stared off through the window at the passing street level shops. Although her son was sponsored, he still had plenty of 'skin in the game' as he liked to call it; she wouldn't mind a repeat of last year's ditched attempt. Having heard enough talk about the mountain for the night, she spoke up. "So, Mr. Kincaid, how long have you lived in Nepal?"

Frank turned around in the front seat and smiled at her. "Call me Frank … please. To answer your question, I guess around forty years. My Pop moved us here when I was just into my tweens."

"And prior to that?" Sarah said.

"Luanda."

"Where's that?" Greg said.

"Angola, Africa," Frank replied.

Sarah was astonished. She never would have guessed he came from that part of the world. "Why'd you leave?"

"Civil war."

"Oh. So, what made you choose Nepal?" Sarah asked, a little curious, but mostly to keep the conversation from reverting back to Everest.

The driver hit the horn and swerved to avoid a motorbike barreling past them. Frank diverted his attention to the road in front of them then turned back to her. "My father had friends here." He fixed her with an enigmatic gaze that put her on guard, as if he already knew her. She smiled, trying to shake the feeling, and said, "So, you live in Kathmandu, I take it?"

"Oh, no. Up in the mountains." He turned to Greg. "When's your O2 supposed to arrive?"

Greg pulled a stick of gum out of his pocket and popped it in his mouth. "Wednesday."

"Got it from POISK, right?"

Greg nodded. "Not cheap either."

"You don't want cheap up there, believe me," Frank said. "How many bottles?"

"Thirty."

"Good," Frank said. He pulled a small pad out of the glove compartment along with a pencil. "Got the flight number?"

Greg dug into his knap-sack and pulled a folder out. As he went through it, Sarah said, "Any idea how much longer to the hotel?"

"Actually, we're here right now," Frank said as the van came to a halt.

As they started backing down an alleyway, Sarah looked around her. Seeing only broken down brick buildings around her, she wondered what kind of hotel it was that Mr. Kincaid had set them up with. It wasn't like she hadn't stayed in one star hotels before, but the building they were headed for right now appeared as though it was ready for the wrecking ball. In fact, from what she had seen so far, the whole city looked like it was ready for one. She could only imagine what the light of day would reveal.

Greg handed Frank the flight itinerary for the oxygen delivery as the van stopped. After Frank wrote it down, he handed it back and opened the door, letting Sarah out with Greg following close behind. Trudging into a small closed-in lobby, Sarah felt her stomach knot up. It was shabbily furnished and there was a foul pungent odor in the air she couldn't quite place. There were a lot of things she could tolerate, but a flophouse wasn't one of them.

She turned to Greg. "You've got to be kidding."

Greg shrugged.

Suddenly Frank was behind them. After chatting in Nepalese with the hotel receptionist, he said, "You should be all set."

Sarah stared back at him, wondering if the man had lost his mind. "Mr. Kincaid, this is not a hotel!"

Frank studied her a moment as the receptionist handed him a pair of room keys. For a minute, she thought he was going to read her the riot act, but he nodded toward the front door and said, "Looks are deceiving in this city. Follow me."

He led her around back into a softly lit courtyard dotted with flowering trees and shrubs. Scattered amongst them were wrought iron tables and chairs. Sarah looked up at the enclosing verandas draped with leafy vines and then glanced down to one of the lower windows that peered into an occupied room with drawn back curtains. Inside was a freshly made bed and on it was a colorful quilt. Beyond the bed, she saw freshly painted pastel walls, dotted with a lovely painting of the mountains. Finally, she said, "Well, I guess I stand corrected."

Frank eyed her impassively. "Right. And don't get too comfy here. It's the best you'll see for quite some time." He turned to Greg. "I put the rest of your gear in storage 'til our flight to Lukla. Breakfast is at six over there under the veranda by the stairway. Just tell the server you're with KJM and go help yourself. We'll meet here in the courtyard afterward; say around eight for introductions and a brief chat on how things are going to go for the next few weeks until we get to Base Camp."

He gave Sarah one last long look then said, "'Night now."

Sarah watched him walk back the way they came in as the bellhop brought their luggage around. As Frank faded into the dark shadows of the passageway, she wasn't convinced she should trust him with her son's life. But there was little she could do about it for the time being.

Chapter 2

Frank opened the door to his hotel room and hit the switch. He hadn't known what to expect when he finally met the Widow and her son, other than he had been determined not to like them anymore than was necessary. Yes, the tragedy on Everest involving Steven Madden had happened a long time ago, and yes, Frank had told himself he had gotten over it, but that didn't mean he'd forgotten it either. Added to that was the fact that the Widow and her son were Americans; expecting folks to lay down the red carpet for them. He snorted. They'd soon find out things didn't quite work that way on the mountain. Frank Kincaid was not a cruise director nor did he concern himself with being their personal valet.

He cleared a pile of regulatory expedition documents from his bed and plopped them on the dresser. Why hadn't he told his front office to call the son back and cancel the American's expedition reservation when he found out about it? And letting the mother tag along and live with them at Base Camp? Sure, the extra $10,000 from her would help in financing the classroom addition he was building with the support of the Hillary Trust in Khum Jung; and yes, he'd occasionally allowed family members to be present during expeditions. But that was generally reserved for repeat clients with enthusiastic loved ones. Greg Madden and his mother were neither of those things.

Was the need to see the son and widow of the man who was responsible for killing his best friend so long ago morbid curiosity or was it that he wanted vengeance? Frank refused to believe it was the latter because it would mean he was vindictive and self-serving. Yet, with every day leading up to this night, the anger he'd worked so hard to repress over the years had grown exponentially.

He took a long look at himself in the dresser mirror as he unbuttoned his shirt. What were the chances he'd be guiding the son of the man who'd brought so much pain to him and those he cared about? Then again, Frank had learned that karma had a way of reconciling itself. He tossed his shirt over his backpack and sat on the bed, pulling his legs into a lotus position. Lying on his pillow beside him was his satchel. In it, was a tattered book of Buddhist stories he'd put down on paper over the years. He pulled it out, leafed through it, and thought of what Ang Tashi-ring would say. The answer the old Buddhist lama would give him back, he already knew; '... what lesson are you about to learn? And are you ready to hear it?'

Frank peered out the window across the courtyard toward the Widow's room. He knew anger was a ghost, an irrational emotion that could control his life if he let it. He took several deep measured breaths to take back control of the angst that was twisting his stomach into knots. As he did so, he realized he had a mountain of his own to climb. It was a different kind of mountain; yet no less dangerous than the one awaiting the young American client. At length, he looked down at the book in his hands, drank in the words on the page and read; 'If you light a lamp for somebody, it will also brighten your own path'.

He sighed.

* * *

The next morning, Frank woke early from a dreamless sleep. He quickly showered and went to work reviewing the expedition climbing permits and the shipping paperwork for the cargo and equipment. On top of the pile were copies of the various alpine clubs attesting to his clients' climbing abilities. He glanced at them one more time, and seeing the American's half way down, pulled it out, and looked it over. Having summited the Matterhorn by way of the south face, along with Denali, Greg Madden was no tenderfoot. But that didn't mean he wasn't reckless either. When pushing for a summit, people often took ill-advised chances. Frank would have none of that on Everest.

Next, he took one last glance at the insurance policies for his Sherpas along with the required Ice Fall and ground transportation fees. Once he was satisfied that all the 't's were crossed and 'i's were dotted, he picked up his cell phone, and called his local rep, Daku, to give him flight numbers and arrival times for client oxygen. Finally, last but not least, he pulled out his schedule to go over the day's tasks.

First thing would be a short briefing with his clients after breakfast to go over upcoming details and to make introductions. Afterward, he would take them to the Nepalese Trekking Ministry to file essential paperwork and pay the fees, along with having a brief meeting. From there, it would be onto another meeting to provide information for the mountaineering historical records.

The afternoon would then be devoted to confirming flights to Lukla and overnight accommodations in Namche and Tengboche. In between these last minute details was a phone call to the Inland Revenue Department (IRD) over back taxes they were insisting he owed, even though he had receipts to prove otherwise. Someone there had it in for him, and he had a good idea who was behind it. The problem was, his documentation of proving he paid the taxes would be swept under the proverbial rug because in this instance, it wasn't about the money; it was about shutting him down and settling a score. That it was jeopardizing his support of the school in Khum Jung pissed him off even more.

He clenched his fist and tried to put the issue with taxes behind him for the moment. It was going to be a long day for sure, so he'd best get to it. He threw his paperwork into his satchel, stepped into his sandals, and went out of his room into the warmth of the early morning sunshine that was pouring down into the courtyard. As he strode down an open-air stairway, he saw Toby and Jakob heading out into the courtyard with their breakfasts.

The Austrian clients had arrived the day before yesterday along with the Aussie. The two Italians, an Irishman, and two Frenchmen came in on Monday. The Widow and her son that he had picked up last night rounded out the climbing permit to nine. Frank preferred small numbers in his expeditions as opposed to one of the larger companies on the mountain. Besides, having smaller numbers allowed him to get to know folks better going up the mountain. That, and it made it manageable for his Sherpa guides. Two or three clients per team were more than enough for one guide to handle.

As he stepped off the last stair tread, he was greeted by his assistant, Sangye, a short, young, wiry bronze-skinned man with a bright smile and friendly brown eyes.

Frank put his arm over the man's shoulder and gave him a good squeeze. "Sleep well?"

"I did, and you?" Sangye replied as they walked in lockstep toward the dining room.

"I'm still kicking, so I guess so," Frank quipped. He withdrew his arm from Sangye's shoulder and dug his cell phone out. As he checked his text messages, he added, "You get ahold of Guna?"

"Yes, he is bringing the van around just now and will park it outside the lobby," Sangye answered.

"Good," Frank replied. He slipped his cell phone back into his pocket and eyed the two Austrians, who were just outside of the dining room sitting in the shade of an overhanging veranda. By the look of their breakfast plates, Frank wondered if there was anything left at the buffet.

Tapping Sangye on the arm, he said, "You go on in. I'm going to go have a chat with the boys over there." Walking over to them, he donned a smile. "Namaste."

The men looked up as Frank snatched a chair from a nearby table. "Good morning," Jakob replied in a thick Austrian accent.

Frank flipped the chair around so the back of it was against his chest and straddled it. "You're enjoying breakfast, I see."

Toby shoveled a fork full of fried potatoes into his mouth, and nodded. Jakob said, "It's not bad. Could use a little more seasoning."

Frank appraised the large fair-haired men. They were in marvelous shape, but being large and muscular wasn't necessarily a good thing for where they were going. "You might want to ease up on the chow. The mountain will make you pay for it."

Both men eyed him quizzically then glanced down at their plates. Jakob set his fork down and leveled a pointed gaze at Frank. "It has never been a problem before."

"Except neither of you have been higher than 6,500 meters. Normally, calorie intake is a good thing up on the mountain because your body works harder up there. But being large and muscular has its drawbacks. Your bodies demand more oxygen and once you're over 8,800 meters with the air volume being a third of what it is down here, it becomes a lot more difficult if you get my drift," Frank countered. "Trust me, ease up the chow. You'll thank me for it later on."

The men darted glances at their plates and then at each other. Jakob frowned. "I had not thought of that before."

Frank got up and slid his chair back under the table beside him. "You'll be okay. Just need to pay attention to intake is all. All right, I'm off to get a cup of tea." He pointed to the far end of the courtyard. There, a small round pool with a stone sculpture of a Lotus flower was adding its burbling voice to the sounds of the waking city. "When you're done, join me for a briefing over there by the fountain."

The Austrians nodded and a moment later, Frank heard them break into their native tongue as he walked into the dining room. Grabbing a cup of Masala tea off the end of the buffet table, he went over to the French and Italian clients who were sitting with the Aussie and the Irishman.

"Namaste, gentlemen," he said, offering them a practiced smile.

"Morning," replied the Italian named Carlo. He pulled a chair out for Frank. The Frenchman named Vicq said, "So, is everyone here now?"

Frank drank a gulp of tea and considered the short, lean man. Vicq certainly got right to the point. Though he could appreciate the man's desire to get things moving along, Vicq needed to understand folks in Nepal didn't necessarily adhere to the schedules of the western world. He patted the man's shoulder. "All here. Relax guy, enjoy the morning."

Vicq sat back stiffly and looked out over the wrought iron rail to the courtyard beyond. Frank ignored the muttered French coming from the Frenchman and turned to Carlo and Rene. After exchanging pleasantries with them, he said, "We'll be heading to the Ministry today for final paperwork. Everyone have their fees worked out?"

"All set," Carlo replied as the Italian, Lanzo, came over and joined them. "So, when are we leaving for Lukla?"

"If all goes according to plan, Friday," Frank said. "Depends on the weather. I'll go over that in our briefing right after breakfast."

Lanzo took a sip of coffee, and setting his cup down, said, "And where would this briefing be?"

"Right outside. It's pretty informal." Frank said. He turned around and called out to Sangye. "Hey, Sangye, could you have someone gang some tables and chairs up outside by the fountain?" As he turned back to his clients, the Widow and her son entered the room.

He watched them wade through the sea of tables to the buffet. The Widow was wearing a crisp, white cotton blouse and tan khakis. As she took up a bowl and perused the offerings under the domed metal lids, he got up and went over to greet her.

"Well, good morning, Mr. Kincaid," she said without turning around. Frank was surprised. "How'd you know it was me?"

"Your cologne. It's quite distinctive."

"I hope that's a good thing," Frank said. He grabbed a plate and piled a spoon-ful of potatoes and onions onto it.

Sarah lifted the lid off the tub of scrambled eggs and spooned out a couple helpings. As she dashed salt and pepper over them, she looked up, and gave him a diffident smile. "It's nice."

Frank sensed her ambivalence as he snatched a napkin. "How'd you sleep?" he said, offering her a friendly smile.

"I didn't," she replied tightly, and turned toward her son, who was standing at the far end of the buffet waiting for the toaster to pop. "Greg, could you throw a couple slices in for me, too?"

Greg looked up. "Sure … Oh, morning, Mr. Kincaid."

"Namaste," Frank replied. "Going to try the porridge, huh?"

"Thought I might. Looks good," Greg said as the toaster popped up.

"It is," Frank replied. "They call it Halwa here."

Sarah rolled back a barrel-topped lid and peered down into a steaming tub. "What are these?"

Frank peered over her shoulder. "Roti — it's fried unleavened bread. It's good, especially with honey. You should try some. The vegetable curry is good, too."

"Hmmm … interesting," she muttered. She grabbed the tongs and took one out. Placing it on her plate, she went around him and scooped some mangos and pineapple up along with a banana. Shooting Frank a thin smile, she added, "I'd better get out of the way and let you boys chit-chat."

"Nonsense, join us," Frank insisted.

"No, I don't think that would be a good idea," Sarah replied, glancing furtively toward her son. "Don't take it personally. I just feel like being alone right now."

Frank nodded, and watched her wend her way out into the courtyard. Things were definitely going to be different up in Base Camp this year.

* * *

Thirty minutes later, Frank gathered his team of climbers and Sangye around two large tables in the courtyard. As they sat by the babbling fountain, sipping tea and mango juice, the sounds of car horns, motorbikes, street people, and shopkeepers hawking their goods beyond the hotel walls trickled in around them. Over a low brick wall beside them, children could be heard playing a lively game of cricket. A rooster crowed in the distance.

Frank leaned forward in his chair and gave his clients the typical opening spiel regarding their responsibilities of looking after their own gear and letting them know what their assigned Sherpa guides would and would not do during the next two and a half months. As he ticked off the list, his glance fell on the Widow and her American son more than once.

When he finished, he sat back. "All right, let's get to know each other a little better. Why don't we start with you, Toby? Anything you'd like to share with the rest of us?"

Toby set his bottle of water down, ran a large hand through his light blond hair, and cleared his throat. "Not much to tell really. I work as mechanical engineer for large firm in Vienna for ten years now." He paused, looked around him then awkwardly went on in his thick Germanic accent. "I enjoy travel, and of course climbing. My brother, Jakob, here beside me, got me into it when I was eighteen and in university, and I've been doing it ever since."

Frank nodded as the big man shifted uncomfortably in his chair. "So, tell us, Toby, what made you decide on Everest?"

Toby took a moment with the question before he said, "When I was young teen, fifteen years old, I was very, very big. People used to make joke about me. One day, I get on train with father and brother to go to Graz for soccer game. As I walk down aisle to find seat, people stare at me. That was okay. I was used to it. Then I see little boy turn to his father and say, 'Wow, look da, the circus fat man is here!' I never forget it."

Glancing at Frank, Toby paused and went on. "The following year I lose one hundred fifty pounds. Start working out; get in shape. Now I eat to build muscle, not because I feel bad about myself. Anyway, I push myself now to be the best I can. This is the ultimate way to find out what I can do."

He reached down and took up his water bottle and as he did so, Frank found himself reassessing the thirty-something year-old Austrian. It was a hell of a thing to lose that much weight. Well, it was clear the man had the focus to get up the mountain, but his six foot four, two hundred and sixty-five pound frame was a strike against him. Next, Frank turned to Toby's brother, Jakob.

Jakob was tall like Toby, and perhaps thirty pounds lighter. The two men shared much in appearances: fair skinned, strong Roman noses, sky-blue eyes, and square jaws. But that was where it ended. Where Toby was introspective and quiet, Jakob was gregarious and out-going. Having never faced a weight problem, Jakob had played soccer and was an avid skier growing up. 'Mountaineering was just a natural extension of his love affair with the slopes,' he said, and so it had led him into his present occupation as owner of a small alpine gear and clothing shop just outside of Vienna called, 'Carabiners'.

Again, Frank asked the question of why he wanted to tackle Mount Everest, and Jakob answered that it was the challenge of testing himself, and of reaping the reward of knowing he could do anything if he achieved the summit.

Next, Frank turned to Aldan, who was sitting beside Jakob. Aldan was a soft-spoken man with bristly short white hair, but didn't appear to be anywhere near his age of fifty-five years. Intelligent and discerning hazel eyes looked out from a thin, chiseled wind-burnt face while he told the team about his time guiding people in the outback.

"I came to climb the beast 'cause I like adventure and this here mountain provides it," Aldan said with a lilting voice.

Frank nodded, but down inside, a flag went up. While the Aussie might be a skilled guide in the Australian outback, this was Chomolungma, not the bush. Experience told Frank, that folks who were skilled outdoorsmen often didn't understand things were different on the mountain than what they were used to. The last thing Frank needed was someone who believed he knew more than his guides.

Sullivan, or Sully as he preferred to be called, had the body of a mountaineer: sleek and sinewy and not too tall. Like Jakob, Sully was an experienced climber, having summited the technically challenging Ama Dablam and K2. But there was more to the thirty-one year old Sully than just being an alpinist. He was a Theoretical Physicist who held a prestigious position at the atomic super collider CERN. That, and he had a young wife and baby daughter waiting at home for him; which was where Frank thought the Widow should be right now. When the question of why Sully wanted to climb Everest came up, he simply said he wanted to know what it was like to gaze out over the world.

The Frenchmen, Rene and Vicq, came from affluent families just outside of Nice, and were partners in their family's vintners operation. Rene said they had taken up climbing several years ago after being introduced to it by a friend, and that they both found it a welcome diversion from running the winery. Since then, it had turned into a passion.

Rene was a tall, sinewy man in his early thirties and had curly black hair and large chocolate brown eyes. A colorful tattoo of a flowering grape vine peeked out from under his shirtsleeve. Vicq was quite the opposite: late thirties, blond-haired, ice blue-eyed, short and angular. With his constant stoic attitude and expression, they made quite the odd couple, Frank thought. But their zest for climbing was evident as was their reasons for climbing.

The two Italians were watchful throughout the conversation as they sat listening to the Frenchmen tell their stories. Lanzo, who was a ski instructor at Andalo, which was located in the north of Italy, was the younger of the two. Late thirties, Frank guessed he was. At six-three with flowing black hair, doe brown eyes, and a sleek build that was almost cat-like, the soft-spoken man was undoubtedly popular with the young ladies.

Next to him was Carlo, a mid-forties restaurateur. The chunky, dark-haired Italian was staring ahead with a far-away look. At last, he turned his attention onto the group, and as he did so, leaned forward and said, "My family lost everything when my papa died of a heart attack at his ristorante. He was a good man and devoted to my momma. I was eighteen when it happened, and I can still remember my momma slouched over him.

"My older brother, Marco, and I struggled to keep the ristorante running, but not knowing how to run a business, we almost ended up losing it. The years that followed my papa's death were hard, many times we were near bankruptcy, but eventually we learned and we made it. Now we are the best ristorante in all of Milan."

He paused, and Frank heard him cough. At last, Carlo cleared his throat and went on. "The one thing I remember most about my papa was his wanting to climb the mountains. I asked him why he wanted to do it one time, and he told me; up there, it's only you, the mountain, and God. He wanted to know what that felt like to be that close to God. So, I climb for him."

There was silence all around the circle of men, and when Frank saw the Widow's stricken face he knew the Italian's story had affected her. He wondered what she was thinking and turned to Greg.

"So, Greg, what about you?" Frank said having a good idea what the young man would say.

Greg shifted in his chair and furtively glanced at his mother. "I've been climbing for the last ten years. Started out facing some of the cliffs in the Grand Canyon before moving onto alpine climbing. My father was into it in a big way before he died. In fact, he was here back in 'eighty-five," he said. "Anyway, I like challenging myself, and I love the feeling I get when I reach the top. There's nothing like it."

"Did your father summit?" Jakob said.

"No, he didn't," Greg answered quietly while fixing his gaze straight ahead. The Widow's face stiffened and looked away. At last, Greg shrugged. "Anyway, hopefully, I can finish what he started."

"A very admirable thing," Toby said.

The Widow pushed her chair back abruptly, scraping metal on the courtyard's brick pavers and got up. "If you'll excuse me, I need to find the lady's room," she said through tight lips, and walked away.

Greg's gaze remained forward and his face darkened as he took his water bottle up and gulped a swig. Frank shot a fleeting glance at the Widow's retreating back, then glanced over at her son. Red flags were waving all over the place. There was definitely more to this young man's simplified reason for climbing than he was letting on.

Chapter 3

Sarah stood looking at the dresser mirror in her room, thinking about her son. Although he was twenty-eight and held an upper management position at Johnson Industries, a subsidiary of Oracle America, all she saw in her mind's eye was a sandy-brown-haired and freckle-faced boy. What had happened to all the years in between when he was growing up? They all seemed like a blur to her now, as if she had been asleep and had just awakened to find him a grown man.

How she wanted those years back. She had missed too much of Greg's life from holding down two jobs to make ends meet. She lamented the vacations they never took when he was growing up because there never seemed to be enough time or money, as well as the long nights spent studying for her Master's degree. She had sacrificed so much to give them a better life, but in the end, the sacrifices had betrayed her, taking away the one thing that mattered most; time with her son.

So here she was, a senior administrator in the Los Angeles school system, pulling down six figures a year and all for what: a modest house in West Covina, a used BMW, and a smattering of creature comforts she had dreamed of having during those long desolate years.

Thinking back, she would trade it all away in a heartbeat to get back just one year with her son. But it was too late now. He had carved out a life for himself that barely included her.

So why was she here, really? Was it because something deep inside her wanted to finally confront the mountain that had stolen her husband? She thought she'd gotten over losing Steven until Greg announced he was going to climb the Monster. Suddenly, all the pent up anger she'd buried so long ago came roaring back and she didn't know what to do with it.

She buttoned the last two buttons on her blouse as her heart roiled. In a minute or two, Greg would be knocking on her door, so she put her game face on and tucked her blouse into her pants. Then turning in profile, she appraised herself. The one benefit to this Godforsaken trip was that she was in the best shape she'd been in, in years.

The knock on her door signaled it was time. "You ready, Mom?" said Greg's muffled voice on the other side.

Grabbing her daypack off the bed, she gave the room a last cursory inspection to make sure she wasn't forgetting anything. Satisfied, she went and pulled the door back to find her son waiting by the balcony railing with his back turned toward her. "Well, I guess we're off and running," she said. She pulled the door shut behind her and stepped into the lamp-lit, humid air.

Greg turned around, took her pack from her. "That we are. I ran into Frank a minute ago. We're all ready to go. There's a continental breakfast downstairs if you want a bite before we head out."

"I'm not hungry," Sarah said, feeling her stomach tighten.

"Okay. It'll be awhile before we eat though."

"Don't worry, I'll be fine," Sarah replied as she followed him downstairs. What she wanted was to pull him aside and hold him. At last, if nothing more than to hear his voice, she said, "You know, they should put some shelving and hooks in their bathrooms, not to mention adding a grab-bar here and there. Those floors are slick as hell when they're wet."

"Mom, this is Nepal, not the States."

"I know!"

"Well then?" he said over his shoulder. "It could've been worse, you know. The toilets could've been just a hole in the floor."

"A fact I'm well aware of," Sarah said.

"Good. Hold onto that thought 'cause there won't be a lot of toilets on the way up to Base Camp," he said.

As he stepped off the final stair onto the courtyard floor, he glanced back up at her. "There's still time to change your mind, you know."

"Yes, I know," Sarah replied. "I'm good."

"Yeah. What I thought," he replied, then turned and stalked ahead toward the dining area.

* * *

An hour and a half later, Sarah and Greg were in the van sitting with the Italians. As the van navigated the maze of narrow empty streets, Sarah listened to the men's lyrical chatter coming from the back seat. Apparently, they had gone out on the town last night and had raised a little hell. As for herself, she had had quite enough of the city's chaotic lifestyle — thank you very much.

The van turned onto what could be barely called an arterial and headed along at a fair clip out of the city, until at last, they turned into the main entrance to the Kathmandu International Airport. As they rounded the serpentine drive that skirted the main parking lot, Frank turned around in his front seat and faced her and Greg along with the Italian climbers.

"Okay, once we're parked, Sangye will go ahead and get the paperwork going. The rest of us will go grab some carts so we can get loaded and into the queue outside the front door. It's going to be a bit crazy out there, but don't worry. Just follow my lead."

As he turned back, the entrance into the drop-off lot outside the domestic air terminal came into view. Along with it, ensued a circus-like atmosphere. Sarah gazed out from her passenger side window at the speeding motorbikes that were threading their way around and through teams of men pushing overburdened carts of supplies toward a growing heap of items near the entry pavilion. Beside this pile, stood a long queue of travelers waiting to go through a security checkpoint.

Although this scene was not so different from what she'd experienced in Mexico, she couldn't help but wonder how anyone got anywhere from this place. She shook her head in wonder as the driver steered the van through the chaos and parked alongside several other off-loading vans.

A moment later, Frank was sliding the passenger side door back. As he helped her out, he barked orders to the driver and a porter who came running up to start unloading bags from the rack on top of the van. As the Italians piled out behind her, Frank pointed to a covered walkway near the queue of travelers lined-up outside the terminal entrance. "All right guys … and lady. Let's go get our carts."

That he made no exception for her didn't bother her one bit. She was used to fending for herself, and besides she expected everyone would be required to carry their own weight. She'd been doing it for the last twenty years, so she hoofed it after the Italians and melted into the confusion of humanity.

* * *

It was two hours before Sangye finally gave the thumbs up that the expedition team was at last clear to move out of the crowded and dingy terminal waiting area toward their gate. In the meantime, Sarah had been standing within the semi-circle of Frank's crew at the far end of the cavernous room, sipping luke-warm coffee from a paper cup as the cacophony of multi-lingual conversations echoed around her.

She followed her son down a narrow stairway to their gate and waited yet again for another twenty minutes until Frank signaled it was time. After lining up for another quick check and handing their boarding passes to an attendant, she went out onto the tarmac under a deep blue morning sky with just a whiff of cloud. As she walked toward the waiting transport bus, the wind tugged at her collar, and the smell of oil and diesel wrinkled her nose.

Ten minutes later, she boarded a revving nineteen-seat Cessna that looked like it should've been retired twenty years ago. After finding her seat, she buckled herself in, and prepared for the forty-five minute flight to a tiny airport at the foothills of the Himalayas.

This airport they were headed to was not just any airport, though. It was named the most dangerous airstrip in the world by just about every website. She thought about the accident that had happened two years ago that claimed sixteen lives on the treacherous landscape before the tiny airstrip. It was not a comforting thought. She pushed it out of her mind though and glanced at her son sitting across the aisle from her. He had been quiet all morning, and while she didn't think he was brooding, she knew he wasn't happy with her decision to push on with him.

At last, she said, "Looks like we're finally on our way. Are you excited?"

Greg shot her a half smile. "Yeah, I am. It's been a long road to this point."

"It certainly has," Sarah agreed. All morning she had been contained in her self-imposed dread of the impending expedition, but now it was raging; push-ing against her chest, threatening to break free from the Teflon shield she had put around herself to deflect others from seeing the terror in her heart. She wanted to be happy for her son — no, that was a lie. She wanted to turn this whole thing around and go home. But digging in her heels now would do no good. She drew breath and forced a smile. "I'm happy for you. You've worked hard for this."

He turned and looked at her hard. "Really?"

"Yes, I am," Sarah lied, studying his naked expression of doubt. It crushed her and yet offered her a small window back to him, so she folded her needs into a dark corner of her soul and said, "Look, I might've been against this all along, but we're here and so it's all done and past. The important thing now is that you succeed."

Greg eyed her and she could feel him assessing her capitulation. Finally, he said, "You really mean that?"

She leaned toward him and touching his arm, whispered, "Yes, I do. You know I love you very much."

He shot her a lazy smile as the plane taxied onto the runway. "I know. Me too." He opened his mouth to say something then looked off as the plane came to a halt. Pirouetting ninety degrees, it revved its engines and drowned out the conversations around them.

Up ahead, the pilot grabbed his microphone and called back to the flight attendant sitting in the back of the plane. "Prepare for takeoff."

The twin-engine aircraft shuddered and suddenly they were racing down the runway and launching into the air.

Sarah peered out the window as the ground fell away. Five minutes later they were above the clouds. In the distance she saw the vast Himalayan range stretching as far as she could see.

Below lay the sprawling, congested city that crawled out to a sparse, rolling land dotted with small farms. As the city gave up and fell behind them, she saw long, winding roads going up into the hill country that was just now beginning to make an appearance.

Midway into the flight, the plane tipped its wing and bore to the left before straightening out. Fifteen minutes later, the mountains were running along beside them. Sarah was taken aback by their sheer size. Though she lived in southern California and had traveled to Yosemite when she was a child, she was unprepared for the view passing outside her window. The mountains were, indeed beautiful, but she reminded herself that the Monster lived here, too.

They followed the snow-covered range for the next ten minutes while slowly banking northward until, in the distance, an imposing dark ridge appeared. As Sarah watched it steadily rise, the plane climbed upward. But as high as they went, it didn't seem to be enough to clear the trees below that were quickly coming into deadly clarity.

As they scraped their ragged tips, Sarah gripped the armrest.

"Attendant, prepare for landing," the pilot called over the microphone. The plane banked sharply to the left and a minute later was headed toward another imposing dark ridge. *Landing? Where?* Sarah thought, peering out the window as the ground below fell away.

The pilot pushed forward on his stick and the plane dipped downward. Sarah leaned toward the window and tried to get a better angle of what they were headed for. But all she saw was a muted landscape looming ahead with no sign of the infamous airstrip anywhere in sight.

As the plane bounced up and down, jostling her side-to-side, she could almost imagine being on a rollercoaster at Venice Beach. Except this was no rollercoaster and she wasn't a kid anymore. All she wanted was to be on the ground, preferably in one piece. She fixed her gaze on the plane's wobbling wings as the deep blue sky dove behind the tree-lined crest beside her. The plane veered left, then dropping like a stone, shuddered.

Chapter 4

Frank sat back and watched the ridge slide past his passenger side window. They'd soon be landing in Lukla and heading for Everest. But there was something else on his mind right now; specifically, John Patterson. John was the Everest Expedition Leader for Andersen Expeditions on the mountain, and the two of them had never gotten along well. The man was just too reckless for Frank's taste, and more than once he had taken on clients who had no business being on the mountain.

That was one of the big problems with Everest. Too many clients had too little experience with high altitude climbing. And while it was true the Nepalese Ministry required evidence of their ability, they often looked the other way once it came to the profitable fees required for the permits. Twenty-five thousand dollars turned heads, especially when an attached bribe was in an envelope along with it.

That left 'Judge Gerry', as she was referred to, as a last defense against folks ending up dead on Everest. As the mountain's historian, she alone collected the valuable data, which was in constant use by the climbing community. Frank liked her. She was a shrewd woman who had seen it all, and it was near impossible to fool her. But she was only one person in this Wild West, as she liked to call it.

That left the final decisions to the expedition leaders as to whether their clients were capable or not. And competition for the wealthy or well-sponsored men and women who wanted to experience the ultimate adventure was fierce, so the leaders often passed the client's lack of experience onto the shoulders of their Sherpa leaders. That, in a nutshell, was where the rubber met the road, or in this case the crampon met the ice. The more experienced the Sirdar Sherpa was, the more coveted he was by the expedition leader.

So when one of Andersen's Sirdars defected to Khum Jung Mountaineering two years ago, it wasn't well received by John. The Sirdar, Ang Da-wa Phu-Dorje, was highly respected and losing him had been a serious blow to John. Suddenly the uneasy but acceptable co-existence between Andersen and Khum Jung Mountaineering on the mountain changed overnight into a bitter war of accusations that erupted into a heated exchange last year between John and Frank.

Frank didn't know for certain if John was behind the IRD's review of his financial affairs, but he had a good idea he was. The question became, how much money was John feeding the IRD's taxation agent, Mr. Karthacharya, and more importantly, how much was it going to cost Khum Jung Mountaineering to make this back tax issue go away?

If John had all of Andersen's vast resources behind him, Khum Jung Mountaineering was toast. But Frank didn't think so. Andersen was a huge trekking conglomerate with outfits all over the world. They would more than likely order John to just find another Sirdar rather than to send a lot of money down the proverbial toilet over what they would perceive as a petty dispute. Still, one never knew. It had been weighing heavily on Frank's mind for quite some time, but the plane shuddering as it touched down on the tiny airstrip ripped the thought away. There would be time enough for that later. Right now, he had clients to attend to.

* * *

After they unloaded the plane and collected their gear, Frank led them into the quaint village nestled in the sleepy foothills of Sagarmatha. Sagarmatha was the national park reserve that encompassed many of the legendary peaks sought after by climbers, Everest not the least of them. As they tramped down the main street dividing the village, Sangye and he bade old friends good morning.

Lukla was one of Frank's favorite oases up in the mountains. Its cozy relaxed atmosphere and unfailing folk provided a welcome doorway into the land he loved. Today, the sun was shining and an endless blue sky soared above.

He hitched his pack up on his shoulder and strode down the broken macadam-paved street for another hundred meters until he came to a small sign with the words Juniper Hotel on it. The Juniper Hotel, or teahouse, was owned and operated by Ang Nyi-ma Lha-mo or just Lotti, as she was known to most. Lotti was a small, venerable old woman of sixty-eight who was beloved by all who knew her, and she treated Frank like a son. Just now, he could see her in his mind's eye standing by the front door looking back at him with laughing brown eyes and a broad smile that lacked a couple of front teeth.

Turning around to make sure he still had everyone with him, he pointed to the narrow alleyway on his left that led back to the three story cut-stone and tan stucco-faced hostel. "Okay, this is our digs for tonight," he called back. "Once we're settled in, you can poke around town if you want to while I check on the rest of our gear and supplies coming in from Kathmandu."

To Sangye, he said, "Do me a favor; call Daku and double check to see if our gear's on schedule to fly out on time."

Sangye pulled his cell phone out and drifted ahead down the street as Frank and his clients ducked into the alleyway and went down a small stairway between the street shops. At the end of the alleyway behind the one-story masonry buildings was a small sun-lit courtyard. Sitting in it and piled against one wall, was a long shoulder-height stack of firewood. His Sirdar, Da-wa Phu-Dorje, who was plucking pieces off of it, turned around just as he set his pack on the ground.

"Namaste," Da-wa said. "How was your flight?"

Frank went over and embraced the short, stocky man. Pulling back to look at his round coffee-colored face, he said, "It was good. So, we all lined up for today? Got a lot of gear coming in."

The Sherpa returned one of his patented broad smiles. "They'll be here right after lunch."

"Good. How many hands do we have?"

"Fifteen, I thought would be enough," Da-wa said, and glanced around Frank's shoulder. "Good looking group we have coming in."

Frank turned back to see his clients piling in behind him. Clearing his throat, he said, "Folks, this is Ang Da-wa Phu-Dorje, your lead guide for the expedition."

"But you can call me Dave," the Sirdar said. He went over and started shaking hands with them until he came to the Widow. Smiling politely at her, he dipped his head slightly in respect before passing by her to finish greeting the rest of the men.

As the Sirdar finished up saying his hellos, Frank saw Sangye had returned. When the man gave him the thumbs up that everything was going as scheduled, Frank spoke up. "Everyone, just leave your packs and gear out here for right now."

Afterward, Frank called Da-wa over. When the Sherpa came close, Frank made his voice low and broke into Lhasa. "Any news on Patterson?"

"Not yet. Something you should know, though. Cho-pal and Sun-jo say Park soldiers checking permits very close now. Something going on in Monjo, I think." He gave Frank a wary glance then bent over and cinched the cloth strap around the firewood that was sitting at his feet. After he picked the bundle up, he took hold of Frank's hand and squeezed it. "Anyway, come. Lotti has tea brewing and wants to get started with lunch."

As her guests passed by single file into the adjacent receiving room, Lotti stood back to get a good look at them. As ageless and enduring as the mountains, she had remained unchanged by the gradual influx of technology creeping up the slopes of the majestic Himalayas.

Wiping her hands on her tattered apron, she handed Frank a cup of masala tea and said, "You've lost weight. Are you eating okay?"

"I'm doing just fine, Lotti, and how are you?" Frank said.

"I'm very good. The rooms are ready upstairs. Come, I'll get the keys for you."

Frank followed her into the main dining room and waited while she dug them out from underneath the transaction counter. Looking around, he noticed she'd purchased new tables and chairs for the large, rectangular wood paneled room. Also, there was a new cast iron pot-bellied stove that had replaced the old worn out drum style one that had stood in the center of the room for over twenty years. As usual, the café style curtains hanging over the long ribbon of narrow windows were crisp and colorful, and fresh flowers were placed in glass vases on the tables.

As she rummaged around behind the counter, her reedy voice floated out. "So, how are things up in Khum Jung? I hear you are building a new classroom at the high school."

"Not much gets past your ears, does it?" Frank replied with a smile, "but, yes, things are going well up in Khum Jung."

She stood up and handed him the keys. "That is good. Well, why don't I let you introduce me to my guests."

Frank drained his tea with one long gulp and headed for the receiving room where the group was busy talking amongst themselves. Getting everyone's attention, he introduced Lotti and gave a bit of history about her teahouse, which had the distinction of having housed Tenzing Norgay and Sir Edmund Hillary several times in the early seventies. As he went around handing out room keys, Lotti followed him, getting their names and where they were from. Lotti loved finding out about guests who stayed under her roof.

* * *

That night after dinner, Frank went for a walk along the main avenue outside their teahouse. He headed out of the village to a spot up in the hills where he could peer out at the valley below and relax. But the peace he sought among the budding rhododendrons eluded him. All he could think about was the threat to his business and he didn't know what to do about it. He closed his eyes and tried to focus on breathing in the clean, cool air and letting the fragrant scents of the hillside flow through him. It was how he went about becoming one with nature and self. Once he was in that place, the answers he sought often became more evident, and from there, he could move forward confident in his decisions.

Stay with it, stay with it, he told himself over and over again. *Let the truth come to you. Don't try to order or alter it. Just let it come.*

But it didn't come and he knew why. He was getting in the way of it. One could not simply arrange peace in the way he wished it to be. It came only when one was truly open to listening, and right now there were too many voices shouting in his head for attention.

At last, he gave up and decided to strike back into town. He stood and dusted the grit off his jeans, then started back down the invisible trail through the tall waving grasses. To the east, stars were just beginning to prick the darkening sky and the mountain air was beginning to nip. As he picked his way along, he looked down at the patchwork of red and green metal roofs and saw the mountain folk beginning to close their shops and stores up. Many of them lived above their establishments, and those who didn't were heading down into the flowering hills beyond where their wives and children tended small farms. More than a few were heading along the trail below toward Phadking.

He picked his pace up and soon after struck the main road leading into town. As he walked, people who knew him stopped and passed along news from those who carried the commerce on their backs up and down the long winding trails.

Business was brisk, they reported, and the trekking trails never better. It was going to be a banner year.

That was good, Frank thought as he pulled his collar up around his neck. Last year's heat wave on the mountain had ditched every summit expedition and that had hit the mountain folk hard. No active Base Camp meant a reduced parade of trekkers hoping to catch a glimpse of the mountaineers. That, in turn, meant less trade for the lesser merchants who supplemented their households by selling jewelry, clothing goods, and various other homemade crafts.

Up ahead was another old friend. Cho-Lin or Cho, as he preferred to be called, had been a staple in Lukla for as long as Frank had been alive, and the two of them spent many an evening sitting outside his small shop swapping tales. As always, the old man was wearing a tattered wool pullover and jeans and was sitting in an old rickety rocker, gumming a cigarette. When he saw Frank, he called out.

"And how is the Lion tonight?" Cho said, preferring to call Frank by his Buddhist name.

"I'm very good," Frank lied. He went over and embraced the old man and asked him how his daughters were doing. Cho's wife had passed on five years ago, and so now his children were looking after him. The answer was the same as always; they were a pain in his behind, always fussing over him.

Frank smiled and perused the table of brightly colored wool scarves that Cho had put out. After a quick inspection, he picked out a green one with a flowering red cascade of rhododendron. After handing Cho four one thousand rupee notes, which was twice the asking price, he looped it around his neck. It was then he saw the Widow step out of the adjacent shop with her head down inspecting something in the bag she was carrying.

He watched her rummage around in her bag and tried to decide whether or not to say "hi." Outside of talking with Cho, he really wasn't in the mood for conversation, least of all with her, but when she suddenly looked up to see him standing there, he was stuck.

"Well," she said, breathlessly, "Good evening, Mr. Kincaid."

"Evening to you," Frank replied. "I see you've been checking out the shops. Found a few things, too."

"As a matter of fact, yes," she said, zipping up her jacket, then pulled out a beaded necklace and a colorful blue buff. She showed him her purchases, then stood back and looked at him with an admiring gaze. "Nice scarf."

"Thank you. My good friend, Cho, over here, sells the very best."

She drifted over to the table beside him and ran her hand over a cream-colored one that was embroidered with curling green stems and orange blossoms. "Oh, that's soft."

"Eighty percent cashmere," Cho piped up. "Very good to have up on mountain when get cold."

Frank smiled. "They do come in quite useful."

The Widow shot him a friendly glance and went back to perusing the goods, flipping back and forth through the scattered pile. Frank knew she knew she was being herded into a sale, but she didn't seem to mind. Finally, she came back to the cream-colored one and turned to Cho. "How much?"

"Two thousand," Cho replied, eyeing her expectantly.

She put her hand to her chin, tilted her head thoughtfully, and paused. "I'll give you fifteen hundred?"

Cho smiled back. "Seventeen-fifty?"

"Done!" The Widow pulled a wad of cash out and peeled several notes off. As she handed them to Cho, she looked back up at Frank. "I must say, I like shopping this way."

Frank liked his way better when it came to doing business with the mountain folk. He watched her pick her purchase up and hold it out in front of her. He knew she was his client — well, sort of; she wasn't going up the mountain. That didn't mean he had to censor himself.

At last, he said, "It might be a bargain for you, but for them it puts food on the table."

She turned, and as she looked at him, her victorious smile melted. Perhaps he shouldn't have said what he did, but it was the way he felt in general about folks who haggled down the small shopkeepers on the mountain, even if it was the expected way of doing business for them.

"Well, Cho, I better be getting along," he said. "You have a good night, Ms. Madden. I'll see you in the morning."

"Yes, you, too," she answered soberly as she folded up her scarf and shoved it in her bag. As he turned away from her to make his way back to the Juniper, she spoke up. "I didn't mean to sound heartless, Mr. Kincaid."

"I'm sure you didn't," he replied, turning back to her. "Most who come here don't see the hidden lives of these people. It's not your fault. You're just being a trekker. I try to remember that fact, but now and then, I forget. I'm sorry. I didn't mean to embarrass you."

Sarah furrowed her brow. "Mr. Kincaid, I'll thank you not to judge me," she said, her tone brittle and pointed. She softened her tone then, and added, "I'm sorry, that was rude of me, but you have no idea how I live my life." She paused and looking back at Cho, continued, "I do understand your sentiments, though. It's easy to forget where we are sometimes. I'll be more mindful of it going forward."

Frank took the implied apology in stride, unsure of what to say next. Women were a mystery to him. Their moods shifted back and forth on a whim, and for the life of him, he couldn't understand why they made so much of so little all the time. After a while he'd just given up trying to figure them out, and that was fine by him. He liked his own company well enough, and had enough to keep him busy without having to deal with their constant, unfathomable needs.

At last, he said, "I guess I get a bit prickly about things now and then."

"So, don't we all," she answered. She was quiet a moment. "Can we start over?"

Frank nodded. "Yes, let's."

"Good," she replied. "You mind if I walk back with you?"

"No, not at all," Frank said, keenly aware to keep a safe distance between them. She joined him and as they walked under the darkening sky, she peppered him with questions about the mountain people; where they lived, what they did during the off-season, and so on until they came to the alleyway leading to the Juniper. Turning into it, they walked down the stair to the front entrance, each in their own thoughts. As Frank opened the door, Sarah said, "Would you like to join me for a cup of tea?"

Surprised at her invitation, Frank glanced down the hall toward the empty dining room. The offer made him nervous. Then again, everything about her put him on edge. But it was hard to say 'no' so he sauntered in with her and found them a table in the corner of the room.

As she removed her jacket and set it on the bench seat next to her, Frank went to the transaction counter and ordered a thermos of tea. When he returned, she went back to asking him about Sagarmatha and the trip ahead, what to expect, how long it would take, and what the shower situation was going to be like going up the mountain. As he answered her questions, the conversation drifted to what he did when he wasn't leading expeditions.

Frank sat back and thought about how much he should tell her as Lotti brought out mugs and a large metal thermos of lemon tea. After Lotti left, Frank poured the Widow her tea, and said, "I have a small construction business in Khum Jung that keeps me busy when I'm not on expedition."

"Khum Jung? Is that far from here?" she asked taking her mug from him.

Frank shook his head. "No, it's a solid day's walk. We'll be a couple hours away from the village when we reach Namche."

The Widow sipped her tea, pulled her jacket off the bench, and draped it over her shoulders. "It's suddenly turned a bit chilly in here."

Frank was quiet, wondering what she'd be saying once they reached Dengboche. They'd be seeing nightly temps below zero Celsius there. But that was her problem. She wanted to come; therefore she had to deal with it.

At last, he said, "Gonna get colder the higher we go."

"Yes, I know," she answered. "Don't worry, I won't be a pest. So, tell me about Lotti. She's quite a lady from what I see."

"She is," Frank replied. "She's known me since I was a kid. Strongest woman I've ever seen. There was a day, not long ago, when she'd split half a cord of wood, then come in, and cook a dinner for two dozen guests."

"Has she always been alone?"

"No, she lost her husband a few years back."

"Oh? Sorry to hear that," Sarah said.

Frank took a gulp of tea. "Don't be. He lived a good long life."

Sarah nodded. "How old was he?"

Frank counted back to when he first met the man. "Sixty-three, I believe, but don't quote me on it."

"Really? Just what do you consider being young?" she said setting her mug down.

Frank shot her one of his practiced half smiles. "Up here, life is a little harder than what most folks are used to."

Sarah was quiet a moment, seemingly absorbing the hardened fact that this was the Himalayas, not the States, where one had the finest medical care available to them. Finally, she said, "How old is Cho?"

Frank shrugged. "Not sure. He's never told me. Not sure he knows himself. But if I were to guess, seventy-five?"

Sarah's gaze strayed over Frank's shoulder. Finally, she looked back and said, "He made me chuckle."

"How's that?"

"The way he sat there, rocking back and forth as I looked through his scarves. There's a lot going on behind those dark eyes of his."

"More than you know," Frank agreed.

She grinned, and as she did so, little dimples formed around the corner of her mouth, bringing a smile to Frank's face. "You know, one thing I've noticed, is how different the people are up here from those in Kathmandu."

Frank poured himself another mug of tea. "It's a different philosophy up here."

"Are you a Buddhist?" she said, sitting back and studying him.

"I work at it," Frank said, suddenly feeling oddly at ease around her. He paused momentarily thinking about the unexpected openness developing between them, then stretched his legs out in front of him. "So, tell me? What do you do back in the States?"

"Right now, I'm a deputy superintendent in the Los Angeles School System, but I used to be a sixth grade teacher," she said, taking up her mug of tea.

"Moved up the ranks, huh?" Frank quipped. But as she looked back at him, her open and confiding expression vanished.

"You could say that," she answered. "If you want the truth, I'd just as soon be back in the classroom. I miss it."

"So, why aren't you?" Frank said.

She gave him a crooked smile as she cupped her hands around her mug. "If only it were that easy. Don't get me wrong; I don't dislike what I do. It's important work, but it's not what I thought it'd be."

"Which was?"

"Having a stronger voice to advocate for the kids and teachers," Sarah said. "But most of the time, my hands are tied. Politics, you know. I'm tired of playing the game. Tired of toeing the Board's party line. Everything's always about how it will look in the public eye. Doesn't matter if it's hurting the kids as long as it brings the votes in. Just massage the message." She shook her head and stared off into the distance.

Frank understood her frustration all too well. He'd been neck deep in politics with the Nepalese government ever since he put in the paperwork for his expedition company years back. What caught him by surprise was that he had just thought of her as Sarah instead of "the Widow." He studied her more closely as she peered into the darkness. There was an unsettled soul behind the self-assured mask she was wearing, and it resonated within him just a bit too much.

At last she came to herself, and for a moment they gazed at each other in the palpable silence. Finally, she shrugged. "Anyway, if there's one thing I've learned in life it's not to wish too hard for something—"

" — because you just might get it," Frank said, finishing her quote.

"Exactly."

Chapter 5

Sarah woke up to sunlight pouring through her bedroom window. Outside, there wasn't a cloud in the sky. She flipped the heavy wool blanket aside and rolled out of her cot. The floor was cool to her feet and the room was nippy as she headed toward the community bathroom to brush her teeth and to take a shower. *Lord knows when I'll see another opportunity at hot water.*

Twenty minutes later she was back in her room digging into her backpack to pull out a pair of thermals and a fresh pair of socks. In the room next door, she heard the Irishman, Sully, moving around. Outside, the hall was filled with the voices of people murmuring as they got around. She glanced at her watch. 6:35 AM. Breakfast was at seven. After they ate, they'd be off on the first leg of their long trek to Base Camp. Today, they would hike to Phadking, a small village seven miles up the trail.

Throwing her clothes on, she heard the sound of Frank's voice down the hall outside her room. As she listened to him chat in Lhasa with one of the Sherpas, she found herself thinking about the conversation they had the night before. He was turning out to be quite different than what she'd expected him to be. For one thing, he cared deeply about the people on the mountain, who were vastly different from those who labored within the dense urban sprawl of Kathmandu. And the other thing was, he'd paid attention to her when she'd told him about her job back in the States. She couldn't believe he had her spilling her frustrations out regarding her inability to effect real change for the kids. While it felt good to unload her thoughts and feelings to him, she wondered afterward if she'd revealed too much.

At length, she pushed her feet into her hiking boots, laced, and tied them up. Not being one to leave an unmade bed, she pulled the blanket up and tucked it under the thin, beaten mattress and fluffed the threadbare pillow. Her sleeping bag, which was stuffed in its compression bag, lay by her bed. She repacked her clothes in her backpack, strapped the sleeping bag on top of it, and grabbed her hiking poles that were propped up in the corner of her tiny room.

Taking one last look around to make sure she wasn't leaving anything behind, she was out the door, and heading down the hall for breakfast. On the way, she ran into her son, who was just coming back from the communal bathroom with a towel draped over his bare shoulders.

"How'd you sleep?" she asked.

"Alright, I guess," Greg replied. "Heading down for b'fast?"

"Yep," Sarah answered, catching a whiff of frying potatoes and onions in the air.

Greg yawned. "Something smells good down there. What I need is a strong cup of coffee. Unfortunately, I won't be seeing one of those for quite some time."

"I hear you," Sarah said. Tea was nice for a change of pace, but as a steady morning constitutional? She didn't think so. She smiled, and tapping the tip of her hiking pole on the hardwood floor, said, "Well, I better get down there while the getting's good."

"Yeah, I'll be right along," Greg said, and shot her one of his rare patented smiles before sliding past her.

Sarah watched him slip into his room then turned away, carrying his smile with her like a banner. Her telling Greg she was going to root for him yesterday, was making a subtle difference between them. Though he was still guarded, she sensed a change in him. She thought of the walk they'd taken down the main street running though Lukla yesterday afternoon. For the first time in weeks, they talked to each other rather than *at* each other, and they laughed. How she loved seeing him smile and hearing his quick-witted humor. For too long, it had been missing between them.

After they returned to the teahouse after shopping, she'd decided that she was going to stay out of his way and let him bond with his fellow climbers. There would be plenty enough time for her over the next month and a half. Besides, she wanted to find out more about this Frank Kincaid, whom she was trusting with her son's life.

Yes, Greg and her were going to be okay, and maybe, just maybe, she could reclaim some of the closeness they had once shared when he was young, before the money ran out, before losing the house and having to hold down two jobs to make ends meet; before the long years moving up the ranks in the school district, and last of all, before the climbing bug had infected him. And she found it paradoxical that the one thing that had driven the deepest wedge between them might be the one thing that could bring them back together again. But she wasn't going to let the dreaded mountain spoil how she was feeling right now, so she drove it out of her mind and lightened her step going down the stairs.

* * *

The dining room was humming with trekkers talking about the day ahead and swapping information about where they were going or where they had come from. Most were just Base Camp trekkers, hiking up to the famous camp and back. But Sarah was actually going to be living there, and her son was going to the summit.

As she took her seat at the reserved Khum Jung table, she smiled, delighting in that secret. Those who went to scale the mountain didn't broadcast it freely, Frank had said. It was better to just blend in with folks or over-curious people might pester you all the way from Lukla to Base Camp. That was all right with Sarah. She was pestered enough at her job back home. That didn't mean she didn't enjoy listening to others banter back and forth though. Just now, a young man was holding court with three young women, telling them about his trekking experience to Base Camp.

"The mountains were so close we had to look almost straight up at 'em to see their peaks," he said, earning 'ooohs' and 'aaahs' from the girls.

"Did you see Everest?" one of the girls said, leaning forward.

The young man sat back and smiled, obviously enjoying the girl's attention. "Yeah, and it was awesome."

"How high did you get?" another girl queried.

"All the way up to Kala Patthar. Fifty-four hundred meters! It was a hell of a slog, lemme tell ya. And the wind was really cold and whipping around. Almost froze the water in my camelback. I made it though and got some great pics." He pulled his digital camera out and showed them a few of his shots and had them eating out of his hands.

Sarah shook her head and looked down at the table with a grin. As she did so, she heard heavy footsteps come into the room. Glancing up, she saw the expedition team trickle in. A moment later, chairs were dragged out from under the table as thermoses of tea and trays loaded with mugs were brought out.

Greg set his pack next to the others that were piled around the pot-bellied stove and found a seat next to the Italian, Lanzo. Sangye and Sherpa Dave came around with bright smiles.

"Namaste! We have lemon and ginger tea here, but there is also Mango juice if anyone would like some," Sangye said, as he handed out menus. As Sarah took it from him and began perusing the selections, Sullivan pulled a chair out next to her.

"Morning," he said. "Mind if I join ya?"

"Not at all," Sarah answered, setting her menu down.

Sully took his menu from Sangye and studied it. "So what's good, ya think?"

Sarah poured herself a cup of lemon tea. "I'm thinking a cheese omelet. So, 'Sully', right?"

"That's me," he said looking up with a winning smile. He grabbed the bottle of hand sanitizer and squeezed a dab on his hands then handed her the bottle.

"Tell me about that family of yours. You have a baby girl, right?" Sarah said, taking the sanitizer from him.

He sat back and smiled the way only fathers can smile when talking about their little girls. "Yeah. Just turned two last month. Her name's Fiona, but I call her Razzy," he said, and pulled his wallet out to show her a picture. "When she was a wee one, she liked blowing raspberries."

"Oh, what a darling she is," Sarah gushed, eyeing the photo of the little girl with mint green giggling eyes and shocking red hair. She handed him back his wallet. "And your wife? What does she do?"

"She's a pediatrician. And you?"

"I work for the Los Angeles School system," Sarah replied as Sherpa Dave came next to them with paper and pencil.

"Okay, what will you be liking this morning?" the Sherpa said, squatting down beside her.

"I'll have an omelet with toast," Sarah answered handing him her menu.

"And I'll have a stack of pancakes and two eggs, sunny side up," Sully added, shoving his menu across the table. After the Sherpa left them, Sully continued, "Teaching?"

"No. Deputy Superintendent," Sarah replied. "But your job — theoretical physicist. My goodness."

Sully smiled, and as he did so, dimples punctuated his long freckled face. "It's a hard mistress, but I love it. The big discoveries come rarely, most of them after years of work deciphering tons of data, but in the end it's worth it. In a lot of ways, it's like golf."

"Oh, really?" Sarah replied, raising her brow.

"Yeah. You keep playing for that one shot that keeps ya coming back. And when it does, ya can't imagine doing anything else."

"Have you made any discoveries?" Sarah asked, inhaling the tangy steam rising off her tea.

"Not yet. But I'm in no hurry. Part of the process is getting there, and I enjoy it well enough." He told her then about how he had been recruited to CERN after getting his PhD at the Dublin Institute of Advanced Studies. "It wasn't a slam-dunk decision either. I'd only been married a year and a half when the offer came, and my wife, Mary, wasn't interested in pulling up stakes in Cork and moving to Geneva," he said, as Sherpa Dave brought their breakfasts around.

As they ate, he continued, "That meant a commute back and forth, spending four days a week in Geneva. With Fiona on the way, I was reluctant to take the position. But in the end, my wife convinced me it was something I couldn't pass up."

Sarah was of divided mind as she thought about what he said. On the one hand, she sensed his Mary as a courageous woman, strong and independent, but sacrificing the most important years at home for a career? She had been there and done that, and look how it had turned out. Finally, she said, "You must miss her when you're away."

"I do, but when we come back together, it's like meeting all over again."

"Except, now you have a daughter."

"Yeah, and that's hard for sure. I'm trying to back my time off at CERN to three days a week now and working from home." He laughed. "Thank God for the Skype and email."

Sarah was quiet as she considered her next question. "Can I ask you something of a personal nature?"

Sully popped a forkful of pancake into his mouth, and after a moment, he nodded. "Sure."

"You said you've climbed all these mountains. Didn't that cut into your time with your wife?"

"Oh, we climb together, though not so much now after Fiona was born. This will be my last summit for a while. We both agreed I could take this one shot then hang my crampons up until Fiona gets old enough to travel with us."

"I guess the family that climbs together, stays together," Sarah said. She took one last bite of her omelet and setting her fork down, pushed the plate away.

Sully wiped his chin with a napkin. "That was pretty good. Well, it was great talking to ya. Time to fill my camelback. See you on the trail?"

Sarah took a last sip of her tea as he got up. "I'll be there."

* * *

After they said their good-byes to Lotti, the team marched off single-file through the village and down a rocky trail into the Rhododendron and conifer forest that cradled the rushing blue-gray waters of the Dudh Kosi River. As Sarah poled along the winding trail at the rear of the column, she peered up at the towering Himalayan and Chir Pine and Birch that flourished on the verdant hillside. The land beside her was not so different than the towering conifer forests of northern California. She dug her hiking pole into the ground, and for the next forty minutes she descended some six hundred feet in elevation before the trail finally leveled off. That probably meant a good slog upward was in the near future. But the skies were a brilliant blue and a pleasant cool breeze was tugging at her upturned collar.

She followed the meandering trail back and forth and up and down for the next hour, and the farther she trekked on it, the more she encountered mountain folk going back and forth carrying their burdens. Many of them offered broad smiles, greeting her with a 'Namaste' as they passed her by. Just now she heard the melodic tinkling of bells coming her way. The expedition team came to a halt, and one-by-one, they moved to the side of the trail as a train of cattle came lumbering toward them. Behind the beasts of burden, walked a short, lean, dark-skinned man wearing a soiled white shirt and carrying a stick. As he prodded the animals forward, he uttered loud whistling bursts and verbal commands that strafed the air. After the train had passed, the trekking column started back up. With Frank being nearby, she decided to have another chat with him.

"Gorgeous day for a walk," she said.

"Yes, it is," Frank replied.

She took a deep breath of the mountain-scented air. "What is that lovely fragrance?"

"Juniper. The local people burn it in the morning to cleanse their homes," he answered. "I do enjoy it."

"Me, too," Sarah said as they walked side-by-side. As they went past flowering Tibetan cherry and maple, Frank pointed out some of the local wildlife. Sarah listened as he talked about the musk deer, tahr goats, and blue sheep that roamed the hills and highlands. Hopscotching over a pile of strewn rocks, she cleared her throat "So, tell me, do you always give guided narratives to your clients?"

He chuckled. "No, not usually. Most are interested in getting where they're going, though I do get questions on and off."

"Well, you're doing a good job of it, narrating, that is," she said, and tried to hike her pack up higher on her shoulders. But the pack wasn't obeying her. She stopped and leaned her poles against her waist, but they went clattering to the ground.

"Here, let me give you a hand," Frank offered. He loosened the straps of her pack, adjusted the cinch tabs and strapped it back up over her shoulders. "How's that?" he said, standing back to regard his handiwork.

It felt like twenty pounds had been lifted off her back. She smiled. "Wonderful. Thank you."

"Not a problem," he replied, picking up her poles and handing them to her.

They walked awhile more passing occasional fieldstone fences wrapping around small homesteads that bellied up to the trail. As they went by them, Sarah found herself being immersed in the simple but difficult life of the Himalayan people. Frank was quiet, his soft, caressing gaze often falling on the stout ruddy people that were toiling in their gardens or caring for their livestock and beasts of burden. Children in dirty, ragged garments played freely amongst the chickens that pecked at the ground around their front doors. Sometimes, the ground ran over the thresholds and into the dark rooms of their rough stone houses. Without fail, the gated entries into the homesteads were flanked with smoldering boughs of juniper that sent aromatic smoke spiraling upward through the ragged limbs of the conifer forest.

It was so easy to fall into the trap of romanticizing this bucolic world, but Frank kept it in perspective, saying, "Behind the visual beauty and peaceful atmosphere, is a world that exacts much from these people."

And it was true. She had things pretty easy back home; a superstore a few blocks away from her house stocked with all the necessities of modern life, a fancy car with air conditioning to get around, a three-bedroom raised ranch with hardwood floors and a built-in pool in her back yard.

At last, she said, "It's like stepping back in time up here."

Frank drew a drink of water from his camelback, and said, "How so?"

Sarah paused, feeling like he was testing her. Any answer she gave was sure to be judged and she didn't like it. She eyed him with a level gaze and said, "Oh, come on Frank. Certainly anyone can see that life in the cities is a huge rat race all the time, people competing with each other trying to make a living?"

"True."

"So, it isn't too hard for anyone with half a brain to see that things are different up here," Sarah said pointedly, letting him know she was onto his little game. "Like I said, stepping back into time when life was simple and focused."

Frank's brow rose slightly as he eyed her, He cleared his throat. "You have to be focused up here, or you get chewed up."

He stepped aside as an old man came toward them carrying a load of supplies on his back. Sarah counted at least six cases of bottled water and a sizable box of canned goods bound to a large wicker basket over his shoulders. All of it was borne down from a wide strap across his head. As the man passed them by, he greeted Frank with a nod.

"My goodness, he must be carrying a hundred pounds!" Sarah said, once the man was out of earshot.

"Closer to one-fifty, I'm guessing," Frank replied.

Sarah shook her head. "How late in life do these people work? He looked to be well into his seventies."

"Actually, he's probably younger than you are," Frank answered and started to walk again. "Don't feel too bad for him. He's likely very wealthy by Nepalese standards. Sherpa porters are the backbone of the system here. This trail we're on is their highway."

As they marched over the up and down winding trail, he told her about the life of the Sherpa; how the first born son was dedicated to the local monastery and those after him either worked the farm or carried the goods up and down the hillsides to the various villages and tea-houses. Some went to school to learn the skill of a guide and if they excelled, went on to attain the status of a Sirdar or an Ice Doctor.

"What's a Sirdar?"

"A lead guide responsible for leading teams up the mountains. To achieve the ranking, they have to have summited the mountain at least once."

Sarah nodded. "And an Ice Doctor?"

"They fix the lines and ladders over the crevasses and up the faces of the glaciers. Dangerous work, especially when it gets warm."

"Yeah, seeing how ice and heat don't mix well."

"Well put," Frank said.

He fell quiet then, and by the time they reached Nachipang for their noon lunch, Sarah's perception of him had moved another notch towards him becoming passable. She was going to keep her distance though. Despite his pleasant demeanor, there was an undercurrent of guardedness behind his cool, gray eyes and easy-going smile.

* * *

After lunch, the team strode out into the mid-day sun, which was now high overhead. Sarah peeled her sweatshirt off, stuffed it in her backpack that sat on an outdoor picnic table where she slathered sunscreen on her face and neck. Then came a quick check of her camelback inside the pack. Having a good supply of water in it, she buttoned everything up, and squatted down to pull her backpack up onto her shoulders. As she did so, her son came beside her.

"How're you doing?" he said.

Sarah smiled up at him as she cinched the straps tight around her. "I'm doing great. What a beautiful country."

He nodded and was quiet a moment. "I saw you talking with Kincaid back on the trail."

"Yes, he's quite an interesting man," Sarah said, feeling Greg's guardedness. She wondered what was running around in his mind. "So, I guess it's up, up for a while, huh?"

"Yep," Greg answered. He reached over and tucked the mouthpiece of her camelback under her shoulder strap so it was positioned near her chin. As he did so, he said, "You talk about my father?"

Sarah stared into his deep blue questioning eyes, gauging him, knowing he was worried she'd stir things up. "No, we didn't talk about your father. It's none of his business."

Greg looked away. "Good. I don't want to —"

But Sarah put her hand up, halting him. "Don't worry. I'm not going to meddle in things." But they both knew it wasn't that simple. She noticed Lanzo looking on, and said, "I think someone's waiting for you."

Greg glanced back at the Italian. "Okay, see you on the trail then." He headed for Lanzo, and as he walked away from her, she bit her lip. Scaling the walls they had built around themselves over the last few years was not going to be easy.

* * *

An hour later, she was bringing up the rear of the team. It wasn't that she couldn't keep up. It was more that she liked the solitude of walking alone under the trees and thinking. Ahead was an upward slope and trudging upward on it was the Aussie. When she came beside him, he said, "Awesome trekking weather, eh?"

"Yes, nice and cool," Sarah agreed. "Aldan, right?"

"At your service," he said, joining her as she poled her way up the steady incline. "You from L.A.?"

Sarah took a pull of water from her camel back. "Yes, I am."

"I have a cousin living there. Encino I think it is."

"That's a little south of me," Sarah answered looking ahead to a pile of large stones that were embedded in the trail before her. As she picked her way over them, she said, "Where are you from?"

"Me, I'm from Bulls Brook, little wop north of Perth." He was quiet a moment then said, "So, you're not climbing, eh?"

"No, I leave that to my son."

Aldan hip-hopped over a couple of large stones and plopped back down next to her. "Seems a shame ta come all this way and stop short."

"Oh, I'm quite alright with it, believe me."

Aldan narrowed a puzzling gaze on her. "So you're here for what then, cheering the young lad on?"

Sarah saw him working things out in his head. Not caring for the conclusions he was coming to, she said, "Actually, my son is a very busy man and so am I, so we don't get a lot of face time together. I asked if I could come along, and here I am."

"That's nice. Kinda like a holiday for ya, then?"

"Something like that." She paused, wanting to get off the subject. "So, help me out here. My geography isn't great in your part of the world. Where's Perth?"

"On the west coast."

"Oh … So, you said you're a guide, right? Must be an interesting life. How'd you get involved with it?"

Aldan shrugged. "I've always been a wanderlust sort, so I guess I just fell into it."

"Family?"

"A brother and sister in Northam. A few kilometers northeast of me."

"No wife?" Sarah said.

"Nah. Had a few gals when I was younger, but that was it. And you?"

Sarah shook her head. "I'm widowed."

Aldan didn't say anything for a minute. At last, he piped up, "I'm sorry."

"It's okay. Been a while."

"I see." He was quiet a moment. "So your son said your husband climbed Everest."

"Well, he tried," Sarah answered, and felt her gut tighten.

"Which is more than most people can say. Must've been a fine memory for him."

Sarah gritted her teeth. "Not really. He died on that damned mountain." She stared off over the river unable to meet the man's gaze for several minutes then took a deep breath. "I'm sorry. You didn't need to hear that."

"No worries," Aldan replied, and for the rest of the hike, he remained quiet as he walked beside her.

Chapter 6

The team arrived in Phadking shortly after 4:00 PM and slogged through the tiny village to a handsome, cut-stone three-story building with red shutters at the northern-most edge of town. The building was 'The Red Rhododendron Inn' and it was one of Frank's favorite teahouses, ranking just behind the Juniper. Not surprisingly, it was also very popular with the rest of the trekking companies. Its spacious rooms and hot showers along with the large deck overlooking the fast-flowing Dudh Kosi River was the last of the cozy homes for quite some time. Knowing this, Frank made sure to book it a year ahead every time he passed through so as not to be shut out.

After getting everyone checked into their upstairs rooms, he went downstairs, grabbed a cup of masala tea, and strode out onto the broad, white stone terrace that skirted the front of the teahouse. On it sat wooden urns of flowering red Devil's Tongue and yellow Cobra Lilies.

He passed by the fragrant honey scented flowers on his way to the stone walkway, which was on the south side of the teahouse, and went down the sloping green hillside to a flight of wooden steps with an old rickety railing leading up to the timber framed deck.

Taking the treads two at a time, he climbed up to find Da-wa and Sangye at the far end by the railing with their backs turned to him. They were chatting about their upcoming plans once the climbing season ended. They turned around just as he stepped up behind them.

"Hey," Frank said, joining them.

"Hey, yourself," Da-wa answered back.

Frank peered down over the low overhanging Chir pine and rhododendron forest below, catching glimpses of the dark blue waters of the Dudh Kosi River cutting through the mountain pass. "Everything settled with Nam Kha?"

"Ho," answered, Sangye. "Only thing left is what clients buy."

"Good. I want to get an early start tomorrow. Who knows what we'll run into at the Monjo gate," Frank said. He glanced over at Da-wa. "You hear anything more about what's going on up there?"

The Sherpa shook his head. "They're looking for someone, that's for sure. 'Who is another question."

Right, Frank thought. 'Who?' was the question indeed. He had the uneasy feeling it was Khum Jung Mountaineering. The last thing he needed was to get held up in Monjo while things got sorted out. Knowing the way the wheels moved in the Nepalese park authority, it could take a couple of weeks. And wouldn't that just put a big smile on Patterson's long ruddy face. He gritted his teeth, hating the feeling of being left out in the dark, especially about such an important matter. Finally, he said, "Well, I guess we'll find out tomorrow, won't we?"

Da-wa fixed him with a knowing gaze. "You think they're looking for us, don't you?"

"The thought has crossed my mind," Frank answered.

"How much cash we got?"

Frank knew where he was going with that comment and shrugged. "Around two hundred thousand rupees."

Sangye and Da-wa exchanged glances. Da-wa said, "Should be more than enough if we need to turn heads."

Frank sighed "Yeah, but I'd just as soon we don't have to."

Sangye said, "Don't worry. It will be okay. You will see."

"Maybe," Frank answered, "but you know as well as I do how things work up here when it comes to greasing palms. If it comes down to it, just make sure our clients are kept in the dark. I don't want anyone thinking we don't have our act together, okay? If things get dicey, we'll feed 'em the standard stock reply; the park authorities screwed up the paperwork and are in the process of straightening things out. Got it?"

The two Sherpas nodded and they all looked off toward the snow-ridden peak of Nupla far to the east, each in their own thoughts as the clouds rolled in overhead.

* * *

That night, Frank tossed and turned. If worse came to worst, he did have the extra fee he'd gotten from Sarah to offset his losses. But he looked at her ten thousand dollar payment as a windfall because he didn't really have to do much of anything to earn it. They were already going to be up to Base Camp anyway, so what was one more person to deal with? Now his plans for that windfall were in jeopardy and it burned him up thinking he might have to give some of it away instead of using it for the school addition he had conceived with the Hillary Trust.

He reached over, and pulling his watch off the windowsill beside his cot, looked at the dim green numbers shining back. 2:30 AM. He needed to get some sleep. Today promised to be a long one and the two and a half hour hike that went up 550 meters to Namche at the end of the day was the least of his problems. Setting his watch back on the sill, he punched his pillow and plunked his head down. As he lay on his back staring up at the ceiling, he thought of all the years he'd put in toiling to carry on his mother's dying wish for the school she loved. "Keep it strong and prosperous," she had told him as she lay on her deathbed. "The Government Education Committee isn't doing their job. Promise me. The children need it so they can prosper and be happy."

"I'll keep it strong, I promise," he had answered fervently as he held her hand. He could still see her withered, careworn face gazing back at him. Her dark gray eyes had drilled into his heart fiercely, searching for an unsaid promise. At eighty-five, she was still as sharp-witted as she was at fifty. But her frail body had given up at eighty-three, and having been waiting for her beautiful mind to catch up, her body was starting to take matters into its own hands. A week later, she had passed away in his arms surrounded by her extended mountain family.

"Yes, mother, I am going to keep it strong," he muttered into the darkness of his room. He leaned over the side of the bed and dug his prayer beads out of his backpack's pouch. Shutting his eyes, he drifted into a meditative state, determined to shed all the negative thoughts and focus on the here and now.

The next thing he knew, it was morning. He sat up and squinted into the bright sunshine streaming in through his window. The meditation work he'd done last night had helped him galvanize his resolve.

After he got up, he stretched, breathing in the cold morning air that carried just a hint of pine and ginger into his room. In the kitchen below, he heard the muffled voices of the Rhododendron's staff as they worked at putting the morning's breakfast together. His stomach rumbled as he pulled on a pair of pants, grabbed a towel, and tracked out of his room bare to his waist for the tiny shower closet at the end of the hall. On the way, he ran into Sarah, who was just coming back to her room with toothbrush in hand.

"Morning," she said as she walked toward him.

"Namaste," Frank replied moving to the side so she could pass in the narrow sunlit hallway. As she passed by, he caught a whiff of vanilla. He quite liked it. "How's the water this morning?"

"Nice and hot," she said. "Now, if they could only put some hooks in there or maybe a shelf or two, that would be wonderful."

Frank laughed. "What, and make life easier?"

She groaned, and as she opened the door to her room, shot him a crooked smile. "See you downstairs."

* * *

Forty-five minutes later, Frank strolled into the immense, wood-paneled dining room and searched for Da-wa and Sangye among the crowd of noisy trekkers. The room buzzed with people telling stories and discussing the trail ahead as their guides brought plates of pancakes, scrambled eggs, toast, and bowls of porridge to their tables. In the far corner, he saw his Sherpa guides in conversation with a young Sherpa porter named Ta Shi. When Sangye noticed Frank, he put his hand up and waved him over.

Frank picked his way around the pile of daypacks and gear, and said, "What's up?"

Sangye said, "Ta Shi, tell Frank what you saw."

Ta Shi nodded respectfully to Frank, and said, "Namaste, Frank Kincaid."

"Namaste," Frank answered bowing back. "What did you see?"

"John Patterson. He was in Monjo yesterday and talking with park ranger. I see papers and a large envelope pass between them."

Frank glanced at Da-wa and saw a knowing gaze coming back. "Was the army soldier with them?"

"No, just park ranger."

Frank nodded. That was good. If the military man was involved in the bribe, things would get dicey. He thanked the young porter, slipped him a thousand-rupee note, and pulled the two Sherpas aside. "Well, I guess Johnny-Boy has played the money card."

"Ho," Da-wa said. "Thing is, how much did he give them and for what?"

Frank threw his Sherpa director a sidelong glance. "I think we can all guess what for," he said matter-of-factly, knowing the drill when it came to playing the complicated game of dealing out bribes. Finally, he said to Sangye, "We'll start with 60,000 and work up from there."

* * *

After they downed breakfast, Frank led the team outside under the deep blue sky that never seemed to quit this time of year. He glanced at his watch. It was quarter of nine. That would put them in Monjo just after the noon hour. If all went well, they'd make Namche right around 4:30 and be settled in by dinner. He knew the men would fare the two and a half hour switchback slog up the steep mountainside to Namche well, but Sarah's ability was doubtful. While she appeared fit, she was a novice, or so she had said when she booked her trek with Daku.

As he went ahead at a leisurely pace, he called Sangye up to him. "Look out for her after we get over the Hillary Bridge, would you?"

Sangye bobbed his head and drifted back down the line behind him. Two hours later, the team came to the tiny hamlet of Dengkar, and took their mid-morning tea break on a flagstone terrace under the arms of an old hoary oak. As Frank sat sipping his tea, Greg pulled a chair up next to him.

"A bit warm out," he said, leaning back in his seat.

Frank looked out over the noisy river crashing against the rocks below the elevated terrace and felt his guard go up. He had been trying to keep his distance from the young man over the last few days while he worked through his own feelings about what had happened up on the mountain years ago. At last, he said, "It'll get warmer as the day goes on."

Greg sat mute and Frank could feel his disquieting presence beside him. Finally, Greg said, "You think we'll have another repeat of last year's disaster on Everest?"

Frank shook his head. "No, I don't think so." He paused, and looked back at the long angular face staring back at him. "So what do ya do when you're not climbing?"

Greg stretched his legs out in front of him. "I'm an operations manager for a company supplying hardware to a giant computing company. Oracle; perhaps you've heard of them?"

"Larry Ellison's little toy. Yes, I have," Frank said. "Sounds like you have quite a future ahead of you."

"Keeps me busy," Greg answered. "I saw you talking with my mother the other day. She sort of invited herself along on my climb. I hope that's not a problem. I wanted her to stay in Kathmandu, but she wasn't hearing of it."

"So, you're not happy with her being here then?" Frank replied, which was no surprise as he had figured that out the moment he met the man last week.

"Nope."

Frank nodded. "Well, don't worry. She's not a problem. I have family members come up from time to time with us." He paused, and peering back out over the river, said, "Your mom is quite a woman."

"That she is," Greg answered, "and stubborn, as you'll soon find out."

Frank cracked a smile, not doubting it for a minute. "So how was the Matterhorn? I saw you tackled the south face. No easy assault, that one."

"Thanks. But it was more because I was testing myself, getting ready for this climb," Greg said. "Everest has always been my main goal."

Frank turned to him and narrowed his gaze. "Does your being here have anything to do with your father?"

Greg stared back with haunted eyes. "Some."

The question was rhetorical, and Frank knew it. Of course the man's father had something to do with it, just like Sarah's insistence on tagging along to Base Camp. What Frank needed to know was if Greg would answer truthfully or not. That was important. He didn't want Greg up on the mountain in denial of what was driving him up there. That was dangerous for everyone concerned. Still, there was something more the man was hiding. Frank could feel it, and it bothered him. He drained the rest of his tea and stood up. "Walk with me a minute."

He led Greg over to the side of the terrace, away from earshot of everyone and said, "I'm going to tell everyone this later on up at Base Camp, but I'm going to say it now because I have a feeling I know what you might be thinking. My cardinal rule is this; No matter what, your Sherpa guide is the boss up there. You obey him at all times. If he says, you're coming down — you're coming down. Ignore him, and you're on your own. Understand? I'm not kidding! I will leave you up there and you will most certainly die. Everest isn't the Matterhorn nor is it like any other mountain in the world. It will grind you up and spit you out. Stronger men than you have died up there and I won't put my Sherpa's life at risk for anyone who won't listen to him."

Greg nodded, averting his gaze to the river and was quiet for a moment. Finally, he looked back. "How many times have you been up?"

Frank considered the young American, wondering if he had heard him. But the pained expression coming back told him the off-track question was posed as a diversion away from some hidden truth. Finally, he said, "Five times."

"Will this be your sixth?" Greg said.

"Maybe," Frank answered cautiously. "I have one more summit left in me, just not sure when it'll be. Why?"

"Just wondered. I'd like to be by your side going up."

That will most certainly not happen! Frank thought. Aloud, he said, "You never know. Come, we'd better get back at it."

* * *

The team arrived in Monjo just after the noon hour and filed into a walled in terrace beside the two story beige stone and stucco park ranger's office. As usual, the checkpoint terrace was humming with trekkers milling about and talking while snapping photos of the snow-covered mountain peaks beyond the gatehouse entrance to Sagarmatha.

The waiting time for people entering the park depended on how well organized their guides were with the permits that needed final approval and processing; that, and the number of park ranger's staffing at the main desk, which was usually minimal. As a guide, you wanted to hit the park office no later than 1:00 PM otherwise the rangers would be taking their lunches, which meant anywhere from an hour to two hour delay. As far as Frank was concerned, he wanted out of here as soon as possible.

As he dug into his satchel to retrieve the permits and park entrance paperwork, his clients unloaded their packs from their shoulders onto one of the many picnic tables set outside the building. Some headed off in different directions looking for restrooms and refreshments. Da-wa and Sangye came over and huddled beside him under the watchful eye of a armed military guard who was lingering nearby. Frank felt his gut tighten. Even though he was accustomed to the army's presence at this checkpoint and others in the park, he always felt uneasy around them. The memory of the civil war in Angola, and the violence against its citizens when he was a child had never left him.

"Okay," he said to his Sherpa guides, "let's go find out if we're in someone's sights." He handed the satchel with the climbing permits to Da-wa and took a quick drink from his camelback before following Sangye to the line waiting outside the park office entrance.

Twenty minutes later, they stood just inside the polished oak doors that were thrown back and wedged in place. Frank's gaze darted around the shadowed lobby that was buzzing with men transacting their business with the park rangers. As he waited their turn, Frank saw one of the rangers watching him. The thin dark-skinned man had a stolid expression as he took the paperwork from one of the guides in front of them.

Frank knew Geet from the few interactions he'd had with him over the last couple of years. Although Geet had been cordial with him in the past, Frank didn't doubt for a minute he disliked him. Then again, the Nepalese authorities were always suspicious, if not belligerent, towards westerners intruding into their fragile economy. This was the one reason all the expedition companies in Sagarmatha used native folk when it came to negotiating the intricate and confusing system of doing business on the mountain.

At length, Geet stamped and signed the paperwork on the counter in front of him and sent a trekking guide on his way. Next in line was Sangye and Da-wa. The man waved them to the counter. "Namaste, Da-wa and Sangye. How have you been?"

"Very good," Da-wa answered.

"And how is your father these days?" Geet said, as Sangye laid the permits on the counter.

"Never better. We're hoping for a good planting season this year," Da-wa answered.

Geet smiled back. "So don't we all after last year. And you, Sangye, how is that young wife of yours?"

"Very pregnant," Sangye replied, which brought a wide grin from the park ranger. "And your brother? I have not seen him since before the monsoon."

"He is good. The monastery keeps him very busy." He glanced over at Frank, barely making eye contact. "Namaste, Mr. Kincaid. You are well, I hope."

"Very good, thank-you," Frank answered.

Geet nodded. "So, let's get you taken care of, shall we?"

As the review began in earnest, Frank went off to the side and watched Geet spread the documents out in front of him, studying each one in detail against the paperwork he had in front of him. Finally, he glanced up and shot a pointed frown at Frank. "There seems to be an informality here."

Sangye shook his head. "Really, what?"

"The dates," Geet said, "They are listed after Khum Jung's operating license being revoked."

Really? Frank mused, though it didn't surprise him after learning that John had been there before him.

"Revoked? By whom?" Da-wa said.

Geet studied his paperwork, but Frank knew it was all for show. There was no way his license had been revoked so quickly. Losing one's license took a lot of time in the complicated and convoluted maze of Nepalese bureaucracies. Finally, the man said, "Wait here, I need to confer with the officer on duty."

Frank watched the man walk over to his partner who was sitting at an old wooden desk going through a stack of files. The two men exchanged knowing looks then stared back at Frank before falling into a secretive conversation. When they finished, they came back to the counter.

The man who had been sitting at the desk looked the permits over with an affable expression on his fat, round face and said, "Namaste. I am Naresh. Geet, here, has told me about your problem, and sadly, I do not think there's anything I can do to help you."

"I don't understand," Sangye said. "How can it be that this license has been revoked? It was in place when we left Kathmandu only two days ago."

"I don't know what to tell you, except that I have documentation that says differently. I'm afraid you will have to take this up with the licensing authority in Kathmandu. In the meantime, I must ask you to go back to Lukla until it can all be straightened out."

Sangye pursed his lips, and after a moment, said, "Perhaps there is a solution."

"And what would that be?" Naresh said, staring back expectantly.

Sangye smiled. "What if I put the permits under my name?"

Naresh and Geet raised their brows. "I did not know you were licensed, Sangye. Since when?" Geet said.

Sangye said, "Just this year."

Which was not the truth, but Frank knew what was going on. Sangye was opening up the intricate game of greasing the wheels with the park rangers.

A tiny smile crossed Naresh's face as he put his hand up. "Let's not get ahead of ourselves here. Whether or not you are licensed has nothing to do with the problem here. The documentation requires the company's and the ministry's signatures to be affixed to it prior to entering the park. Therefore, I do not think it will be possible to transfer the permits in this manner. However, I am willing to look into it. Do you have your documentation?"

Sangye nodded. "I do, but how long will it take?"

"A couple of days, maybe more."

Sangye was quiet a moment then said, "Maybe I can move that along a bit."

"And how is that?" Naresh said, eyeing Sangye pointedly.

The two of them fixed each other with knowing gazes and Frank saw the unspoken words going back and forth between them. When the silent exchange was played out, Sangye said, "I have some documents I think you will find most useful."

When Naresh nodded, Sangye opened the front pouch and pulled a folder out with an envelope tucked underneath it and pushed it toward the man. "I think this will be of great help to you."

Naresh opened the folder and furtively slid the envelope out from underneath it. As he pulled it under the counter, his gaze went downward. A moment later, he looked up. "Hmmm … this is very interesting. Maybe something *can* be done. Is there another document that can support this one?"

Sangye glanced at Frank. "Why, yes, of course," he said, and pulled another folder out, again with an envelope attached to it and handed it to the man.

Naresh subtly smiled as he slipped the envelope out and brought it below the counter. Frank saw him counting the money tucked inside. A moment later, a wide, friendly smile was on his face. "Well, this does certainly change things," he said. "I did not know that you have been given special dispensation by the authorities in Kathmandu. Very well, everything does seem to be in order here, except for one thing."

"And what is that?" Sangye said.

"I need this document in duplicate for my files."

Meaning an equal portion for Geet. Frank bristled. He wasn't sure how much money Sangye had pushed across the counter, but he trusted it was a decent amount. Although he had promised himself to accept any outcome in the Buddhist way, he couldn't hold back the surging anger inside him. He shot the portly Naresh a withering frown and stomped out of the building.

Chapter 7

Sarah swept her gaze over the steep trail meandering down into the lush green valley beyond the Sagarmatha gatehouse. Since they left Phadking, the trail had been fairly level and an easy walk beside the Dudh Kosi River. But the sparkling glacier-fed tributary had lost itself in the trees over the last hour leaving the travelers behind. Straight ahead of her was a vast panoramic view of the conifer forest that stretched its dark green fingers up onto the shoulders of the gleaming snow-covered spikes. The raw power of the land spreading before her pierced her heart. *Truly, God dwells within this land,* she thought.

She closed her eyes, basking in the warmth of the noonday sun and breathed in God's resinous fragrance that wafted about her. Although she was not the devout Catholic her mother had been, she'd never gone a day without raising her eyes upward in supplication. And right now, more than any other time in her life, she felt God's awesome majesty by her side. Suddenly, she felt something 'click' inside her, but she didn't know what it was. Only that she felt a presence settle over her troubled heart.

As it cocooned her, her thoughts drifted back to the swift reaction she'd had to the Aussie when he asked her about her husband's climbing of the Monster. The visceral hatred she harbored toward the mountain all these years had reared its head, and as she stood there, she tried to reconcile it with what she was feeling right now.

Why was God doing this? His ways had always been a mystery to her. Him doing one thing when she had asked for another, and wasn't He doing that right now? Spreading out His masterpiece before her knowing that in this place was the source of so much grief. She didn't understand it, except that something was telling her to leave things in His hands — that all her fears were for nothing.

She wanted to trust in that more than anything, but after so many years of fighting Him, she didn't know how. She felt her throat tighten and bit her lip as His unspoken words whispered in her heart; then opened her eyes to find Carlo standing a few feet away staring out across the valley. As she turned to go back through the enclosed gatehouse, he stirred.

"Did I disturb you? So sorry," he said, turning toward her.

"Oh no, not at all. It's beautiful, isn't it?"

"Yes, it is," Carlo replied. He took a deep breath and said, "My papa would have loved this land. When I was just fourteen, he told me about our ancestors, how they came across the Northern Alps and settled on the foothills near Milan. They were mountain people, like the Sherpa people here, loving the highlands."

"I thought I might travel to Milan someday," Sarah countered as they strolled through the gatehouse passed a row of tall, bronzed metal prayer wheels. She ran her hand across their raised Sanskrit writing while she walked, turning the drums clockwise like Frank had showed her.

"Oh, absolutely you must come," Carlo said. "And you shall be my guest."

Sarah smiled. "Why, thank you. I shall keep that in mind." She was about to ask Carlo more about his restaurant when she saw Frank stalk out of the park office. He didn't look happy.

* * *

A half hour later, she was following the Italians down a winding rock stairway embedded into the narrow Sagarmatha valley. As she poled her way along, taking two steps ahead and one down, squirrels chattered in the lofty boughs while birds sang high overhead. If she didn't know better, she'd say she was hiking one of the trails in Yosemite. It had been years since she'd been there, and the thought of it brought back a fond memory of the camping she had done with her parents on the banks of the Merced River. She had just graduated from high school that summer, and her gift from them was a vacation up in the mountains, tramping about on the trails.

She smiled as she plodded along behind the men. Frank set an easy pace and she was glad for it. The afternoon sun was heating things up and she was sure that sooner, rather than later, they'd be going up — that is if they ever found the bottom of this earthen stair they were on. She looked downward, searching for some indication of it leveling out and saw a column of trekkers heading up toward her. More than a few had stopped to wipe their faces.

As they passed the trekkers on their way down, Frank met up with their guide. The man was around forty, she guessed, and his wide, inviting smile crinkled his tan, weather-beaten face. She watched them exchange greetings in Lhasa, then break into a friendly animated conversation. When the team came to a halt behind him, Frank stepped aside and waved them past. *Another one of Frank's mountain family,* Sarah supposed as she went by; but as she did so, she saw him nod in the direction of the Park office and shake his head. Something had happened back there, and she couldn't help but wonder what it was.

Drawing a sip of water from her camelback, she continued down the steps for another ten minutes until at last she heard the rushing waters of the Dudh Kosi in the distance. Before she knew it, she was picking her steps through and around the rocks that were scattered along the banks of the river. Here, she felt a welcome breeze sweeping over the sloshing rapids. At length, Frank and Sangye came trotting along from behind and caught up with her.

"Another friend?" Sarah said amiably.

Frank fell into step with her as Sangye followed them. "Yeah, we go back some. How you doing?"

"Alright. But it seems like we're always going down. I would've thought quite the opposite."

Frank grinned. "Don't worry, you'll be heading up soon enough." He drank a gulp of water and as he walked, re-tied his ponytail. As he did so, Sarah eyed him furtively.

Finally, she said, "Everything alright?"

"What do ya mean?" he answered, shifting his pack up on his shoulders.

"Well," Sarah said, treading cautiously with her words, "You looked upset when you came out of the building a little while ago."

"Oh, that? It was nothing. Just a tiny hitch; happens all the time. Not to worry, it's all taken care of. Well, I better get up front. You take your time. It's not a race." He turned to Sangye. "I'll see you at the break-point."

"Ho," Sangye replied.

Sarah watched Frank hike on ahead, unconvinced he was telling the whole truth, but it was essentially none of her business. What caught her attention was the gentle way he'd looked at her when he told her to take her time. While it was his job to look after those he led, the manner in which he addressed her seemed to be more than just the standard check-in she'd seen him have with the others. True, they were men, and men were men, never wanting to appear anything other than having everything under control, but still there was something different — perhaps a shift in attitude toward her?

She walked on with Sangye quietly trailing her. He was a soft-spoken boy — well, a boy to her anyways — and behind his doe-brown eyes, was a very observant mind. She wondered what he made of her, and for that matter, Sherpa Dave as well. When they looked at her, it felt as if they were almost afraid to get too close. Frank had said it was a cultural thing. Men in this part of the world took great care to maintain the socially accepted distance from women, meaning; you didn't show outward affection, hugs and so on in public. But there seemed to be more than that going on with the two Sherpa guides, as if they deemed her a threat or a bad omen. Whatever it was, she hoped it wouldn't last the entire two months they'd be together.

Twenty minutes later, the trail started upwards, and it wasn't long until Sarah saw a thin, gray bridge stretching out like a flimsy spider web over the raging current.

Her heart thumped as she took in the knitted cable and chain-link mesh expanse whose handrails were dressed with faded prayer flags fluttering in the wind. While she had crossed other bridges like it after leaving Phadking, this one was well over a hundred and fifty feet over the surface of the water. As the people walked over it, the bridge swayed and bounced back and forth.

Sangye came beside her. "Hillary Bridge," he said, smiling. "It is very safe. You'll be okay, you will see."

I'll be okay once I'm across it, Sarah thought. Aloud, she said, "I'm sure it is. I'm just not a fan of heights." After the words came rushing out, she laughed nervously. "You must be wondering what I'm doing here then."

"You come to see the mountain, I think." Sangye said.

Sarah kept her gaze fixed on the bridge and was quiet a moment. Finally, she muttered, "Something like that," and started back up the rising trail that wove back and forth through the trees. As she went, her thoughts returned to why God had brought her here. In the beginning it was all so simple. She came because of Greg, because she couldn't bear to wait an ocean away while he put his life in peril. But now, she wasn't so sure it was all because of him, and it cast doubt on her motives, leaving her uncomfortable.

She came to the crest of the hill. Although it had only been a short haul of fifteen minutes, it was the first real ascent she'd encountered so far and she had managed it without any trouble. She jabbed her hiking poles into the ground and, looking down a flight of several stone steps, started off after the team who was strung out onto the bridge in single file. As the men trod over it, the sound of the metal creaking and rasping came whispering back over the din of the cataract below.

"Just keep your eyes straight ahead," Sangye said behind her as she stepped off the last tread.

She stared down the long, narrow expanse and closed her eyes, steeling her nerves then opened them back up. Stepping onto the swaying bridge, she felt tiny vibrations run up her legs and into her chest. By the time she was at the sagging mid-span, it felt as if she were walking on a mattress.

"Crossing is like a dance. Time your steps," Sangye said, encouraging her.

Sarah nodded, and it wasn't long until she got the hang of it. When she reached the other side, she turned to him and smiled.

"See, I told you, you could do it," Sangye declared.

As Sarah looked back at the wiry Sherpa, a wave of triumph ran through her. Her heart danced with sudden exhilaration. She'd done it! She clenched her fists over her head shook them in victory over her fear. But as fear fell on its knees behind her, brute lack of sympathy raised its head in front of her. She stared at the countless switchbacks zigzagging up through the forest as far as she could see and took a deep breath. Glancing back at Sangye, she said, "Well, I guess there's no rest for the weary, huh?"

"No, no rest. We will go slow so take your time. No rush."

An hour later, Sarah felt like the mythological Greek king, Sisyphus, who rolled a boulder fruitlessly up the hill over and over, only to have it roll back down. She struck the tip of her hiking pole into the hard clay soil beneath her feet and came to a halt on what felt like the bazillionth switchback. As she did so, Sangye came beside her. "Not long now before we come to a break. How you doing on water?"

Sarah drank a gulp from her camelback, and nodded. "I need to peel a layer off." She squirmed out of her backpack and set it aside then pulled her sweat-soaked fleece top over her head. Wiping her face with it, she rolled it up and stuffed it into the pack's side pouch. "There, that's much better," she uttered as fresh air rushed over her shoulders and arms.

"Don't forget to protect skin," Sangye warned. "Even though we walk under trees, sun will still burn you."

He was right, and Sarah knew it. The sun would have a field day with her fair skin if she weren't careful. She dug out her bottle of sunscreen. After applying a generous amount to her face, shoulders, and arms, she took another drink and lifted her pack onto her shoulders.

"Okay, back at it," she muttered, and started off up the unforgiving slope that never seemed to end. Back and forth, over and over, up and up she climbed and as she went, she marveled at the heavy-laden porters who seemed to run up the hill cutting paths through the briars and scrub and across the switchbacks, some of them bearing loads well over a hundred pounds. How they did it was beyond her comprehension. Her back ached just watching them.

"Almost there," Sangye announced in an encouraging voice from behind.

"You said that fifteen minutes ago," Sarah grumbled, though she meant it all in fun.

"Little bit more. You will see."

"Uh-huh. I don't suppose there's an outhouse up there."

He stared back at her puzzled for a second then smiled. "Ho. Toilet."

Sarah could hardly believe it, but she wasn't arguing. She spiked her pole down between two long woody roots and hauled herself up over a small boulder. As she did so, Sangye called out, "Last switchback!" and, there it was when she turned around and peered up, daylight pouring down through the trees ahead onto what appeared to be a gentle, grassy slope. *Hallelujah!* She thought and marched toward it.

* * *

After a quick trip to the toilet, she joined the rest of the men who were sitting on a fieldstone wall under the trees. The Frenchmen were chatting amongst themselves in their flowing language and laughing at some unknown comment one of them had made. The Italians were quiet, each occupied with his own thoughts. Frank was talking with Sully, asking him questions about CERN as Greg listened in. Aldan nibbled an apple as he sat beside Toby and Jakob who were rummaging around in their backpacks. Sherpa Dave stood off to the side with Sangye looking out over the hillside beside them.

A little way off, a Tibetan woman wearing a woolen tunic with red and blue stripes on a background of black was selling apples and mangos to the weary trekkers coming up the trail. Sarah went over to her and bought a couple of mangos then went and sat in the shade of a large overhanging oak on one of the many boulders littering the site. As she bit into the fruit, she watched the coming and goings of people. Many of them were Europeans, coming from all over. A woman with a British accent was taking pictures of her trekking group. A man chugging from his water bottle nudged his partner beside him and pointed to a porter coming up the trail carrying a load of plywood on his back.

When she came to Nepal she never dreamed the trails would be so populated with people, to say nothing of the cattle and horses bearing supplies going up and down as well. Instead, she had envisioned an empty wilderness with broken-down hovels for homes. And the idea that the Internet and cell phones had found their way so far up into this lost world had never entered her mind. She didn't know whether to be glad for the conveniences at hand or sad to see people glued to their smart phones reading email and texting while the awesome beauty of this land was right in front of them.

She cast her gaze over to her son and wondered if he felt the same way, then eyed Frank. Her first impression of the enigmatic expedition leader had changed somewhat over the last few days. He didn't fit the mold she'd envisioned after reading the material Greg had showed her. She had expected a gung-ho adventurer, interested only in the thrill of the climb. What she found was a man who'd endeared himself to the indigenous people of the highlands. The kind of affection they had for him couldn't be bought. It had to be earned.

Frank glanced her way then stood and pulled his backpack up. "Okay everyone, *sammma hami haru Lae Jau Cheen.*"

Those were the words of onward and upward, and Sarah was coming to the point of dreading them. She finished her mango and got up as the team across from her gathered their packs and struck off behind Frank and Sherpa Dave into the forest. As Sarah watched them slip into the shadows, Sangye stepped beside her. "Rest of the way not so steep. You want me to carry anything for you?"

"Oh, no, but thank you," Sarah answered, hoisting her pack up. After she put it on, snapping the straps together and cinching them tight, she pasted a smile on. "Shall we?"

Sangye nodded, and the two of them started off up the long winding incline through the trees to Namche. As they slogged ever upward onto the back of the Himalayan ridge, Sangye began to open up, asking her about the States: where she lived, what she did, and did she like it?

After she answered him, she said, "What about you? Where do you live?"

"Down below Lukla in village called Tingla."

"And family?"

"Ah, five brothers, one sister. Oldest brother, live in Monastery up in Tengboche. You will meet him when we go through," he said.

"And are you married? Any children?"

Sangye broke into a wide grin. "Yes, very soon I will have first child."

Sarah reveled in his delight and asked him what they planned to name the child. But Sangye told her that much of it depended on the day he or she was born. Each day had its own virtue, and that determined the child's destiny. She thought about that a moment and decided she liked the custom. It made her think what name she would have chosen for Greg had she been raised over here. She walked a bit more without saying a word, then asked a question that she hoped would lead to another that had been on her mind since the night in Lukla when she opened up to Frank.

"So how long have you been with Frank?"

"Oh, long time now. Seven years, maybe."

"You like working for him?"

"Oh yes, he is best expedition leader on mountain."

Sarah wondered if she should ask about what happened back up in Monjo, but decided not to and asked instead the question that was foremost on her mind. "Sangye, what's he like? I mean when he's not running expeditions?"

Sangye shrugged. "Same. Why?"

"Just wondered," Sarah muttered. Disappointed, she tried to think of a way to rephrase her question; to get a peek through Frank's armored façade. But short of coming right out and asking Sangye if Frank was really a nice guy, which she knew she wouldn't get a straight answer on, nothing came to mind. Huffing, she took a quick drink from her camelback and picked her way over a pile of rocks on the narrow trail that cut across a sharp drop-off tumbling down into the forest. After a while, the forest blended into an ongoing kaleidoscope of green. They should be nearing Namche, but she didn't see anything ahead that indicated it.

Looking back over her shoulder, she said, "How much further?"

"Oh, not far, maybe … ten, fifteen minutes. Oh, careful," he cried, and ran up to her just as she felt the ground give away under her feet. As she felt herself going over the edge, he grabbed her arm and steadied her.

Sarah caught her breath. Looking down the steep slope that ran away through the dense understory of the forest, she felt her heart thump. "My goodness!" she said.

"You okay?"

"Yes, thank you. I guess I need to be more careful," she replied and backed away weak-kneed from the edge.

Sangye let go of her arm. "Just take your time, use poles, and watch where you're going, eh?"

"Yes," Sarah answered, blowing out a deep breath. But inside, she was shaking. She stood there, waiting until she had control of her nerves then pushed back onto the trail. As she went, she felt Sangye close behind until at last the trail widened and came out onto a broad level opening with a row of wood-framed shops built into the hillside. On their porches were tables holding hand-crafted jewelry, handheld prayer wheels, and other trinkets, and dangling from the rafters above were chiming cowbells on colorful braided straps of wool. Out in front of the shops, children played under the watchful eyes of women hawking their wares to the bypassing trekkers.

Feeling much better to be on safer ground, Sarah breathed in the cool mountain air and watched the kids run around playing some version of tag. As she stood there enjoying their fun, she saw Frank sitting under the shade of a large maple tree with his pack beside him.

When he saw her, he got up, and threw his pack on. "You made great time," he said, coming to her. "Dinner will be in an hour. Here, let me take your pack. Sangye, would you take care of business with Thami while I help Ms. Madden here?"

Sangye nodded, and hurried on ahead. Sarah eyed Frank sidelong. There was nothing more she would like than to be then relieved of the burden grinding down on her shoulders, but she was determined to carry her own weight the whole way. At last, she replied, "Thank you, but no. Please don't take this the wrong way, but I want to finish this myself."

He considered her a moment, before breaking into a winning smile. "Very well then, after you."

They strode past the shops to the end of the village and up a winding stair that spilled out onto the foot of a funneled plateau overlooking the valley far, far below. But it was the village with its colorful red, blue, and green roofs with matching trim on the windows and doors that caught Sarah's eye. She stopped and breathlessly took in the scene before her.

Suddenly, she heard, "Kincaid, Kincaid!" She looked down to see a young boy run into Frank's arms. Picking him up, he tousled the boy's long, raven hair and broke into Lhasa as a throng of children came running down the path toward them.

Chapter 8

Frank set the boy down as the children swarmed around him begging for attention. Many of them he had known since the day they were born. He slid out of his pack, and digging into one of its many pouches, pulled out several candy bars as Sarah stood back and watched. As he passed them around to his eager audience, he eyed her from time to time. The intensity of her gaze unsettled him. It had been years since a woman looked at him like this, and the end-result that time had been a painful lesson in placing too much trust in someone you gave your heart to. Compounding his unease was the growing awareness of her understated beauty. Up until now, he had done his best to ignore her soft oval face and imploring eyes that were as blue as the Himalayan skies. But now, he saw the impossibility of ignoring her shining face anymore, so he looked away and sent the children off back to their homes. Finally, he motioned toward the three-story teahouse waiting for them at the end of the narrow lane cutting across the village. "Come, let's get you settled in."

* * *

After dinner, Frank pulled Da-wa outside and told him he'd be heading up to Khum Jung first thing in the morning. He wanted to check on the addition to the high school, but more than that, he wanted to get his head back on straight. To do that, he needed time away to think about a lot of things, chief among them, John Patterson and Sarah Madden. In that regard, Ang Tashi-ring's quiet wisdom would be invaluable in helping him get his grounding back. The venerable old Nyingmapa Lama always seemed to know the right questions to ask, and when to remain silent.

He looked up at the failing light over the towering ridge across the valley. "Make sure Sarah's on the acclimatization hike tomorrow. She's a strong woman, but I don't want to chance her getting in trouble when we head up to Tengboche. I'll be back in time for our departure on Thursday."

"Ho," Da-wa replied. The Sherpa studied Frank a minute, then said, "You okay?"

Frank shrugged. "I don't know. It just seems like things are ganging up against us."

"You mean Andersen?"

Frank nodded, but kept his growing affection for Sarah to himself. "Yeah. Look, I'm going to go for a walk around. See you in the morning."

The Sherpa bade him good night and walked back into the teahouse leaving him alone. Frank stood on the terrace outside the building, listening to the murmuring village set upon the steep slope behind him. Below, the terraced landscape dropped like a stone into a dark valley that was partially obscured by thick strewn clouds hanging on the treetops. He stared out over them to a dark ridge beyond, and as he did so, thought of a time not so long ago when life seemed so clear and unencumbered by messy feelings.

Back then, he knew who he was, or at least he thought he did. But now, he wondered. Had he simply been fooling himself, believing he was happy living alone with no one to share his hopes and dreams with? He suddenly found he couldn't answer that question. And while he'd had his issues with Kate, who was the only woman he'd ever allowed close to him, he had to admit there had been times of great joy with her as well. Did he miss them? Did he miss her? For a long time after she left to go back home to New Zealand, he'd told himself he didn't. But after the last few days with Sarah, whom he'd looked on as the enemy — yes, an enemy — and had sworn to keep at arm's length, he found he hadn't been as happy as he supposed.

He drew out his prayer beads and fingered them in his hands, and a minute later set off into the hills behind the teahouse, turning the large metal prayer wheels on the stone walls beside him as he went while reciting their soothing words. As he walked, he eyed the sacred mountain of Khumbila and wondered what questions his Buddhist mentor and friend, Lama Tashi-ring, would leave him with.

Frank was a teen when he met the Lama, and it was after Pasang died on the mountain that he really got to know the man. But it was during his stay in

Khum Jung afterward, as he tried to figure out who he was and why the world was dealing him such a difficult lesson that the Lama became a permanent fixture in his life.

The old man's withered brow, scraggly white beard and hair that seemed to float over his golden dome came to Frank's mind. But it was the red-robed lama's all-seeing dark eyes and unflappable expressions that resonated the most. Nothing ever bothered the man as far as Frank could tell and his peaceful easy manner seeped into all who met him.

Frank smiled as he found a place to sit and look out over the hillsides below that were deep in shadow. As he sat there amongst the scrub pine and black-berry briars soaking in the earthy smells of the montane grasses around him, his gaze settled on a small upright cairn of stacked stones a couple meters away. The mountain folk erected them to send prayers and hopes up to Khumbila, and they were all over the high places of Sagarmatha, waiting to be toppled, whereby the god of the mountain was thought to have sent back his answers.

It had been a while since Frank indulged in building a prayer tower, but suddenly he felt compelled to. Getting up, he collected several flat stones nearby and brought them back. Dumping them on the ground, he sat beside them. Ten minutes later, he had erected a tower half a meter high. He leaned back, regarding his cairn then closing his eyes, sent an unsaid prayer upward into the last pale light of day.

* * *

The next day Frank was up early, and after a quick breakfast of porridge and toast, he grabbed his backpack and headed out to meet a brilliant blue-skied morning. As he strode down the narrow lane back the way he'd brought the expedition team in the day before, he ran into Sarah, who was out with her camera taking in the sweeping vista.

"Well, good morning, Mr. Kincaid," she said, offering him a smile.

"You're up and about early," Frank said as he headed toward her. He stopped a safe distance away, careful to not get too close, but she had other ideas and slid over next to him.

"I thought I'd take some pics of this gorgeous valley below," she said. He heard her take a deep, refreshing breath. "My goodness, what a beautiful day — not a cloud in the sky."

"Yes, it's like that this time of year. Clear skies in the morning and cloudy in the afternoon," Frank put in, taking a step back from her.

Her bright smile dimmed. They stood there a moment in silence, each in their own thoughts. Finally, she nodded toward his backpack. "Going somewhere?"

"Well ... yes. I'm heading to Khum Jung for the day to check on my project," Frank replied and glanced off toward Ama Dablam, whose icy peak glistened from the sunlight raining down over its shoulder. Sarah suddenly went quiet. As she stood beside him, he could feel her nervous tension. At last he said, "I'll be back by tomorrow morning."

"Oh, you're staying overnight?"

"Yeah." Again he paused, not knowing what more to say. He frowned. *Why am I suddenly tongue-tied?* Finally, he said, "By the way, make sure you join the guys on the acclimatization walk today. Very important."

"I'll do that," Sarah said, but her answer came off as stilted. She rubbed her shoulder. "I must say, I'm feeling muscles I didn't know I had this morning."

"Little sore, huh?"

"Sore doesn't begin to describe it," she replied. "I saw they have a deal on massages at our teahouse. Think I'll take them up on it."

He fought back the image of her lying on the table in semi-undress. "Well, I'd better get going. Got a bit of a slog ahead of me."

"Okay. I guess I'll see you tomorrow then," she said. As she turned back toward the stone fence beside them, he found himself wishing he had ended the conversation another way. But he hadn't, so he headed for the main north-south passage cutting up through the terraced village.

On his way up through Namche, he stopped by one of the many small mercantile shops and loaded his pack up with pens, pencils, pads of paper, and anything else he could purchase as gifts for the kids as well as something nice for the teachers. A chunk of chocolate for himself to snack on his way rounded out his shopping spree.

Twenty minutes later, he stood looking down at Namche. From high above, the village took on the appearance of a spattered rainbow laying face down in a large brown bowl that had been cut in half. At the deepest part of the bowl was a funnel like spout that threatened to pour the village out into a five hundred fifty meter drop to the Dudh Kosi River below.

Then, from a distance, he heard the thwapping of chopper blades heading for the dirt landing strip on the upper bluff behind him. He turned and skirted the rim of the Namche bowl counter-clockwise. After another twenty minute hike, he was walking on a broad level field. On it, a half-kilometer or so away, was a large S-76C Sikorsky transport helicopter with people ducking their heads under it.

Frank smiled and shook his head. Some big hotshot had just landed, he supposed. He always laughed when one of them came in on their flying chariots. Especially when they landed on the mountain ridge across from Namche to spend a night in a ridiculous resort some idiot had poured millions of rupees into. Funny thing was, they didn't last long before they came down puking their guts out or complaining of a mind-numbing headache from ascending to the sky-high altitude resort to quickly. So much for the high life!

The remaining hike to Khum Jung was mainly downhill cutting through the rocky terrain pocked with stunted chir pine. Here and there, rangy scrub and wild berry bushes ran along the maintained path of stone pavers and steps. The trekkers and expeditions would be heading east toward Tengboche so he essentially had the trail to himself. Occasionally, he met up with a porter or a solitary hiker.

As he went, he entertained himself with the latest Nepalese tunes coming off Sangye's iPod. Frank wasn't much of a music man, but it was good company when he hiked alone. An hour later, he stood staring down at a sea of green roofs with a tall, white Buddhist Stupa out in front. He hoofed it down the fifty steps of pitted camel-colored sandstone and onto a narrow straightaway path toward the village.

Meeting him at the edge of the settlement was the school grounds, and on them stood a sculptured bust of Sir Edmund Hillary on a tapered stone pedestal. He went to the white wrought-iron fence surrounding it and stopped to look at the larger-than-life man who had started it all back in 1961, back when Frank was just four years old and living in the port city of Luanda, Angola.

The first school building was conceived shortly after Hillary arrived in Khum Jung, haggard and suffering altitude sickness. Taken in and cared for, Hillary had asked what he could do for the locals. The answer had been unanimous; 'we need a school for our children'. In a whirlwind, money was raised and soon afterward, a small one room, prefabricated building was standing twenty meters to his left. Frank glanced over at the work of love, toil, and sweat that had been brought up piece by piece on the backs of village Sherpas, and felt humbled.

Across the yard, the sounds of hammers chipping away at the quarried stone signaled ongoing work to the addition whose exterior walls were now half way erected. He bade the statue 'Namaste', and headed over to his foreman who was setting the front door frame in place. The dark man whose bare arms were dusted with powdery chalk looked up as he came near.

"Namaste," the man said. "Wasn't expecting you until June. Everything okay?"

Frank nodded. "I was just in the neighborhood. Thought I'd stop in. She looks great," he said standing back and taking in the progress of the stonemasons.

"Ho, she is coming along," the man said, joining him. He took Frank's hand and walked him around to the other side, showing him the window frame he'd been working on. "What you think? You like?"

"Very much," Frank said, eyeing the detailed dentil moldings that had been painstakingly carved by hand around the perimeter of the frame. "Oshon, you never cease to amaze me."

The Sherpa smiled. "I have word roof arriving in two weeks."

"That's good," Frank replied, and was about to say more when a flock of children came running across the yard toward him. Frank patted the man on the shoulder and went out to meet them. Setting his pack down, he knelt on one knee as they crowded around him, calling his name and asking him questions.

One of the boys named Harka got right to the point. "What you have in your pack, Mr. Kincaid?"

Frank smiled and pulled the lad toward him. "Let's find out, shall we?" He opened the top flap and dug out a handful of pens and pencils, and began handing them out. As he did so, other children started arriving. Word traveled fast when gifts were being given and it wasn't long until he was handing out the last pad of paper. "That's all, kids. Now show me what you've all been up to."

They led him to the elementary school and five minutes later he was busy perusing their nature discovery projects as the teacher stood by with a beaming smile. This was what Frank lived for, seeing their young inquisitive minds at work, looking at the world as a beautiful place to live and discover, unfettered by the fear of violence that pervaded so many cities of the world. At last, he turned to the teacher and handed him a paper bag with thank-you cards, each signed by him and holding five, one-thousand-rupee notes inside for the staff.

* * *

That evening, Frank made his way from his three-room simple stone-built home along a winding street to the modest wood-framed and stucco-clad monastery located on the north side of the village. Its gabled roof and salmon-colored walls looked out over the village with a paternal-like presence. Rounding a bend, he came to a courtyard nestled beside the monastery. In back of it was a small, whitewashed building with a dark green band running under its eaves. An old water pumping station was housed within it. A sign nearby proclaimed it as a Hillary project.

Frank walked past the courtyard up to the monastery's front door and entered a broad stone-tiled courtyard. Sitting on a carved wooden bench across the courtyard, was the old lama reading from his book of prayers. He looked up as Frank strode out toward him. Grabbing his long dark staff, the lama stood and shuffled out to greet him.

"Namaste, Frank. What brings you back so soon? You miss me already?" the Lama said.

Frank dipped his head in reverence to the red robed man. "Namaste, Tashi. May I sit with you for a while?"

The Lama eyed him pointedly, but nodded toward the bench he had gotten up from. "Something the matter?"

"Yes," Frank said, going over and taking a seat. He paused, waiting for Tashi to join him as ginger and juniper incense wafted about the courtyard. When the lama sat, Frank looked off toward the monastery gate, then back at him. A minute later, he proceeded to tell him everything that had happened over the last two weeks regarding John Patterson and his unexpected change of heart regarding Sarah. As he did so, Tashi remained quiet and hardly moved a muscle. But there was plenty going on behind his wizened eyes. "I do not understand this karma," Frank said, coming to the end of his tale.

Tashi remained still for another five minutes, as if letting Frank's story soak in. Finally, he leaned forward and softly said, "Frank, destiny is a mystery. It does not make sense until you look back upon its tapestry and see its perfection. It is not up to you to direct it, only to accept it. This Patterson, he will do what he going to do, you know this. All you need to do is accept it and to continue doing what you know is right in your heart."

"Even if it means ending my charity-work at Khum Jung? The school depends on what I bring in from my expeditions."

"I do not mean to lessen the work you do here for the children of Khum Jung, but school was here before you came and it will be here after you are gone."

"But —"

"But nothing. The Trust and people here will find other ways to keep it running, and besides learning does not confine itself to buildings and computers. Its classrooms are everywhere: in forest, the cities, the mountains, the deserts, and most important in the heart." He paused letting the words settle into Frank, then continued, "It may be that karma has a new road for you, hmmm?"

Frank sighed. "I've done this all my life, I don't know anything else."

"Sure you do." Tashi retorted. "Do not limit yourself by your fear. Fear is nothing unless you make it so."

"I know."

"Then why are you letting it run you around like a squirrel in the forest?"

"I don't know."

"Oh, you know. You just won't admit it. Until you banish it from your heart, you will look over your shoulder all your life. Is that what you want?"

"No."

"Then what do you need to do?" He put his hand up. "Do not tell me. Tell yourself. Ask yourself why you run from your heart, when it knows what it wants to do?"

"You mean Sarah?" Frank said, guessing his intention.

"I did not say that, but it is interesting you did. What do you think that means, hmmm?"

Frank thought about that a moment. "I don't need the complication in my life."

"What you call a complication may be an answer. You ever think about that? Maybe she has a part to play."

"Except she lives clear across the ocean, ten thousand kilometers away."

Tashi smiled. "Ah, so. Hmmm … I wonder what that mean?" He let the words hang between them then got up. "You have a good night Frank. I'm taking these old bones to bed."

Chapter 9

Sarah stood by the stone knee-wall on the teahouse terrace retying her pony-tail while peering out over the Namche valley below. Beside her, Greg was going through his backpack looking for something. She glanced down at him, wondering what he was after before peering back up at yet another pristine, blue-skied morning. Finally, she said, "What are you looking for?"

He glanced up, perplexed. "What ... oh, my power adapter."

"I have mine if you need it," she offered.

"Thanks, but I want mine."

Sarah smiled. Though he never really knew his father, he was so much like him when it came to his belongings. She knew enough to leave him alone and suppressed the urge to help. "So, we're on to Tengboche today."

Greg ducked his head back into his pack. "That's the plan." Over his shoulder, he added, "How ya feeling? Still sore?"

"No, the massage was wonderful," she replied, which brought his head back out. He leveled a crooked frown at her, as if to say, 'I didn't really need to know that, did I?' She shook her head, and rolling her eyes turned back toward the valley. "Anyway, I feel great. By the way, did you find your internet café yesterday?"

"Yeah. It was a joke," he snorted and went back to rummaging in his pack.

"How so?"

"The computer server kept bombing out. Took me over a half hour to get into my email account," he muttered then exclaimed, "Ah, there it is." He held it up. "I need to go charge my phone before we skate this morning. Be right back."

Sarah watched him trot into the teahouse and mulled over whether or not to ask him if his girlfriend had contacted him. Her son was rather tight-lipped about his personal life where it concerned matters of the heart. But she wanted to be there for him if he wanted to talk.

When he returned, he had a bottle of water in hand. As he opened it, she said. "So, anything from Jenny?"

Greg frowned. "What are ya talking about?"

"In your email?" Sarah said. "Did she write you?"

"No. And haven't we been over this a couple of times already?"

"I'm sorry, it's just that —"

He stood up and pressed his lips together. At last he said, "Mom! Please. I'm fine, don't worry," he answered as Frank came around the corner.

"Namaste," Frank said, shedding his pack.

Sarah quickly composed herself. "Morning, Mr. Kincaid. You just get back?"

"About fifteen minutes ago." He gave them a quick glance and looked northward over the Namche ridge. "Khumbila is beautiful this morning, isn't it?" he said, nodding toward the looming peak rising over the distant trees.

Sarah put her hand over her eyes to shade the bright sun. The tall conical mountain to the northeast was swept of ice and snow save for the peak, which blazed in the sunlight. "Yes, it is."

"It's called the Protector and it's sacred to these people," Frank said, coming close beside her.

Sarah inched back. After yesterday morning's stilted meeting on the path outside their teahouse, she got the feeling he didn't like her getting too close. Yet here he was, standing next to her and acting like it never happened. Then again, why had it bothered her? It wasn't like they were going to be close friends, except that it was nice to be around someone who was not obsessed every minute with the looming climb ahead. The rest of the climbers, including her son, were living in that world right now, talking about the summit attempt every chance they had, and the weather as it pertained to it.

Finally, she said, "Why's that?"

He eyed her companionably. "It's believed to be the essence of an old god that was subdued and converted to Buddhism," Frank said. "One legend has it that Khumbila stretched out its arms and held back a thundering glacier that broke off Phuletate beyond to the north, saving the lives of all within the Khum Jung valley below."

"Phuletate?"

"A mountain north of Khumbila." He waved in its general direction and turned to her. "Please call me 'Frank'."

"Okay," she answered, but the fragile trust that had been building toward him was wary of his sudden back and forth attitude.

Frank paused, and as he stood looking down at her, she sensed his uncertainty, as if he was afraid to say what was on his mind, making his formless thoughts real by adding the weight of the spoken word to them. At last, he took a deep breath, removed the thong tying back his long graying hair and shook his head, splaying it out over his shoulders. "And your acclimatization hike yesterday, how was it?"

"It was great," she answered as she watched him run his long fingers through his thick mane. He combed it out and tied it back into place, then pulled his sunscreen out.

As he slathered it on his arms, neck, and face, he said, "So, did you get your massage?"

Now it was Greg's turn to roll his eyes. "I'm going in to fill my camelback and get my phone," he announced then turned to Frank and added, "When we shooting out?"

"As soon as everyone's ready," Frank replied.

After Greg went inside, Sarah found she couldn't keep from grinning. Frank eyed her quizzically. "What's funny?"

"My son. I think the idea of his mom getting a massage is just a little too much visual information for him," she said.

"Ah, we boys don't like imagining our parents doing anything resembling, you-know-what," Frank agreed. "Some things you just don't want to know." He flipped the tab shut on his bottle of sunscreen and offered her the bottle.

She took it, and as she went about applying a douse of it to her face and neck, she said, "How was Khum Jung?"

"Khum Jung was great."

"And your project?"

"Moving along wonderfully."

Sarah handed him back the bottle. "Mind if I ask what it is?"

"Not at all. It's an addition onto the high school. Enrollment has skyrocketed, and things were getting tight up there for the kids."

Sarah blinked. "You have a high school up there?"

"Yes, and an elementary school as well."

"Really?" Sarah replied. Suddenly her mind was racing ahead with questions. "Tell me about them. How many students?"

"About 300 now, but the way things are going, it'll be up to 350 before long," Frank replied. He pulled his fleece shell over his head and rolled it up.

"And what is the curriculum?"

"Name it. We try to incorporate it all."

Sarah caught the reference to 'we'. *Oh, my goodness, does he teach, too?* Aloud, she said, "You are full of surprises."

"How's that?"

"I never suspected you were in the classroom."

Frank chuckled. "Oh, I don't teach."

"Just build additions?" Sarah said, and felt a smirk come to her face.

"Something like that," Frank said, offhandedly. He pulled a buff out of his backpack, folded it into a makeshift hat, and pulled it over his head. "Well, I'd better get folks rounded up."

As he left her to go inside, Sarah sat on the knee wall and thought about all he had said. She admired people who worked behind the scenes, doing the necessary things no one else wanted to do that made the quality of life better for others, children especially.

* * *

Two hours later, the expedition team had hiked to an elevation of 11,650 feet. Strung out single file on a narrow dirt path skirting the mid-section of a towering treeless ridge, they had clear views as far to the north and east as the eye could see. To their immediate left was a scrubland that rose sharply toward the deep blue sky and to the right it fell away at a dizzying rate. Sarah kept her head down focused on the trail as much as possible, though from time to time she peered across the chasm at the tan gossamer trail lines that were etched into the distant ridge.

Since the team had left Namche, the temperature had dropped into the low fifties and the steady north wind blew unimpeded by the lack of trees that had given up on the narrow ridge they had traveled alongside an hour ago. In the distant northeast, glimpses of Island Peek and Ama Dablam, which Frank had pointed out a half hour ago, could be discerned. At length, the trail swung westward in a great sweeping bend, and when at last they came around it, they stopped and took in the first glimpse of the Monster.

Behind the massive ice and snow packed wall of Lhotse, it loomed casting a cloud of blowing snow to the east. Sarah stared at it, seeing and feeling more than the men around her. As they pointed and gestured to the white plume streaking off its peak, the memory of the day long ago came roaring back to her. Except now the memory took on a new meaning, and that meaning was standing ten feet in front of her, high-fiving his climbing buddies. She closed her eyes trying to ignore the visceral reaction running through her and as she did so, felt someone slide up beside her.

"You okay?"

Hearing Frank's voice, she nodded. "Sun's a little bright." She averted her gaze downward, unwilling to let him into her private moment and dug her sunglasses out. Putting them on, she said, "There, that's better." She paused, stared northward in contempt, and added. "So that's it, huh?"

"Yep," Frank said.

She felt his gaze and wondered if he knew how she felt being here. Panning to her right, her gaze settled on the leaning conical peak of Ama Dablam. As she studied it, she wondered if her son would add it to his list of conquests. Pointing below it, she said, "And Tengboche is over there, somewhere, right?"

"A little more to the right," Frank replied, directing her gaze to a point just over the ascending wedge of a distant dark ridge. "We'll be there in a few hours. You been drinking your water?"

Sarah nodded, and looking back forced a smile, glad for the anonymity her sunglasses provided.

"Good girl," Frank said, his tone soft and inviting. He cleared his throat. "Okay, time to go now."

"I know, *sammma hami haru*," Sarah said, and paused trying to remember the rest of the Nepalese words that meant, 'to get this train going'.

Frank smiled. "*Lae Jau Cheen.*"

* * *

The trail gradually dipped down to around 10,650 feet and leveled off until at last they came to Phunki Tenga. There, they had a light lunch of noodles, rice, string beans, and fried potatoes, then headed off under a bright sky toward the long climb to Tengboche. Again, the team was met with switchback after switchback as they slogged up through the trees that had since returned after their descent an hour ago.

Unlike the hot and humid climb to Namche though, the resinous mountain air here was cool, and a steady northeast wind funneling up the valley beside them kept the humidity at bay. Sarah made a point of taking short breaks often, then after a quick drink, would push on. Again, Sangye tagged along after her, and like before they fell into an easy conversation, talking about the land and the people of the Himalayas.

Poking her hiking pole into firm soil, she hopped up onto one of the many large rocks that studded the ragged trail before her. "So, I hear there's a school in Khum Jung," she said. "Did you go there, Sangye?"

"Ho," he replied. "Long time ago."

Sarah smiled at his reference to 'long time'. He was only thirty years old, if that. She came to the end of the steep switchback and stopped; more to face the young Sherpa than to catch a quick breather. "I bet you have a lot of nice memories of it."

"Many, yes. I met my wife there when we were in fourth grade," he answered as a smile came to his face.

Sarah loved seeing him smile. His whole face lit up. As she took in his revelry, the memory of her first meeting with Steven came to mind. It was the fall of 1980, her first year at UCLA. Her roommate at the dorm had heard about a frat party off campus, and so they went, and there she met a tall, brown haired cocky senior with a magnetic personality and a quick wit. At last she said, "I met my husband in school, too. I was a freshman in college."

"Ahhh. So, your husband, what does he do?"

Unwilling to dampen the friendly moment between them, Sarah pasted on a tiny smile. "My husband is no longer with me."

"Oh, so sorry."

"Don't worry about it, it's okay," she lied. She cleared her throat and pushed the memory away. "So, Frank told me he's building an addition up at the school. That must keep him very busy. How does he have the time to do it and run this expedition?"

Sangye shrugged. "He not build it by himself. He pay others to do it for him from money he make guiding people up mountain."

"Really?" Sarah said, intrigued.

"Oh, yes. He donate everything he make to school, except enough for him to live on."

Sarah took a minute to digest what he told her. At last she said, "How long has he been doing it?"

"Oh, long time," Sangye answered. "Since I was in school."

Sarah eyed the Sherpa's enigmatic expression discerningly, finding it hard to believe what he told her, yet quite sure Sangye was telling the truth as he saw it. If it really were true though, she owed Frank a lot more respect than what she had been giving him. She collected herself and said, "I assume that is where you met him, then?"

"Ho. He came to the school often. Fix things when they broke, built stuff for us, and make toys," he replied.

Sarah nodded, open mouthed and started back up the trail. "Toys. I bet he was popular."

"Very popular," Sangye answered. "He tutor me in English. Got me interested in books."

"Books?" Sarah said. *My goodness, how much more is there to you, Mr. Kincaid?* "So, what book did he get you hooked on?"

Sangye was quiet a moment as he walked behind her. Finally, he laughed and replied, "You not believe, but *Moby Dick*."

"A classic," Sarah answered. She peered back over her shoulder at him. "And what did you think of *Moby Dick*?"

"Very provocative story," he said quietly. "Melville show how karma becomes clear for Ahab as it is for all of us."

"Oh, really?" Sarah said, interested to hear what the Sherpa derived from Ahab's death.

"Ho! By Ahab's lust for vengeance over the whale, he reaps the reward of death, taking down all who are around him. Anger ate his mind, leaving only madness. Buddha teaches that anger is a ghost and is nothing unless you give it substance. The whale was only being what a whale is, doing what a whale does, but Ahab chase the whale to feed his anger, therefore the whale ultimately became his anger made real. And when anger turn on itself, death is the ultimate outcome."

Even though Sangye's interpretation of Ahab was tainted by his beliefs in Buddhism, Sarah's heart skipped as he finished talking. The Sherpa's simple wisdom had dug down and reached into her, shining a light into a dark place she had avoided going into for the last twenty-eight years. She stabbed her hiking pole into the soft earth and continued up the long winding path.

* * *

An hour later, the trail leveled out under a cloudy sky and turned into a steady-easy going slope through the pine and deciduous forest. The temperature had taken another dip and the conifer-scented air nipped at Sarah's nose and ears. She pulled her buff up over her nose and ears to ward off the cold as she tossed Sangye's logic over in her mind. Obviously, the story of Ahab had resonated with Frank at some point in the past. She wondered if he had identified with the tormented captain of the *Pequod*, and if he still did. If so, that would explain a lot of what she was sensing in him. As much as he would deny it, there was anger there, and it was swimming in his veins like a predator searching out an unwary victim. Then again, the giving of the book to Sangye might not have anything to do with Frank's demeanor other than his wanting to share a good story with the lesson it teaches. Somehow, she didn't think so. Moreover, she felt that his ambivalence was directed at her at times; but why?

The chiming of bells drifted down the trail as Sangye came beside her and pointed to a large grey stone building with blue trimmed windows. "Our teahouse," he said. "And over there is monastery, where my brother live."

She started at his voice, and coming to herself, tried to settle herself to look through the trees. There, she saw a prominent three-story red block cloister with a wide band of deep green under its large overhanging eaves. She took a deep breath and shelved her musings as she passed a waist high wall of piled stones bearing engraved Buddhist symbols.

The temple dominated the tiny village that nestled into the palm of the treed landscape. Around it were small basic white stucco structures with green metal roofs. Just inside the entrance walls to the village, she saw the members of her expedition team huddled together and staring out at the mountains beyond. Frank was with them, and when he saw her, he strode out to greet her.

"Welcome to Tengboche," he said.

She slipped out of her pack and set it down on the ground, taking in Ama Dablam's leaning tower of snow and ice looming over the top of the teahouse roof. Having come to the foot of the mountain's roots, its sheer size rising through the misty clouds clinging to its sides made her feel impossibly small.

"Isn't she beautiful?" Frank said.

Chapter 10

Frank stood by as Sarah drank in the beauty of the great mountain to the east. Partially shrouded in cloud, Ama Dablam was more than just a mountain to him. It's symbolic shape and name represented much of what he said his mother had stood for. At last Sarah stirred beside him.

"It's overwhelming," she muttered.

Frank gazed at the pinnacle, absorbing its splendor, then came to himself. "It's called the 'Mother's necklace'." He raised his arm and pointed to it. "See those long ridges flanking her peak on either side? Those are her arms protecting her children, and the glacier there, hanging down the front of her is the Dablam."

"Dablam?"

"A traditional pendant worn by Sherpa women that holds pictures of their gods," Frank replied.

Sarah was quiet a long time. "Do people climb it?"

"Yes. It's a very difficult ascent, some say harder than Everest." He glanced down at her, sensing something was wrong. "You okay?"

She shrugged and tossed him a tired smile. "Yeah, just a little beat." She turned her gaze back up to the mountain and said, "Have you —"

"No," Frank said. "Ama Dablam, I leave alone." Now it was his turn to be quiet. As he stared up at the noble peak he thought about what Tashi-ring had said about Sarah possibly being an answer to something, but what kind of answer? For the last ten years, he believed his destiny was to fulfill his promise to his mother. Now suddenly, it all seemed so unclear. If John had the full backing of Andersen, all he worked for would melt away like an early spring thaw.

Tashi's words rang in his ears. *Do not limit yourself by your fear. Fear is nothing so why are you letting it run you around like a squirrel in the forest? You must banish it from your heart or you will look over your shoulder all your life. Is that what you want?*

"No," Frank muttered.

"No, what?" Sarah said beside him.

Frank came to himself. "Oh … nothing. Just thinking."

He dug her room key out of his pocket and handed it to her. "Your room is downstairs in the basement. Number 9. Why don't you go and get settled? There's a menu on your bed. Bring it up and hand it to the man at the front desk when you're done. Dinner will be in an hour or so. You hungry?"

"Starved. I don't suppose there's a shower?"

Frank shook his head. "'Fraid not. From here on in, things are going to get pretty basic."

"Right. Okay. See you in a bit."

She picked her pack up, hoisted it over her shoulder, and trudged to the stark masonry building that would be their home for the next two days. After she went inside, Frank rubbed his neck and sauntered back to the team who were still out in the open field within the village conclave. As he listened to the banter between the Italians and Frenchmen, Da-wa tapped his arm and nodded toward the small café at the far side of the field. Coming out of it, was a tall, lanky man wearing a black fleece and a light blue baseball cap. Under his hat, dirty blond hair flowed out and poured down over his broad shoulders.

Frank glanced at Da-wa knowingly. He had half-expected to run into John Patterson before they reached Base Camp, so it wasn't a huge surprise. He braced himself as the man marched toward the teahouse with long purposeful strides. Whether or not John saw him he didn't know, but he knew it wouldn't take long before he realized his little game of bribery with the park rangers hadn't worked.

As John neared the teahouse, he came to a stop and looked over toward the Khum Jung team. Though Frank couldn't see his face, he definitely felt the visceral reaction coming back. A moment later, John was tromping toward them. When he came beside the Italians, he smiled and said, "Hey Frank. Didn't know if I'd see you up here this year." But Frank knew the man was seething inside.

"Oh, you know me. Can't stay away from the action. So how many are you taking up this year?"

"The usual, twenty-four. This your team?" John said, sizing them up.

"Yep. You know how I like to keep things small."

"Right." John shot Da-wa a withering glance. "Well, just make sure you don't get in our way."

From the corner of his eye, Frank saw Lanzo, Toby, and Jakob's brows furrow. "Wouldn't dream of it," Frank replied, ignoring the man's idle threat. "So, you on acclimatization today?"

John turned and spat, and as he did so, Da-wa grunted and walked away. As John watched the Sherpa retreat from him, he wiped the remaining spittle from his lips with the back of his hand. "Yep. You taking the standard southeast ridge?"

"Thinking on it. You?"

John shrugged. "Well, let's see. I have a dozen heading for the standard ridge route, eight for the South Pillar and four itching for the Southeast Pillar."

"Aggressive," Frank said.

"Yeah, but they can handle it." John puffed. "Hey, look … gotta go score some grub. Glad to see ya up on the mountain though. Hang loose."

"Yeah, you too," Frank said. He watched the man strike back across the field to the teahouse and turned back to his team. "That man, gentlemen, is John Patterson, aka the 'Hound of Chomolungma'. He's very territorial when it concerns his team, especially his Sherpas, so do yourself a favor and stay away from them."

* * *

That night after dinner Rene and Vicq along with Toby, Jakob, and Da-wa collected themselves in the far corner of the teahouse's dimly lit dining room. Like the other teahouses, Tengboche's dining area was arranged with long wooden tables skirting the perimeter of the room with bench seating against the wall. Simple wooden chairs were scattered about, many of them having seen too many years.

As expected there was a lot of discussion among the men about their upcoming assault on Everest, not to mention John Patterson whom they all decided they didn't like. But overall, the mood was lively as the Frenchmen battled the Austrians in a game of cards Da-wa was teaching them, and which the Sherpa excelled at. Off to the side, Sully and Sangye plotted against each other in a game of chess as Carlo and Aldan looked on. Beside them, Greg sat with

Lanzo, swapping stories about their careers and comparing life in their native countries.

Frank pulled a chair up next to Sarah in front of the pot-bellied stove putting out heat in the middle of the room and a minute later, they were nursing mugs of Masala tea. As they fell into conversation about the land and the people he loved, he saw Greg glancing toward them now and again out of the corner of his eye.

At length, Sarah set her mug down and stretched her legs out. "So, who's this 'Hound of Chomolungma,' John Patterson, I keep hearing about?"

Frank considered his answer then looked at her. "He's one of my competitors up on the mountain."

"From what I hear, he's a bit of an ass," Sarah said, eyeing him pointedly.

"Let's just say, he's abrasive," Frank answered.

"Hmmm." She was a quiet a moment as the men erupted in laughter behind them. Someone had just scored a winning point at cards.

"So, how were your dumplings?" Frank said.

"They were excellent, although I wish they had a better dipping sauce. I like a little spice in things." She paused then taking up her mug, continued on, "So, how long have you known this John Patterson?"

Frank shrugged. He really didn't want talk about John, but he didn't know how to extricate himself from her growing curiosity without appearing abrupt. "About ten years, give or take."

She was quiet, and he could sense her mulling over her next question. "Greg said he threatened you; something to the effect of 'stay out of his way'?"

Frank rubbed his neck, thinking how best to answer her probing question. "What he was referring to; was not to crowd his climbers going up, which is something that sometimes happens with other outfits. Up on the mountain things are tense, so people tend to forget their manners."

"I see," she said. "Still, I see no reason to act that way down here. We're not even there yet."

"True."

She took a sip of her tea. "You're being very diplomatic."

"I try not to judge others," Frank replied.

"But you don't like him, do you?" Sarah pressed.

"Let's just say, John and I have our moments," Frank answered, "but I respect him as a mountaineer, and the others ought to as well. He might be a lot of things, but he's a man they'd want in their corner if things get dicey."

"So, he climbs with them?"

"Oh, yes, though not always to the summit," Frank answered. He could see her next question coming, so he continued, "And so have I, though not so much anymore."

She nodded and after a moment, said, "How many times have you been up *all* the way?"

"Five."

She sipped her tea, and as she did so, he could sense her ambivalence toward the mountain. "And will you be going up part way or all the way this time?"

"I don't know. Usually, I stay back at the command tent and run things, checking weather reports, et cetera and let my Sirdars do the legwork, so to speak. Why do you ask?" he said, knowing he had a good idea why.

"Just wondered," she replied off-handedly. She yawned and turned a weary smile his way. "Well, I think I'm going to turn in."

"Good idea," Frank agreed. "And as soon as I'm done going over paperwork with Sangye, I'll be doing the same.

* * *

The next morning Frank rolled out of bed and sat up. The temperature had dipped down below freezing last night in his room, chasing him out from under the heavy wool blanket and into his sleeping bag. He stretched and looking through his rising misted breath, saw a wintery world outside his tiny bedroom window. He rubbed his eyes with his palms then reached down, snatching his fleece off the floor. Pulling it over his head, he heard the Austrians stirring in the next room. A muffled conversation was taking place. More than once he heard the name John Patterson uttered in their stark accented tongues, which was immediately followed by sharp retorts against the Andersen director.

Frank pressed his lips together as he retied his hair. The last thing he needed was a war on the mountain, especially with Khum Jung Mountaineering on shaky ground with the governing authorities. He folded his buff into a cap and fitted it over his head, stuffing his hair underneath it and went out into the cold darkened hallway. On the way upstairs to breakfast he caught Aldan slogging up ahead of him with his head down.

"Hey there," Frank said coming up behind him.

"Aye. A mite nippy last night," Aldan said. He blinked and a tiny grimace ran across his grizzled face.

Frank had a good idea what the grimace meant. "Headache?"

"Yeah. Back of my head is pounding and I feel a little queasy."

"It'll pass. Hang in there. I have some Tylenol in my pack if you need it," Frank offered.

"Thanks, I'll be alright though," Aldan said. As they came to the top of the stairs, he added, "I see we have ourselves a bit of snow out there."

"Little bit. It'll be gone by lunchtime," Frank answered. "You feeling up to our acclimatization hike today?"

"Gonna give it a go," Aldan replied.

They headed into the dining room, which was nearly empty except for Da-wa and Sangye who were sitting in the corner, and the inn keep who was stuffing firewood into the pot-bellied stove. When the Sherpas saw Frank, they got up and pulled chairs out. Sangye headed for the transaction counter and called for a thermos of tea through the kitchen pass-thru in the wall.

Ten minutes later, the rest of the team started to trickle in, taking seats nearby. Vicq and Rene dragged chairs over from a nearby table and sat next to Frank. Frank eyed the two men. They were both bleary-eyed and their hair was in disarray. When he turned in late last night, the Frenchmen were still playing cards with the Austrians and indulging themselves in the house wine. By the looks of it they'd had a snoot-full.

Vicq ran his hand through his dark mop and yawned. "I don't suppose there's any chance of getting a cup of coffee here."

Frank chuckled, shaking his head. "What time did you boys get to bed last night?"

Vicq turned to Rene who was snuffing. Rene shrugged. "After midnight at least."

"Well," Frank said, "better make that your last party 'til we get back."

"Believe me, we will," Vicq replied closing his eyes. "My God, my head is splitting. Can someone please shut those damned drapes? That sun is killing me."

"Those Austrians drink like fish," Rene muttered, and right after he said it, Toby and Jakob came strutting in as if on cue.

They came up behind the Frenchmen with shining faces and broad smiles. Jakob slapped Vicq on the shoulder and said, "What happen to you last night?

One minute you kicking our ass in cards and the next you lay down like a heel hound."

Vicq groaned, which elicited a booming laughter from Toby. "It is okay. Wine affect me that way, too." He turned to Frank as Sangye brought tea and mugs over. "So, when do we head out for acclimatization hike?"

"I was thinking we'd trot over to the monastery around nine for morning prayers and shoot up afterward," Frank said. He shot a passing glance at Greg. He hadn't said a lot to the young man who was buried in conversation with Lanzo. Then again he hadn't intended to. He had wanted as little to do with him as possible, except now, after being around the man's mother for a while, he decided he ought to start cutting him a break.

"Hey, Greg, how you doing?" Frank said.

Greg turned away from Lanzo and shot him the thumbs up.

But Frank wanted more than just 'a thumbs up'. He got up and went over to him, pulling a chair up alongside Lanzo. "I see you two like matching wits at chess. So, who won out last night?"

Lanzo smiled. "I wiped his butt."

"Really?" Greg said. "Seems to me, it was the other way around."

"Who got mated, bub?" Lanzo shot back and winked.

Greg leaned toward Frank. "I was just feeling him out. We'll see who comes out on top tonight. Do you play?"

"Not often, why? You interested in a challenge?" Frank said.

"Sure, why not? You can have winners."

"Well, that leaves you out," Lanzo chuckled.

Greg gave the Italian a friendly swat. "We'll see."

Frank smiled, liking the friendly banter between the two men. They would definitely make good teammates going up the mountain. He sat with them a while longer, listening to their back and forth chatter about kicking each other's butt until it veered into something called March Madness. Apparently, it revolved around basketball, of which he knew nothing. As he tried to make sense of what they were talking about, Sarah drifted into the room. She was moving rather slowly, he thought, so he excused himself and got up.

"Gentlemen, until tonight," he said, then went over to Sarah. "What's up?"

She shook her head and whispered back, "More like what's been going down."

"Oh. You have the runs."

She shot him a tightrope smile. "That doesn't begin to describe it. I think I got maybe two hours sleep last night. Thank God the toilet was across the hall. Anyway, I think I'll take it easy today and hang around close-by if that's all right."

"Of course," he answered. "You have anything for it?"

"Yes, I took something a couple hours ago."

"Well, hopefully, it'll ease off," Frank replied. "And make sure you keep drinking. You don't want to get dehydrated. I'll let the boys know to use the upstairs toilet until it passes."

"Thank you. Now, what to eat? I really don't want to add insult to injury, but I suppose I should at least try."

Well, so it begins, Frank mused as he watched her find a seat at the end of the table. From here on out, people were going to start getting ill at certain points. Even he'd had headaches and tummy troubles from time to time going up. These maladies were only a nuisance at this altitude but once they reached eighteen thousand feet and up, it'd be a different story. And with Sarah being a novice, who knew how her body would handle it? He thought back to when they'd just met. It was only last week. How things had changed between them. No longer did he feel ambivalent toward her. In fact, he discovered he quite liked her, which surprised him. On the other hand, he couldn't afford distractions up at Base Camp. At the rate things were going between them, it could end up being a problem. He shook his head as Tashi's maddening questions continued to echo in his ears.

* * *

After dinner, Frank dug out the chessboard and rounded up Greg and Lanzo. Sitting in the far corner of the dining room, the two young men set up their pieces and began moving their men over the board. As Frank watched them play, he looked to see who was the aggressor. Chances were they'd be the same way on the mountain. It didn't take long to find out. Lanzo went straight for the queen and rooks and was doing quite a bit of damage to Greg's forces. Fifteen minutes later, the Italian seemed poised to claim checkmate, when from out of nowhere, Greg sprung his trap.

"Mama mia," Lanzo cried, sitting back and running his hands through his hair.

Greg smiled as he watched his rattled friend trying to cope with what had just happened. Finally, Lanzo gave up and conceded the game.

"You sneaky little bastard," Lanzo said, getting up. "How did I miss that?"

Frank was impressed. He didn't figure Greg to play that kind of game. All the same, you couldn't play it twice. And having seen it, Frank knew to be prepared for it. To Lanzo, he said, "He back-doored you."

Greg looked up at his friend innocently, and said. "I believe we had a wager?"

Lanzo laughed. "Yes, a beer I know. Mr. Kincaid, something for you?"

"Oh, no. Not just yet, my good man. I think I want to have my wits about me when I play your pal over here." Frank slipped into Lanzo's chair and went about setting his pieces up. As he sat back, he said, "I believe white goes first."

Forty minutes later Greg and he were in a tug of war as Lanzo and Sully watched from the sidelines. "I see what you're doing," Frank said, nodding toward the knight that Greg had just moved.

"Do you?" Greg replied. "Then I assume you realize you're going to be mated in the next four moves." He sipped his beer and looked up at Frank with a challenging grin.

Frank studied the board and saw Greg's rook and bishop poised and ready to swoop in on his king. They weren't the issue though. It was the knight that was troubling him. But what else was he missing, because he didn't doubt Greg's threat for a minute. He searched the board, diagramming each play and counter play in his mind until he saw it. A stinking pawn was going to be the death of his king and there was nothing he could do about it. He sat back and laughed. "Very, very good, Greg. Who taught you to play chess?"

"I did," Greg confessed. "You play a good game yourself."

Frank got up and eyeing all three men, said, "Can I get you guys another beer?"

"After seeing Vicq and Rene this morning. I think I'll pass," Greg said. But Lanzo was all for it, and Sully threw his hat in the ring as well.

Frank called over to the inn-keep and after he ordered, sat and listened to the guys talk about sports, politics, and finally, women. As they did so, Frank found himself warming up to Greg. The young man was thoughtful and smart, but more than that, he reminded him of himself when he was around Greg's age.

* * *

After breakfast the following morning Frank led the men across the enclave to the revered monastery. As he walked with them, he told them a bit of its history and of its destruction and reconstruction twice over the years; once by an earthquake in 1934 and the other by fire in 1989. Coming to the sanctuary's broad front gate, they passed under an ornately painted orange pagoda roof with yellow ribs reaching up from the eaves to a raised ridge plate. On the plate were two golden musk deer facing each other in repose and between them, a golden wheel of life. Ahead of Frank, lay a walkway and a stair of stone pavers to an enclosed courtyard.

The men quietly followed him in and gazed up at the intricate masonry dentils and yellow trimmed windows stretching around the perimeter of the courtyard walls. Beyond their facades, were the living quarters of the residing monks. Directly ahead, was the monastery prayer hall main entrance. Cloaked by a pair of long, deep brown curtains bordered in white that hung down from a wide valance, the monastery had brought him through a dark time in his life when he was angry at the world. He had come here seeking answers to questions and had found the Buddhist path instead. And now, destiny had seen fit to bring the son of the man liable for his search and of finding 'the way' next to him. The irony was so thick he could cut it with a knife.

The men gathered around Frank as his thoughts swirled. Suddenly, Vicq said, "I heard that Tenzing Norgay was from Tengboche. Is that so?"

Frank started then looked at him. "I'm sorry?"

Vicq repeated his question.

"Yes, and it's largely because of him and Hillary, that we, as mountaineers, come to pay tribute here."

Sangye, who was standing nearby with Da-wa, added, "This place, and all around us is considered sacred ground to Tibetans. It is written that Lama Sangwa Dorje prophesied this monastery long before it was built based on a footprint left by him while meditating."

"There used to be a stone that had that footprint, too, as I remember," Frank said.

"Yes, before the fire," Da-wa answered as a young, red robed monk pulled back the curtain and came out.

Frank smiled as Sangye's brother came trotting over. "Namaste, Bajay,"

"Namaste, Kincaid," the monk said dipping his head to Da-wa and his brother. "You are here for prayers, yes?"

Frank dipped his head. "If it pleases the Lord Buddha, we should very much like to join you."

"Ho, you come," Bajay said.

The team followed the bald-headed, lean monk up the stone stair and past the tall brown curtains. Inside the vestibule leading to the main prayer hall, they removed their shoes and went in single file around the perimeter of the two story wood paneled room. As the monks came in and took their places on the long wooden benches in the middle of the candlelit hall, Frank put a candle to a flame and set it on the mantle before a large brilliantly painted Buddha. When he finished, he bowed to the presiding lama who wrapped a long, flowing saffron khata around his neck. Having received his blessing, he proceeded to the far wall, sitting lotus-style on the floor. Sangye and Da-wa followed with the rest of the team behind. Once they were all seated, the monks opened their prayer books and chanted, and as they did so, Frank closed his eyes and sent the conflicted thoughts upward along with the monk's sonorous voices.

* * *

That afternoon after the team returned from their hike, Frank went in to check on Sarah. She'd had a quite a morning of it, but was feeling fine now. Afterward, he returned upstairs to join the team and make a phone call to Daku in Kathmandu to find out what was going on with the IRD, and to check on his licensing status. He couldn't believe his license had been revoked, but one never knew.

An hour later he was sitting with Da-wa and Sangye in a quiet corner of the teahouse dining room, going over receipts and checking on the status of the expedition's supplies and gear going up the mountain ahead of them. Their camp Sherpa, Tembe, who was up in Lobuche, and in charge of their gear and supplies, told him over the phone that everything was proceeding smoothly. The command and supply storage tents at Base Camp would be up and waiting for them when they arrived.

"Okay, we're all set," Frank said, putting his cell phone in his pocket.

"Has Daku called back yet?" Sangye inquired, looking up from running numbers on the receipts.

"Not yet, but it should be soon," Frank answered.

Da-wa leaned back in his chair and peered through the window, his thoughts seemingly far away. Frank wondered what was on the Sherpa's mind, but knew it was probably John. Since the Sherpa had parted ways with the Andersen director to come work for Frank, John had been spreading lies about his competence on the mountain and creating all kinds of problems for Khum Jung Mountaineering. It was bad karma, Da-wa confessed to Frank once; alluding that maybe he'd been responsible for it by leaving Andersen. Frank didn't have an answer for him other than to let him figure things out for himself. But down inside, Frank knew he'd circle back to his original decision and stick by it. It was plain and simple; Andersen was forcing John Patterson into taking too many chances with people's lives and Da-wa didn't want to be a part of it anymore.

At last, Da-wa turned back. "When we get to Base Camp, I am going to settle this," he said.

Chapter 11

The following morning it had snowed again, dusting the grounds and trees that were putting out the first buds of spring with a fluffy white powder. Sarah got up from bed, feeling like she'd lost twenty pounds the hard way, but at least she had gotten a good night's sleep. The medicine had done the trick, but in its wake, it had left her with an unsettled stomach. It was nothing serious, but it was enough to steer her away from wanting breakfast. Frank talked her into a couple of hard-boiled eggs and half a bowl of porridge, which she was picking at while the men gobbled their food around her.

Beside her, sat Aldan. The Aussie was staring ahead, looking through the window. He had hardly touched his breakfast either. Sarah spooned a mouthful of porridge and leaned toward him. "Not feeling well?"

"Yeah, got me a nasty headache." He reached into his pocket and pulled a bottle of Tylenol out, dumping a couple of tablets in his hand. Popping them in his mouth, he took a slug of water. "And you? Heard ya had a touch of the runs."

"I did, but it's done with. Now, I have to deal with the side effects of the meds."

"Ahhh, yeah, I hear ya."

Sarah glanced down the table at Greg. He had hung with her last night after dinner, encouraging her to drink every ten minutes or so it seemed until she thought she would burst. She smiled as she remembered telling him, she was not a fish, and the laughter they shared afterward. Just now, he was looking down the table toward her as he bit into his slice of toast. She gave him the thumbs up, which elicited a grin on his stubbly face that hadn't seen a razor in four days.

For the most part, Sarah had triumphed in leaving her son alone to bond with the other men. Yet, it was hard being on the outside looking in as he prepared himself mentally for the upcoming climb. And harder yet, to pretend she was excited for him. But that was the pact she had made with herself and so she had gritted her teeth and plowed ahead.

Fifteen minutes later, the table was being cleared as packs were hoisted up onto the team's shoulders. Sarah grabbed hers, along with her hiking gloves and poles and went outside into the cold, crisp mountain air to join the men who were going through last minute preparations for the hike to Dengboche. As she climbed into her pack and pulled her hat on, she surveyed the snow-covered grounds. At the far end of the conclave, a stream of gray smoke drifted out of a small café's chimney up over the treetops, staining the brilliant blue dome. To her right, a pair of yaks with black matted tresses hanging down over their broad bellies nibbled at grass hiding under a thin blanket of white snow. Musical brass bells pinged and dinged on the straps hanging around their necks as they sought their morning breakfast.

As she listened to the restless men chatter about the land, a steady thwack, thwack of an axe chopping wood echoed in the pristine silence enveloping the valley. At last, Frank, Sangye, and Sherpa Dave came out and joined them. Frank came close to her and quietly said, "How's business?"

Sarah nodded as the scent of juniper comingling with the fresh hay, wrinkled her nose. "I'm good. What a picturesque scene with the snow draped over everything. Reminds me of a Kincaid painting."

When Frank cocked his brow quizzically at her, she realized his confusion over her reference to 'Kincaid'. "Oh, sorry. I forgot you both share the last name. Kincaid is a famous artist back in the states. Paints wonderful winter landscapes."

"I see," Frank said, nodding. "Well, a painter I'm not, unless you call slopping varnish on a cabinet, art." He glanced up at Ama Dablam. "Well, time to push off, I guess." He called over to Sherpa Dave, and told him to lead the way and a moment later they were funneling single file into a large swale under the snow-laden branches.

For the next thirty minutes, the only sounds in the deepening woods were the snapping of fallen twigs under the trekker's feet and the click-clacking of their hiking poles on the sloping snow covered terrain. As Sarah picked her way around the rocks and muddy snow covered ruts, she cast her gaze over the simple understated world all around her and breathed in its cold, resin scented air.

This was the closest thing to 'peace on earth' that she had felt since childhood and she reveled in it.

"Everything, okay," Frank said coming up beside her. He stabbed the tip of his hiking pole in the snow and adjusted his pack.

Sarah turned to him, unaware he had stopped. "Oh, yes, more than okay." She tilted her head back, closed her eyes and as she absorbed the sun's rays went on, "When I was little, my dad took us camping every year up to Yosemite. We'd hike the trails along the Merced River and fish for trout while mom hung out back at camp. It was the best time in my life."

"The forest is a magical place in a child's mind."

Sarah sighed, feeling the euphoric moment slip away. "Yes, and then we grow up and forget the magic."

"But it doesn't forget us. The magic lives in our hearts, and they don't forget it even if our minds do," Frank offered.

"Maybe for you," Sarah countered. "But me; it's been a long time since I've felt any magic in my life." She shot him a quick glance and started back off. It wasn't long afterward that the trail leveled off and the thin blanket of snow gave up. A half-mile later, they were crossing broad clearings of montane grasses and flowering sedum. While Frank walked beside her, Sarah asked him about the monastery and the prayer service he went to yesterday. Greg had told her a little bit about it, but her son was no Buddhist, and so much of what went on during the service was more than likely lost on him.

As Frank told her about the history of the monastery, they came upon a shoulder height wall of jumbled stone tablets inscribed with Tibetan writings. "Pass on the left," he instructed.

Sarah obeyed and as she went by them, said, "I saw these in Tengboche and other places. What are they?"

"They're Mani walls."

"Do you know what they say?" Sarah said, coming to a halt to get a better look at them.

Frank stopped beside her. "Om mani padme hum. It's a Buddhist mantra, meaning, 'Hail to the jewel in the lotus'."

"Which means what?" Sarah said.

Frank eyed her, seeming rather delighted that she had pressed him. He pointed to the first inscribed word and said, "'Om', is the practitioner's impure body, speech, and mind, and 'Mani', means jewel. That is the altruistic intention to become enlightened with compassion and love. Then here, 'Padme', the lotus, wisdom, and last, purity that is achieved by indivisible unity in how we approach life, called, 'hum'."

Sarah nodded. As a Catholic, she could easily compare this thought to how Christ lived his life. She looked up and seeing a banner of prayer flags waving in the tree branches ahead, said, "And the flags, what is the writing on them?"

"The same," Frank answered.

"And why do you always pass them on the left?"

Frank took a drink of water from his camelback and urged her to do the same. "We pass them this way according to how the earth and universe revolve. And when you turn the prayer wheels, it is the same as reciting the mantra. But it is better if you also recite the mantra aloud as you do it."

"There's a lot I need to learn about this Buddhist way," Sarah said, starting back off down the trail. Not that she really wanted to learn it. Buddhism was a bit complicated for her tastes, unlike Catholicism, which was pretty much straight forward.

As Frank followed her, he said, "So, what path do you follow?"

"The path of Christ. To be more specific, though, I'm a Catholic, although I'm not very good at it."

"Meaning?"

"Well, I haven't been to Mass in sometime," Sarah answered.

Frank was quiet a moment. Finally, he said, "I always found it puzzling why people feel they're sinners when they don't go to church as much as they think they should."

"How so?" Sarah said, wondering what he was getting at.

"Well, to my way of thinking, if what you believe is in your heart, then that's all that matters," Frank replied. "You practice what you believe by how you live your life. There is no good or bad about it."

"But isn't it important to also spend devotional time, like … like reciting the mantra back there for example?" Sarah said, as the trail dipped back into the forest.

"Well, of course, but it's not an end all if you don't. To tell you the truth, I've never quite understood the whole concept of sin and how it relates to the Christian hell either. It seems very harsh that all your sins are tallied up at the end of your life and used against you."

"That's rigid orthodox Old Testament stuff, and there are some who would have you believe it. But Christ changed all that by dying on the cross and cleaning the slate for us."

"Yes, I'm familiar with the concept," Frank said, "But to me, it sounds rather barbaric to have this loving God, as you refer to him, require that an innocent man die on a cross to atone for the sins of the world."

"But Jesus was His son, and to my way of thinking, it was Jesus' time. He had done what God had sent him here to do, and so he was called home, as we all are at some point. Through his crucifixion, the Father and the Son were making a statement, showing us what sacrifice and love is really all about," Sarah answered.

"Sacrifice is not important in my way of life. I give because it reminds me of the true source of unhappiness, and that is, desire. Think of it this way; when you get what you want you perceive yourself as being happy, but how long until there is something else you want? It is quite maddening. Thus being unattached to things frees us from suffering desire, which can never be quenched." Frank said coming along beside her. He pulled out a candy bar, unwrapped it and offered her a piece.

"Oh, thanks," Sarah said accepting it. She stopped and took a bite, then started off again. "Okay. I can see your point. But I think it's impossible to not have some attachment to something, like your school in Khum Jung for example."

Frank's eyes widened and he stopped and looked at her.

"Something wrong?"

"No, nothing," Frank said starting after her again.

"But back to what we were talking about," Sarah went on, "Devotion and church are important, I think. They remind me of the great sacrifice that was made, and to be thankful for it, sort of like when you turn your prayer wheels in reverence to Buddha, remembering him and his teachings."

"Not in reverence to Buddha, but to achieve enlightenment and perfection," Frank corrected.

"But it's the same, don't you think?" Sarah posited.

Frank shrugged. "To a point."

Sarah stepped over a large root and heard the chinking of bells coming their way. "Sounds like we have another train coming toward us," she announced, and moved to the side. A moment later, a herd of cattle appeared through the trees. As they passed, it occurred to her that he had never spoken of a higher power once in all the time they had been together. She turned to him. "Do Buddhists believe in God?"

"No, not in the sense you talk about," Frank replied, nodding to the Sherpas passing by them who were driving the team down the mountain. "We have instead deities that are associated with Buddha. All of them are there to help guide us on our path."

"Hmmm … for me, God is my path. If He wasn't in my life, I'd be lost."

"Ahhh, but you are never truly lost," Frank said. "Being lost and getting lost are false concepts, as you are always where you are supposed to be. Rather, it's the fear of being away from familiar things, family, and friends that frightens you."

That made Sarah think for a moment. Finally, she said, "I never thought of it that way. But that only applies to the earthly realm. With God it's different. If he didn't exist, I'd be —"

"Lost? But how could you be lost if He didn't exist? I would postulate you wouldn't be here talking to me about it," Frank replied.

They walked a little further up the gentle slope as Sarah pondered the maddening logic. At last, she said, "Then, using that logic, it would mean that neither of us would be here."

"But we are," Frank replied.

"Therefore, God exists," Sarah volleyed back.

"That is your truth," Frank answered. "Not mine."

His tone, though gentle, was firm, but Sarah couldn't understand how or why he rejected the notion of the heavenly father. She walked on, thinking about how to get across to him what she felt was an infallible truth. Finally, she said, "Haven't you ever had a yearning inside to connect with something larger than yourself?"

"Yes, of course," Frank replied.

"Well, then, couldn't it be your spirit reaching for God?"

He was silent a moment, then said, "What you speak of, for me, is enlightenment. For me, truth and purity of mind are what I seek. It's a matter of my letting go of all my petty human needs, fears and wants and living a life that accepts the entwined nature of things, which, I might add, I'm not very good at — yet. But I'm striving to let go of them and all the other things that diminish my life, and look instead to the truths that are outside and inside of me."

Although Sarah couldn't wrap her mind around a world without God or Christ, she accepted his response. That left one puzzling little question. She said, "I heard some of the Sherpas refer to you as the 'lion'. Care to share?"

"It's a name given to me by my lama, Tashi-ring," Frank replied.

"Really? Hmm, so is there a meaning behind it?"

Frank smiled. "As my teacher would say, 'Look and discover for yourself.' "

Sarah rolled her eyes. "You're a brat."

"I've been called worse," Frank said, grinning.

* * *

Four hours later, after taking a lunch of noodles, rice, and fried potatoes in Orsho, Sarah was back out on the trail poling her way amidst the men who were slogging single file into a barren land of stunted pine and scrub. No one said much as they walked except for a random comment now and then about the vast brown landscape and the approaching mountains before them. Frank was now in the lead, and Greg was following close behind him. Sarah could see them chatting every once in a while as the narrow path wove back and forth through the rocky terrain that now followed the Imja Khola River. Having joined with the Khumbu just north of Orsho, the Imja zigzagged down from the Lhotse Nup Glacier northeast of them.

As she went, Sarah occasionally glanced up into the hill lands that reached for the endless blue sky. On them, almost invisible to the eye, one might see blue sheep or tahr goats nibbling at sedum and montane grasses. However, most of the time all that was there on the sheer slopes were brown and gray rocks. Some of them were massive, and they seemed to teeter on their foundations, threatening to come rolling down at any minute.

Eventually, the team came to a series of relentless embedded stone steps that went ever upward, and as she poled her way along, she made sure to stay far to the left away from the precipitous drops on the other side. How they had been built into the mountainside was beyond her, and she marveled at the amount of effort that must have gone into the work. At length they reached a modest plateau, and there, Frank called for a breather. Sarah went and sat beside Alden, who was rubbing the back of his neck and wincing. After she took a long pull from her camelback, she said, "How are you doing?"

He nodded. "Just the damned headache. Can't seem to shake it."

"I have some Tylenol in my pack here."

"Awe, thanks, but I got me some right here," He said, pulling out a bottle of his own. "How you doing?"

"I'm ready to see the end of this day."

Aldan chuckled. "Me, too."

Just then, Frank came walking back. "Not long now, folks, another hour or so. You drinking?"

Sarah lifted her camelback tube and gave him the thumbs up.

"What about you, Aldan?" Frank said, narrowing a critical eye on the Aussie.

Aldan blinked. "Got it all under control, mate."

Frank shot Sarah a look, as if to say, keep an eye on him, then pulled Sherpa Dave aside. As they broke into Lhasa, Sarah got the feeling Frank was more than concerned over the Aussie, and for the first time she realized that maybe the man from Down Under was in over his head, which surprised her. Didn't everyone who attempted the Monster, already have immunity to the effects of altitude? Apparently not.

* * *

The team arrived at the valley of Dengboche under a cloudy sky and a chill wind a little after 4:00 PM. As Sarah poled behind the men down the path running along the outskirts of the tiny settlement, she eyed the helter-skelter grid of empty corrals that sprawled out over the sloping dun landscape. Viewing the lain stone pens, she suddenly found herself thrown back to the days when she watched John Wayne and Henry Fonda westerns on Saturday morning TV. If she closed her eyes, she could almost imagine sagebrush rolling over the empty hard-packed soil along with the sounds of horse-drawn wagons rolling into town.

A hundred yards further up, Frank turned and led the team around a wide bend passing small shops and stores selling their wares out in front. As they went by them, Sarah noticed signs for Internet cafés, tea shops, and bakeries ahead, and for the first time, thought about checking her email and maybe posting a pic or two on her Facebook page. Now, wouldn't her friends at home get a kick out of that. And the thought of a nice piece of chocolate cake made her mouth water. Perhaps tomorrow she'd step down after their acclimatization hike and spoil herself.

Right now, she just wanted to get to their lodgings for the night and she wondered how much further it was to a bed. They were near the end of the village and there were only a couple of buildings that had any chance of housing them. One of them sat up on a foothill overlooking the valley, which was falling into shadow. Frank pointed to it. "Our home for the next two nights," he announced.

But to Sarah, it was more like a motel than a teahouse, at least those she had been accustomed to. She appraised the large main building that was flanked by a long arm of rooms that sat back from the front of the property. Off to one side was a large fenced-in yard hemmed in on the north by what appeared to be a large storage building of some sort.

Ten minutes later, she was shuffling along behind the block and mortar teahouse to a small gate with a stair leading down onto a walkway of stone. As she went out onto a broad patio behind the men, she saw tables and chairs set out in front.

"Okay," Frank said, "Dump your packs out here and come on in and get warmed up while I get your keys. In the meantime, Sangye will be bringing around menus for tonight's dinner."

Sangye dipped his head and whispered up into Frank's ear.

"Oh, right," Frank spoke up. "Sangye tells me there's goodies set out to go along with tea, so don't be late getting in."

Sarah set her poles against one of the chairs and removed the pack from her tired shoulders. As she did so, Greg came beside her. She watched him stretch as she pulled her gloves off.

"That was quite a hike today," she said.

"That, it was." Greg snuffed, and looking back, continued, "You're doing really good, Mom. How're you feeling?"

"Oh, much better," she replied cheerfully. "And you?"

"I'm great. It's awesome up here, don't you think?"

"Yes, it is," she answered, although awesome wasn't exactly the word she had in mind. More like, 'harsh', she would call it. Yet, she could see his point, too. There was nothing like this place anywhere in the world.

Greg was quiet a moment, seemingly absorbed in the landscape, then said, "You and Kincaid seem to be getting along well."

"I like him," she said, guardedly, wondering what had brought the comment on.

"Yeah, he's a real straight shooter." He turned toward her and nodded at the teahouse side entry door. "Well, we'd better get in there, before Lanzo, Sully, and Jakob scarf down all the goodies."

* * *

The following morning, the team gathered on the patio and went out on their acclimatization hike. It was another bright day and the air was cool and crisp with an earthy smell to it. As they went up into the foothills behind the tea-house, Sarah thought about her growing interest in Frank and she wondered if he felt it, too. She eyed him up ahead as he led the team single file up the grassy hill, remembering their conversation yesterday. For a man who didn't believe in God, he portrayed a hell of a peaceful presence except she knew there something more lurking underneath his easygoing persona, and that in a nutshell, gave her pause to be wary.

At length, the team came to a promontory that looked out over the Dengboche valley below. As Sarah found a seat within the rocky outcropping, she pulled out a granola bar and bit into it. Beside her, a few feet away, Greg stood deep in thought, gazing northward. She watched him surveying the mountains, sensing something was troubling him. Her first thought was that it had something to do with his girlfriend, Jenny. She didn't know what had happened between them but she knew whatever it was, it had hit him hard.

Suddenly, he looked back at her. "Hell of a view, huh?"

"Yeah," she answered, resisting the urge to ask him what was going on. "I was thinking of taking a walk around the village when we get back, maybe stop in and check my email. Interested in joining me?"

Greg shrugged. "Sure, why not?"

"So, tomorrow it's on to Lobuche, is it?"

"Yep." He pointed to a wide swath of barren land behind them that was nestled between the soaring brown hills. "Frank says, 'we head back northeast that way to join back up with the Dudh Kosi River. From there, we go up again to around 16,000 feet'."

"And how much further after that to Base Camp?" Sarah said.

"Another seven hour hike, give or take," he replied, then came and sat beside her. "Aldan's having a rough time of it."

"Yeah, I noticed. You think he'll be alright?"

"I don't know. Hard to say," Greg answered. "Everyone's body reacts differently in high altitude. What about you? How are you feeling?" he said, and took a long pull of water from his camelback.

"I'm good," Sarah replied. They fell silent a while as the stiff wind tugged at their collars. Finally, Sarah cleared her throat. "I heard someone retching pretty hard last night."

"Yeah. Lanzo said it was Carlo. Apparently, his dinner didn't agree with him. Poor bastard. The last thing you want up here is tummy trouble. Anyway, I heard he was feeling a little better this morning."

A little ways away, Frank gave the signal to head back down. Greg stood, and holding his hand out, helped her up. Ten minutes later she was scrambling down the slope with her son. As they picked their way down the treacherous hillside, she felt the distance between them had inched a bit closer. She smiled as she followed along behind him.

Forty-five minutes later, they walked through the gate and onto the teahouse patio. Sarah pulled her pack off, and as she set it down, heard playful chatter coming up from the yard below. Curious, she went to the railing and saw a ball game getting organized between the locals and the expedition team. As she watched the men fan out in the grassy yard, Frank stepped beside her.

"Want to join them?" he said.

Sarah glanced at him and cocked a brow. "Oh, I don't know. I'm not much on baseball."

Frank shot her a crooked smile. "Baseball? Perish the thought. It's Cricket! Come, it's a lot of fun. Greg, you too," he called over.

Before she could protest, Frank grabbed her hand and pulled her along. Rolling her eyes, she followed.

When they stepped onto the field, Frank turned to her and said, "Now Cricket is very easy, so just watch and you'll soon get the hang of it."

"We'll see," Sarah replied, grinning and shaking her head as Toby took up a weird banana-shaped bat and held it cocked over his shoulder. Behind Toby was a stake and behind the stake, stood Sully. In the field some distance away, stood Sangye, and in his hand was a blue ball about the size of an apple. Spread out strategically in the field behind Sangye, were the locals, along with Vicq and Rene and Sherpa Dave. Sangye backed up a step, and running forward pitched the ball, bouncing it a few feet in front of Toby. The Austrian took a mighty swing, but missed, eliciting laugher from the fielders. Sully tossed the missed ball back to Sangye, who wound up and tossed another pitch. Again, another miss.

"What's-a matter, Tob? Can't connect?" Jakob taunted.

Toby groaned, and waving the bat, said, "Come here and we'll see who connects with who."

Sangye grinned as Sully pitched the ball back to him. Toby wound up, and as the ball came hurtling toward him, swung and caught it square, launching it over the roof of the adjoining building. Looking back at his brother, Toby broke into a toothy grin, which brought about more laughter.

Frank went out to Sangye and waited as one of the locals ran out back to fetch the ball. As they stood there, Frank whispered something into the Sherpa's ear, then came back and stood beside her. For the next few minutes, Sarah watched Toby miss the ball more than he hit it, which brought on more jeering, until at last he caught it again and sent it over the fence.

She assumed that was a home run, but wasn't sure just what was going on. It appeared there was no such thing as striking out. She mentioned that to Frank, and he told her that Toby's turn ended when the ball either hit the stake behind him or when it was caught out in the field. To Sarah, it looked more like a glorified game of batting practice.

"So, how do you keep score?" she said.

"Well, we aren't keeping score here, but if we were; when the ball is hit there would be running of bases back and forth," Frank answered.

"Oh," she replied, still confused, but it didn't really matter. Everyone seemed to be having fun.

"Okay, Mr. Pieterson, you proved your point, now give up the bat to the young lady," Frank said to the Austrian, then nodded to her and added, "Your turn."

"Me, oh no."

"Yes, you can," Frank retorted with a grin.

"You can do it, Mom," Greg added as Toby came over and handed her the bat.

Reluctantly, Sarah took the club and shot Greg a playful threatening look.

But Greg ignored it and turned to Jakob. "By the way, who's Pieterson?"

Jakob laughed. "You kidding, right?" When Greg gave him a dumb look, Jakob shook his head. "You Americans. You think baseball is only game in the world. Mr. Pieterson," he said, adding some emphasis to the name, "is greatest cricket player in the world."

One of the locals standing nearby spoke up. "No. Sachin is best."

Whatever, Sarah thought as she strode over and took her place beside the plate. She lifted the bat over her shoulder — it was heavier than it looked —

and saw Frank go out to Sangye. Taking the ball from his Sherpa, he broke into a devilish grin. She stuck her tongue out at him and dropped her shoulders into a hitting position. "Okay, Kincaid," she called out in a daring tone, "bring it on."

Oohs and ahhs followed as Frank backed up and studied her. "Knock it out of the park, Mom," Greg said.

A moment later, Frank sent the ball her way. She swung, and missed. Frank winked, waited for Sully to return the ball and went back to the pitching position. Sarah crouched down and set her jaw, getting into the spirit of the game. The pitch came and she swung again, dribbling it off to her right.

After a few more misses, she frowned. Now it was getting personal, and her competitive nature took over. She set her jaw and waited, and when Frank sent the ball her way, she caught it square and rocketed a line drive back at him, beaning his chest. As the ball fell to the ground, everyone roared in laughter. Sarah stuck her finger in the air triumphantly.

"Atta way, Mom," Greg shouted, bending over in laughter.

"Better watch out everyone, I think we got another Sachin here," Sherpa Dave said.

Frank tipped his head back and laughed. "I think so, Da-wa."

Sarah took a few more swipes, before launching one in the air, which Frank tracked down. She handed Sully the bat, and decided she'd go play out in the field. She was having the most fun she could remember in some time. As she passed Frank, she leaned in and whispered, "Lucky catch."

Next up was Greg. He took the bat from Sully, and got into position as Sarah flexed her legs and arms, ready to chase down anything that came her way. "Okay, Greg, let's see what you've got," Sarah said.

"Coming at ya, Mom," Greg said.

Frank pitched the ball and he took a big swipe and missed.

Toby yelled out from the sidelines. "Hey Greg, open your eyes next time, it helps."

Again Frank pitched, which was followed by another miss. Greg backed away from the plate as more jeers followed. Sarah said, "Come on, Greg, you can do better than that."

Frank received the ball back and rubbed it with his hands. "Hey Greg, want me to slow it down?"

"Kiss my butt, Kincaid," Greg retorted as he returned to the plate and took his stance.

More laughter came from the sidelines. Frank got into position, ran up, and fired the ball. This time Greg connected and sent the ball high in the air toward Sarah. She moved to her left, keeping her eyes and hands upward as the ball started its downward arc and just as it came near, another pair of hands went up beside her followed by a thud. As she started to fall back, a powerful arm caught her as the ball bounced free to the ground.

"Are you, okay?" Frank said.

She caught her breath as she peered up into Frank's flashing gray eyes. For a minute, the world suddenly went away and it was just the two of them. It had been a long time since she felt a man's arm around her, and she wasn't sure how she felt about it.

"Yeah, I'm fine," she said, as he straightened her up. After he let go of her, she swatted his arm. "By the way, that was my ball," she said, giving him a quirky smile then went back and took up her position.

* * *

That night, Sarah lay in bed peering up into the inky blackness as she thought about all that had happened so far on this trek. And as she did so, the memory of Sangye's interpretation of Ahab's anger came back. She mulled Frank's erratic behavior toward her over in her mind wondering if she was seeing things that weren't there. Maybe it wasn't anger he was hiding behind that smile. Maybe it was uncertainty. He lived alone, or so she had heard. No girlfriend as far as she knew. Could it be he was afraid to get close to her? It wouldn't be the first time that had happened with men in her life, which for the life of her she couldn't understand. She wasn't a bitch. She just knew what she wanted and went after it. As for Frank, she had no intention in going after him, or did she? It had certainly felt nice being in his arms for just a moment. What was she thinking, though? Nothing good would come of getting too chummy with him and the last thing she needed was to fall into bed with a man she had looked upon as an enemy when this whole odyssey began. But her body nagged at her, wanting to feel his arms around her again.

She folded her pillow and buried her head into it, determined to push the thought away. But the sleep she sought came in fits and spurts, and what little she had between her restlessness and disjointed dreams, wasn't enough. At last, she gave up and wandered out onto the patio outside her room under the ever-brightening dawn sky. As she went to the fence and gazed out over the deathly quiet land, she heard a door open behind her. Turning around, she saw Greg heading her way.

"Having trouble sleeping?" He said, coming beside her.

She nodded, and pulling her jacket collar up around her neck to ward off the cold, said, "Headache."

Greg put his hands on the fence railing and looked out toward the mountains. "It's the altitude. The higher up we get, the more it happens. You'll get used to it."

Sarah eyed him sidelong. "Oh, great. Well, I suppose there could be worse things."

"Oh, yeah," he said, "and let's hope they don't happen. Anyways, it won't be long now until we're there."

"You must be excited," she said, panning a corral below them. In one of them, she saw a yak lying down, methodically chewing his cud.

"I am," he muttered, but in his tone she detected a bit of anxiety. She debated on whether to pry further when he suddenly cleared his throat. "But there's a part of me that wonders if I'm doing the right thing."

Sarah's heart thumped and she reached over and touched his arm. "What do you mean?"

Greg turned and fixed her with a grave expression. "Can I tell you something without your going nuts on me?"

She swallowed and braced herself for whatever was coming. "Of course."

"Promise?" Greg said emphatically.

"Yes, I promise," she answered him firmly. "What is it, Greg?"

He averted his gaze back over the valley toward the mountain. "The reason I'm climbing is because of Dad. I never knew him, other than what you told me. I just wonder what it would've been like hanging together and doing stuff like going fishing or out to a ball game. Most people get a chance to say one last good-bye to their parents when the time comes, but I never had that." He sighed. "I guess what I'm saying is, I just want to be near him, just once. And he's up there." He turned a hopeful gaze back onto her. "But now that I'm here, I wonder if I'll find him. It's a big mountain up there. Frank said, it's important to know why you're climbing, and if the mountain says 'no', then to call it off. The others climb for glory or God, or whatever, but I'm climbing because of Dad. What if all this is for nothing? What if I don't find him? Then what?"

At last the real reason came out, and Sarah took a deep breath as she looked at her precious son. He was more vulnerable than she'd seen him in years. Every fiber in her body wanted to tell him to call the whole thing off. It wasn't too late. But she knew if she did, the 'not-knowing' would haunt him for the rest of his life. Looking upward, she searched for the strength to tell him what her heart was railing against. "It's not all for nothing. Look, you know how I feel. But this isn't about me. It's about you, and I love you, so you're going to have to answer that question for yourself and make your own decision. But whatever that is, I'll stand behind it. And if it's to climb, then climb — damn it!"

He turned back to her and pulling her into him, hugged her fiercely for several minutes. When he backed away, he smiled and said, "For Dad."

"No, for you." Sarah said as her throat tightened.

Chapter 12

After breakfast, Frank led the team into the hill land above Dengboche, and as he did so, he thought about Sarah. In fact, she had occupied his mind all night. He wondered if the others noticed. He'd seen Greg look on yesterday with a curious gaze after his collision with Sarah out in the field. But the truth was, he liked her more than he should, which he knew was a disaster waiting to happen. There were so many reasons to back away and forget her he could hardly count them. For one, she lived half way around the world. For another, she was a Catholic — not that he was against it, but still. And finally, she hated Everest. Now, that was big. He made his living off the mountain, which supported his charity work. For the life of him, he just couldn't understand why destiny was drawing the two of them together. It didn't make sense.

But here she was, and she wasn't going anywhere for the next forty-five days, give or take. Up until now, he hadn't been considering one last stab for the summit to see his old friend Pasang, but now he wasn't so sure about that. Or rather, his heart wasn't so sure. He could hear Tashi right now. 'I wonder what that mean?' The old lama could frustrate him to no end with his open-ended questions. So what did he want? As he tramped up the steep hillside toward a small Stupa fifty meters above the Dengboche valley, he thought about it, and the answer that came was muddled with uncertainty.

At length, Da-wa came up and joined him as the wide barren swath of land heading toward Lobuche came into view. They walked silently in tandem for a while as the mountains slowly inched their way closer. Finally, Da-wa broke into Lhasa and said, "Have you given any thoughts to pairing the men up?"

"A bit," Frank answered back. "We'll have five teams. What do you think of Toby and Jakob?"

"Big men, but strong. Who knows? They may make it all the way to the summit. At least to Camp 4," Da-wa answered. "Maybe have Ke-tsum and Ong-cho lead them?"

"Good choice," Frank agreed. "Now Vicq and Rene will want to stay together so that's a done deal. Pair them up with Nam-kha and Nanga."

"What about the American?" Da-wa said.

The north wind funneling through the wide trough they were walking suddenly kicked up. Frank pulled his buff up over his mouth and glanced back behind him. Greg and Sarah were flanked out to his right twenty meters back striding along side by side. In the beginning, he had thought to pair Greg up with Aldan and send him up in the first grouping, but over the last five days watching him interact with Lanzo, he'd changed his mind. Turning back to the Sherpa, he said, "I think Lanzo would be a good teammate for him, with you and Nga-Wang leading. Any objection?"

The Sherpa shook his head.

"So, that leaves Aldan, Carlo, and Sully," Frank said. "I'll send Aldan up with the Austrians and Carlo and Sully up with Sangye or myself with Yang-dzum."

Da-wa came to a halt and eyed Frank warily. "You thinking of climbing?"

"I don't know, depends on how things shake out," Frank replied coming to a stop. "It's been awhile, and I'm not getting any younger." He glanced back at Sarah, mindful of his rules when it came to climbing. Everest was not to be taken lightly, ever. He had told Greg that just after they left Phadking. He hiked his pack up onto his shoulders and started back ahead on the meandering trail. As he went, he thought about what life would be like at Base Camp if he stayed behind. With Sarah being nearby, it could get complicated. Before he got to know her, he had intended to hang back, but now he was of divided mind. If he manned the Command Tent, he'd have to deal with his growing attraction to the woman. *Am I looking for an excuse to climb?* He thought. *It was my decision to man the tent in the beginning, but it was to be away from Greg. But now if I stay —*

They walked another hundred meters in silence until Da-wa spoke up, "So, who you think will summit?"

Frank shrugged. "If I had to put my money on it, I'd say Sully for sure, followed by Lanzo, then possibly Jakob, and finally Greg."

"The American? Hmmmm … you may be right. Strong kid, but I wonder if his head is in it."

"What do you mean?" Frank said, turning toward him.

"I watch him. He seems troubled to me, like he have big things on his mind that aren't about mountain."

That was Frank's feeling, too, though he couldn't quite pin it on anything Greg had said so far. But, now hearing Da-wa voice what was already on his mind about Sarah's son doubled the warning in his heart. If he were in Greg's shoes, he knew what he'd be thinking. Finding his father. In fact, he himself had drifted off course each time on his way to the summit to look in on Pasang. At last, he said, "I'll have a talk with him on the way to Lobuche. Which brings me to you, my good friend."

"What about me?" Da-wa said, shooting Frank a bemused grin.

"This chat you've decided on having with John at Base Camp. You sure you want to go there?"

Da-wa lost his smile and stared off over the hills. "Ho, he needs to understand it was my decision."

"Good luck with that," Frank said, eying him sidelong. "He's not one to let go of grudges easily."

"True," Da-wa answered. "Yet, sometimes, a voice can be heard through the clanging of an angry heart, no?"

"Ho, sometimes," Frank replied. Reaching over, he took Da-wa's hand in his. "I'll send positive thoughts with you when you go."

* * *

Two hours later, they came to the Dudh Kosi River. Frank came to a halt before a long, sagging, metal bridge crossing the sloshing rapids ten meters below and looked upon the lonely outpost of Thukla. A little way off behind it was a 300-meter climb up a steep, rocky escarpment. As he viewed the distant thread of trekkers scaling the zigzagging trail amidst the boulders, he thought of Aldan and Sarah. The next few hours would be a real test for them and he wondered how they'd do. Up at this altitude, it was easy to get dehydrated because the cool air fooled the body into thinking everything was fine, while stealthily sucking the life out of it. He took a drink of water, stepped onto the sweeping metal span crossing the Dudh Kosi River, and strode over it to the hostel waiting on the other side.

The owner of the Yak Lodge, who went by the nickname of 'T', was standing outside smoking a cigarette and talking to one of the trekking guides who was leading a group of Chinese tourists up for a quick view of Base Camp. Sherpa Tse-ten and Frank went back a long way to the days when Frank worked for Andersen. Back then, Tse-ten ran Andersen's cook tent before leaving to take up ownership of the Yak.

When Tse-ten saw Frank, he broke into a wide grin and came over to greet him. "Namaste, Frank."

Frank dropped his pack and put his arm around the short, round man. In English, he said, "And how is my good friend?"

Tse-ten nodded. "Very good. You get here just in time. I have fresh batch of rice and lentils just come out." He peered over Frank's shoulder. "How many you lead up mountain this year?"

"Nine, plus a lady observer," Frank said, turning around to watch his expedition team file onto the broad stone terrace flanking the lodge. As they climbed out of the packs, Frank motioned them inside out of the sunlight.

The Sherpa watched them go in with a critical eye and leaned toward Frank. "So, I assume tall brown-haired man is Madden's son."

Frank frowned. Did everyone on the mountain know his business?

Tse-ten's wizened eyes looked back from under heavy brows. "Ahhh, you wondering how I know. Tembe tell me when he come through with your supplies. He say you guiding son of man who die on Chomolungma with Sherpa Pasang. You think that wise? Much bad karma there."

"He'll be okay," Frank said, tempering his surprise at Tse-ten's finding out about it. It wasn't like it was a huge secret in the beginning, but now, with his change of heart toward Sarah, it occurred to him that he might have a little problem. How would she take it, if she found out he had known about her husband and never said anything about it? But she was an intelligent woman. Surely she would see his point of not mentioning anything about it in the beginning. What good would there have been in doing it, except to create more problems? No, he had made the right decision, and she would see the logic in it.

* * *

Two hours later they were climbing the escarpment up to the ridge that would take them to Lobuche. Frank had put Da-wa in the lead so he could hang back with Sarah, Greg, and Aldan. To his surprise, Sarah was doing great and Aldan seemed to be getting on as well, but there was still a good slog ahead until they reached the top. The rest of the team had traveled on ahead of them and were nearing the crest of the ridge.

"Clouds are moving in," Greg said.

"Getting colder, too," Sarah added.

Frank checked his hand-held altimeter. They were about 4,700 meters above sea level and halfway up the slope. By the time they made the Lobuche outpost the temps would drop another twenty degrees Celsius.

Sarah stabbed her pole into the unforgiving ground, and searched for a place to put her foot on the strewn rocks before them. But the step up was too much for her. She turned back to Frank. "Any suggestions?"

Greg came back and put his hand out. "Here, Mom, grab hold," he said, and hoisted her up.

"Whew, this is quite a jaunt, isn't it?" she said, as she let go of Greg's hand. She turned and looked down at the Yak Lodge, whose rooftop had shrunken to a small green dot on the vast brown landscape.

"One step at a time," Frank encouraged. "How you doing Greg?"

"Great!" Greg looked up and surveyed the mountains to the north. "The views are awesome. What are those mountains over there?"

"The one that looks like an inverted cone would be Changri, and to its left would be Lobuche," Frank said pointing toward the jagged, ice covered peaks. "What about you, Aldan? How're you doing?"

"I'm good," he said, and took a long pull of water from his camelback.

"Headache still there?" Frank said.

"Getting better, I think," he answered. He looked up ahead at the stream of trekkers going back and forth on the hill. In the buffeting wind, the sound of bells could be heard coming toward them. "Looks like we have a train coming at us," Aldan said.

Frank nodded. "We'll head over there by those rocks and wait 'em out."

Sarah said, "How do they do it?"

"How does who do what?" Frank said.

"The yaks," Sarah replied. "Going up and down these steep slopes."

"It only looks hard," Frank said. "Actually, they're more sure footed than you or I could ever dream of being."

She shook her head and started off to where he'd pointed. As she went, Sherpa porters went marching past them; some of them going straight up, ignoring the barely recognizable switchback trail. Frank followed and waited amongst the jagged rocks as the yaks picked their way down, stopping now and then to decide their next step. When the train had passed, he roused his companions and started back up the escarpment. To help make the last two hundred meter climb easier, he got them bantering about their hobbies and asking about their families back home. Sarah bragged about her gardens and her pottery, Aldan talked about the outback, noting that the walk they'd just taken from Dengboche to Thukla reminded him of the bush except for the mountains of course. Greg made little mention of his life back home other than to comment about not missing the smog. But after a while everyone ran out of things to say, and so they fell silent as they negotiated the final leg of the climb.

When they reached the top, Frank found the team sitting on their packs, munching energy bars and drinking long draughts off their camelbacks except for Carlo, who was bent over heaving.

Da-wa stepped beside Frank. "What you think? Dehydrated? He come up awful fast."

Frank dropped his pack and went over to the Italian. "Hey, man, what's up?"

Carlo wiped his mouth with the back of his hand. "I think I eat something in Tengboche that not agree with me."

"Like what?" Frank said.

Carlo nodded and sat back on his heels. "A small steak, not big. I be alright. Just need a minute."

"Sure," Frank said, pissed that the man had failed to take his advice about eating meat. "We're in no hurry. Sangye, bring me my pack, would ya?"

As the Sherpa went and picked it up, Sarah came over and stood beside them. Sarah said, "You okay, Carlo?"

The Italian nodded as Sangye returned.

Frank pulled out a bottle of pills and popped a couple into Carlo's hand. "Here, take these. They'll help settle that tummy of yours. Next time, stay away from the steaks, eh? Your body isn't used to 'em."

Standing, Frank called everyone around him. "Listen here, folks. Stay away from the meat, all right? Your body isn't used to the natural bacteria occurring in it. Last thing you want is to get sick at Base Camp. It's hard enough up there getting acclimatized, without having to deal with nausea on top of it."

When they all consented, Frank marched off behind the rocks. As he stood amongst them relieving his overflowing bladder, he shook his head. *Why can't folks follow simple little rules? They better learn though, 'cause later their lives'll depend on it.*

* * *

After Carlo dealt with his upset stomach, the team filed out onto a land of scattered erratics running along the earth-encrusted glacier. As they poled along, Frank dropped back and joined Greg. "So what are your thoughts on Sagarmatha so far?"

"Different than what I expected."

"I bet," Frank said, shimmying his pack up his shoulder.

Greg scuffed along on the hardpan soil. "It's crowded up here."

"We do get a lot of trekkers going through the mountains."

Greg shrugged. "Yeah, more than I expected. I'm glad I don't live in Kathmandu, I couldn't deal with that mess every day."

"Me either," Frank agreed staring off over the barren terrain leading up to the foothills. He took a drink from his camelback. "It's why I live up here."

"You always been up here on the mountains?"

"Most of my life, give or take a few years," Frank replied. "What about you; LA always been your home?"

"Yeah, though I don't live in the city anymore," Greg answered. He hopped over a large flat rock crossing their path. "I'm up north near Glendale now. Mom is down the pike from me in West Covina. So, what's it like living up here?"

Frank considered the question. It had been asked before. Usually, he changed the subject, deflecting the inquiry, but he decided to reach out to the young man and told him about how his family came to the mountains when he was a boy. "Up in the mountains you depend on your neighbors, especially in the winters. Nothing comes easy up here, but I wouldn't trade my life among the Sherpa for anything. They're the salt of the earth and there's nothing I wouldn't do for them."

"Mom told me you're building a school for them."

Frank looked away. "Did she?"

"Yep. It definitely got her attention," Greg said. "She used to teach, you know."

"Yes, she told me that," Frank said, wondering where Greg was heading.

Greg was quiet a moment. "Yeah. We're not real close these days." He paused, said, "You like her don't you?"

The question caught Frank sideways. He glanced at Greg, wondering how much the kid had made of Sarah and his conversations. Finally, he said, "Sure, I like her. Smart lady. So, how come you two aren't close?"

"Don't know; we just aren't. Could be because she sees the world one way and I see it another. With her, it's always been about the next step up the ladder. That's not me. I like my job, don't get me wrong, but there's more to life than promotions and status. Now a job like yours, I'd jump on that in a heartbeat."

"It's not all adventure, you know," Frank said. "Lots of paperwork and planning."

"But you like it," Greg persisted.

Frank smiled. "Yes, I do."

They were quiet a moment. Finally, Greg said, "Were you up here when my father died?"

Frank drew breath and felt his gut knot. This was one question he didn't want to answer, but he wouldn't lie, and his silence would only confirm it anyway. "Yes, I was. Didn't know him very well, other than a few exchanges."

"My mom used to talk about him all the time when I was little. But at night she cried in her room. I'd run in and put my arms around her, asking her what was wrong. She'd always tell me she had a bad dream and not to worry. But I knew it was more. Then one day, she just stopped talking, so I stopped asking. Wasn't long after that before she began throwing herself into getting her Masters. She told me she was doing it for us, but I know it was more for her."

Frank said. "How much does your mother know about the accident?"

"Some. She knows he died on the south summit. Knows there was a freak storm involved. Why?"

Frank closed his eyes as he mulled his decision over. Should he tell him the truth? The kid was laying himself wide open to him. Had this been twenty years ago, he would have cruelly run the blade of truth into him and twisted it, and to be truthful right now, he couldn't deny that it wouldn't feel good to do it. The smoldering embers of that day so long ago that had been banked into a dark corner of his heart suddenly burst into a bright flame and it took all his resolve to smother it. Coming to a stop, he turned to Greg and collected himself. "There's more to it."

"Like what?" Greg said stopping beside him.

Frank paused and carefully considered what he was about to tell him. "Your father was liked on the mountain by everyone as far as I could tell. And he was no tenderfoot, like a lot of folks up here. He knew his business and he was careful. Anyway, he and his Sherpa were at Camp 4, and were socked in for two days waiting for a window. It wasn't looking good for a summit bid. If the weather didn't clear the next day, they'd have to come back down. But as luck would have it, if you could call it that, the weather improved on the third day and gave them a shot at making it. But with their O2 supply tanks dwindling in number, they'd have to hoof it pretty good. With that in mind, they pried themselves out of their tent around midnight and hauled ass up the mountain. Maybe, your father pushed himself too hard or something went wrong with his O2 regulator, who knows."

"He had summit fever didn't he?" Greg said with a pained expression that stabbed at Frank's heart.

"I'd like to think it was HACE," Frank said, wanting to soften the blow and keep the young man's vision of his father intact. "Anyway, he wasn't thinking clearly, and in the end, it cost him his life and that of his Sherpa."

Greg took a deep breath, bit his lip and looked away. "That's why you gave me the business earlier about me listening to my Sherpa, isn't it?"

Frank nodded. "Look, I can't tell you not to say anything to your mother about this. But I don't think she needs to know he lost it up there."

"No, I don't think she does," Greg agreed. "So, where were you?"

There it was, the question Frank was dreading from the moment the subject shifted to Steve Madden. He felt his chest tighten as he cleared his throat. "I was working the tent."

Greg's gaze remained fixed on the mountains. "So, you heard everything go down, then?"

"I did," Frank answered, hating the memory, yet pitying the son.

"Did he —"

"He went peacefully," Frank lied, wanting to find a way out of this terrible conversation. "I'm sorry."

Greg turned back and shrugged. "It's not your fault. Thanks for telling me." He started back off on the trail and for the next half hour a cavern-sized silence separated them until Greg said, "You're probably wondering why I *really* want to climb Everest, aren't you?

"The thought has crossed my mind," Frank said, and waited to see what Greg would say.

Greg came to another stop, collapsed his hiking poles and tucked them in his backpack. After he took a drink from his camelback, he stared at Frank, and the haunted look on his face was devastating. "Yeah, mine too. I used to know exactly why I wanted to climb Everest and part of me still does, but there's this doubt now. Like, what if I get all the way up there and I feel nothing. What then?"

Frank couldn't give him an answer to that because he knew from experience it could crush him. "My teacher, if he were here, would tell you not to let the fear of tomorrow diminish the beauty of today. Easier said than done, I know. But it's the only way I know how to approach life and be happy now."

Greg shrugged. "You're probably right, but like you said, easier said than done." He started back off and they fell into a comfortable silence between them as they walked side by side.

* * *

The expedition team strode single file into the sparse settlement of Lobuche a little after 5:30. The village, if that was what it could be called, squatted beside the receding edge of the frozen Dudh Kosi River. The sky was overcast and the wind was stiff, ruffling the collars of their down jackets. As they made their way to their teahouse along the stone path, Frank pointed out Mt. Nuptse and the edge of the Lhotse wall they would eventually circle around behind. There, they would come upon Base Camp at long last, where they would spend the next month preparing for the assault on Everest.

For now, they would hunker down in the large stone built teahouse with blue trimmed windows and doors that was coming up on their left. He stepped to the side as they came to the front door and waited as the crew passed by him into the darkened interior. There, they unloaded their burdens in the dim lit hallway leading to the dining room, and went to rest their bones within the circle of chairs that were gathered around an old potbellied stove.

While everyone was getting warmed up, Frank checked them in while Dawa and Sangye handed out menus for the evening meal. To be honest, he was tired, too. It had been a long day, and tomorrow would be longer. But a burden had been lifted from him he didn't know he was carrying. The talk with Greg had been cathartic in ways he couldn't have guessed. He felt a tiny smile come to his face as he looked the men over from where he stood by the transaction counter. Lanzo had connected with Greg and they were huddled in a corner talking and Sully, Carlo, and Jakob were plowing into a bowl of popcorn. He glanced at Sarah, who was sipping a mug of tea, and wondered if she knew how wounded her son was.

Chapter 13

That night the temperature dropped to well below freezing. Burrowing down into the warmth of her sleeping bag, Sarah left just a crack of it open, but the Diamox she'd been taking to combat the altitude was now showing its other face to her. She groaned as her bladder woke her up for the umpteenth time. Groping for the button on her battery-powered headlamp she had worn to bed, she clicked it on and fumbled her way out of her warm cocoon into the frigid night air. *How much water could a human being put out in one night?* she wondered as she pulled back the toilet lid, whose only saving grace was that it was of western persuasion instead of just a hole in the floor.

As she hovered above it, waiting for her body to do its business, it was becoming quite apparent that life was going to be rather uncomfortable for the next month. Already, she'd been living in the same fleece, pants, bra, and thermals for the last three days. She drew the line on panties though. At last, she scampered back to her room and the comfort of her sleeping bag. As she pulled the zipper up, closing out the cold, she wondered what she had gotten herself into, but it was too late now and she wasn't going to complain to anyone about it except her pillow. *Well, at least we'll be in Base Camp tomorrow*, she thought — then realized what that meant and felt her stomach knot. Taking a deep breath, she fruitlessly tried to banish the thought of coming under the eyes of the Monster, and clicked her headlamp off.

But as she lay there curled into a fetal position, trying to get back to sleep, her brain wouldn't let go of the fears that had haunted her since this whole thing began. She gritted her teeth, trying to consume herself with the nine hour slog ahead, imagining what life was going to be like at Camp, how the toilets worked, whether or not she could stomach another month of Dal Bhat, noodles, and potatoes, and did they wash their clothes or just continued living in them until they rotted off their bodies? Up until now, the trek had been a scenic feast for her eyes — except for the grueling marches up the hillsides — and an awakening to the world of the Sherpa people. But now, the cruel reality of the Monster was pressing down on her, and for the first time she wondered if it would have been better had she stayed home.

And then there was Frank.

Never could she have imagined finding someone here in this wilderness, living in the lap of her husband's murderer, who could tug at her heart like he could. She couldn't understand why she felt her pulse quicken every time he came around. He was guarded, complicated, frustrating, and reserved to the nth degree, to say nothing of leading her son to the one thing she'd hated more than anything over the last twenty years. But, oh how she loved listening to him talk about the Sherpa people and watching him laugh with the children they met along the way.

He was a man of compassion and confidence, a man who was shaped by the land he lived in, and his dark gray eyes and weather-beaten face drew her to him unwittingly. Whether he knew it or not, he was touching a hidden place inside her that had been closed off since the day Steven had left her so long ago, and it frightened her. Yet, it was too late, and she knew it. Whether she ever saw him again after she left the Monster didn't matter; his indelible mark had already been branded into her memory.

* * *

The next morning, a knock on her door woke her out of a nonsensical dream. "Up and at 'em, breakfast is waiting," Frank said from the other side.

Pushing the flap of her sleeping bag off her face, Sarah squinted into the bright sunlight pouring through her window and glanced at her watch. 6:30 AM. She'd overslept. She rolled out of bed and cleared her throat. "I'll be right down."

She heard Frank's footsteps trail away as she took her headlamp off and dragged a comb through her hair. Seeing her breath in the beam of sunlight streaming into the room, she sighed and forced herself to strip down in the icy cold room and change. Ten minutes later, she gathered her pack and poles and headed downstairs into the crowded dining room. Sitting around three long tables in the far corner, were her team members. She set her pack down with the rest of the packs that were lying by the potbellied stove and went over to take a seat next to her son.

"Okay," Frank said, speaking up and getting everyone's attention. "Today we finally get to Base Camp. We have a long slog ahead of us, so we need to get going fairly shortly. Remember your sunscreen and do wear your sunnys today. It might be a bit chilly out there, but the sun can still bake you and burn your eyes, so take care."

A bit chilly! Sarah thought. *Understatement of the century.* She poured herself a mug of ginger tea as Sangye put a plate of pancakes and a hardboiled egg in front of her. The cakes didn't look half bad, and she found her appetite coming back a bit. She sipped her tea and setting the mug down, doused her cakes with whatever they thought maple syrup was up here.

As she ate, Frank came over and set a large bottle of water in front of her. "Drink *all* of this before we leave," he said quietly.

She looked up, wondering if he was serious. His firm expression told her he wasn't kidding. She pursed her lips and unscrewed the cap, taking a healthy mouthful. "All of it?" she said, setting the bottle down.

"All of it. I heard you getting up all night. You don't want to get dehydrated, believe me." He shot her a tiny smile then headed off outside.

Greg nudged her elbow. "You were running laps last night, huh?"

"Very funny. Finish your breakfast," she said, peeling the shell off her egg. She bit into it and added a sprinkle of salt. "How'd you sleep?"

"Alright, I guess. A little nippy."

"Nippy doesn't begin to describe it. I can only imagine what it'll be like up at Base Camp," Sarah said, popping the last of the egg in her mouth. "Wish they had coffee. I could use a thermos of it."

Greg chuckled. "Me, too. Hey, you want me to fill your camelback?"

"Would you?"

"Sure." He got up and gave her shoulder a squeeze. "Almost there. Tomorrow you can sleep all day if you want."

"We'll see," she answered, and shoveled a forkful of pancake into her mouth.

Greg winked and smiled at her wickedly. "Don't forget to finish your water."

She groaned. "Don't you have something to do?"

* * *

They left the settlement of Lobuche shortly after 7:30 AM under another incredible blue sky. The terrain was now nothing but brown earth and tiny scrub ferns and grasses along with mosses and lichen clinging to the strewn boulders and rocks. The desolate landscape rolling up to the mountains was like walking on another planet as far as Sarah was concerned. Yet, it was beautiful in an alien way. She glanced from time to time to the frozen Dudh Kosi River they'd been following. The swath of ice was barely discernable under the thin blanket of grit that capped its undulating and fractured surface.

Then, Sangye, who was a few feet ahead, pointed upward at a 'V' shaped formation flying northward. "Asian geese," he called back.

The team stopped and Sarah took out a small pair of binoculars. Through her lenses, she saw nine tan-feathered birds with white heads gliding silently overhead. She followed their flight, entranced by the graceful command of the whispering wind overhead until they were but specks in the sky.

Four hours later, the team was tramping on what Frank called, *sammma ra tala trail Cheen*, or the up-and-down highway. It was a bit like taking two steps forward and one backward, Sarah thought as they poled their way back and forth around the huge stone erratics that had been laid down by the glacier millennia ago. But always, the mountains were before and beside them as they marched over the vast wasteland single file like a parade of ants following an invisible sugar trail to its hopeful end.

Frank had noted they'd be in Gorak Shep in an hour or so a half hour ago, but Sarah could see nothing ahead indicating a settlement, just ice, rock, and blue sky. She came to a halt, and drank from her camelback, fighting a nagging headache in the back of her neck. Carlo came up and joined her.

"*È bella*," he said.

Sarah's Italian was a bit rusty, in fact, it was nonexistent. She looked back at him. "I'm sorry?"

He paused and she could see him searching for the English words. Finally, he said, "Ahhh … beautiful. The mountains above Milan are like these, except not so *grande*. My papa would have loved seeing this."

"Your father sounds like a romantic. You said he thought about God and the mountains. Tell me about him," Sarah said.

"Oh, my papa was in love with God. He start every day talking with Him. When I was *piccolo* … ah, little, I could hear him downstairs in the morning before he go to *ristorante* having long conversations telling Him how *grato* he was for all that he have."

Sarah was quiet; suddenly remembering her own father who had died way too young when she was a teen. He had been larger than life to her, a man of duty with a fierce love of God and family. Even now, after all these years, she could see his shining face dotted with freckles and his deep blue eyes looking back lovingly in her mind's eye. And if she listened hard enough, she could hear his booming laughter when the two of them had sat watching Roadrunner outwit the wily coyote on Saturday mornings. But friendly fire had taken him away from her, leaving a void that could never be filled. But that was the way it had been in her life. The men she loved were taken away from her before their time. She looked over at her son and felt the weight of that reality pressing down around her.

At last she said, "You must miss him very much."

Carlo nodded. "*Sì, molto.*" He reached into his pocket and pulled his wallet out. Opening it, he showed her an old faded picture of the man. Looking at it, Sarah could definitely see the resemblance between father and son.

"What about your mom, is she still living?"

"No, she pass a couple years ago, God rest her soul," Carlo said, crossing himself and putting his wallet away. "What about you? Are your momma and papa still alive?"

Sarah shook her head. "My father died years ago when I was thirteen. My mom never got over it; fell into clinical depression, She passed on fifteen years ago."

"So sorry," Carlo said. "But they are back together now, so that is something."

"Yes," Sarah answered. Why was it people didn't know how to deal with death and loss? Sometimes it felt like their ill-conceived platitudes were nothing more than breath mints being passed out to cover up an unpleasant taste of grief that was left on the pallet. "Well, we better get back at it before the slave driver cracks the whip."

Carlo grinned. "After you."

* * *

The team arrived at Gorak Shep just after 2:00 PM and there they had a light lunch of more rice and more noodles along with a mix of carrots and green beans, before heading back out on the last leg of their hike to Base Camp. But for her son and the rest of the men, it was just the beginning. Ahead of them was a month of reaching for the sky hiking up a perilous and unforgiving mountain with a quick temper. At least that's how she looked at it; although the further she had come up, the more the beauty of the Himalayas had gnawed away at her pre-conceptions.

At first, the subtle admission that she saw any beauty up here had surprised her but the more she thought about it, it made sense. Many things in God's creation that were beautiful were also very dangerous. Perhaps, more than anything, it was the lure of beauty that attracted men to their death. At this point, she didn't know, only that her son was heading into that lure. But at least she knew why he was climbing now, and to a point she could understand it. In any event, the die was cast and she had made a promise to stand by him. She just hoped Frank would bring her son back to her alive.

An hour later, she caught her first glimpse of the Khumbu Ice Fall, and before it, the tiny yellow specks of Base Camp. She climbed over a large boulder and slid around another to get a better look at it with her binoculars. The sloughing ice sheet that was slowly tumbling down the mountainside was enormous, and it appeared ready at any minute to squash the tiny colony of tents stationed before it.

Frank pointed to Base Camp. "Home for the next forty days," he called back then struck off into a far-reaching sea of brown and gray boulders ahead. From here on in, there was no trail, just a maze of erratics to wend around and climb up and over against a chill, stiff wind coming off the mountains. Oddly, Sarah found this was proving to be one of the hardest parts of the trek and by the time they came walking into the tented outpost of Base Camp, she was exhausted.

As she pulled her pack off and caught her breath; Frank came over to her. "How you doing?"

She nodded under his watchful gaze. "Okay, I think."

"Well, why don't you take a breather, and if you need help with your tent, come find me. I'll be around."

"Thanks, I appreciate it, but I'll be fine. Got to pull my own weight," she said and watched him march off toward a large yellow tent, whose sides shuddered in the wind. As she stood watching her son and the rest of her team empty their gear and start pitching their tents, she took in the multitude of prayer flags fluttering all around the busy camp. Men and women dressed in down jackets and Gortex leggings were going back and forth on some errand or other. Some were pulling sleeping bags off the tops of their tents and stuffing them back inside their canvas homes. Others were washing plates and cooking utensils out in metal basins. A man nearby was examining gear he'd laid out on the ground in front of him. As soon as she got her wind back, she'd be at it herself. Sarah Madden was no slouch.

CHOMOLUNGMA

Goddess of the Snow

Chapter 14

Frank strode across the large square plot of land that his camp cook, Tembe, had secured for Khum Jung Mountaineering and headed for the command tent. As always, Tembe had done a bang-up job of getting things set up. The cache of four hundred and twenty bottles of oxygen had been neatly stacked, chained, and locked up waiting to be tagged and labeled. Twenty solar panels were laid out nearby and wired to batteries. The climbers' personal tents and gear had been broken down and piled beside the command tent. And last, but not least, their camp latrine had been set up and ballasted to the ground.

Pulling the Command Tent flap back, he went in to find his old friend with his nose buried behind a clipboard. The man was going over the inventory that had been brought up to Base Camp by yak caravans. Ang Lhak-pa Tembe dorje had been with Frank for the better part of twenty-five years going back to the days when they worked for Andersen. The Sherpa had a good deal of Chinese in him from his mother's side of the family. Outside of the old lama in Khum Jung, Tembe was one of his closest friends and one of few who knew the whole story behind the disaster that occurred up on the mountain back in '85.

"Namaste," Frank said with as much enthusiasm as he could muster after the nine-and-half-hour-long slog.

The rail thin Sherpa looked up, giving Frank a broad toothy smile. Laying his clipboard down, he cleared his throat. "Namaste. How was your trip?"

"It was great. I see, once again, you've outdone yourself," Frank said, scanning the ring of four-foot long folding tables placed around the perimeter of the tent. On one of them sat sixteen portable communication devices hooked up to chargers along with the camp base station. In the center of the tent stood a long table with a cooking stove with a large propane tank beside it. Pots and pans, mugs and bowls, along with cooking mitts and utensils were stacked underneath the table.

The Sherpa shrugged. "How long you know me? You expect anything else?"

"Nope, just letting you know I appreciate it."

"Humph," the Sherpa grunted back. "Well, you gonna sit there all day, or you gonna help? Lots to do. Don't have time to make chit-chat."

"Sure, give me the clipboard," Frank said, getting up. Taking it from the Sherpa, he went on, "Okay, where were you?"

Tembe pointed half way down the page. "Need to check in medical supplies and food."

"Speaking of which," Frank said, looking up knowingly, "did it make it in one piece?"

"Ho. It over there in cooler," Tembe said, pointing over his shoulder as he started up the stove for the evening dinner.

After checking in on his little surprise to the team, Frank strode over and knelt down beside a large plastic crate. Pulling it out from under the table, he untied the straps holding the lid down. He opened the crate and started going down the list of first aid items. Checking them off one by one, he said, "You run into Patterson yet?"

"Oh, yeah. He here. Set up on other side of camp. He didn't look too happy when he came in. What you do, kiss him on the lips and try to make nice?" Tembe scoffed.

Frank couldn't help but laugh. "Yeah, something like that. Hey, is this all the Dexy we have?" Frank said, losing his smile. He held up two small bottles above his head.

"Should be more in there. Check around."

"Oh, I see 'em," Frank said, digging them out. He eyed the expiration dates on them and set them aside with the other two. Twenty minutes later, he had everything back in place and checked off on the med list. Next was the food, which was stored in the supply tent next door. He went outside, and as he did so, saw John Patterson stalking across camp with his long blond hair flapping in the wind.

The Andersen Expedition leader was headed straight for a group of gawking tourists who had crossed the Base Camp boundary line. By now, Frank thought the trekking guides should have known better than to let their trekkers cross into the protected zone. But every year, there seemed to be someone who hadn't gotten the memo. Frank shook his head as John tore into the poor bastard leading the scattered band of tourists. The Andersen leader wasn't the most tactful man when it came to certain things, especially when it involved endangering his gear and equipment.

But it was important to enforce the boundary zone that went around the climbing community. Those who poured so much money into their one chance of climbing Everest didn't need light-fingered tourists added to the mix, to say nothing of the potential for infecting the camp. It was hard enough staying healthy up here as it was.

Frank turned, and as he went to inventory the provisions of rice and vegetables, he glanced over to see how Sarah was making out with her tent. It was up and pegged down by the numbers on an elevated section of moraine twenty meters or so away from the men's tents. Suddenly he saw her pop outside wearing a fresh black fleece and gray trekking pants. The colorful scarf she'd picked up in Lukla was loosely wrapped around her neck and fluttering in the wind. He watched as she stood, tying her hair back and tucking it up under a bright red cap. She was unaware of him until she turned and caught him looking on. He quickly averted his gaze and ducked into the supply tent. But it wasn't so quick that he didn't see her wave back to him.

* * *

Forty-five minutes later after finishing his inventory, he gathered his team for introductions. "Okay, everyone," he said carrying his water bottle and heading to the center of the circled tents. "I have a few folks I want you to meet." He pulled Tembe next to him and put his arm around the Sherpa's thin shoulders.

"This man here, is Tembe. He's your camp cook and he'll be the most important person in your lives for the next six weeks," Frank said, and with a playful but serious tone, added, "Cross him at your own risk."

Lanzo and Toby chuckled and there were smiles all around as Tembe bowed politely to them. "Namaste, Namaste," the Sherpa said.

Frank then turned to the group of rugged, hard-bitten Sherpas standing behind him. Dressed in faded jeans, tan woolen shirts and down vest jackets, they typified those who carried the commerce up the down the mountain. But these men were not porters. All of them had summited Everest more than once.

Sweeping his hand in their direction, Frank said, "And now I want you to meet your guides." Nodding to a robust, chisel-faced man wearing a knitted gray hat with earmuffs, Frank said, "This is Sherpa Ang Tu-chi."

The man stepped forward and dipped his head respectfully, then stepped back. Next was a round-faced man, sporting a thin, dark mustache and beard, whom Frank introduced as Sherpa Ang Nam-kha dorje. Beside Nam-kha was Sherpa Nga-Wang. Both men had square-jaws with broad noses. They stepped forward in tandem and bowed respectfully. After them, was Sherpa Ang Ke-tsum, who was the tallest of the Sherpas as well as the youngest. His long, flowing black hair framed a thin ruddy face.

"These men, along with Sherpa Dave, Sangye and his assistant Chok-pal here will be with you the rest of the way," Frank said. "I can't impress upon you enough how much these men know about this mountain. Listen to them." Taking a drink from his water bottle, he paused, letting his words sink into them before clearing his throat. "Now tomorrow, after breakfast, we'll be meeting right back here to go over pairings and groupings. It won't all be written in stone because the weather will have a lot to say about how things shake out. But the good news so far is things look great this year for a successful summit."

That brought a lot of wide beaming smiles and a couple hoots and hollers from Jakob and Lanzo. As high fives went around, Frank quietly observed his clients, letting his gaze fall on each one until he came to Greg's thoughtful expression. It put him on edge. He made a mental note to keep his eye on the young man.

"Okay, okay, one last thing. Everyone — make sure to wear your masks during the night from here on out. It'll go a long way in preventing Khumbu Cough. You don't want *that* if you can help it."

Suddenly, it occurred to him that Sarah might not have a mask. As people dispersed back to their tents, he saw the wide-eyed look on her face. He went over and pulled her aside. "You don't have one, do you?"

She shook her head.

He paused, debating his thoughts on summiting. If he went, he could probably get away with just one spare. At last, he said, "Not to worry, you can use one of mine."

* * *

The following morning, the team gathered outside their tents. As they ate their breakfasts of porridge, Frank mentally went over the logistics of the next two weeks. For the majority of it, they'd be spending their time acclimatizing to the 5,300-meter altitude of Base Camp. Many of them would probably suffer sleep deprived nights, headaches, and a loss of appetite until their bodies adjusted — or not. Sometimes you never acclimate and that made for a long, uncomfortable forty-five days at the top of the world. His one huge mantra, which he would continue to emphasize over and over, was to drink, drink, and then drink again. Nothing did more to help their bodies deal with the stress they were under than a steady dose of water to replenish what the thin air siphoned away. Beyond that, it was just 'grit it out' and eat as many high carb meals as you could; especially for Aldan. He was struggling big time and wasn't eating nearly as much as he should. He'd have to keep a sharp eye on him. With his thoughts in place, he got down to business.

"All right folks," Frank said, putting his clipboard down, "Here's how things are going to shake out. First off, as I said yesterday, I like to pair folks off with my Sherpas. I do this because there's a lot to deal with when you go for a summit bid and I don't want my Sherpas overwhelmed."

He paused to make sure he had everyone's attention then scanning his audience with a meaningful gaze, announced the pairings and groupings. When he was done, silence followed. At last, Rene said, "Does that mean we're climbing separately?"

"Yes. Once you're above Camp 2, I like to space folks out a bit," Frank said. "I don't want folks on top of each other."

"How far apart do you space us?" Jakob said.

Frank turned to the Austrian. "An hour or so, depending on the weather and how folks are doing."

That brought a puzzled frown to Vicq's face. "Who decides how folks are doing?" he said pointedly.

"Me, and if I'm not there, my Sherpas. I don't want folks getting in over their heads up there."

"So, if you're not there, the Sherpas can say this or that, and that's it?" Vicq said, deepening the furrow on his brow.

Frank turned to the Frenchman. "Exactly!"

Vicq bristled. "I've a lot of money invested in this expedition. I find it unacceptable to be denied a summit bid because some Sherpa, who knows nothing about medicine, can decide I don't look good!"

Frank paused, watching to see how the Sherpa guides were taking the challenging remark. The Frenchman had no idea how close he was to skirting a dangerous, thin line with them. Finally, seeing that the Sherpas were letting the comment slide by, he said, "Then you'll be climbing alone, *mon ami*. I wouldn't recommend it, though. You could end up dead long before you reach the summit."

A long uncomfortable silence followed as the warning sank into Vicq. Finally, Frank surveyed the entire team, and said, "Folks, I know you all have a lot riding here, but the important thing's to come back alive to try again if it doesn't work out." He swept his hand toward the Sherpas. "These men here beside me, know these mountains. They live up here, and so do I. We have no vested interest in seeing you fail. When you summit, it's a win-win for us."

The argument he put forth got heads nodding after a while so he went on, "Good. Now, I was going to wait on this, but I think it's a good time to bring it up and get it over with." He paused and narrowed his gaze on Vicq and Aldan, who were still frowning across from him. "Now, listen up, 'cause I'm only saying this once. After you reach Camp 3 and above, your Sherpa is the boss. If he says you're coming down, you're coming down, no questions asked. If you insist on disobeying him, I will tell him to leave you there, and you will die. I will not sacrifice a man who is putting his life on the line looking out for you because you decide you know more than he does. Understood?"

Not a word was said for several minutes as the men turned their gazes inward, until at last, one by one, they nodded. There was one however, who was sitting to his right who was of a different opinion. He didn't need to look to know whom it was frowning back at him either. He could feel it. But then, he expected no less from Sarah considering what had happened to her husband so long ago. Well, it was her decision to come up here, and though he'd gotten to really like her, his duty was to his Sherpas first and his clients second.

At last, he broke into a smile and pointed to the stacked bottles by the command tent. "Now, your O2 is waiting over there to be weighed, labeled, and tagged. It's all chained together and locked up so it doesn't grow legs. Tembe has the key for the padlock." He eyed the Italians, who seemed to him to be a bit free and easy about their gear so far. "Important; make sure that after you're done tagging and weighing your tanks, you put them back and have Tembe lock them up. Think of O2 as gold up here. Desperate folks will want it so act accordingly.

"Second; your communication devices are all juiced up in the command tent. From now on, it'll be your responsibility to do your own charging. Third; if you start feeling ill, come see me and let me know. I'm not the enemy, and do remember, just because you're feeling like shit doesn't mean it's permanent. I'm not going to send you back down the mountain unless there's a damned good reason. And believe me, if I do send you down, you're feeling really, really bad and won't want anything to do with this mountain anyway. Again, there's no reason to suffer if I can do something about it. Additionally, there's going to be a meeting later on this week to go over first aid and emergency medical issues, which by the way is mandatory for all," he said, turning and fixing Sarah with a 'you-too' look.

She raised a brow but made no objection.

Moving on, he continued, "Now, in this meeting, I'll be introducing you to Robert Cranston. He's a skilled medic who'll be here to look after all the folks at Base Camp who come down with serious issues. Not the sniffles or the rumbly tummies.

"Fourth; meals are offered at 7:00 AM, noon and at 6:00 PM. Bring your own plates and eating utensils and clean up after yourself." He was about to say, 'Your mom isn't here to pick up after you', but caught himself just in time.

"Finally, we're going to be living in close quarters from here on out. Use your sanitizers religiously. No one wants to get sick up here. Also, folks are going be tense; not sleeping well due to the altitude, so there's bound to be things that'll irritate you more than usual. Remember that, before you go launching into someone, and that goes double for members of other expedition teams up here. Life will be so much easier if you do.

"That's all I have for right now, except for one little thing. It's my tradition to have a small kick-off dinner the night after we arrive at Base Camp to get things started on the right foot. Sherpa Tembe will be working his magic in the kitchen and I have a little surprise to add as well, so be on time tonight and bring your appetite." He bent over, picked up his water bottle and stood.

The men got up along with him and went with Tembe to their oxygen tanks to get on with their work. As Frank watched them leave, Sarah came beside him. "Well, that was quite the speech."

"There's a lot to go over, and this is just the beginning," he said. He studied her circumspect expression wondering if she was going to bring up the issue of his cardinal rule. "How'd you sleep last night?"

"On and off," she said. "Couldn't get comfortable."

"You use your pad?" Frank said, folding up his chair.

"Oh, yes. It's just these old bones of mine complaining. I'll get used to it." She paused and he could see her thinking. At last she said, "Have you ever come close to invoking this rule you just mentioned?"

"No, not really," Frank said, warily. "Most folks know their limitations. It just takes some folks a little longer than others to realize it."

"Hmm …" She stared off toward the spewing glacier on their doorstep a kilometer away. "So, how'd this rule come about?"

Frank chewed his lip, knowing what this conversation could easily lead to. While he knew his presence up on the mountain twenty-five years ago had to be talked about with her, he wasn't prepared to do it right then. Besides, he wanted privacy and there were too many folks around. At last he said, "It's really more of a cautionary threat. If I can prevent just one disaster on the mountain, it's worth it."

"Would you ever follow through with it? I mean, leave someone there to die?"

"If all else failed, yes. But only after my Sherpa and I had done all we could to convince them otherwise," he said, knowing what was on her mind. "Don't worry, I'm sure your son will do just fine. He's been climbing awhile from what I've read and I'm certain he'll come down if he sees things aren't working out. It's the folks who aren't so skilled, I worry about."

Sarah nodded, but he felt it was forced. He motioned her to follow him over to the command tent. "You wear your mask last night?"

"Yes, but it's not too comfy," she said, following along behind him.

He pulled the tent flap back and allowed her to duck inside ahead of him. As she went, he said, "I know, but you don't want Khumbu cough if you can help it."

"You mentioned that before. What is it, exactly?"

"It's a nasty cough that can develop into a real problem if you don't take care of yourself," Frank said, pulling out a chair from under one of the tables and offering her a seat. She sat and crossed her legs as he plopped his chair down next to her. "What happens is the linings in your lungs get exposed to the super dry, cold air up here," he continued, and went over to the large plastic water bubbler across from them. "That results in dried out membranes and bronchi, leading to excessive heavy breathing when you exert yourself up here." He refilled his water bottle and came back. Taking a swig from it, he sat down. "Not long afterward, you'll end up with a persistent cough that won't go away. Then before you know it, you're hacking up a lung. I've seen guys bust a rib from Khumbu cough. Not a lot of fun."

"My God, that's awful!" Sarah replied. "Should I be wearing my mask now?"

Frank shook his head. "We're high, but I think you're okay wearing it just at night when the temp really drops."

Sarah's brow arched up. "Just how cold does it get?"

"Minus twenty sometimes."

Her eyes nearly popped out of her head. "Minus twenty?"

"Give or take," Frank said then realized she was thinking in terms of Fahrenheit. "That's minus twenty, Celsius."

"Oh!" she said visibly relieved then added, "That's what the web sites I checked said."

"Good, then no surprises then," Frank said. He shot her a playful grin and winked, which brought a diffident smile to her face.

"We'll see," she volleyed back. "In any case, I'll be sure to wear my mask along with every stitch of clothing I have."

A visual image of her waddling to the latrine, made him laugh. "Better watch out when you go out to use the toilet at night. You might be mistaken for a Yeti."

"Very funny," she replied as her smile broadened. She tagged him on the arm. "You're an itch!"

"And you need to keep drinking," he said, pointing to her bottle. She hadn't drunk more than a quarter liter from it, which wasn't nearly enough since they'd gotten up this morning.

* * *

Two hours later, they were still talking about life at Base Camp. Sarah wanted to know every little detail about how things worked and what was in store for her son in the next few weeks. For someone who'd never climbed or had an interest in it as far as he could tell, she soaked up the information he dispensed like a sponge.

Just now, he was sitting next to her at the table with his laptop open. As she moved in closer to see the weather forecast he'd pulled up on the screen, her leg brushed against his knee, stealing his breath for just a second. He paused, fairly sure it was an accident, but she made no effort to move away. Well, if she didn't mind then neither did he, so he continued on and showed her the maps and the associated data that would become a critical factor in determining a summit attempt.

"FL100, for example, means 10,000 feet above sea level. FL240, 24,000 feet, and so on," he said, scrolling over the line of text. "And this here below is the wind direction and speed. 230/02 — the 230 being the polar direction and 02 indicating the wind speed in knots."

Sarah nodded and pointed to the next line below: PS20. "What's that mean?"

"That is the temp in Celsius," he said and decided to give her a little test. "So what do you think MS08 means?"

"PS could mean plus. If so, then MS might be minus, so minus eight, Celsius?"

"Bingo! Now it's very important to know Everest's global position because we use it in determining the jet stream's relationship to it. Last thing we want is to be climbing into a blizzard. So, we have Everest at 28N and 87E. The forecast on the day this was sent last year shows the jet stream at 26N and 80E with a direction of 280/57 at FL270 with a MS35. Question: is this a good day to try and summit?"

Sarah pursed her lips, studying the screen. At last, she said, "No, the jet stream is too close to the summit and the wind is too strong and persistent. Visibility would be nearly zero."

Frank sat back and patted her on the shoulder. "Very good. Maybe I ought to put you to work here."

Sarah turned back to him as he took a swallow of water from his bottle. Returning his smile with one of her own, she said, "Hmm … I don't think you can afford me."

He chuckled. "Oh, really?"

She elbowed him, and in a playful tone that feigned insult, said, "Hey, I don't come cheap."

"I wouldn't doubt it for a moment," he quipped. "So, what will it cost me?"

She cocked her head. "I'll have to think about it. But for starters, you can let me in on your little surprise tonight."

"Nice try," he said wagging his finger at her. "Speaking of which, I have things to do before Tembe comes back. He'll give me the business if they're not done."

She appraised him with a raised brow. "I think you're giving me the bum's rush, Mr. Kincaid."

"And you'd be right, Ms. Madden. Time to go. I'll see you later," he said getting up. He went over and pulled back the tent flap and waited for her to collect her water bottle. As she passed him by, he winked and added, "Don't forget to drink."

* * *

Frank looked on as Sarah headed for her tent under the waving streamers of prayer flags. Although he knew it was a mistake to continue down the path he was heading with her, he couldn't stop himself. He liked her and he could sense the feeling was mutual for her as well. In fact it was becoming more than just liking her. He could still feel her leg brushing against his knee as they sat huddled together perusing the weather data on his laptop. And it didn't help that her vanilla essence still lingered in the tent about him. He drew a deep breath, soaking in the delightful fragrance.

He shook his head, but all he could think about was what it would be like to wake up holding her in his arms. Oh, yes, he was attracted to her, though he had tried to deny it from the first night they met. But it was more than physical attraction. She had a way of looking at him at times that took his breath away.

And then there was Greg, who along with his mother had brought back all the anguishing memories he'd tried to bury in the past. Except now, after talking with Greg and seeing him for more than just the son of Steve Madden, it was impossible to continue his misplaced anger for the guy. That, along with his mounting feelings for Sarah left him with nowhere to focus his stirred up emotions.

He shuffled to the back of the tent where Tembe had stowed away his surprise for later that night. As he bent over to pick up the cooler, he tried to whisk away the nagging thought of her becoming a part of his life. But the memory of the two of them colliding out in the field vying for the fly ball, came instead. In his mind's eye he could see her gazing back up at him as he prevented her from falling to the ground. Her soft, poignant gaze and the feel of her in his arms for that brief moment had stirred a wave of tangled emotions he hadn't been ready to deal with. But now those feelings were roaring.

He opened the cooler lid and pulled out the cake he'd shaped into a mountain. As he set the confection on the table, he appraised his future. For some reason karma had brought Sarah and Greg into his life. Tashi suggested Sarah might be an answer to something, but for what, he had no idea.

Chapter 15

Later that afternoon, Sarah went out and joined the team around a dung fire for the evening meal as her sleeping bag dried on the top of her tent. As a treat for them on their first day at Base Camp, Tembe made a platter of vegetable momos; dumplings stuffed with spinach, cheese, and rice served with a tart tomato dipping sauce. To go with them, was a pot of traditional dal bhat, which had been a staple coming up the mountain. The dish of rice with lentil soup poured over it was tolerable, though not her favorite. But the spicy mix of potatoes and peppers seasoned with garlic that was served on the side was delicious. Last of all was a selection of fresh mangos and apples.

As for a drink, Frank, who had been scarce for the last half hour, provided a cask of *jaand*, a Tibetan beer made from whole grain millet. Sarah and Aldan passed on the beverage, preferring to stick with tea. But the rest of the men more than enjoyed the beer, except for Vicq and Rene. Unfortunately for the Frenchmen, wine wasn't on the menu.

As they ate, the men chatted about their gear; swapping information back and forth about the merits of the harnesses, crampons, carabiners, or jumars they had brought with them. Sarah had heard the names of these tools used for climbing from Greg over the years, but had never really paid attention to what they were until now. She watched and listened as Lanzo did his show and tell with the men.

The harnesses were elaborate contraptions of nylon straps with steel clips and rings that wrapped around the men's waists and legs. *And they think women's clothing is difficult?* Sarah mused with a half-smile.

The carabiner was an elongated metal loop that reminded her of an oversized safety pin. Greg told her it was to clip onto the ropes going up the mountain that were fastened into the ice and rock.

Jumars were a bit more complicated than the carabiners. To her, they looked like miniature heavy-duty staple guns. Sully picked one up and demonstrated how it worked for her.

"The line goes up and in through here," he said passing a piece of nylon rope up through a slot in the jumar's headpiece and nestled it in a round hole. "Now, you lock the line in place by sliding this pin here over the slot so the rope doesn't come out." He pushed a small lever on the side of the jumar forward with his thumb until the pin clicked in place, closing off the opening.

"Okay, now when we climb, we squeeze these handles together and reach ahead of us like this," he said, clutching the jumar's lower handle upward. He pushed the device ahead along the line passing it through the hole with ease. "Then, when we let go like this …" He relaxed his grip on the lower handle. At once the rope went taut in his hand, unwilling to budge an inch despite his tugging hard on it. "We can pull ourselves forward and up, as the case may be."

"Oh," Sarah said, trying it out for herself. "So, when you let go of the jumar's handle, the do-hickey in the hole clamps down on the rope."

"Something like that," Sully said, smiling. "It's what we call a fail-safe. In other words, it automatically stops you from falling without your having to think about it. But in order for that to happen, we need to clip ourselves onto it." He reached down beside him and grabbed one of the harnesses lying on the ground. Drawing out one of the straps, he hooked the metal clip that was attached to the end of it to the steel ring of the jumar. "There, now you're ready to rock and roll."

Sarah nodded, liking this jumar gadget. "And those would be your crampons?" she said. "They look more like bear traps than footwear to me."

The men all laughed. Greg said, "Want to try one on?"

Sarah cocked a brow and setting her plate down, said, "Sure why not?"

Greg picked the pair of crampons up and brought them to her. Five minutes later he had them strapped to her boots. After a couple of faltering steps, she came to a stop. "My God, how do you walk in these things?"

"Very carefully," Frank said, coming out of the command tent.

Sarah turned to see the expedition leader walking toward them with a large, white frosted cake that looked as if it been thrown together by a five year old.

But it was cake!

Frank motioned to a small aluminum fold-down table beside the supply tent. "Carlo, bring that over here would you?" As he waited for the Italian to retrieve the table, he added, "This, here, is my little surprise. Every year I make a bit of tasty fun so we can all get a little piece of Everest regardless of whether we summit or not."

Sarah stared dumbfounded at Frank then at the cake in his hands. After Carlo brought the table over, Frank set the cake down and called back to Tembe. A moment later, the Sherpa cook came out with a frosted white tub in his hands. Sarah's eyes widened. *If that's chocolate ice cream, I'm pigging!*

Tembe lifted the lid off the tub and handed it to Frank, who pulled a large spoon out his jacket pocket. "Can't have a mountain without a glacier, now can we?" he said. He carved out several large dollops of vanilla ice cream and placed them strategically on the concaved front side of the cake.

Oh, well, vanilla, but it'll do, Sarah thought. "Hey Greg, mind helping me out of these contraptions?"

Frank grinned. "I don't know, I think you look pretty damned good in them. Besides, aren't shoes all the rage with American women these days?"

The comment brought a raucous round of laughter from the men. Greg rolled his eyes and even Tembe grinned.

"Very funny," Sarah shot back sarcastically. She clomped over to Frank in her attached footwear with the intention of throwing back an age-old Nancy Sinatra retort concerning boots, but when she stared into his laughing, gray eyes, she found herself at a loss for words. Her heart thumped as he stared back down at her.

"Yes," Frank said, seemingly waiting for her to say something.

Suddenly, Sarah realized everyone was watching her and felt warmth spread over her face. "Well, are you going to slice me a piece of that or are you going to stand there all day? The ice cream's a-melting!"

* * *

Three hours later, Frank and Sarah were sitting alone, side-by-side out in front of the command tent. With the sun having just set, the barren land of rock and stone around them took on a spectral quality. She pulled her collar up around her neck, warding off the chill wind buffeting the land. All was still and quiet, except for the murmurings of climbers upwind who had yet to retire to their tents.

Picking up her water bottle, she took a swig and said, "Back home, this is my favorite time of day. Just sitting on the deck with a glass of pinot and watching the stars come out."

"A time for reflection," Frank said. "To think about all that has happened during the day and to let it pass away."

"Or to hold onto it as a fond memory. I've had some good ones here thanks to you," Sarah said turning her gaze onto him. "I came here hating this place, but you changed my perspective. I still don't like that mountain up there, though."

"I don't expect you ever will," Frank said. He turned and fixed her with a playful gaze. "So, did you like the cake?"

"I did." She smiled and leaning toward him, whispered, "Next time, have chocolate ice cream."

"Chocolate?" Frank cocked his brow. "Hmm … not sure if that would work. Ice and snow aren't exactly brown, my dear."

Sarah grinned. "Trust me, chocolate works," she said, then shot him sidelong glance and added, "Dear?"

"I'm sorry. I guess I got a bit too friendly there."

"Not to worry. Actually, I kind of like it. Just keep it between us though."

"Right, wouldn't want to traumatize your son," Frank said.

Sarah laughed and sat there a moment thinking about what it would be like to have Frank in her life. Despite all he'd told her, there was so much more she didn't know about him, such as how he organized his home. Did he sleep on the right or left side of the bed, did he have hobbies and talents he kept hidden, and a billion other little subtleties that interwove themselves into relationships?

Finally, she said, "Can I ask you something?"

"Sure, fire away."

Sarah leaned forward. "How did you end up here?"

Frank was quiet a moment, as if he were gathering his thoughts. Finally, he said, "You mean on the mountain?"

"Well that, but also Khum Jung," Sarah said.

Frank shot her one of his trademark half-smiles. "That's a long story. How far do you want me to go back?"

"As far as you can remember, if you want to, that is," Sarah said, and sat back to burrow into the warmth of her jacket.

"Okay … well, let's see; my family arrived in Kathmandu in '66 fleeing the civil unrest in Angola. I was ten years old at the time, just old enough to remember the carnage. We lived in Luanda, south of the fighting so we weren't affected right off, but it was coming and quickly, so we got out. Anyway, we ended up staying with a friend of my father for most of the first year in Kathmandu. But mom didn't care for the city, especially after coming from all the insanity of Angola. So, the first chance we had, Dad looked for a place out in the country, except there wasn't a lot out there either."

"Yes, I noticed that," Sarah said, thinking back to the flight coming in to Lukla. All she had seen looking out her window was a rolling dun landscape with desolate farms out in the middle of nowhere.

"Anyway," Frank continued, "we got out of the city and ended up renting a sharecropping farm just below Lukla. My mother referred to it as a 'chicken shack'. It was a hard life. My father wasn't exactly a farmer, and my mother hated it. Then one day, my father heard of an opportunity in Namche, which at the time was nothing like it is now. A dozen scattered buildings and a few teahouses here and there was all there was. Khum Jung was where the real settlement was. But, it was to Namche that folks were coming to on their way up to the mountains, and with Sir Ed and Tenzing's historic summit, big expedition outfits started teaming up with the locals to provide mountaineering supplies. My father, who had a mind for running a business, hiked up here and was hired on the spot. A month later, Mom moved me up here and we never looked back."

"So, you lived in Namche first?"

"Yes, above the store my father worked in." Frank paused, and smiled as if he were reliving some fond memory. At last, he went on. "I loved it up here. Being around all the legendary men who were traveling to the top of the world. Their stories of adventure and survival on the mountains were larger than life to me.

"But my mother was more interested in my education, so it wasn't long until she started asking about town if there was a school nearby. The next thing I knew, we were in Khum Jung living in a three room stone house with old plank floors and a big cast iron stove. The rest is history."

"So, your father quit his job?" Sarah said.

"Oh, no. The climbing season wasn't all that long. A couple of months at best, so he stayed down in Namche until it was done with, then came home. Mom's job didn't pay much, but it included our rent and more importantly, my education in the one room schoolhouse, which by the way is still there and in use."

"Was it hard integrating with the other kids?" Sarah said.

"In the beginning there was the language barrier, but it didn't last long. By the time I was thirteen I was fluent in Lhasa, and they had picked up a great deal of English. You would've found it real interesting, I think."

"How's that?"

"Well, we mixed the two languages together, drifting back and forth between them as we talked. For example, when I was rattling something off in Lhasa and came to a word or phrase I didn't know, I barged into English without missing a beat. And for them the opposite was true. Anyone listening would have thought we were speech impaired but we understood every word we were saying to each other."

"So, you had a lot of friends then?" Sarah posited as she imagined being there and listening to the magical conversations going around the playground.

"A few, yes."

"Have I met any of them on the way here?" Sarah said, wondering if the man outside of Monjo might have been one.

Frank thought a moment. "The inn-keep at Thukla was one."

"Any girlfriends?" Sarah said, feeling a grin come to her face. She wondered what kind of girl would've turned Frank's head.

He cocked his brow and waved his finger back and forth in front of her. "Nice try, but I don't kiss and tell."

Sarah frowned. "Okay, keep your secrets." She took another swig from her water bottle. As she did so, she noticed Frank had turned his gaze out over the shadowed landscape with a troubled expression on his face. "What's the matter?"

He didn't say anything for a minute then turned back to her. "I think now would be a good time to tell you something you need to know."

Sarah drew back guardedly when she saw the grave look in his eyes. "What is it, Frank?"

He took a deep breath as if to compose himself. "First off, I need you to hear the whole story before you say anything, okay?"

"Yeah, sure," Sarah answered as she braced herself.

"Okay. There's more to how I got into this business than my father's store and the men I revered marching up the mountain. A long time ago, during my second year at school I met a boy named Pasang. We hit it off from the moment we first saw each other in class. It was like suddenly having the brother I always wanted, and we did everything together."

He glanced at her tentatively and went on. "Anyway, I got into climbing because of him. He was a Sherpa Porter for one of the expedition companies on the mountain. Anyway, he wanted to be a guide, and seeing how I followed him around like a puppy, it only seemed appropriate to me at the time that I follow him into it."

"So, you were a porter?" Sarah said.

"For a time, yes, until we'd saved enough to put ourselves through Guide school."

"You go to school for that?" Sarah said.

"Well yes, remember what I told you before?" Frank answered.

"Oh, that's right. I forgot," Sarah said.

"Anyway —" Again, he looked at her and she could see him taking a deep breath. "We ended up landing a job with Frontier."

The name 'Frontier' clanged in Sarah's ears. Although she hadn't heard it spoken in twenty-five years, it sent a bolt of apprehension rocketing through her.

"Pasang was hired on as a guide, and I worked the tents for them. It was like living the dream. Suddenly we were the legends I grew up admiring. Going to places most men could only dream of. We were twenty-six and full of ourselves. But then ... " Frank closed his eyes and she saw him struggling to get the words out. "It was May 15th, 1985, and I remember it like it was yesterday. Pasang was at the south summit guiding a young American mountaineer on his first attempt. I had come off the first watch three hours before and was in my tent resting. The weather at the summit had been clear when I'd sent them up for the summit bid.

"Suddenly, I heard a lot of commotion around the command tent. Someone said a storm was brewing at the summit. Another person said, 'Who gave the go-ahead for the attempt?' I got up and ran inside and saw Jack on the radio ordering the men down, but it was too late. The storm was barreling down on them. I kept looking at the numbers. Nothing made sense. They had a good window when I sent them up."

He went silent then as Sarah tried to comprehend the weight of his words that were sagging his shoulders. She fought the impulse to strike back, to ask him why she was just learning about this now as the image of her husband dying in the snow flashed before her. But the tragic look on his face sliced to her very core. Here was the man who had sent her Steven up the mountain on that terrible day and all she could think of was what he must have gone through.

"I'm sorry I didn't tell you until now," Frank said, quietly. "I know I should've but I just didn't know how to do it. I hope you can forgive me."

Sarah sat with his story and apology. At last she reached over and laid her hand over his and got up. She motioned him to stand and as he did so, she drew him into a hug. As she stood holding him, feeling his raw emotions in his embrace, she knew he was a man of conscience who suffered terribly from that decision so long ago, no less than she had.

At length, she pulled away and gazed at the haunted eyes looking back at her. She put her hands to his face. "Frank, it's okay. We'll talk more about this later. Right now, let's turn in."

He nodded and as he looked up studying the star spattered sky, she saw in the spray of the lantern light, a man who could crush her heart. And at this moment, she wanted to say what was on her mind, or rather how she felt about him. She had never known a man like him. He was like day to her night, and yet every part of him felt like a puzzle piece that had been stamped especially to fit the missing hole in her life. But more than that, she had come to trust him with her heart and the most important thing in her life, her son. She didn't know when or how she had come to put her belief in this man, but she clung to it fiercely under the looming presence of the Monster. Then, as if on cue, a sharp crack in the distance pierced the air and echoed down the highland.

* * *

Sarah woke up early the next morning and peeked out of her tent from the warmth of her sleeping bag. It was another clear, crisp morning. Prayer flags fluttered overhead, flapping in the wind rushing over the glacial trough that sat at the knees of the Monster. She peered eastward toward the rising sun hiding behind the shoulder of Lhotse. Its bright cascading rays were igniting the tips of the icy ridge in flaming alabasters and burnishing the moody land below in burnt reds and yellows. Removing her heat exchanging mask, she rolled it up and shoved it into her backpack, then pulling her jacket sleeve back, glanced down at her watch. It was a few minutes before 6:00 AM. Breakfast would be in an hour, not that it mattered. She wasn't hungry. In fact, the thought of eating mildly nauseated her.

With an effort, she forced herself to climb out of the warmth of the cocooning bag and pulled her boots beside her. As she pushed her feet into them, she could hear the murmurings of the camp that was just beginning to wake. A scent of frying potatoes nearby slipped into her tent as she tied her laces. Grabbing a comb she dragged it through her hair and stared into the small index card sized mirror hanging on the side of the tent. Her face was thinning and she had lost weight, which normally wasn't an issue. But the kind of weight she was losing now wasn't in the places she preferred, and things weren't going to be improving anytime soon along those lines. She shook her head, allowing her shoulder-length brown hair to splay out over her jacket collar and dug into her pack, searching for her toothpaste and brush. Finding them, she snatched her water bottle and headed to the latrine.

Twenty minutes later, she was sitting on a small boulder a hundred yards from camp. Peering through her sunglasses, she eyed the bivouac of bright yellow tents sprouting out of the barren landscape. This was her home for the next six weeks. It was hard to believe she was sitting here, half way around the world in this stark unforgiving environment. Yet for all of the land's harshness, there was a hallowed serenity here that spoke to her. She turned her face into the chill wind and closed her eyes, contemplating her troubled emotions. She didn't understand herself or for that matter, anything else now. It was as if God had set her adrift, rudderless and without a compass.

Looking upward, she said, "Dear God, heavenly Father, help me. I don't know why you've dragged me here, but here I am. I give up. Please tell me what it is you're trying to show me by bringing me here and having me re-live the past, because I don't understand any of it. Please, give me some kind of sign. Anything, so I know which way You want me to go."

She sat with that a moment, listening to the wind rasping at her jacket. All she ever wanted was a normal life, to be happy and loved. Was that so wrong? She was tired of living alone, tired of fighting with her son, tired of hating this damned mountain, but she didn't know how to change any of it. Then she remembered Frank telling her about the prayer towers the Sherpa people built; how they put their prayers into them and left them for the God of the mountain to answer. It certainly couldn't hurt to build one of her own to her God, the God who loved her so much, He gave his only begotten son to save her soul.

Chapter 16

Frank sipped his morning tea in the command tent, watching Sarah stroll out onto the moraine. He wondered what she was thinking as she went. He had done the right thing and told her he was there at Base Camp when her husband went on his ill-fated journey to the summit and she had taken the confession as well as he could've hoped. More important, was her compassion for him after he told her. As he watched her, visions of her reaching out to him and pulling him into a hug flashed before him. He could still feel her embrace and hear her soft comforting words. There were lots of questions he still needed to answer, but they would take care of themselves.

And then there was Greg. He thought about their long conversation during the march to Lobuche. During it, Frank had learned more about himself than he did the kid. How ironic, he mused, that it had taken the one person in the whole world he had never wanted to meet to rid himself of the monkey he had carried around on his back all these years. One thing was for sure, he could certainly identify with what Greg was going through.

Behind him, he could hear Tembe preparing the morning meal. The Sherpa cook was busy humming an old mountain melody Frank had no name for, but had heard it on and off over the years about working the fields. He let go of the tent flap, letting it drape back over the opening and turned back to his computer. On the screen, the weather forecast was showing projections out for the week ahead. The temps were good, ranging from minus ten to minus fifteen degrees Celsius and dropping into the minus twenties at night. *So far, so good*, he thought. He opened his logbook and recorded the events of the last two days. Nothing major yet. The Aussie seemed to be getting on better, a few complaints of headaches from the Frenchmen, and of course the loss of appetites and difficulty sleeping, which were to be expected.

"So, Frank, what goes on between you and the woman?" Tembe suddenly said.

"What'd' you mean?" Frank replied startled, wondering where the comment had come from. He didn't think he was giving anyone any reason to think his relationship with Sarah was anything but professional.

Tembe ran one of his large spoons around the pot of rice on the stove. "You out there pretty late with her last night."

"We were just talking," Frank answered as casually as he could.

Tembe looked up and gave him a discerning stare. "Hmm … looked like more than that to me."

"What're you getting at, Tembe?"

"It none of my business, but I know you long time. Last time you look at woman like that, was Kate."

"And?" Frank said.

"And I just wonder if it wise. You have expedition to run. No time to make funny business," Tembe said, wiping his hand on his apron.

If it had been anyone else making a comment like that, he would've lit into him, but Tembe had been there through it all with him over the years, including his ill-fated involvement with the woman who left him because he hadn't been able to fully commit.

At last, he said, "Thanks for the reminder, but I'm not planning on making any funny business. Don't worry about me, okay? I'm fine."

"Hmm … That what you say last time," Tembe said. He stirred the rice and shrugged. "Okay, I don't say no more."

Good, Frank thought, *'cause I'm not interested in talking about it.* He went back to his journal, re-reading his entries, but couldn't quite take his mind off Tembe's astute observation. If his Sherpa noticed his paying attention to Sarah more than he should, certainly the others did, too.

That afternoon, Sarah came into camp hobbling with her arms draped over Greg and Lanzo's shoulders. As they helped her along, Frank went out to meet them. When he came alongside of Sarah, Greg said, "She turned an ankle."

"I think I broke it," Sarah rasped through her teeth.

"Can you put any weight on it?" Frank said to her.

She shook her head.

Frank directed them into the command tent so he could get a better look at the leg. As Lanzo pulled a chair out, Greg helped her to sit. In the meantime, Frank went over to the medical supply crate and grabbed a couple of instant ice packs and an ace bandage. A moment later, he knelt down in front of her and gently palpated her foot, before he carefully unlaced the boot and removed it. Upon rolling her sock off, he saw considerable swelling around the ankle, but there was minimal bruising and no deformities he could see. At first glance he didn't think it was broken. He grabbed a pair of her toes and pulled them.

"Ouch," she cried. "Easy there, mountain man."

Frank looked up into her deep blue eyes. "Sorry about that. Quick question, did you hear a crack when you fell?"

"No, just the sound of my camera biting the dust," she said, and paused to catch her breath. "Damn it, I think I lost all my photos."

"Don't worry about the photos," Frank said, sitting back on his heels. He lifted her foot, and placing it on his lap, set an ice pack on the swollen joint. Wrapping the pack tight to the ankle with the elastic bandage, he said, "You're gonna need to have this elevated, Sarah. You want to go to your tent or hang out here?"

"I'd rather hang here, if it's okay," she answered.

Frank nodded, then surveying the limited space in the command tent, saw there wasn't enough room for her inside. Pressing his lips together, he said, "Or maybe not. Looks like it's going to be outside. Still interested?"

"Yeah. Tent's fine for sleeping, but hanging out in it all day, isn't my idea of fun," Sarah replied.

"Lanzo, could you go grab Sarah's pad and sleeping bag? Greg, there's a blanket over there in one of those compression bags beneath the table holding the base station. Would you grab it for me?" To Sarah, he said, "I'll get you set up outside by the command tent then." He put her arm around his shoulder and helped her up. "So, mind telling me how this happened?"

"She climbed up on a rock to take a few pics and decided she needed to get just a little bit higher," Greg interjected.

Sarah glanced back over her shoulder as Frank walked her outside. "I was trying to get a better angle," she retorted.

"Hey, Frank, everything alright?"

Frank brought Sarah and himself to a halt. Turning to his left, he saw John Patterson standing a couple of meters away with his hands on hips. "Yes, she took a tumble. Might be a bad sprain. Something I can do for you?"

"No. Just saw her being carried into camp and wondered if I could lend a hand," John said, eyeing her up and down. "You call for a chopper?"

"Not planning on it, why?"

John cocked his brow. "Well, climbing's a bit out of the question, isn't it?"

"I'm not here to climb," Sarah chimed in. "I'm here with my son."

"Oh," John replied. "Well, I guess that's fortunate for you then — that you're not on a summit bid, that is." To Frank, he said, "We need to talk … later."

Frank nodded. "About what?"

"Like I said … later," John replied. To Sarah, he said, "Nice meeting you. Good luck." He turned about face, and as he strode away, Frank wondered what was stirring in the Andersen expedition leader's mind.

"So, that's the infamous Mr. Patterson," Sarah said, as Lanzo headed toward them with her sleeping bag and pad. "He is rather abrupt, isn't he?"

"Just John being John," Frank replied as he waited for Lanzo to spread the pad out on the ground. "Okay, you want to get into the bag or lay on top?"

"I'll lie on top." She hopped on one foot using Frank's arm for support and plopped down on the makeshift bed. As Lanzo handed a pillow to her, she winced then broke into a crooked smile and said, "You know … a body could get used to this."

"Is that so?" Frank replied, squatting down by her feet. He opened the compression bag Greg had handed him and pulled the blanket out. "Okay, Ms. Lilly Lightfoot, lift your leg so I can put this under it."

"Very funny," she replied, and propping herself up on her elbows sent him a feisty glance.

Damn, you're lovely, Frank thought, *and would you stop looking at me like that?* "You comfy?" he said, getting up.

"Very," she announced, biting her lip. Laying her head on the pillow, she added, "I'll take a piña colada, please."

Greg groaned. "You're a piece of work, Mom."

Frank went in and grabbed her water bottle and took it out to her. "Your piña colada, shall I get an umbrella for it?"

Sarah grunted. "Humph … kill joy!"

The following afternoon, Frank strolled over to the Andersen Camp to find out what John had to say. It probably had something to do with Da-wa's conversation just after they came into camp. Last night, Da-wa had said that John listened to his overture of peace, but that was all. Maybe there could be talk of a truce, but Frank wasn't betting on it. He stepped up to the Andersen command tent and called in.

"John, you in there? It's me, Frank."

He heard a few muffled voices come from inside, and then the tent flap was pulled back. Standing on the other side was John, with his hat in hand. He pulled it over his head. "Walk with me," John said, and strutted out ahead, marching toward the receding Khumbu glacier.

As Frank followed, he felt the eyes of the Andersen Camp Sherpas following him. He got the distinct feeling there was trouble coming, but he wasn't fretting about it. As Tashi had said, 'John is going to do what John is going to do.' Frank knew that the question became 'how was he going to react to him?' In answer to that he would have to wait and see. His Buddhist teaching told him to let it pass through noticed but then released, like snow blowing off the mountain high above.

At last John came to a stop. They were about a hundred meters from Base Camp. He turned around and fixed Frank with a withering gaze. "Your Sherpa paid me a visit the other day. Did you send him?"

"No," Frank answered.

John stiffened his jaw. "Really?"

"I don't tell my Sherpas what to do or interfere in their business," Frank replied, knowing John would bristle at that.

"Don't give me that shit," John snapped back. "You have something to say, you come say it to me. And keep Da-wa the fuck away from my Sherpas, understand? I saw him chatting with the boys, and I don't want him filling their ears with your fucking bullshit, understand?"

"Perfectly, but I'm afraid that's out of my hands. Like I said, I don't tell 'em what to do. And you'd be wise to lighten up on your crew as well. They're not slaves, John."

"I pay 'em a fuck of a lot of rupees. They'll do as I'll tell 'em. I'm warning ya, keep Da-wa and the rest of your trolls away from Andersen, or else."

"Or else, what?" Frank said, fighting a powerful urge to retaliate. He drew breath as his body stiffened.

John stepped up to Frank, leaving mere centimeters between them and stared back belligerently. "Or else, I'll run you off this mountain!"

"You mean like you tried to do in Monjo?" Frank replied, staring back defiantly.

"Oh, you haven't seen anything yet," John growled. "Andersen has lots of friends in Kathmandu. All I gotta do is pick up the phone and you're fucking toast."

"Really?" Frank retorted. "So, how come it hasn't happened yet? How come you had to bribe the boys down in Monjo with your *own* funds? How much it cost ya, John? Must've stung, I mean seeing your own personal stash go down the toilet like that. You know, you really ought to learn how things work here."

Frank backed away and regained control of himself, knowing this conversation was going nowhere if he let it continue on its present course. "John, I never stole Da-wa from you. You lost him 'cause you take chances on the mountain. You're a good mountaineer. I don't understand why you do the things you do."

"What I do and don't do is my own damned business," John fired back. "Don't you judge me, don't you dare fucking judge me!"

"I'm not judging you, John. Just saying. Is Andersen pressuring you? I used to work for them, so I know how can they can be."

John paused, and for a split second, Frank saw the truth in his eyes. Andersen was indeed pressuring him. "Look, John, you're the boss on the mountain when it comes to your clients. Don't let anyone interfere with that."

"You're damned straight I'm the boss," John said. "No one tells me what to do, and that goes double for you!"

"I'm not telling you what to do, John."

"Well, it certainly fucking sounds like it," John replied. "Just keep away from my Sherpas. You stole Da-wa from me, what more do you want?"

"I never stole Da-wa from you. He works for me because he wants to. If he were to decide tomorrow to work for you or anyone else, that's fine, too. And that goes for all my Sherpas. They work for me at their own pleasure. Period!"

John laughed sardonically. "Oh, you are rich! You and your fucking noble bullshit are hilarious."

Frank shook his head. "You know, coming to meet with you, I was hoping we'd find common ground between us. I still hope for that. My tent's always open to you, John."

"That'll be a cold day in hell."

Frank nodded. "Well, since I don't believe in hell, I'm encouraged. I trust we're done here?"

John spit. "For the time being."

Frank walked away. He hadn't weathered John's tirade as well as he'd hoped, but it had turned out better than it had two years ago when they'd ended up rolling on the ground throwing haymakers at each other.

* * *

Frank returned to the Khum Jung Camp deep in thought. As he headed for the command tent, he saw Sarah and Sangye chatting by the fire pit. She looked up as he went by. "Hi, where you been all morning?"

"Just out and about. How's the ankle?"

She lifted her foot and rubbed the back of her neck. "It aches, but it's better."

"Headache?" Frank said.

"A bit. I popped a couple of Tylenol," she replied.

Sangye said, "Cranston called in. Said he's in Lobuche and will be here tomorrow."

"Oh, good," Frank said. Turning to Sarah, he added, "He's the EMT I told you about. I'll have him check that ankle of yours as soon as he gets here. Right now, I need a cup of tea." He winked at her, which brought a smile to her face, then left them to continue with their conversation.

Inside the command tent, Tembe had just started the preparations for the evening meal. Frank went over and grabbed his mug. As he dug through a box of teabags, the Sherpa said, "So, Patterson give you earful, huh?"

Frank looked up. "In a manner of speaking."

"Well, I don't see no blood on your shirt. So you making progress in peace talk, huh?"

Frank grinned. "Your powers of observation never cease to amaze me."

"Ha! I hear things, also."

"Like what?" Frank said, getting up and stealing some hot water off the pot on the stove.

"Word has it, there may be bad *ju-ju* on mountain," Tembe said.

Frank furrowed his brow. He knew from experience that when the Sherpas got nervous, there was a good reason. Yet, the weather was behaving. "What do you mean, what's going on?"

Tembe looked up. "I hear there been couple close calls on mountain fixing ropes in Ice Fall."

"When?" Frank said, surprised. *And why am I just finding this out?*

"This afternoon, when you out trying to make nice with Patterson," Tembe said. He pushed Frank out of the way, and lifted a large bag of rice. Pouring it into the boiling water, he added, "Some say mountain angry. Too many people come, make big mess."

Frank didn't know about that, but he knew from experience that many of the Sherpa folk were superstitious when it came to the mountain's behaviors. Buddhist or not, people were people. And when people felt threatened by things they couldn't understand, they succumbed to fear, and all the explanations born of science weren't going to change that fact.

"Anyway," Tembe said, "Da-wa say he talk to you later when he see you."

"Where's he now?"

"What am I, his keeper? How I know?" Tembe grunted. "Now shoo! I have work to do."

* * *

That night, Frank helped Sarah back to her tent. As she flicked her battery-powered lantern on, he turned back the flap of her sleeping bag so she could get in. When he got up to go, she said, "Can we talk?"

Frank shrugged, having a good idea what it was she wanted to discuss. "Sure. What's on your mind?"

She crawled into her sleeping bag and pulled her pillow under her head. "Steven. How well did you know him?"

Frank knelt back down beside her and sat on his heels. As he set her water bottle next to her, he said, "Not very. We spoke a couple of times in passing. He was a real go-getter as I remember. Very enthusiastic."

"That was him. Always a hundred miles an hour. I remember him coming home one day about a year before coming to the mountain. He was all excited, telling me he had gotten a sponsor for the climb. Wouldn't shut up for the rest of the night. I tried to be supportive, but with Greg having just been born, I was thinking, 'do you really need to do this right now?'"

Frank peered into her liquid blue eyes and took in her delicate chiseled face, imagining her sitting on the couch listening to her husband prattle on about the adventure waiting before him. She was an attractive woman at fifty-five, what must she have looked like at thirty?

"But, it was something he had wanted all his life. So who was I to pour water over it?" she said.

"How long had he been a mountaineer before he came here?" Frank said.

"I don't know. Before I met him anyway. He tried to get me involved in climbing, but for the life of me, I couldn't see anything fun about freezing my butt off and living in my clothes for days on end," Sarah said. She turned on her side, pinned her elbow on her bag and propped her head up with the palm of her hand. "So, when did you know Steven was my husband for sure?"

"Not for a while," Frank said. "Your son's last name rung a bell with me, but I didn't think much of it until your name showed up. I knew Steven was married at the time, and I remembered him telling me a bit about you. On a lark, I called Jack Trammel and ran your name by him. He said, you sounded like one and the same. That got me really thinking, so I started researching. To answer your question though, I guess I wasn't really sure until about a week or two before you came."

"I remember how you acted when we first met. You didn't seem happy to see me."

"I wasn't," Frank replied. "You were a reminder of the past I had tried hard to put behind me. I didn't want either you or your son on my expedition. But it was too late. Then as things went along, it turned into not knowing what to do with you until I realized, I was judging you for something you had no control over."

Sarah nodded then reached over and took her water bottle. After she took a drink, she said, "And my son? What is your opinion of him now?"

"I like him. He's a lot like me when I was his age," he said, acutely aware of her hand being centimeters away from his fingers. "I want to thank you for accepting my apology. I wasn't sure how you'd take it."

"I wish you had told me earlier," she said, searching him with a guarded, yet compassionate gaze. "At first, I felt betrayed and angry, but the more I listened to you talk about what happened, I realized how hard it was for you." Slowly, her hand reached out and covered his. "We've both suffered from a loss of someone we loved."

Frank felt the warmth of her hand radiate up his arm and caught his breath. Suddenly, he could hardly breathe. He wrapped his hand around her fingers and felt his heart drum. He knew he should get up and leave but he couldn't find the strength to do it.

Sarah said, "Do you think we were brought together to put this all behind us somehow?"

"Maybe. Destiny and karma have their ways," he said. "Everything that happens is born out of choice. It's what we do in the present time that matters most, I think."

Sarah's gaze darted over his face. "I've never been someone who could live in the moment. I couldn't afford to."

"I know, except now —"

"Except now, what," Sarah rasped.

He gazed down at her unable to contain himself any further and bent forward. Taking her up in his arms, he said, "Now is forever." He kissed her tenderly then, and as he did so, felt her arms wrap around his neck.

* * *

The following morning Frank stood by the command tent watching his clients eating their morning meal. As he sipped his tea, his gaze darted back and forth to Sarah as he watched the circle of men pick at their food. The affects of living at high altitude were catching up to them. But it was Rene who caught his attention most. The man coughed, and as he did so, winced. Frank wondered what was going on with the man. It wasn't Khumbu cough. He knew what that sounded like. His gut tightened. Had the man picked up a bug? If that was so then he was a menace to the whole Base Camp. But where, or rather from whom, did he get the damned thing?

Frank eyed Da-wa who was sitting nearby. He went over and squatted down beside him. "Keep an eye on Rene over there, would ya? I have a bad feeling he's picked a up bug." When the Sherpa's brow lifted, he continued, "Keep this between us until Cranston gets here."

Da-wa nodded. "Might be best to make him stay in his tent until we know for sure."

"That's my thought. In the meantime, we'll go on as usual."

* * *

Three hours later, Bob Cranston came lumbering over to Frank. As the Base Camp medic, he was the last and only line of defense when it came to serious medical issues. The tall, dark, curly-haired man put out his hand to Frank and the two of them shared a quick hug. "How ya been, old boy?" Bob said.

"I'm good. How was the trip coming up?"

"Was great," Bob said. "I hear we have a casualty in camp."

Frank said, "I see word gets around."

"Yeah. John told me about it. Where is she?"

"In latrine," Sangye piped in from behind them.

As they waited for Sarah to return, Frank filled Bob in on Rene. "It may be nothing, but I wanted to keep him under wraps until you got here."

"Good idea," Bob agreed.

"Ah, here she comes," Frank said, seeing Sarah pop out of the latrine. After she washed her hands, she hobbled toward him using her hiking pole as a crutch. As she came near, he introduced Bob and helped her sit.

"My goodness, a house call," Sarah quipped, looking up at Bob with a broad smile.

The man laughed. "And at Base Camp of all places," he said. "Now let's have a look at that ankle." He knelt down before her and unrolling the bandage around the swollen foot, gently turned the joint side to side. "Well, no broken bones from what I can tell," he said. "You're in luck, too," he added glancing up at her. "I just happen to have an ankle brace here in my bag." He dug into his gear and pulled it out. "Oh, look, it's a sexy yellow!" he said holding it up for her to see.

After he fitted it to Sarah's foot, he stood up. "Okay, stay off the foot and keep it elevated for the next day or so. I'll check it out then and we'll see how you're doing." To Frank, he said, "Okay, where is my next patient?"

Frank nodded towards Rene's tent a few meters away. Outside of it sat Vicq. As they headed toward the man, Bob whispered to Frank, "If, um, Rene — is that his name? — has picked up a virus, I'm quarantining him for the next 72 hours except to use the latrine. The only ones I'll want going anywhere near him are you and myself."

Frank nodded. "It'll be hard to keep his countryman Vicq away, though."

"Okay, I'll include him in on the mix. But that's all," he said, coming to Rene's tent.

"Are you the doctor?" Vicq said, getting up.

"Camp medic," Bob corrected.

Vicq lowered his voice. "Rene's burning up. I'm worried."

Bob shot Frank a wary glance. Digging a surgical mask out of his pocket, he put it on and ducked inside Rene's tent with his medical bag. Fifteen minutes later he came back out and his expression was guarded. He glanced at Frank warily and said to Vicq, "It's strep. I've given him an antibiotic so he should start feeling a little better by nightfall. In the meantime, he needs to drink like a fish." He reached into his bag and pulled out another surgical mask. "Here, wear this whenever you're in there with him and make sure you use your sanitizer."

Vicq nodded.

"Okay, I want your friend in there wearing his mask at all times. The last thing he needs right now is a dose of Khumbu cough. If he comes down with it, we're gonna have to call a chopper in. Got it?"

"*Oui.*"

"Okay, the less exposure you have with him the better until the antibiotic kicks in. And," Bob glanced back at Frank, "for the time being, we need to be discreet. I don't want a panic up here. If someone is carrying this bug around, it could spread like wild fire. The good thing is, it's not a virus, so it's treatable. But it's also highly contagious. Once I make my rounds, I'll be back and wanting a meeting with your folks right away."

"One last thing," Bob said. "Since you only have one latrine, you all need to be wearing your masks whenever you go to it. And the less you have to use it, the better."

Chapter 17

Sarah sat listening to Bob Cranston reading the riot act, as she liked to call it, to the team. As she watched Frank listen in on the conversation going on across from her, she thought of what Frank had told her last night. Had God brought her here to heal? When she signed up for this adventure into hell, it had never occurred to her that it might not be about her son. And then there was the kiss. It had only been a simple kiss — okay, a long fervent kiss — but now there was no going back to just being friends with Frank. They had crossed the line and now she was wondering where things would end up with them.

Conflicted, she stared off over the mountains. In her mind's eye she could still see him pulling her up into his arms, and feel the desire and need in his embrace.

"Sarah?" Bob Cranston said. "You still with us?"

She started and looked back. "Sorry."

"This is important, Sarah," Bob said. He cast his glance around at the men. "Everyone needs to be extra diligent about using their hand sanitizers and keeping interpersonal contact to a minimum until we know we have this bug nipped. And another thing; keep this under your hats. I don't want people getting all nervous and jerky up here."

"But shouldn't they know?" Sarah interjected.

"If someone else comes down with it outside of Rene, then yes. But I'll be the one letting people know. For the time being, I'm treating this as an isolated case. He may have picked the bug up in one of the villages. There are lots of trekkers going back and forth down there that are coming from all over the place. Simply put, they aren't as mindful as we are here."

Sarah nodded. She had maintained her distance from those who weren't involved in the Everest expeditions, and to a degree hadn't been close to Rene, but that didn't mean anything. Strep throat didn't discriminate, she reminded herself. And she did kiss Frank, but he was in good health, and if he were feeling otherwise, he certainly wouldn't have put her at risk. It was going to be a long couple of days until people knew how things were going to turn out.

* * *

An hour after dinner, Frank snagged her as she headed off to her tent. He had understandably been busy all day, but beyond that, he had felt aloof to her.

"Well, hi there, stranger," she said.

Frank smiled. "Miss me?"

She loved the tiny dimples that formed on his face when he curled his lips. "No, not really," she said, feigning a yawn.

He winked. "Yeah, I figured. I saw you gawking at old Bob during our meeting."

"Well, he is nice to look at," Sarah agreed.

"Hmm ... I guess I'd better watch out then." He chuckled. "Anyway, I see you're getting around pretty good on that bum ankle of yours."

"Yes, I'm doing fine, thank you. But I need to get it up and elevated so the good doctor won't yell at me. Care to walk me to my mansion?"

Frank peered over his shoulder. "Um, sure."

Sarah knew what his furtive glance back toward the men meant, and to be truthful she shared his feelings. After all, her son was sitting with them. "Frank, I don't want the rest of our conversations to be on the sly from now on, okay?"

Frank paused and she could sense him debating an answer. Finally, he said, "No, Sarah, they won't be. But I have to be careful of how things look."

Really? God, man, it's conversation, not climbing all over each other, Sarah thought. Aloud, she said, "I understand that completely," She stared at him hard, not wanting to say what she had to, but knowing it had to be said. "Frank, I'm not going to walk around on eggshells here, worrying about everything I say. If it's going to be like that, I'd rather you just leave me alone," she said quietly and held her breath.

He didn't reply for several moments as he fixed her with a longing gaze. Finally, she saw him swallow and clear his throat. "Understood. What do you want me to do?"

Men. Really? "Just be yourself."

He grinned sheepishly. "Well, that shouldn't be too hard."

"There you go."

He leaned toward her. "So, you're not upset I kissed you last night?"

"No. It was nice, but —"

"I know, it won't happen again," he said. "I hadn't planned on it. It just sort of happened." He paused. "Mind if I drop by tonight?"

Sarah eyed him as she debated her answer. Last night had been special. She had connected with a man in a way she hadn't thought possible. This was no frivolous dalliance. This was the real deal and she didn't know what to do about it. Her mind screamed at her to say 'no'. It was too dangerous being alone with him like that again, but her heart longed for the intimacy of reconnecting with this man who had slipped under her walls. She swallowed. "Um … sure."

* * *

That night, as Sarah lay on her sleeping bag reading, she heard feet shuffle up to her tent. She book-marked her novel and sat up, watching the tent flap pull back. On the other side, wreathed in moonlight, was Frank. "It's me," he whispered.

She grabbed her brush and ran it through her hair as Frank crawled in and sat beside her. "Hi," he said. He glanced at the novel sitting beside her. "What're you reading?"

She picked the book up. "Seven Years in Tibet."

"Oh, Heinrich Harrer. Good read," Frank said.

"Yes, I'm liking it very much so far." She set the novel down. "So, you had a busy day."

"I did," Frank said. He looked at her a moment then averted his gaze to her book. Finally, he said, "I thought about you a lot, though."

"And what were you thinking?" she said as the feeling of nervous anticipation reverberated in her body.

He smiled. "I was wondering what it would be like to wake up next to you every morning."

Sarah sighed. She'd been wondering the same thing, and had been fighting it all day. "Frank, please don't say things like that. We both know that can't ever happen."

"I'm sorry," he said. He paused. "Foolish thinking. It's just that, I've never met a woman like you. You're special."

"Thanks, and so are you. We shared something special that I'll never forget."

"Maybe I should go," he said.

It was probably the right thing to do, but Sarah couldn't help herself. "No — please stay." She moved to one side on the sleeping bag and patted it. "Here, why don't you get off your knees and sit beside me."

He hesitated then smiled. "You sure?"

She nodded, and a moment later he was lying down on his back next to her, telling her about his conversation with John. As she sat beside him listening, she thought about how nice it would feel to be in his arms again. Her better judgment warred against it, but her heart won out, so she abandoned her wariness of things she couldn't control and joined him, laying her head on his shoulder. As she did so, she felt her body melt into him. It felt so right, yet it frightened her because there was no future for them. Still, she couldn't help wanting to feel everything was going to be all right, if just for one night.

As they lay there in the dim lantern light casting shadows about them, he stroked her hair and told her about his history with John and why the man was trying to run him off the mountain. Up until the night he confessed his prior knowledge of her, she had never seen or felt anything but certainty in this man who had touched her deep inside. She drew her head back from his shoulder and gazed at the troubled expression staring off into space.

At last she said, "What are you going to do about him?"

"I don't know," Frank muttered.

She reached up and put her hand to his cheek. "I wish I could help you."

"You already are, just being here in my arms," he said, placing his hand over hers.

She looked up and saw a tiny smile and snuggled in tighter to him. It felt so right being in his arms; safe and secure that he was a man she could trust. If only. She lay her head on his chest, inhaled the remnant of smoke on his jacket and listened to the wind buffeting her tent.

At last, she said, "So tell me about your school."

She felt Frank's fingers run through her hair, and a minute later he was knee-deep in the past, telling her about the Hillary Trust and the Government Education Committee that ran the schools. Eventually the conversation came around to his simple life in Khum Jung and the children he loved. Yes, the two of them had much in common.

At last, it came to half-past midnight. She felt him plant a kiss on her head and pull away. As the cold air rushed into the void he left behind, she thought about what it might be like to make love with him. She braced herself and said into the night, "I'm scared."

He put his arm around her. "Of what?"

"Of falling in love with you, Frank." There, she said it. She waited for him to respond.

Several moments passed before he finally said, "Sarah, a very wise man told me once not to let the fear of the future steal away the present. Destiny is what it is. We cannot change it, no matter how we try. But yes, I share your feelings as well. Perhaps the morning will tell us new things, hmmm?"

"I guess," Sarah said wanting to believe him.

He kissed her tenderly. "Namaste, dearest," then slipped out of her tent.

* * *

The following week dragged by and as it did, she spoke with her son about her feelings for Frank; that she liked him a lot and would be spending as much time with him as she could. That she liked Frank way more than she should — that, she kept to herself. For Greg's part, he was relieved that she had struck up a friendship with Frank. Probably because it meant she wouldn't be nosing around his tent every day asking him how he felt and was he wearing his mask.

In the meantime, Frank had worried about Rene. If the strep had started spreading around Base Camp, he'd have a lot to answer for. The last thing he wanted was to end up becoming a pariah up here. But Rene steadily improved, and no one seemed the worse for having been around him.

It was now Wednesday, four days since Bob had diagnosed the tall, wiry Frenchman. Sarah followed Frank into the command tent with her tea. "I think you dodged a bullet with him," she said.

"That's an understatement," Frank concurred, putting his phone on the charger. "If that bug had spread, we'd all be in a mess. I'm not sure what to do about him now, though, or for that matter, Aldan."

"What do you mean?"

"The guy's respiratory system has been compromised, and Aldan — I just don't think he has it in him. It's just a gut feeling, but I don't see him making it very far. I think I'm going to have to ask them to hold back from trying a summit bid."

"They won't like that," Sarah said.

"No they won't," Frank agreed. "I'll give it another day and see how they're doing. The rest of us are faring pretty well. How are you doing? Sleeping okay?"

"I'm fine," she said, then grinning, added, "Probably because of a late night visitor who's wearing me out."

Frank smiled back. "And the ankle?"

"Coming along fine. Bob said that I can start putting some weight on it tomorrow."

"Great. I'll let your physical therapist know before he stops by tonight," he replied, straight faced. But the devil was in his eye. "What about your headache?"

"It's not going anywhere, but Tylenol helps."

"You've lost a bit of weight," he said, eyeing her with apparent appreciation. "Next time you shower you're gonna have to run around in it to get wet."

"Oh, really?" she said. She glanced down at herself. The pants that had fit her so nicely back in LA, now had to be cinched back to keep them from falling down around her ankles. At the rate the pounds were coming off, it wouldn't be long until the belt ran out of holes to buckle into.

She crossed her legs and studied the drawn face with the beginnings of a gray beard looking back at her. "You're thinning down, too," she said. "Perhaps all this exercise we're getting isn't such a good idea. You're going to need to conserve your strength if you decide to climb."

"Just toning myself, dear," he replied, shooting her a wink.

* * *

That night, as Sarah sat in her sleeping bag waiting for Frank to make his usual ten o'clock arrival, she thought about the education that had occurred earlier in the day regarding all that could go wrong on the mountain. Up until then, she'd tried to convince herself that Greg would be fine, but today her fear for him had struck back and was staring her right in the face, up close and personal. She fought to believe in what Frank had told her about the team approach of looking out for each other, but the fact was; when you got above Camp 4 no one could protect you. Each man or woman up there was on his or her own when it came to paying attention to how they felt. The problem with that was the psychosis of believing you were only feet away from your dream.

But for Greg it wasn't the summit so much as it was his father being buried up there in the ice and snow that worried her. She would have to tell Frank about it, even if meant betraying her son. She couldn't risk his life knowing what she had learned today.

Frank's voice whispered in through the tent flap. "May I come in?"

Sarah dimmed the light on her lantern. "Yes, please."

The zipper went up and a moment later, he was sitting beside her. When he kissed her though, she didn't return it as ardently. He pulled back and eyed her. "Something wrong?"

"Yes, it's Greg. I need to tell you something."

His brow furrowed.

"Not what you're probably thinking," she said. "It has to do with his climbing. There's something you to need to know."

"What's that?" He sat back on his heels.

Sarah paused, not wanting to go on. "He's not going up the mountain just to summit."

"Meaning?"

Sarah looked up, avoiding the pointed gaze coming back at her. "He wants to find his father."

Frank was a quiet a moment, then said, "I see."

"I'm worried he'll get summit fever; only for a different reason, if you know what I mean," she said, looking down and turning back to him. "If he finds out I've told you, he'll hate me. I just don't know what to do about it."

"I'm glad you told me," Frank said. He reached out and took her hand. "I won't say anything."

"Thanks, but he's bound to find out. I mean —"

"Let's not borrow trouble, Sarah. Besides, I'm pretty good at fishing information out of folks."

"So I've noticed." She tried to smile, but it wasn't coming easily. "Hold me?"

"Of course." He got off his knees and stretched out beside her. As she buried her head in his shoulder, she said, "Promise me you'll look out for him."

"I'll do my best."

"So, you're going to climb?"

He paused. "Yes."

Sarah hugged him tight. "Be careful."

"I aim to," he said stroking her hair.

Chapter 18

Frank sat in his tent grappling with his feelings. There was no other explanation for how he felt, other than he was getting too close to Sarah. *How did I let this happen? There's no future for us — at least none I can see.* And now, he had another thing to contend with; Greg's reasons for climbing. In the back of his mind, the thought of Greg doing something stupid on the mountain worried him. He pressed his lips together. He didn't want Sarah's son anywhere near Pasang. But having seen how Greg struggled with his mother shutting his father and hearing Sarah's confession about the young man's heartfelt desire to see the man he'd never known, he was conflicted. *Doesn't the kid deserve closure? And who am I to deny him of it?*

He untied his shoelaces and dumped his boots in the corner of his tent, then unzipped his sleeping bag. As he pushed his legs down into the cool microfabric of the bag, he punched his pillow. He'd deal with things in the morning. Right now he had a driving headache.

* * *

Frank was woken by a stiff wind rattling the sides of his tent. He opened his eyes, pulled his heat-exchanging mask off and sat up. Suddenly, the headache was back, and along with it came the memories of making love with Sarah. He sat with them for several minutes, reliving the torrid experiences, then rolled out of his sleeping bag and dragged his boots on. It had been a long time since he had been with a woman and the thought of making love to Sarah gave him pause to think of what he was doing.

He stepped outside into a chill wind under the saffron glow of an impending sunrise. The camp was quiet. Voices murmured from the tents. He glanced up towards Sarah's tent wondering if she was awake and thinking about him. A smile came to his face. She certainly got his body revved. In his mind's eye, he imagined her beneath him. But there were things that needed doing around camp, so he marched over to the command tent.

Inside, he found Tembe sitting by the stove busy peeling potatoes and garlic. The Sherpa glanced up as he came in, but didn't say anything. Frank grabbed his mug off the table beside the front flap and walked over to the cooking table in the middle of the tent. Squatting down in front of Tembe's tea box, he dug a bag of ginger tea out and dropped it into his mug. As he did so, he felt the Sherpa's eyes boring into him from behind.

Frank knew what Tembe's look meant. He'd seen it more than once over their twenty-five year friendship. Essentially, Tembe was saying, '*What the fuck you doing to yourself*', with the implied screw-up de-jour as he saw it, which in this case Frank was pretty sure had to do with Sarah.

Frank ignored the condemning stare, stood up, and poured himself a cup of tea. "Is everything ready to rock and roll up at Camp 2?" he said, using his spoon to crush the teabag against the inside face of the mug.

"Ho, everything ready. When you start acclimation climb?"

"First thing next week, depending on the monk's arrival in camp." Frank glanced at Tembe, meeting the man's direct gaze. In answer to the Sherpa's unsaid question, he said, "By the way, I've decided on a summit attempt."

"Hmm … why?"

"What do you mean?" Frank replied, although he had a pretty good idea of what Tembe was driving at.

Tembe scraped his knife over the potato in his hand and dashed the peeling off into the pail between his legs. "Just wondering. You pretty *'busy'* these days, have lots on your mind. Maybe not good idea to climb mountain."

"Actually, my being *'busy'* is the reason I'm trying a summit. I need to get away from all this," Frank said, waving his arm toward the electronics and weather forecasts on the tables.

The Sherpa got up and gave him a discerning look. "Get away or run away?" Tembe said, softening his ever-present rigid expression. "Make sure you know difference, my friend. You always say to me, know why you climb. So, I ask you same question. Only you know answer." Tembe put his finger on Frank's chest then and gazed back at him with concern on his brow. "Make sure your heart knows." Then as suddenly as the tender expression had come to the Sherpa's face it dissolved back into his practiced frown. He backed away. "Now, you go. I have work to do, humph?"

An hour later, the men were sitting around taking their morning meal of fried Spam, fried garlic seasoned potatoes, eggs, and rice. As for Sarah, she hadn't come out of her tent yet. Frank bit into his hard-boiled egg, wondering if she was alright. As the thought of going to find out about her crossed his mind, her tent flap opened and out she came. A moment later, she was hobbling toward them with her plate in hand while the other hand clutched her hiking pole.

"Namaste," Da-wa said, getting up and offering her his chair.

"Namaste, and thank you Sherpa Dave," she said coming into their circle. The men all said their good mornings to her and she replied likewise. She turned to Frank and gave him a saucy smile.

"Namaste," he said. "Can I get you some breakfast?"

"Yes, thank you." She handed him her plate and fork.

As her hand brushed against his fingers, he felt his breath catch. How he wanted to hold her close in his arms and embrace her. "So, how'd you sleep?" she said.

"Restless," he answered. "And you?"

"Hardly a wink."

"It's the altitude," Frank said, knowing that was as far from the truth as the earth was from the moon. "You want some tea, or are you set with your water?"

"Oh, I forgot my mug."

"Not to worry, I think there's an extra one in the tent somewhere. I'll be back in a minute." He turned and went inside. As he dished a helping of eggs and potatoes onto her plate, Da-wa stepped beside him.

"Tembe told me you're going for a summit bid," the Sherpa said.

"Yep," Frank replied.

"So, we will still follow the plan? You taking Sangye's place?"

Frank had been considering switching with his lead Sherpa and guiding Greg and Lanzo for their summit bid for most of the night. It was the right thing to do. The young man deserved some kind of closure with a father he never knew. But Frank just couldn't do it. He gritted his teeth, hating himself, and said, "Not unless you see a reason to."

"No reason I can think of," Da-wa said, and paused. "So, you want to have a meeting. Go over how things are gonna shake out for the next two weeks?"

"Yeah, I'll gather the guys together this afternoon to give them the low-down," Frank answered. "About Rene. I don't know about him going up the mountain. What do you think?"

"Hmm … he don't look too good to me. You may be right. You think you can talk him out of it?"

"I don't know. I would prefer he come to that conclusion himself, rather than me try and force him into it," Frank said as he dashed pepper on Sarah's potatoes the way he knew she liked.

Da-wa said, "There's always Bob. He could put the thumbs down on it."

"True," Frank said. "Any news I need to know regarding the Ice Fall?"

"All seems good, but ropes are needing more attention than usual. Some say, not safe to go up," Da-wa said.

"What's your opinion?

"Hmm … I will have to see. First acclimation climb will tell," he answered. He eyed the plate of food in Frank's hand. "Her breakfast is getting cold." Turning, he headed out of the tent, leaving Frank to follow behind.

* * *

That afternoon, Frank gathered the men together to go over the details of the climb. He sat down with his Sherpa team flanked beside him and went over the list of team assignments once again and informed them of his intention of replacing Sangye.

"Okay, this is how things are going to go next week. Your Sherpa guides will arrange for your O2 to be brought up to Camp 2 and 3 this weekend. Leave a couple bottles down here with you though, just in case. Next, the forecast for Tuesday through Saturday looks favorable for our first two acclimatization climbs to Camps 1 and 2. We'll all be going up at the same time on them. Now these hikes are going to take us over and through the Khumbu Ice Fall. They are not to be taken lightly. In fact, outside of the last 800 meters of this mountain, the Ice Fall is the most dangerous area we'll encounter. I have a short video on my computer if you want to get close and personal with it before we head out. It bears watching if you've never seen it, and even if you have, it's a good refresher."

"Once we've done those two hikes, we'll pop up to Camp 3 the following week, weather permitting, before coming down to rest. I prefer dropping all the way down to Dengboche for a couple days to get our wind and appetites back, but we can stay in Lobuche as well. It's all up to how our bodies are feeling. After that, it's back up to Base Camp and hopefully shooting for the summit sometime around May 6th or 7th."

That brought smiles all around, except for Sarah, who was sitting off to the side. He ignored her frown and continued on, "Now before we begin our acclimatization hikes, we have a rite up here on the mountain, which you are more than welcome to join in with. It's called a *Puja*, and it'll be happening sometime this weekend after the monk arrives from Tengboche. Even if you decide not to join in, I would encourage you to attend. It's not something you want to miss.

"So, with all that said, double check all your equipment and gear, and remember to keep drinking. Any questions?"

"Yes," Toby said. "How long will summit bid take? I heard someone did it in less than one day."

Frank smiled. "Yes, but that man was a Sherpa Guide who lives up here year round. You're not that man. To answer your question though, if all goes well, we'll be on the mountain for about a week, give or take a day."

Greg put his hand up.

"Yes, Greg," Frank said, calling on him.

"Any avalanches lately? I haven't heard of any."

Da-wa spoke up. "A couple of small ones, but not on our route. Still, you never know, so be alert going up and pay attention."

"That's right," Frank echoed. "It's all about being aware of where you are. I don't want anyone to get hurt. Finally, I want to be honest with all of you. Not everyone is going to make it to the top. In fact, none of you may get there. There's a lot of what-ifs when climbing this mountain. Weather is a big one, but there are others. Your stamina and your body's acclimatizing to the altitude are just a couple challenges, along with whatever else the mountain throws at us. The important thing, though, is to come back alive. So park your egos in neutral, guys. There's no place for it up there and it will get you in trouble."

* * *

Two days later, Frank sat outside chatting with Da-wa about the climb when Sangye came up to them and pointed to a party of red-robed monks headed their way over the western moraine. Frank stood and shading his eyes with his hand saw a Sherpa driving a couple of yaks carrying supplies. As they neared

Base Camp, he noticed an old man wielding a dark staff leading them. Frank blinked, wondering if his eyes were cheating him. *Tashi?* He could hardly believe it. The old lama rarely left the monastery these days, and to come all the way from Khum Jung up to Base Camp dumbfounded him. But he had come nonetheless.

Fifteen minutes later, the old lama was standing in front of him with Sangye's brother, Bajay, along with another young monk Frank hadn't met before. "Namaste, Frank," Tashi said.

Frank bowed. "Namaste, Master Tashi," Frank replied, addressing the lama with the honorific title. "Welcome to Base Camp. How was your journey here?"

"Refreshing," Tashi said. "Is there a place for me to rest these old bones?"

"Of course," Frank replied, and as he said it, Sangye came running up with a chair. "May I get a cup of tea for His Holiness?"

"Ahhh … that would be most welcome. So, how are things with the Lion? Has he discovered any answers?" The lama said, resting his staff on the ground beside him.

"Some; others still elude me, I'm afraid."

"Hmmm … they will come," Tashi said. He looked over to Bajay and the young red-robed monk. Nodding toward a small hill with a level top north of Base Camp, he broke into Lhasa and said to them, "Cast our tents there while I catch my breath." Switching back to English he said to Frank, "So, you probably wondering why I come."

"It did cross my mind, Master," Frank answered, as Sangye came back with the lama's tea.

Just then, Sarah came out of using the latrine. As she washed her hands and looked up at the men, Tashi's gaze drifted down the sloping moraine toward her. When the lama looked back at him knowingly, Frank knew at least part of the reason. Tashi smiled, took his tea from Sangye and after sipping it said, "I think it more than cross your mind." He paused, drank another sip of tea. "So, when you want me to perform *Puja*?"

"I was thinking Sunday," Frank answered, watching Sarah head to her tent from the corner of his eye. "We're planning our first acclimatization to Camp 1 on Tuesday."

"Okay, Sunday then. What about other camps? They join with you, or I need to check?"

"Winslow and Eckert expeditions will be coming. As for Andersen and the others, you'd better check with them," Frank replied, noticing a growing audience gathering a few meters away from them.

The lama nodded, finished his tea and got up. "Well, I better be up and about," he said. Then bowing slightly, he walked toward his eagerly awaiting congregation.

* * *

That evening after dinner, Frank went out onto the barren moraine to think. As he walked amid the scattered rocks and boulders, he tried to focus on the mountain and mentally prepare for the grueling ascent that would test his fifty-seven-year-old body, but all he could think about was Sarah and Greg. He had spoken with Tashi briefly telling the lama about his struggle to do the right thing and lead Greg up the mountain, as well as his feelings for Sarah. *Why can't I let go of the need to keep Pasang and Steve Madden's whereabouts on the mountain to myself?* The young man deserved to have at least one moment with his father. As for Sarah, how could he tell her he loved her, knowing that she would be going home, never to see him again? It just seemed cruel to put that on her.

He sighed and peered up at the brooding clouds hugging the icy peaks. *How has my simple, uncomplicated life become such an emotional mess?* He scrambled up a pile of strewn erratics and took a seat upon a sloping pedestal of gray schist. Although the camp was a couple hundred meters away, he knew where Sarah's tent was. He trained his eye on it, watching her and Greg sitting together outside her tent, then closed his eyes and took his prayer beads out. Fingering them, he recited the *Om mani padme hum* mantra over and over, trying to quiet his troubled heart. When he looked up an hour later, he found Tashi sitting a couple of meters in front of him with his back turned, gazing off into the darkening sky.

They remained silent for some time, until the lama said, "You will not find the answers you seek if you keep yelling at yourself."

How does he get into my head like that? Frank thought. "Is it that loud?" he said.

"Deafening," the lama replied. He turned and eyed Frank. "I have story to share with you. Once, long time ago there was a champion archer. He think he best in all of Tibet. But there is one better, the people of his village said. A

Master Zen Monk who live near mountain. So, champion archer, he go to home of Zen Master to challenge him. Zen Master, he follow him out into forest. Champion archer, he set up target long way away and then comes back and says, 'Watch me pierce the heart of the rice paper on that tree'. He draw out his bow and putting an arrow to it, shot and hit it perfectly in the center. Then he pulled another arrow out and shot, hitting the target perfectly again, slicing through first arrow. He say to Zen Master, 'can you do better?' "

"Zen Master say, 'Follow me', and he led him back to his home and up the mountain to a very high place that looked out over all of Tibet. Clinging to the narrow ledge was a thin oak that extended a narrow branch over a deep abyss. Zen Master then took out his bow and climbed the tree. Walking out on the narrow branch that was swaying in the wind, he said, 'Look there,' and pointed to another tree a stone's throw away. Putting his arrow to his bow, he shot and hit it dead center. Coming back to join the champion archer, he said, 'Now you try'."

Tashi held Frank in his gaze for some time then. At last he went on. "The village champion looked down into the abyss, terrified and backed away. Zen Master say, 'You have much skill with your bow, but not the courage to wield it when it matters.' " The lama paused, as the words sunk into Frank, then added, "You think about that." Tashi stood up. "Nice night for a walk. See you tomorrow, okay?"

Chapter 19

Sarah watched Frank walk out onto the vast glacial moraine toward a tall mound of rocks a couple hundred yards away. Something had been bothering him all day, and she had a good idea what it was. But how could they ever be together? She went over every possible scenario in her mind last night and had ended up coming to the same conclusion; whoever left their home to be with the other would be a fish out of water. And no matter how much you loved someone, there had to be more than being in love to be happy.

She sighed as she sat in her chair, waiting for Greg to join her. He'd been sticking close by all afternoon, which she thought was odd. Usually he hung out with Lanzo, Toby, Jakob, and Sully. He strode up and sat beside her, water bottle in hand. "Want an energy bar?" he said, digging into his pocket and taking one out.

She feigned a smile. "No thanks. So, did you meet the monk?"

"Nope," Greg replied, as he pulled the wrapper off the chocolate bar.

Sarah looked off. Why hadn't Frank introduced her? Instead, he'd just glanced down at her when she was washing her hands by the latrine.

Greg stirred beside her. "You alright?"

"Yes, why?" she said, turning back to him.

"You just feel 'far away' to me."

She smiled, trying to hide her feelings of despair. "I'm good, really. Just have a few things on my mind."

He bit off a chunk of his energy bar and was quiet a moment. "You worried about us summiting?"

"Always," she said, gazing at him adoringly. "No, I was just thinking about what life was going to be like once we get home. So, what's up with Lanzo?"

"What'd'ya mean?"

Sarah nodded towards the Italian's tent. "Well, usually you're over there swapping war stories."

"Oh, nothing. I just thought I'd spend some time with you tonight. Besides, he's hyped on the Ice Fall. He's big into extreme sports. I told him he's nuts. Four times up through that horror chamber is way, way over the top. By the way, I recommend you don't watch that video Frank was talking about. Scary shit."

Sarah groaned. "Thanks, but I Googled one before we came here so I've already been terrorized."

"It'll be okay," Greg said. He looked at her hard. "You sure you're alright?"

Sarah studied her son's probing gaze, loving his concern. "Yes. Don't worry about me, okay? You need to focus on what's ahead." Then, from the corner of her eye, she saw the old lama heading out over the moraine towards Frank. As she watched him, it occurred to her that he just might be the lama Frank had told her so much about.

"Okay," he said. He got up. "I'm going back for my jacket. You want anything?"

"A blanket for my foot maybe? It's a bit cold."

"Sure thing. Be right back."

He left her, and as he did so, her gaze turned back to the mound of rocks Frank had perched himself upon. In the distance his small black form was silhouetted against the backdrop of the failing cloud ridden sky. Soon, she'd be alone at camp with the exception of the expedition crews that remained behind to man the command tents. She thought about what her time would be like while they were gone as she sat there peering out over the brooding landscape that threatened to swallow her up. Would Frank's absence give her the clarity to think? Was she really falling in love with him or was she just drawn into the struggles they both intimately shared?

* * *

Sunday morning, Sarah stepped out of her tent to see a two-tiered stone altar erected before the small, elevated hill behind her tent. She eyed the two monks that had accompanied the old red-robed man for a couple of minutes as they strung a streaming prayer flag over the ceremonial table. Watching them from the hill above was the wiry Tibetan with Frank by his side. The two of them were discussing something, and she had no doubt the old man knew she was looking up at him.

She hobbled over to the common area in front of the command tent for breakfast. She wasn't hungry, not that she had been the last five or six days. And the emotional upheaval over what to do about her future with Frank wasn't helping, nor was the lack of sleep over the last few nights. Waking up every hour on the hour with the constant background headache was beginning to wear thin.

"Namaste," Sangye said, as she came into the circle of men who were picking at their plates of spam, fried potatoes, and eggs. "You want some tea?"

She greeted the Sherpa guide, and nodded, which sent him into the command tent. As she took her seat next to Greg within the circle of men, Greg stabbed a piece of potato, popped it in his mouth. "I see they're getting ready for the ceremony this afternoon."

Greg coughed and cleared his throat. "That, they are."

"Here you go," Sangye said, returning with her tea.

Sarah looked up and thought she'd give the Nepalese reply for 'thank you' a try. "Dhan'yavāda."

Sangye grinned. "Welcome. So, you coming to *Puja* later?"

"Sure, I'd love to." She paused and turned back to the monks who were busy stringing the prayer flags. As they went about it, people from the various expeditions started to gather near the Khum Jung Camp to watch. When Greg got up to take care of his dirty dish, Sarah leaned toward the Sherpa and said, "Sangye, what is the *Puja* about?"

"Oh, it is about receiving blessings for whatever is important to you. In this case, safe return back from the mountain."

"Blessings from whom?"

Sangye shrugged. "Depend. Could be a deity or important person, like lama. When you come, I will explain to you."

She nodded, watching Frank, who had just now taken up working with the monks. By the looks of it, he was going to be busy until things got underway. Well, that was okay. He probably needed something to throw himself into. Lord knew she needed something to take her mind off things as well.

* * *

Three hours later, the three camps were gathered in front of the *Puja* altar that was draped in a deep blue cloth and holding several yellow and orange ornate iconic items Sarah had no name for. She eyed a large silver bowl trimmed in brass that sat at the far end of the altar. Out of it, fragrant juniper incense swirled and rose into the deep blue sky. On the other end of the altar, sat four small red and blue dishes that were filled with what looked like flour. Small cakes of fried dough sat beside them. At the rear of the altar, stood the Winslow, Eckert, and Khum Jung expedition company banners. Rising above them, was a wooden pole with boughs of juniper bound to the top.

What caught her attention most was a large headless gray bust sitting front and center on the altar. It was perhaps eighteen inches high and at least that much across its torso. To one side of it, sat a large skein of red and yellow twisted thread and on the opposite side, a slate blue bell with a golden handle. Scattered around the bust were red and pink rhododendron flowers.

Turning to Sangye who was standing beside her, she said, "I take it the statue represents the deity?"

Sangye leaned toward her. "Ho."

Sarah thought back to what Sangye had told her earlier as the members of the three camps brought their gear to the altar and laid them on the ground before it. The notion that it could be whatever god the seeker sought blessings from gave her pause to think that Christ could be included as well. She eyed her son and Frank, who had just laid their ice axes and harnesses at the foot of the ceremonial altar. *Well, I can work with that,* she thought.

As the old red-robed man made his way to the altar from his tent, Da-wa went around offering the celebrants bags of rice. When he gave Sarah her bag, Sangye said, "We throw it as His Holiness conducts ceremony. You will see."

Sarah nodded. *So, he is the lama Frank was telling me about.* The gathered crowd tightened up around her. To her left, a few yards away, stood Frank and beside him were Greg, Lanzo, and Sully. The Frenchmen, Vicq and Rene were behind them, and to their left stood the two Austrians along with Aldan. Carlo was nearby to her right. She glanced back at the Italian restaurateur. The two of them had shared much about God coming up the trails. She wondered what he was thinking of this strange ceremonial rite.

For that matter, she wondered what Greg thought about it. Although she had raised him to be a Catholic, he wasn't much on God. But the ceremony was beginning, so she pricked her ears and listened to the sound of the altar bell being rung by the lama's monks. As the young red-robed man did so, the lama took up one of the dishes on the altar and stood in front of the statue. Sarah turned to Sangye and quietly asked him what was going on.

"His Holiness is symbolically washing the deity."

Sarah nodded, thinking it wasn't so far-removed from Jesus being anointed by Mary. Next, the lama removed a long saffron colored scarf from around his neck and draped it over the statue. Backing away, he picked up the skein of red and yellow thread and turned around. As he did so, the Sherpa guides approached and put their hands out.

"What's he doing now?" Sara whispered to Sangye.

"He's tying the sacred thread to their wrists for protection," the Sherpa said. They will wear it for a whole day or longer after the ceremony. Most of us will wear it until it falls off."

As Sangye left her to join the procession of men going up to receive the sacred thread, Sarah looked on wondering if it was proper for her to join them. When she saw a woman from the Winslow Camp go up, she pocketed the bag of rice and joined the line of climbers going up to receive their sacred threads. As she did so, she caught Frank eyeing her tenderly as he walked back to take his place in the crowd.

A moment later, she was standing before the old lama as the fragrant juniper incense wafted about them. The sharp-featured man held her in his pointed gaze for a minute, and as he did so, she felt strangely at ease. Finally, the man tied the thread around her wrist. Smiling, he nodded and sent her back into the crowd.

Once the sacred threads were tied, the lama broke into a chanting mantra over the gear placed in front of the altar. Sangye tapped her shoulder and said, "He is blessing the climbers equipment. He say, 'By the declaration of truth — may all these things have the blessing of success.' Now is time to start throwing rice little bit at a time."

The lama continued the mantra above the gear and as he did so, a Sherpa raised the pole behind the altar with the attached juniper boughs. More rice was thrown. The lama then turned back and blessed the climbers and the banners as Bajay came forward with several long white scarves. Taking his place beside the attending monk, the lama turned and nodded to Frank to approach.

As the expedition leader went up to him, Sangye said, "His Holiness is now bestowing the blessing. He do this by putting *khata* over his shoulder and tying in front like so."

Sarah watched the lama tie the loosely laid garment around Frank's neck. One by one, the team members followed, dipping their heads to receive the garment then walking off. When at last they had all been blessed, the climbers were invited forward to share in the fried dough and fruit that were on the altar, as well as the food that was stored below.

Sangye said, "Time to rejoice, come."

"Is that the end?" Sarah said.

"Ho."

He waited a moment for her, but she waved him off. "I'll be along in a bit." She watched him go join the climbers as they partook of the dough and fruits. A few of the Sherpas were horsing around, smearing their faces with something white coming out of one of the bowls. The rest were talking with each other and laughing; happy or so it seemed.

Suddenly Frank came running over and stood before her. His bristled face was a white, powdered mess. Sarah laughed. "You look like a circus clown. What is that on your face?"

He reached up and dragged a finger across his cheek. Licking the powder off his finger, he said, "*Tsampa* flour. Want some?"

"I'll pass," Sarah said.

"Oh, no you don't," he said, and putting his hands to her cheeks, slathered her face with it.

Sarah dropped her jaw, feeling like she just got a face full of wedding cake. "Frank! You dickens!" She ran a finger across her chin and dipped it in her mouth. "Ummm … It's good."

"Of course it is." He shot her a wicked smile. "Want some more?"

Sarah put her hand up. "Don't you dare!" But it was too late. He grabbed her hand and dragged her into the merriment of the men who were plastering each other with the flour. As her son pasted her face for the third time, she called over to Frank, "So, is this a food fight or part of the ritual?"

"A little of both," he answered. "It symbolic."

"Of what?" she said, striking out and slathering Frank's face with a handful of flour.

"Of our hopes to see each other again when we're old," he replied. Suddenly, he stopped and stared at her wistfully as the crowd laughed and frolicked around him. "Anyway, that's the gist of it." He paused. "So, umm … I should introduce you to his Holiness."

"Sure ... okay," she said. He put his hand out to her. "What? Now?"

"No time like the present," Frank said.

"Maybe in your world," Sarah replied, wondering if the man had taken leave of his senses. "I'm not meeting anyone looking like the Pillsbury dough girl."

* * *

Five minutes later, Sarah stood looking down at the lama who was siting lotus style on a wooden bench. The lama broke into a wide smile. "So, this is the Sarah you have been telling me about," Tashi said. He looked back at her as if he was meeting her for the first time.

"Yes, Master," Frank said, standing beside them.

Sarah studied the old mottled face of the lama. It was in direct contrast with the bright, insightful eyes. *Why do I feel I've just been brought home to meet dear Old Dad?* She thought. "Very nice to meet you ... umm?"

"Call me Tashi," the old lama said. "This Master and His Holiness stuff get a bit stuffy, don't you think?" he said looking up at Frank and shooting him a pointed stare. He turned his attention back to her. "I hear you are educator. Very noble profession."

"Thank you," Sarah replied. "Unfortunately, I don't get into the classroom anymore."

"Ah, you make big decision now, eh?" Tashi said. "Much responsibility in that. Buddha say, children wonder about life, happiness, and beauty in nature, so is important to teach them right place to look. As teacher once, you had big job. Not to be taken lightly. We have school in Khum Jung where these old bones of mine live. Perhaps when Frank all finished here, you come down and see."

"I would like that very much if I can make it," Sarah said, although she doubted it would happen.

"Oh, I think you will. But you see me many times before then."

The lama's remark brought a puzzled expression to Frank's face. The lama turned to Frank and flashed him an innocent and obviously pretentious expression of horror. "Oh, I not tell you?"

"Tell me what, Master?" Frank said.

"That I stay 'til you come down from mountain."

Sarah saw Frank's jaw drop. Obviously, he wasn't in the know. She grinned and tossed Frank a wink as the lama smiled.

* * *

Sarah woke Tuesday morning to find the men gone for their first acclimatization hike. They'd left well before dawn, before the sun came out to warm the ice up. She removed her heat-exchanging mask and rolled out of her sleeping bag. *So it begins,* she thought, popping her head out through the front flap of her tent and peering out at the glacier. She wondered where they were on the ice just now as the bright sunshine streamed across the Ice Fall.

She caught a whiff of breakfast being prepared. The usual fried potatoes, only they were being cooked by Sangye now. Tembe had left the day before to finish setting up Camp 2. She got around, combing her hair and tying it back, fixing her face, pulling on a fresh pair of socks, and fastening her ankle brace onto her bum foot. After a quick trip to the latrine, she grabbed her mug and ambled down into the encampment for tea.

As she entered the command tent, Sangye and Chok-pa looked up from where they were sitting at one of the tables lining the walls of the tent. Beside Sangye sat his brother Bajay and beside Bajay, the lama, Tashi. The two young men both got up and greeted her. But it was the voice of the lama behind them that caught her ear.

"Namaste," the old man said, remaining in his chair.

She greeted them back and started over to the stove. But Chok-pa put his hand up. "I get for you. Here, sit."

Sarah relented to the young Sherpa's insistence and giving him her mug, found a chair near Tashi, who was busy reading from his prayer cards. As he recited the Lhasan mantras, she glanced at the inlaid, ornamental flowering tendrils that were carved into the sides of the oak box. It was a stunning work of art, and she could imagine having something like it on her mantle back home as a keepsake. Chok-pa brought her tea, and as he gave it to her, Tashi looked up from reading a strip of Lhasan text.

Setting the box aside, he said, "So, how is Sarah this morning?"

"I'm fine, thank you. What a beautiful box."

"Ah, glad you like." He took up his mug and extended it toward Chok-pa. "One time more." To Sarah, he continued, "It was given to me by my grandfather and to him, from his father." He paused while she leaned forward to study it closer. A minute later, he said, "So ... you like mountains?"

"I do," Sarah said, leaning back in her chair. *The mountains are the last thing I want to talk about.* She sipped her tea. "Tell me about your school in Khum Jung."

Tashi considered her behind a half-lidded gaze. Finally, the lama explained to her how Frank's involvement in the school began and how far it had come over the years. But he made little mention of how Frank's involvement in it began, which puzzled her. As Chok-pa brought him his tea, he said, "Frank tell me you Catholic. Very good way."

Sarah drew back surprised. That Tashi would revere her faith never would've entered her mind. "I'm not a very good one, but I try to get to church as often as I can."

Tashi sat with that a minute. "It is intention that matters. Very easy to go to church or temple, harder to hear the message coming back."

Sarah thought about that. All her life she viewed being a Catholic through the lens of following the sacraments and learning about the ways of living a good, penitent life. She eyed the old lama discerningly and nodded. "You're right. I've never really thought about it that way."

They were quiet a moment, then suddenly she found herself launching into her beliefs of Christ and God as Tashi listened. As she spoke she discovered how easy it was to talk with him. It was like being in the company of a long-lost friend who was letting her be herself instead of besieging her with questions on why she thought this or that. Frank had been like that, too, when they came up the trails. What impressed her even more was Tashi's vast knowledge of the Christian scriptures. He recited many of them, almost word for word when they discussed spiritual matters, leaving her to wonder if at some time he had gone to seminary school. Then, she brought the matters up that were closest to her heart at the moment. What to do about Frank and her fears and concerns for her son on the mountain? He was quiet for a long time after she told him then stared at her hard.

"These are difficult things for all of us. We worry about people we love, but one thing we must understand is we cannot control anything except our own decisions. Your Jesus, he was very wise man. Great teacher on many things. One thing he say is very much like Buddhist teaching."

"What's that?" Sarah said, wondering what the lama was leading to.

"He say do not worry about tomorrow, for tomorrow will take care of itself."

Sarah knew what he was getting at. "Yes, I know. Easier said than done."

Tashi studied her. "Ho, I know." He paused and took a sip of tea that Sangye had brought to him while they were talking. Finally, he said, "I have story for you. Once, there was famous dancer, known throughout all the countryside.

She was beautiful and everyone want to see her. One village, they petition her to come to dance for them, and she say, 'yes'. So, date is set and as time approach, people in village get very excited.

"Same time, a certain man in the village fall into very big trouble with the law and is condemned to die. But Judge, he give him one chance. He say, 'If you can walk with bowl filled to brim with oil and not spill any of it through village on same day she come, you may live. But, lose just one drop and guard behind you will draw out his sword and take your life'.

"So, what you think he will do on that day? Hmm? He not look at dancer or people celebrating. No, he pay attention to what is front of him. Life is like this. If we look away from it, we will lose it. All we can do is live one day at a time. No more," the lama said.

He stood up and eyed her compassionately. "Do not let the future you cannot control steal away the present you have, Sarah. The destiny you worry about will take care of itself. I have to go now, prepare for *Puja* ceremony for Andersen Camp. We talk more later, hmmm?"

Chapter 20

Under the cloak of twilight and a bright moon, Frank led his team across the moraine to the glacier. As they threaded their way through the sea of erratics with their headlamps shining, Frank's mind was a mess of conflicting thoughts. What was he going do about Aldan and Rene? He had spoken with them about their condition and warned them that if things didn't improve for them after the acclimatization hikes, he would pull them off the mountain. He hoped it wouldn't come down to a test of wills with the two men, that they would see for themselves the impossibility of going on if it came to that.

And then there was John and his determination to drive Khum Jung Mountaineering off the mountain, and who knew how that would turn out? Last of all, was Sarah. He'd gone back and forth over his feelings for her during the last three days. Part of him said let her go before he got hurt. Another part of him knew it was already too late, that he was falling in love with her. But how could it ever work? She had her family in the States, a son she loved. He knew if she pulled up stakes to come and live in Sagarmatha, where the mountain she hated reigned, she would never truly be happy. And then there was her career.

As for him, he could never see himself anywhere but up here in the cradle of the great white peaks, where the air was clean and life was easy to understand. He knew who he was up here, knew the simple expectations of daily life. And there was the school and the promise he'd made to his mother. How could he ever break that? Finally, there was Pasang. Although he was gone, a part of the Sherpa still existed on Chomolungma high above. Every day Frank spent at Base Camp, he could feel the Sherpa looking down from his final resting place on the south summit.

But right now, he needed to be centered on the upcoming Ice Fall. It was bad enough traversing it by day, but in the dark it was a trip though the fabled Christian hell. If he wasn't focused, it could turn out to be a real bad day. He stepped up onto the edge of the sprawling ice sheet. For the next three hours, the crunch, crunch, crunch of his crampons digging into the ice under his feet would be a constant companion and reminder to pay attention to what he was doing. Marching ahead, he waited for the rest of his team to join him then clipped onto the long nylon line stretching up into the twilight-shrouded glacier.

An hour later, he was in the midst of the dark glacial field, creeping in and around the massive fractured sheets of ice. Above, the star-studded cobalt sky was just beginning to lighten. Frank stabbed the hilt of his ice axe in the glacier beneath his feet and started toward one of the many crossings over the yawning crevasses. He glanced behind him and saw Sully just now poking his head up over the wall of ice he had climbed up. The Irishman was a good mountaineer, slow and methodical, judging each footstep carefully. Frank thought he'd be a good addition to his expedition company if he ever had a mind for it.

Turning back to the crevasse ahead, Frank walked out to the outstretched aluminum ladder that bridged it and peered down into a dark abyss. Focusing his head lantern on the narrow ladder-bridge, he stepped onto it, careful to span his foot over the rungs. Taking hold of the two fixed nylon lines, he slowly walked ahead to the other side, where a narrow one-meter wide plank of ice met him. He stepped onto it and traversed the ice bridge with a daunting drop on either side. And, as expected, there was another ladder fixed to the end of it over another crevasse. After crossing it, the route was up, up, up another fifteen-meter wall of ice. After he climbed to the top, he turned to watch his clients slowly choose their steps across the teetering ice bridges. One of them, Aldan perhaps it was — he couldn't tell in the dark — froze as he stepped onto the ladder spanning the deep crevasse.

Frank called down to him. "You alright?"

"Just need a minute," came a muttered reply.

"Take your time, Aldan," Frank said as he watched the shrouded figure step out onto the ladder. As the yellow light from the Aussie's headlamp crept across the yawning black abyss, Frank turned back to the fractured landscape in front of him. It often took some time for folks who weren't familiar with climbing over glaciers to get their nerve.

And so it went for the next three hours until at last the Ice Fall gave up under a bright blue sky with the sun blazing down. Looking back over it, he watched the climbers crawl along the last hundred meters like tiny black and red ants over a mound of sugar.

He arrived at the Western Cwm and the Valley of Silence where they would set up Camp 1 four hours later. The glacier below and the heavy snow pack could be heard clicking and cracking as the wind whipped the powdery surface into whirling dervishes. To the east and west, towering bare walls of gray schist showed their faces to the climbers, and at their bases were the remnants of avalanches they had thrown off their backs.

Frank led the men to a safe flat space in the open expanse away from jagged fissures in the snow and there they set their tents up and started preparing the evening meal. While he and Da-wa cranked up tiny gas stoves, Sully, Lanzo, and Greg went off with shovels and bags to gather snow for melting. Aldan and Rene looked like hell, but did their part. Everyone had mind crushing headaches. Rene had developed a raging cough.

They retreated out of the diving temperatures into their tents around seven and quietly chatted with each other as the sounds of the moving glacier below them murmured in the distance. Occasionally, a loud crack would ring out nearby, reminding them of the dangers lurking below. Frank pulled out a book as he snuggled down into his sleeping bag and read under the dim yellow lantern light hanging above. Greg, who was bunking with him in order to not bring extra tents, wrote in his journal.

Despite the impending dangers of this Valley, Frank found it one of his favorite places in the world. The utter quiet of the nights he had spent here in the past had given him time to reflect on how lucky he was to be living within this vast swath of land that would never give itself up to the machinations of man. At length, he marked his page and set his book down.

As Greg wrote in his journal, Frank said, "Recording your trip?"

"Yeah. I like to keep a log of my experiences so when I get home I can relive them," Greg answered.

"You did well out there today."

"Thanks. Quite the adventure coming up."

"Yeah, it is, and just think, you'll have three more opportunities," Frank added. "A little different each time."

"I heard that. What'cha reading?"

Frank picked up his novel and looked at the tattered and faded cover. "*Shogun.*"

"James Clavell," Greg said. "My mom's a big fan of his."

"Really?" Frank said. "I'll have to remember that. Who do you read?"

Greg rolled off his stomach and on to his side, pinning his elbow on the ground and resting his head in the palm of his hand. "Well, I like Tolkien and Asimov, Clark and Pohl."

"A fantasy and sci-fi fan, I see."

Greg chuckled. "Yeah. My mom likes her Historicals. Used to tell me to get my head out of the clouds and come down to Earth once in a while. What about you, who do you read besides Clavell?"

Frank reached into his jacket pocket and pulled out an energy bar. As he unwrapped it, he heard someone burst into a coughing fit in the next tent. It was Rene, more than likely. He shook his head, knowing it was going to be long three weeks for the Frenchman if he made it that far. "Tolstoy, Melville, and Hemingway mostly."

"The big boys," Greg said.

"Yeah, the big boys," Frank agreed.

Greg was thoughtful for a moment. Finally, he said, "So, how'd you get into mountaineering?"

Frank shrugged and told him a little of his growing up in the Himalayas; how he came to Khum Jung and got involved in the expeditions. But his friendship with Pasang, he kept to himself.

When he finished, Greg said, "Never been married, huh?"

"Nope."

"How come?" Greg said.

"Guess I never met the right woman."

Greg was quiet a moment then said. "My mom likes you."

Frank nodded. "I know."

"It's been a long time since I've seen her happy. She doesn't let people in easily," Greg said. He eyed Frank pointedly. "We live halfway around the world. Don't promise her shit you can't deliver."

Frank knew he was right to call him on it. He paused as he considered his answer. Finally, he said, "Believe me, that's the last thing I want."

They locked their eyes in mutual understanding until Greg finally looked away, leaving Frank with a lot to think about.

* * *

The team came slogging into Base Camp the following afternoon, arriving shortly after two-thirty. They shed their packs, down jackets, boots and crampons and plopped down on chairs in front of the command tent. Frank headed inside to check weather reports and found Sarah sitting in front of the computer. She looked up as he dumped his pack on the ground.

"You're back," she said. She pushed her chair away from the table and stood. "How'd Greg do?"

"Did fine," Frank answered.

She grabbed her hiking pole, and reaching out, took his hand and squeezed it. "Talk later?"

"I'll be around," Frank said as she let go of him and hobbled outside. He went over to Chok-pa, who was reading the latest weather data. "So, anything to be concerned about?"

The Sherpa shook his head. "Everything look pretty good."

"Great. Well, I'm gonna pay Master Tashi a visit. Dinner at five?"

"Ho."

Frank turned, grabbed his pack, and left Chok-pa to his business. As he headed for his tent to drop his gear off, he saw Sarah and Greg walking together just outside camp. He smiled as he watched Sarah reach out and take her son's hand. Mother and son had come a long way toward finding peace between them over the last three weeks.

* * *

That evening after people had eaten, Sarah snagged Frank and they found a quiet place to talk away from camp. As she poled her way over to a large flat rock and sat down, Frank thought about the conversation he'd had with Tashi just before dinner. He told the old lama he was afraid of falling in love with the woman. Tashi listened as he debated what he should and shouldn't do. But as always, the lama left him to ponder a question. *Perhaps it is not the fear of falling in love, but rather the fear of waking up and living, hmmm?*

"I had a long talk with Tashi yesterday," she said, rousing him out of his musing.

He took a seat beside her and splayed his fingers over the cool, gritty surface of the rock. Looking into the fading blue sky, he leaned forward and said, "What about?"

Her hand found its way over his fingers. "A bunch of things: church, God, Buddha, feelings, fears. He likes to tell stories, doesn't he?"

"Oh, he's full of them," Frank said, and smiled. "Lots of open-ended questions, too, in case you haven't noticed."

"Didn't hear too many," Sarah said. "Must be he saves them for you."

Frank sensed a grin coming back. "Yeah. He likes poking me with a stick. Says it makes me think. So, what was the story about?"

"Living in the moment," she said.

Frank nodded as he watched the phalanx of Asian geese trace a path across the horizon. "And what did you think of it?"

"It gave me pause to look at how I've gone through life. I've always lived a day or a week ahead of myself, running here and there."

He glanced at her and saw her staring out toward the darkening horizon as well. "I've always struggled with the past."

"Me, too," she said. "Seems like we both have a problem living in the here and now. You know, funny thing is, I always thought I was living in the present. I went to work, took care of Greg, attended meetings, coordinated functions, put out the proverbial fires that constantly arose in the district; all that stuff, never realizing I was going through the motions. Even when I was in church, it seemed I always had something on my mind, yelling for my attention. Life for me, 'just was'."

"Instead of, 'just is'," Frank put in.

"Right."

Sarah paused and he felt her hand squeeze his fingers. "I don't want to do that anymore."

He eyed her, wondering what she was leading to. "A journey begins with a single step."

She turned her head and looked back. "Yeah", she muttered. "I need to be more mindful of that. There's a scripture about how the birds don't sow or reap, yet are fed by the Heavenly Father."

"And you're no less than they are in His eyes," Frank said.

"Right," she answered, leaning into him.

* * *

After two nights at Base Camp, the climbing teams left for their second acclimatization hike to Camp 2. Again, it was an early 4:00 AM start. The trip through the Ice Fall went a bit quicker this time as the men knew what to expect having traveled through it already, but there were variations here and there where the glacier had spread and closed up fissures and crevasses over the last two days.

They reached the Western Cwm around 11:00 AM and started for Camp 2 under a deep blue, cloudless dome. An hour after they had passed Camp 1, the temps skyrocketed from the streaming sunbeams bouncing off the walls of snow and ice onto the powdered surface. The valley was becoming a huge solar oven.

Frank came to a halt and peeled off his fleece. Rolling it up, he added it to the down jacket he'd already put aside in his pack. Adjusting his sunglasses, he retied his ponytail and waited for his climbers to make their own accommodations. From here on out, it was going to be a slow march up the valley to the *bergschrund* that separated the glacier from the base of the Lhotse wall. There, before the treacherous, yawning crevasse that spanned over a hundred meter drop, they'd come to Camp 2 and stay three nights before heading back down.

As the men walked single file in a long, winding path around fissures crisscrossing the snowy plane, Frank thought of Sarah. In the stillness under the vast star-filled dome the night before they'd made a silent pact between them to let things unfold as they would.

He looked about him, drinking in the land with its overpowering majestic peaks. The soaring gray walls that were frosted with cakes of snow waiting to slough off onto the snow-covered glacier below, made his heart drum. Ahead, the 1,000-meter Lhotse wall leading to the *Geneva Spur* and the South Col dominated the deep blue sky. But that was several days away, so he put it out of his mind and listened to the snow crunch under his feet and the sound of his lungs breathing in the clean, rarified air. As many times as he'd come here over the years, he never tired of this valley nor were there any words in any dictionary that could adequately describe his feelings for it.

Three hours later, the climbers came into Camp 2. Tembe had been there for almost a week now, and had set up their tents in a clear open space well away from the snow covered shoulders of the mountains. Frank removed his pack and entered the small cooking tent to find Tembe busy melting snow on a small gas stove.

"Namaste," he said to the Sherpa.

Tembe set his plate of steamed vegetables down and looked up. "How was trip?"

"It was wonderful," Frank replied, inhaling the permeating aroma of garlic. "How have things been up here?"

"Not bad. Hot yesterday. So, you hungry?"

"I could eat."

"Okay, I start dinner. Need more water though." He turned around, grabbed an empty nylon bag and held it out to Frank. "Tell someone go get snow for melting."

Frank took it from him, and as he was about to leave said, "We had an interesting guest show up for our *Puja*."

"Is that so," Tembe said, returning his attention to his plate of food.

"Yeah. Master Tashi. Anything you care to tell me about?"

The Sherpa shrugged. "Nothing to tell."

"Are you sure?" Frank said, narrowing his gaze on his Sirdar. "I think a little birdie's been whispering in his ear."

The man kept his eyes focused on his plate, and said, "No birdies here. Too far to fly."

"Right," Frank said, knowing now for certain why his old friend and mentor had shown up at Base Camp. But how could he be upset? Tembe was just looking out for him, and wasn't that what friends did for each other? And besides, he had been glad to see Tashi, though he still hadn't been able to figure out exactly how the parable about the archer applied to him.

* * *

After dinner on the third night, Frank took the team out to see the *bergschrund*. As the men stared across the ten-meter wide chasm, Frank eyed Aldan and Rene's faces, gauging their health. Aldan, who was dealing with a monstrous migraine along with Rene's grinding cough, concerned him.

On their way back to their tents, Frank pulled the men aside. "You alright?"

The Aussie gave him a half smile. "Yeah . . ." He licked his lips and eyed Frank tentatively. "Umm . . . maybe not. I feel like shite, to tell ya the truth."

"What about you, Rene?"

The Frenchman nodded, but Frank knew he was hurting pretty bad.

"Maybe you guys ought to call it a day. No shame in turning around," Frank said, sympathetically. "Not all our bodies are cut out for this."

"Yeah, I hear ya there. Let me think on it a bit and I'll give ya my answer tomorrow," Aldan said.

Rene coughed and shook his head. "I be okay. Don't worry about me."

"Fair enough," Frank said, and watched the men shuffle off to their tents, quite certain they'd never summit.

* * *

The following afternoon Aldan pulled Frank aside after they had eaten. The Aussie looked no better than he had the day before but his spirits seemed to be up. Looking back at the Lhotse wall, he said, "Think I'm gonna give the last hike a go and see where I end up. Seems a shame to come all this way and not give it a shot."

Frank eyed the man. He couldn't blame him. There probably wouldn't be another opportunity for him in the future, with so much of his funding for the attempt coming out of his own pocket. "Okay, Aldan, my man. Just keep drinking and eating as much as you can, and we'll see what happens," Frank said.

"Plan on it, mate."

Frank slapped the man's shoulder encouragingly. "Gear up. We'll be heading back down in twenty." As he said it, Rene broke into another coughing fit behind them.

Aldan glanced back. "Khumbu cough?"

"Yep," Frank said. "Once it grips you, it's like a snake and it rarely lets go." Frank shook his head sadly and turned back to the tents where the rest of the men were getting ready for the hike back to Base Camp.

They were a little over a kilometer away from Camp 1, when Rene's cough became untenable. As the Frenchman broke into another rib busting spasm Frank knew the Frenchman's summit bid was over. He wouldn't say as much though until Bob checked the man over at Base Camp. Better to let the medic make the call. Rene would listen to him, or so Frank hoped. In any event, he wasn't going to lead the man to his death.

But right now, it was about getting Rene back down, so Frank and Da-wa dropped back and brought up the rear of the line, helping the Frenchman negotiate the eroding snow packed landscape to Camp 1. There, they would bunk down for the night, and hit the Ice Fall first thing just before daybreak. The one thing they had going for them was they were moving downhill.

* * *

The next morning, Frank awoke to a stiff wind rattling the sides of his tent. As he sat up, he saw Greg packing things up. They darted glances back and forth, saying nothing, each of them knowing the drill. Thirty minutes later, the team was standing outside in darkness with their headlamps on. Frank motioned to Sherpa Ke-tsum to lead the way and waited with Da-wa for Rene to get around.

When the Frenchman came out of his tent, he looked like he'd been beaten half to death. Frank worried about getting him down through the treacherous *Ice Fall*. But he'd had done it before with sicker clients. It was one step at a time. Clip on to the ropes and pay attention. To make things as safe as he could, he placed Da-wa in front of Rene with himself in back.

The saving grace was Rene being aware of what he was doing; otherwise it would've been a call down to Base Camp for a chopper, which no one wanted. Even though the land was level on the Western Cwm and could be landed on, the snow pack was still riding on a moving glacier that could open up underneath the weight of a chopper at any minute.

But they made it down. The three-hour decent, however, had turned into a five hour odyssey. Bob came by to check on Rene as soon as they arrived at camp and pronounced him unfit for any further climbing. It was a sore blow to the Frenchman and his traveling companion, Vicq. The mountain had claimed its first victory over the Khum Jung expedition team, and it probably wouldn't be the last.

* * *

The following morning was brisk and cold. The chill wind blowing down over the Khumbu glacier ramrodded through the camp like a herd of frightened yaks. Frank crawled out of his tent and strode to the latrine under the lifting gray clouds that were retreating to the east. It was early, maybe 6:00 or 6:30 and the rattle of yellow tent skins shuddering in the wind drowned out the stirrings of the camp around him. As he marched over the moraine to take care of his body's business, he saw Sarah poking her head out of her tent.

She scanned the surrounding encampment as her hair whipped around her shoulders, lashing her face. Frank shook his head. She had turned into a real trooper; and in many ways she was stronger than some of the men he'd seen lumbering around camp. Had she a mind to climb, he didn't doubt for a minute she could've summited. He stepped into the portable tent to relieve himself wondering what it would be like to climb with her. If she could see the Valley of the Silence, he was sure she'd have a different opinion of the mountain. But then he reminded himself that her husband was buried up on the mountain along with a reminder of all that could go wrong, and had.

He finished up and headed into the command tent. Sangye was already up and had put on a pot of water to brew for tea. A power bar lay half-eaten on the table beside the Sherpa as he went about booting up the computer. Frank dug a teabag out of the box by the stove and tossed it in his mug. The two of them glanced at each other, saying nothing and went about their business. That was the way it was most of the time when he and Sangye were alone together; enjoying the silent comforts of each other's company, knowing each other's thoughts almost before the other one did.

At length, Frank sat beside the man and together they perused the weather forecasts for the next week. The jet stream was starting well to the northwest of Everest, which made for great opportunities ahead, but that didn't mean things couldn't change. After reviewing the data, Frank pulled out his journal and made his entries about the expedition's progress. Rene would be flown back to Namche later this afternoon as soon as the clouds cleared overhead and the wind had died down. He felt bad for the man. He had believed the Frenchman more than capable of summiting but bad luck had befallen him.

As he finished penning the entry, the tent flap pulled back and Sarah entered. "My goodness, it's windy out there," she huffed, setting her hiking pole to the side.

Frank looked up. "Namaste, Light-foot."

She shot him a saucy smile and hobbled over to the stove.

"You'll have to crank old Betty up I'm afraid," Frank said getting up. "Here, have a seat."

"Dhan'yavāda," she replied, and plopped down into the canvas chair.

Frank chuckled. "My, you're turning into a regular Sherpa."

"I'm learning. Sangye here and Tashi have been schooling me a bit. So, how are you doing this morning? You were pretty wiped out yesterday."

"It was a long one to be sure," Frank replied. "But we got everyone down."

Sarah nodded, obviously knowing he meant Rene. They were quiet a moment. Finally, Sarah spoke up. "Well, one acclimation hike to go, right?"

"Yep. Then down to Dengboche for a well-deserved breather." He glanced down at her ankle brace. "I don't think you want to try the trip down with us though."

"No, I think not," she answered, and pouting added, "It's not fair."

Frank felt a smirk come to his lips. "No one told you to go jumping off that rock."

Sarah frowned. "Don't rub it in."

Just then, Da-wa came in. He shot Frank a wary glance and nodded subtly toward the front flap. Frank caught the hint and excused himself. Once he was outside, Da-wa said, "There's been an accident on the Ice Fall."

"How bad?" Frank whispered, feeling his heart sink.

"Man fell off ladder crossing crevasse, broke leg. Bob on way up."

Frank bit his lip. "Damn. Whose camp?"

"Eckert's. I'm going up now to see if I can help. You want to join me?"

"Absolutely," Frank said, then trotted off to get suited up.

Chapter 21

Sarah wondered what Da-wa had said to Frank. When she came out of the command tent, he was nowhere to be seen. A couple of Winslow climbers were talking nearby about an accident on the Ice Fall. Her heart thudded and she raced to Greg's tent. She pulled back the front flap and found him inside lying down and reading an *Outdoor* magazine. Sitting up, he shot her a startled look.

"There's been an accident," Sarah said breathlessly.

"What kind of accident?" Greg said in alarm.

"I don't know!"

He shoved his feet into his boots and climbed out of his tent. As he stood, his glance darted around. "Where's Frank?"

"I don't know," she said. An image of someone lying dead in a crevasse flashed before her. She eyed her son anxiously. "He was talking with me in the command tent, then all of a sudden, Sherpa Dave shows up. Next thing I know, he's gone."

"He's probably gone to see what he can do," Greg said, looking off toward the glacier. He chewed his lip, looking like he was thinking about heading toward it.

Sarah grabbed his arm. "Don't you dare go off to that thing."

Greg turned back to her with a withering gaze. "What?"

"You heard me."

He ripped away from her. "Start thinking of others just for once, will ya?"

Stunned, she backed away feeling like she'd just been slapped across the face. "Really? Well, excuse me for worrying about you," she fired back.

"That's just the problem. You worry too much, and it's a distraction I can't afford." He shook his head. "I'm not your little boy anymore. Stop treating me like it!" He turned about face and stalked away toward Lanzo's tent, leaving her to look on perplexed.

* * *

An hour later, she was sitting outside eyeing the glacier. Its deceiving frozen mass of ice spilling out onto the moraine stared back at her impassively. That Greg was on it right now, gave her pause to re-think what she said to him in Dengboche a week ago. Why had she told him to go ahead and climb the damn mountain?

The lyrical murmurings of Vicq talking to Rene, brought her out of her musing. She turned to the emaciated Frenchman who was hunched over in his chair hacking his guts out. The man would be airlifted to Namche in an hour or so. She felt bad for him, but at the same time envied his being transported away from here. To be honest, she couldn't deny wishing Greg was in his place, flying off, too. Then this could all be done and over with.

Then, suddenly, Tashi was standing beside her. His thin face was watchful as he stared into the wind that was pressing his red robe into his body. She watched him, thinking back to their previous meeting. The man was an enigma to her. He spoke simply, but there were layers of meaning behind his words. Did the lesson he taught her about living in the present apply here? She didn't think so.

* * *

By the time Frank and Da-wa returned with Greg, Sully, and Lanzo it was after 5:00 PM. As Frank shed his crampons, he announced a meeting that everyone was expected to attend.

An hour later, the team gathered outside the command tent. Clipboard in hand, Frank said, "Okay folks, listen up. The good news is the man only broke his leg. As for what happened, he lost his balance on the ladder and took a tumble. Fortunately he was clipped on. Now, I've spoken with the Ice Doctor and he's gone over the lines and the condition of the ice. As far as we can tell, the walls are solid and the lines are secure."

That brought a sigh of relief from the Austrians, but Sarah didn't share their sentiments.

Frank went on. "I can't tell you guys enough about how important it is to take your time out there. If you're not feeling the love with the ice, then back off until you're comfortable going on. It's not worth getting hurt because you're in a hurry or letting your testosterone make the decisions." Frank panned the men around him, holding each of them in a stern gaze. "No one is going to think less of you."

When nodding heads looked back, he continued. "Okay, then. We have our last acclimatization hike coming up tomorrow. We'll be heading for the Lhotse wall. Get a good night's sleep and be ready by 4:15 AM. I'll see you out front here."

The team dispersed back to their tents except for Sarah. When they were alone, she said, "So, this *Ice Doctor* said, 'as far as he could tell'? What exactly does that mean?"

"It means it's safe as far as he knows."

"And that's good enough for you?" Sarah said, narrowing her gaze on him.

"Sarah, these men who run the lines up the mountain know more than anyone concerning the ice. But they're not gods. No one can know for sure what the ice will do on any given day, only what it *might* do. Right now, the temps are good and the glacier is acting accordingly. That's all we can hope for." He paused and studied her with compassion. "I know you're worried about your son, but Greg's a good mountaineer. What happened out there this morning was a man being in a hurry and not paying attention to what he was doing. People who take their skills for granted get hurt. It happens."

His assurance didn't help, but she accepted it. Besides, it wasn't like she had a say in anything. "Okay."

"Good. Everything's going to be all right. I've never lost anyone on any of my expeditions."

"There's always a first time, though," Sarah put in.

"Yes, there's always a first time," Frank admitted. He took her hand in his and looked back pointedly. "Do you trust me?"

"It's not you I'm worried about. It's the damned mountain," she answered. "Promise me you'll be careful. I don't want to go down this mountain alone."

"I aim to be. Now, I need to get a bite to eat and then off to bed. I have an early morning tomorrow."

Did he know what she meant about her going down alone? Did he know he was part of that equation? She studied his face, trying to discern his comprehension of what she had just told him. When she saw his knowing expression, she said, "I'll be there sending you off, then."

* * *

The following morning, Sarah roused herself at the ungodly hour of 4:00 AM to see her men off. After she watched the climbers stream out into the dark twilight of morning, she closed her eyes and sent a prayer upward to bring them back safe and unharmed. But the hike to Camp 3 would be no picnic, or so her son had told her. It would take them all day and into the early part of the evening, before they reached the camp stationed on the steep slope of the mountain.

She turned away from the fading stream of lights heading out for the sheet of ice somewhere in the gloom and struck for the command tent. Groping around inside the tent, she found the LED lantern and turned it on. Its pale white light sprayed over the darkened interior, casting eerie ghost-like shadows over the electronic equipment and scattered reports. The sight before her was reminiscent of one of those deep-sea underwater videos she'd seen of old forgotten shipwrecks being explored by robotic subs. Pulling a chair out, she sat in front of Frank's computer and booted it up.

A moment later, she was breathlessly watching a report about an avalanche claiming the lives of seven Chinese men on Annapurna. The video had caught the cascading snow rolling down the mountain and wiping out everything in its path. Several times, her hand went to the mouse to close the video, but she just couldn't do it. And what was worse, her son was going to go up into that hellish nightmare looming above her. Finally, mercifully, the video ended, leaving her sufficiently terrorized for the rest of her life. This was madness. She pushed away from the table just as Sangye and Chok-pa came into the tent.

"Namaste," Sangye said.

Sarah swallowed, trying to find her breath. She was quite sure if she tried to stand, she'd collapse. Sangye glanced at the computer screen in front of her with the open video window.

"You saw report on avalanche, huh?" Sangye said.

Sarah nodded. Finally she said, "Why do men climb these God-forsaken mountains? It's insanity!"

The Sherpa could only shrug. Maybe it was for not knowing what more to say about it that Chok-pa asked her if she wanted tea.

She eyed him incredulously, wondering if she had lost her mind. "Does anyone have a clue of what they're doing? Or do they really have a death wish, hmmm? 'Cause that's what this news boils down to! Risking your freaking life for a God-damned view!" She got up trembling, threw her empty mug across the tent and stalked out.

Returning to her own tent, she dug her rosary out. It had been a while since she'd held the beaded string in her hand. She clutched it, reciting Hail Marys while praying; no, *begging* God to hear her plea and end this odyssey into hell. Even the reason Greg had given her for climbing the mountain no longer mattered. But the only answer that came back was the wind rattling her tent.

* * *

Three hours later, Sarah was back in the command tent picking at a plate of vegetables and warmed up fruit. Sitting across from her with his back turned, was Sangye. He had left her alone since her tirade earlier that morning, busying himself with going over the weather forecasts and checking in with the climbing team via the base radio. Sarah watched him, feeling a mixture of anger, fear, and regret. At last she cleared her throat. "Sangye?"

He turned around and faced her with his ever-present smile. "Ho?"

"I'm sorry about this morning. I was upset and I took it out on you."

"Is all right. How you feel?"

Sarah shrugged. "Like I've been kicked in the stomach."

"You sick?"

She coughed a couple of times. "No." She popped a carrot in her mouth. "Can I ask you something?"

"Sure."

"Have you ever summited?"

"You mean Chomolungma?" Sangye said.

"Yes."

"Ho, couple times."

"Why?" Sarah said. "I mean, what is the lure of that mountain for you? I don't understand."

"Ahhh ... Many reasons I climb, sometimes for job, other times for me, still others for keeping mountain clean. But time I like most is for me. Very peaceful up there. No distractions, just you and mountain."

Sarah shook her head. The ways of men were a mystery to her. As she set her plate aside, the tent flap pulled back and Tashi came strolling in. The two men bowed to each other. As the lama asked Sangye about how things were going on the mountain, he turned and saw her.

"Oh … Sarah. Did not see you there."

"It's okay, Tashi." She grabbed her mug and stood. "I was just thinking about getting another refill. Can I get you a cup of tea?"

"Ho, I would like that very much," he said finding a chair to sit. "So, how is Sarah doing?"

"Not very good, I'm afraid," Sarah said, pouring his tea and handing it to him. As he took it, the lama shot Sangye a look. A minute later, the young Sherpa was gone from the tent, leaving the two of them alone. After he left, Sarah sat and told the lama about the report she saw on the web.

At last, she said, "I'm scared to death for my son."

"I see … and for Frank as well, hmmm?"

"Yes," Sarah said. "Seems I'm the only one who's worried though."

"Ahhh … ho. But you have no control over what might happen to them. For Christian, faith in God is very big … hmmm? You pray for his protection. In prayer there are four parts. Three things are absolute: one, you pray; two, He hears, three, He answers. Last thing hardest of all; you hear His answer and accept … hmmm?"

The lama took a sip of tea and continued. "Sometime, answer is not what you want to hear. And here is where faith is tested most. Sometime, you see only door closing and not one that opens elsewhere. You remember story I tell you about condemned man? For Buddhist, we see things that way. We know destiny is out of our hands and so we pay attention to the moment at hand. Our choice then is thus; to push against the current and suffer or sink into the water's depth like stone and let it flow over us. Buddhist allow for mindfulness of things that are here around us and constantly evolving. That do not mean we not feel loss or grief. Only that we do not let fear steal the present moment from us."

He picked up a pencil and paper from the table beside him. Putting a tiny mark in the center of the page, he showed it to her and said in a reedy voice, "This dot is fear.

The white around it is life and destiny. Fear is hardly nothing, yet it blot out everything else in our sight. To see the white, you must first look past the dot that clouds the mind." He paused and getting up added, "Do not let this dot steal away the present moments with those you love."

Sarah thought about that as he looked upon her with his soft brown eyes. "I like you Tashi, but you don't have a child and therefore you can't begin to understand how I feel. I do appreciate your trying to help, but I can't logic away fear like you. People died out there today and though it's a different mountain, it doesn't change anything."

"Ho, I know. I only try to remind you that there are things you cannot control and to spend your time loving him when he is with you," Tashi said. "I need to go now, but I will keep you and your son in my thoughts."

"Thank you," Sarah said.

* * *

Four days later, the team returned from their third and final acclimatization hike. Sarah met them as they came in and pulled Greg aside. As they walked back to camp, she deferred from getting right into the issue of going forward with the climb and asked him how things went. But all Greg could talk about were the spectacular views he'd seen up on the Lhotse face. Finally, unable to endure another word about the mountain, Sarah said, "I saw a report about an avalanche on Annapurna that killed several men."

Greg stopped and eyed her dubiously. "Yes, I heard about it."

Sarah reached out and took his arm. Searching his drawn face, she took a deep breath and said, "Greg, I'm worried. What if —"

"Mom, please!"

"I'm sorry," Sarah begged. "But I'm freaking scared here. I know what I said before, but —"

"I'm going to be all right," Greg said. "The avalanche you saw happened on Annapurna, not here on Everest. If it isn't safe to climb, Frank will say so. So stop worrying!"

"I can't help it. You're my son," Sarah said.

"You see, this is exactly why I told you not to come, but you wouldn't listen," Greg said. He sighed. "I don't need this shit, not now! I need to stay focused, and you're not helping. Why are you doing this? You know what this means to me."

"I'm doing it because I love you!" Sarah said fiercely.

Greg stared back at her. "Then back off. Just for once, will ya?"

Sarah eyed the scudding clouds overhead. "I see. So, I guess my feelings mean nothing then." She knew she was playing the guilt card, but she couldn't help herself.

"I can't believe you just said that," he said. He pulled away out of her grasp. "But if that's the way you want to look at it, go ahead. But this isn't about you! Not this time. This is about me — my life!"

"And you're needlessly risking it," she retorted.

"No, I'm not!" he said hotly. "I need to get settled back in and check my equipment now, so I'm done talking."

"Fine, you go ahead and do that," she said as her throat tightened. She opened her mouth to say, 'it appears that your dead father is more important than me', but stopped herself.

She watched him retreat to his tent wishing there was some way she could get through to him and change his mind. But he was hell-bent on climbing. To be honest, she understood his burning need to find his father, but what was it that ran through his veins, driving him to risk his life climbing mountains? Over the last ten years, a stranger had entered him, replacing the brown-haired, blue-eyed boy she had always known, and as she stood there with the wind tugging at her hair, she wondered if she really knew him at all, anymore.

Ten minutes later, she headed toward the command tent. As she hobbled along, she thought of what she wanted to say to Frank regarding Greg. If anyone had the power to persuade her son from climbing it was he. She pulled back the front flap and saw Frank going over a schedule on his clipboard. Sangye and Chok-pa stood beside him, listening in.

Frank turned to her. "Well, hello there Light-foot," he said.

Sarah pasted a smile on. "Hi, I know you're busy, but can I have a moment, please?"

"Yeah, sure," he said, waving her in. "What's up?"

She glanced at Sangye and Chok-pa hesitantly. Frank set his clipboard down and motioned her to go back outside. When they were alone, she said, "I saw on the web that there was an avalanche on a mountain a ways away from here yesterday."

"Yeah, I know about it. Tragic."

"It's more than tragic, Frank. People died!"

"I know, Sarah. Avalanches are a part of life up here. Every mountaineer knows that. We assess the mountains as best we can, checking temps, and make decisions accordingly. But in the end, the mountains will do what they're going to do. It's the risk we all take."

"Right. I keep hearing all the reasons for it, but none of them make sense to me. It's just crazy stupid."

"I guess you have to be a mountaineer to understand," Frank said. "You're worried about Greg, aren't you?"

"You have to ask?" she said a little more sarcastically than she intended.

Frank caressed her face with his fingers. "We'll be all right. The mountain is solid and the weather looks good."

"Solid?"

He put his arm around her shoulder and drew her close to him. "It's a term we use to describe stability regarding snow and ice cover. We've had a good cold, dry spell with not a lot of snow this season. That, in turn, keeps the ice from moving a lot, as well as limiting accumulations of snow on the slopes where it can become unstable."

"So, I assume, you're not worried about going up?"

Frank paused and as he stood next to her, she sensed him crafting a careful response. "I'm always concerned, Sarah. People who aren't don't last long up here."

Sarah pulled away and stared him straight in the eye. "What would you say if I asked you to ground my son from going?"

Frank wrinkled his brow. "I can't do that."

"Why not? You sent Rene back down the mountain."

"Rene was sick," Frank said. "I have no basis to ground Greg."

Yes you have. Me! Sarah thought, but resisted saying it.

Frank studied her. "Don't look at me like that, Sarah."

"Look at you like what?" Sarah said, feeling the bond between them stretch.

"You know what I'm talking about. That look that says, I care about you. I won't be coerced, though. Besides, I couldn't stop him even if I wanted to."

Sarah didn't know what to say for a minute. He was right. No one could stop Greg from climbing if he was hell bound to do it. At last she said, "I'm sorry, but I'm frightened."

Frank softened his voice. "Can I ask you a question?"

"Yes."

"Why did you come to Everest? I don't get it. Certainly, you knew what he was getting into," Frank said.

The question had been asked before, but not by him. She averted her gaze and looked off over the barren moraine feeling powerless and frightened. When she started this whole thing, she knew why she wanted to come, but Frank and the people of the Sagarmatha valley along with the majestic land they lived in, had blurred the lines between anger, loss, and love. Finally, she looked back at him, knowing what the real answer was.

"I came because of Greg," she said. "I didn't want to be home waiting for a phone call like I did with Steven. But more than that; I wanted to keep hating this land. I wanted it to be ugly and cruel the way I always imagined it. But it's not! Remember when I said I didn't like you in the beginning? Well, it was more than that. I had made up my mind to hate you."

Frank nodded. "Yeah, and I thought of you as the Widow." He paused, and studied her tenderly. "Sarah, I won't tell you not to worry, but I will do everything in my power to make sure Greg comes back to you safely. You have my word."

She stepped forward and melted into his arms. "I know."

Chapter 22

Frank led his team back up to Base Camp from their trip down to Dengboche. The camp, for the most part, had emptied itself and was heading up the mountain for their summit attempts. The Winslow and Eckert Camps, however, still remained. That didn't bother Frank, though. He liked bringing up the rear because it meant they would avoid much of the inevitable traffic jams that happened near the summit, especially at the Hillary Step.

Although pushing the backside of the weather window was a risky move, in that it could mean an aborted summit if the weather closed in, he was willing to take it. He didn't want his clients standing around in the death zone for an hour in sub-zero weather with their oxygen running out on the way down.

The first thing on Frank's agenda was to check in with Sangye to see what the forecasts were for the upcoming week. Now that most everyone had left the camp, he wanted to get a quick start while everyone was feeling good. After that, he would have one long last chat with Sarah. Once things got rolling, he wouldn't have the time to tell her what he'd had on his mind for the last two days.

He'd been working up the courage to confess his love for her since the night before he left for Dengboche. That he would ever fall in love again had never entered his mind when the expedition began, but he had, and he wanted her to know it. But another part of him railed against it, saying, *Let it be. She doesn't need to know.*

He sighed and went into the command tent. There, he found Sangye at the computer scrolling down the page of the weather report for the next three days. Sangye looked up.

"Namaste, Sangye. How are things looking at the top?"

"Good, right now," he said, sending the page on the screen to the printer. "Jet stream is still moving north. I think you will have a good window to summit. How was Dengboche?"

"Refreshing," Frank said. "Did a world of good for the guys."

"You hungry? I start fixing dinner."

"I could eat," Frank said, taking the page off the printer tray and scanning down the numbers. They looked solid. "When did folks start heading up?"

"Two days ago. John left this morning with his team. Eckert and Winslow teams going tomorrow," Sangye replied, getting up. "So, you go tomorrow too, maybe?"

"Planning on it," Frank muttered.

Just then, Sarah came in. "You're back!" she rasped.

Frank looked up. The altitude was finally beginning to have its effect on her bright, affable voice. She flashed him a brave smile as she hobbled in, tea mug in hand. The moment she'd been dreading since this expedition began was almost upon her and he knew she was struggling to keep her fears in check for her son. When she came close, he caught a whiff of vanilla and saw that her drawn-back, brown hair was damp. A hint of pink splashed her cheeks.

"Namaste," he said, caressing her delicate sculptured face with a tender gaze.

"I spoke with Greg," she said, and put her hand to her mouth and coughed. "He looks so much better than he did a couple days ago."

Frank set the weather forecast page in his hand on the table beside him. Maybe now would be the best time to tell her what he had on his mind. He'd be leaving early in the morning, and being up late wasn't a good idea. He shot Sangye a knowing glance and nodded toward the front flap. As the Sherpa went out, he said, "That's what dropping down to lower altitudes will do for you. You wearing your mask at night?"

She cleared her throat. "Well, most of the time. I … accidentally fell asleep the last few nights and … ummm … forgot about it," she said as her gaze slipped away from him.

Frank pursed his lips. "Sarah."

She coughed again. "I know."

Frank shook his head. "I want you to wear it from now on, all the time, understood?"

She glanced back at him. "I'll be alright, really. It's just a little cough, nothing to be concerned about. If it gets worse, I'll wear it, I promise."

Stubborn woman! "I want you to check in with Bob. If he green-lights it, then okay, otherwise you're wearing it all the time or I'll send you down the mountain on a chopper."

Startled, she dropped her jaw and stared back at him with a 'you wouldn't really do that, would you' expression. But he was dead serious. He didn't want her getting sick. He had enough things to think about, so he repeated his threat with more emphasis.

She frowned. "Okay, okay, you win."

"It's not about me winning, dear, it's about you staying healthy." He reached out, put his hand on her shoulder and stared down at her indignant blue eyes. "You remember what I told you about Khumbu cough? You don't want it. Believe me. If nothing else, wear it for your son," he said, knowing a little guilt added in couldn't hurt.

At last, she nodded and a tiny smile crossed her face. "If I didn't know better, I'd say you just used the famous Catholic guilt against me."

Frank backed away, letting go of her and chuckled. He had heard about it, but decided to play dumb. "Maybe I should look into it. Could come in handy down the road."

"That's what you think," she said. She dug into her pocket and pulled out a tea bag. Popping it in her mug, she removed the pot of steaming hot water off the tiny stovetop and poured herself a cup of tea. She turned and eyed him and the expression on her face was wistful, as if she wanted to tell him something, but didn't know how to say it. He waited for her to make up her mind. Whatever it was, she decided against it and looked out the open front flap. At last, she said, "I've been talking with Tashi a lot while you were gone."

"Really?" Frank said, and turned to look for his own mug, which he kept somewhere amidst the clutter of reports and journals on the table beside them. "What about?"

"You," she said.

Frank looked back at her not sure whether to grin or be straight-faced. "Me? Hmmm … pretty dull subject there," he replied, wondering what on earth she could've learned from the lama that he hadn't already told her himself.

"Oh, I don't know about that," she said, crushing her tea bag against the inside of her mug with her spoon. "Do you know if there's any honey in that box over there?"

Frank shrugged. "Maybe, let me look."

"Anyway, seems you and I are quite alike, or so he says. I'm just wondering what he might've meant by that."

"So, he didn't tell you?" Frank said over his shoulder as he dug through the box. He knew Tashi would never divulge a confidence, but why bring it up at all? *What was Tashi up to?*

"No," Sarah answered. "He's a bit tight-lipped about certain things concerning you, and what he does say is wrapped in riddles. He's quite maddening to talk to sometimes."

Don't I know it! Frank thought. "He does like to make people think," he replied. "Ah! There you are," he muttered finding the honey buried under a box of cookies. He got up and brought it to her.

Sarah said, "Yes, he does." She paused, then finally went on, "Anyway, Tashi said he talks to you all the time about being afraid. So, I'm curious; what are you afraid of?"

Frank averted his gaze, not sure how to answer. He wasn't sure what he was afraid of, only that when it came to letting people into his life, he had felt exposed. At last he said, "Never gave it a thought."

"Hmmm … I wonder what Tashi would say to that?" Sarah said, eyeing him as she sipped her tea. She stepped over and took a seat in one of the chairs that were scattered about the tent.

"Quite a bit, I imagine," Frank said, knowing the answer and went over to grab a power bar from the box he'd just dragged the honey out of. He felt Sarah looking at him. He sighed, sensing that this was his chance to tell her how he felt and he could sense her waiting to hear it. Swallowing, he turned back toward her and studied the open expression gazing back at him from across the tent. "Ummm … I've been thinking," he said shuffling toward her, "things are gonna get real busy around here pretty soon, and with my leaving just before first-light and all … ummm, that it might be a good time to let you to know … that I … " He tried to get the words out, but they just wouldn't come. He saw her draw breath and her hand tighten around her mug.

"What?" she said, barely a whisper.

He forced a smile. "That I'll be thinking a lot about you up there."

She smiled and nodded. "I'll be thinking about you too," she said, and looked at him. "Is there something the matter?"

He felt his heart thud. "No, everything's fine."

"Okay, you're sure," she said.

"Yes, absolutely."

But her expression told him she wasn't convinced. She got up, shuffled toward him and wrapped her arms around him. As she held him tight, his heart screamed at him to say he loved her. But he just couldn't.

He drank in her expectant gaze, and steeled himself. "Everything will be all right."

"I know. Well, I'd better let you get down to business," she said. She reached up, kissed him on the cheek. Flashing him a tiny smile, she turned and left.

* * *

Frank led the men out of camp the next morning a little after 4:00 AM for their summit bid. Everyone was upbeat and chatting amongst themselves as they marched toward the glacier. But Frank was quiet as he walked along side of Da-wa. All he could think of was his failure to tell Sarah how he felt. He replayed the memory of their conversation over and over in his head.

He shimmied his backpack upon his shoulder as the crisp, cold air bit his face, and glanced back toward the camp that was shrouded in darkness. It was time to put Sarah out of his mind, so he pricked his ears and listened to the clicks and clacks of the murmuring Chomolungma as its mighty heart thrummed beneath his feet. The colossal up-thrust of rock, ice, and snow was like the sleeping two-headed dog of Greek mythology lying before them. Once awakened, it showed no mercy to those who dared enter its den. Da-wa stirred beside him.

"You alright?" he said to Frank.

Frank eyed his stout Sirdar, who was walking beside him. The man obviously knew something was on his mind and had probably guessed what it was already. "Yeah, I'm good."

Da-wa was quiet a moment. Finally, he said, "You like the American woman, don't you?"

Frank considered the man. He didn't owe his Sherpa leader an explanation, but he couldn't help saying, "Yeah, I do."

Again Da-wa went quiet. Frank sensed him turning the answer over in his head. At last, he said, "What you gonna do about it?"

"I don't know," Frank said.

"Tembe worried about you."

"I know. Don't worry, I'll be fine."

The man fell silent and eyed him for several steps. Frank knew Da-wa was more than concerned, but what Da-wa didn't know, was that when it came to climbing, Frank pushed everything out of his mind and got down to business. Gritting his teeth, he stabbed his hiking pole into the moraine and picked up his pace.

* * *

Two hours later, they were climbing over the tumbling glacier spilling down the mountain as the first light of day splashed down upon them. The route over the ice had changed since their first acclimatization hike. New crevasses had opened and others had closed. Frank flexed his fingers in his Gortex glove and gripped the line beside him. His clipped-on carabiner dangled off it like a fish on a hook as he stepped onto the aluminum ladder. The bridge shivered under his weight, sagging, then rising with each step. On the other side was a narrow ledge. On it stood a line of climbers waiting their turns at another ladder that was pinned to a wall of ice that tilted back at an uncomfortable angle.

Frank headed toward them as they slowly ascended up and over the dangerous impediment. He wasn't feeling the love with this particular bump in the route, but there was no other way past it. Da-wa came beside him.

Frank said, "Whose idea was this?"

Da-wa shrugged. "Only way up."

"Right," Frank said. The next ten meters going up were going to be tricky.

One of the Winslow expedition leaders stepped over and joined them. His name was Brian and he was from New Zealand. Frank had chatted with him around camp off and on during the last four years. The tall lanky man was a damn good climber. They shook hands as Brian's clients slowly made their way up the tenuous escarpment.

Brian said, "Let's hope there aren't too many more of these, eh?"

Frank nodded as Sully, Carlo, Greg, and the rest of his climbing team piled up behind him on the ledge. "How's things down-under these days?"

"Aw, they're great. So, you're doing the standard route, I assume?"

"Yep," Frank replied. "You?"

"The same," Brian answered. "I heard a few blokes in the Andersen outfit are shooting for the South and Southeast Pillars. Gotta try one of them sometime." He glanced over toward the ladder on the wall. "Well, looks like my turn's up. Have a good climb and I'll catch ya on top."

The Kiwi strode ahead, and clipping on the ropes, headed up the ladder. As Frank watched him, Toby came near and said, "That ladder makes me nervous."

"Me too, Toby, but that's our route. Just take your time," Frank said, and moved ahead. Once Brian was up and over, Frank clipped onto the line and started his ascent. As he went up the backward incline, he could feel the twenty-kilo backpack pulling on his shoulders. He gripped the ladder rail, sliding his hand along it, inch by inch. The ice doctors had fixed the ladder tight to the wall, for which he was glad. But it fell a meter shy of the top. He came to the last few rungs; stopped, clipped on with his jumar and pulled himself up and over. When he stood on top, he let out a breath he didn't know he'd been holding. That was the way it was though, when negotiating your way through this horror chamber, as Jack Trammel used to refer to it. Always a new challenge, daring you to cross it, climb it or walk its narrow planks over yawning gaps diving deep into the massive ice sheet. And every year, someone inevitably paid the price for not paying attention to what they were doing, or not listening to the mountain when it was yelling at them to stay the hell off it. This year, they'd been lucky — so far.

* * *

Once over the Ice Fall, the team headed for Camp 1 and a quick lunch. They arrived there shortly after 1:00 PM and met back up with the Winslow Expedition teams. Here, under a blazing sun reflecting off the snow and ice, they stripped out of their down jackets and stowed them away. Frank grabbed his sun block as he stood gazing up the Western Cwm. As he applied generous doses of it to his weather-beaten face, he listened to the men rib each other about the antics they'd employed getting over crevasses and fissures. Yet, each of them knew it hadn't been a laughing matter at the time.

At length, he roused his team for the five-hour march ahead of them and by the time they had put a kilometer behind them they were strung out fifty meters apart on the hard-packed snow. Vicq caught up with Frank and they walked for some time until the man said, "I cannot believe what happened to Rene."

"Yes, I'm sorry about that. He'll get another shot, I'm sure," Frank said, encouragingly to the Frenchman.

"Oh, oui," the man said. "Is just, we were looking forward to doing it together."

Frank nodded. "I'm gonna need to place you in another team. How would you feel about climbing with Toby and Jakob?"

"Okay, I guess. Don't have much choice, do I?"

"Sorry, but no." Frank answered. "By the way, how you doing? Feeling okay?"

Vicq shrugged. "Oui. Trip down to Dengboche helped a lot."

"Good ... Watch yourself. There's a fissure right over there," Frank cautioned, pointing to a crack in the powder. He moved to his left and went around it. "So, I saw you shooting a few movies. You have folks back home tracking your ascent?"

"Oui. Set up a website before I came," Vicq replied.

"I'll have to check it out when we get back," Frank said. They marched along slowly as the sun beat down on them. As they did, Frank asked him about home and their winery, which got the man's mind off his partner. Up until now, Vicq hadn't said a lot to him, or anyone else for that matter. But once Frank got him talking about the family's prized Merlot, the man wouldn't shut up. Frank wasn't much on wine, so he didn't know half of what the man was talking about, but he didn't mind the distraction either.

* * *

It was around 5:00 that evening when Frank led his team into Camp 2 under a cloud-ridden sky. He wiggled out of his backpack and set it down in front of the Khum Jung cooking tent as his teams piled up behind him. He looked back at his men who were dumping their packs on the snow and stretching. They were all tired, but were in good spirits. As they started breaking out their tents, Frank went hunting for Tembe and found him standing behind the Khum Jung cook tent with one of the Eckert Expedition Sherpas. The men were smoking and chatting in Lhasa about family life back down in Phadking and the upcoming farming season. As Frank came up to them, the Eckert Sherpa took a drag on his cigarette and flicked it off into the snow.

Frank broke into Lhasa and joined them.

Tembe said, "Namaste. How was trip?"

"It was good," Frank answered. "Since when did you take up smoking again?"

"Since you start being pain in butt," the Sherpa said, shooting him a flinty glance.

Frank laughed and introduced himself to the Eckert Sherpa and said, "Any news on the Spaniard?"

"He down in Namche now," the man said. "Compound fracture of tibia. He okay."

"Good," Frank replied. To Tembe, he said, "The guys are out front setting up tents. Dinner in thirty?"

Tembe frowned, but a tiny smile cracked his lips. "What you think? This fast food joint?"

"Just wondering," Frank said, patting his Sirdar on the shoulder.

Tembe butted his cigarette and bade his Sherpa companion good-bye. As he started back around the tent, he said, "I hear Frenchman choppered down to Namche."

"Yeah, he got the cough pretty bad. Aldan hung back too. He stayed at Base Camp though."

"I send their O2 back down tomorrow then," Tembe said as he entered the cooking tent. "So, you go for Summit?"

"Gonna try."

"Humph ... and woman, what you do about her?" When Frank didn't answer right off, Tembe eyed him pointedly. "You got your head screwed on straight?"

"Tembe!"

"I just ask."

"I'm alright," Frank said, though in truth he knew he wasn't. "Radio juiced up?"

Tembe nodded toward the tiny folding table then went over and grabbed a couple of white nylon *snow bags* off the stack of rice sacks. As Frank shuffled over to the com-station, Tembe came up from behind and jabbed him in the arm. "Before you go make mushy-mush with her, I need more water. You go fill first ... hmmm?"

"Right," Frank said, rolling his eyes. He grabbed the bag and the small hand shovel and went out. Ten minutes later, he was busy on his knees packing the bag. As he did so, Tashi's story of the archer came back to him. He sat back on his heels as the hidden meaning about the archer slammed into him. *How could I have been so ignorant?*

* * *

The next morning, Frank led Sully and Carlo under a shocking blue sky out to the *bergschrund* with the rest of the men and their Sherpas following in their groupings. The great crevasse at the Lhotse wall, where the glacier detached from the mountain, had grown since their third acclimatization hike up the mountain. Frank eyed the ladder that crossed it, which had since been replaced with two overlapping six-meter aluminum ones that were lashed together. Steeling his nerve, he clipped his carabiner to the fixed lines that draped over the wide chasm and slowly walked out onto the narrow bridge that spanned the great crack. As he went forward under the bright sunshine streaming down over the gleaming Lhotse wall, he focused on every step, assessing the dips and sways. At the end of the span, a near-vertical face of ice went up twenty meters to the ledge that sat beneath the base of the Lhotse wall. From there, they would undertake a grueling steep climb rising twelve hundred meters up the mountain's iridescent, icy blue shoulder. In the distance, the telltale sounds of ice axes digging into the wall's frozen surface could be heard.

But right now, he had to pay attention to the danger below. Even clipped on to the ropes, a tumble off the ladder could lead to a grave injury, and possibly death, so he put his thoughts to the task ahead and finished the crossing. As he stepped onto the narrow stretch of ice on the other side, he clipped his jumar to the fixed line and shifted his 'biner over. Digging his ice axe out of his pack, he swung it and buried its spiked tip into the mammoth ice face that went up and out on either side of him for as far as he could see.

Two hours later, he was clawing up the ice-encrusted slope into the rarified air and pristine world of Everest. But the long exhausting slog ahead wasn't on his mind. Instead, it was on the moments at hand as he dug his crampons into the ice and snow and marched ever upward. For Frank, this was what he lived for; immersing himself in the moment as he plotted his next step.

Up here, his world demanded only one thing; that he pay attention to what he was doing. Climbing was easy to understand, unlike the messy feelings that churned inside him. But as much as he loved this realm, he knew it didn't have the answers he sought in life.

He stopped for a breather, and as he did, he glanced back. Sully was about twenty meters behind him and Carlo and his Sherpa Yang-dzum, another fifteen meters behind Sully. The other groupings followed them close behind, trailing off into a guess.

Ahead were the Winslow and Eckert teams and beyond them a long line of climbers stretched for as far as he could see. The mountain was busy this morning, and would be for the next seven days. Over two hundred and fifty men and women were fighting to slide into the weather window at the summit.

Many would make it; many more wouldn't. A few unfortunates would pay the price for inexperience, hopefully suffering nothing more than a bruised ego. But that was wishful thinking. Every year, someone paid the ultimate price for either being careless or not listening to their bodies.

The mountain didn't take prisoners with people who had no business being there. Frank understood that and that was why he hadn't lost anyone in over twenty years. He released the grip of his jumar, slid it ahead on the fixed line and started back up. Climbing the vast featureless and barren Lhotse wall that went on and on was an exercise in meditation. It was a process of leaning into each grinding step and taking a few breaths before the next step. A full stop and rest came perhaps every half-hour along the way, and when he did stop, it was for only a brief moment.

As he went, the one thing he was mindful of was falling rocks and ice that could come tumbling down the steep slope at a moment's notice, and because there was a base of powder on the wall, avalanches. He kept his ears pricked for the eerie howls that often announced their impending arrival. But the mountain was behaving today, and so he and his teams made good time against the brisk chill of the fifteen-knot head wind, arriving at Camp 3 at late afternoon.

There, on a pitch of ice that overlooked the Western Cwm far below, the weather turned sour as Frank and his teams fought to set their tents up in the blustering, swirling winds that rampaged down the icy slopes. An hour later, exhausted and battling a mind-bending headache, Frank crawled into his tiny domed nylon shelter and took refuge. The rest of the day and throughout the night, he tossed and turned on the unforgiving slope. The rapid rat-a-tat-tat thwapping of his tent's nylon skin cracked and snapped in his ears, and what was worse, his body was nagging him to take care of some necessary business every hour on the hour it seemed.

Grudgingly, he flicked his head lantern on and dragged himself out of his sleeping bag. Going outside for any reason up here was just insane except for the utmost need, because the fixed ropes weren't always fixed as well as one would hope. Finally after he had geared up, he pulled back the flap of his tent and crawled out onto the dark, menacing slope where he clipped his harness 'biner onto the thrashing rope. Then stomping his foot down, he stood and walked a few meters out under the blackened sky. As he relieved himself in the freezing wind, he noticed a ghostly pale image shifting across the snow several meters down wind. Whoever it was, they weren't clipped on to the ropes. His heart thumped and just as he was about to call out, the image vanished. Frank rubbed his eyes. He was tired and it was dark. It was probably just a trick of his lantern light on the snow. He zipped up and shuffled back to his tent for the rest of the long night ahead.

Chapter 23

The next morning Frank woke at 6:00 AM, if he could call it waking up. He hadn't slept more than an hour at a stretch all night. The persistent headache that had been dogging him since leaving Camp 2 had grown into a raging firestorm between his temples. He pulled his heat-exchanging mask off, polished off the last of his water, and forced down a breakfast of oatmeal. Today was going to be a long one, fraught with dangerous drops and mixed tool climbing up sheer walls of ice and rock into the *land of spirits*. The Death Zone, where mistakes were not forgiven.

Gearing up, he crawled out of his tent. Sunrise was just pricking through the charcoal gray dome above. Thin clouds were streaking across the tips of the Lhotse wall above. As he stood breathing in the arid bitter-cold air, his gaze went to the treacherous yellow band of limestone that loomed ahead on the slope. The formidable stretch of rock girded with a tangle of old and new ropes presented a frightening 1.300-meter slide down the mountainside.

At length, he started tearing down his tent and packing it away as the Sherpa guides and climbers stirred around him. Greg was already out and had stowed his tent away. He stepped beside Frank and slathered a healthy dose of zinc oxide on his nose. "Freaking cold last night," he muttered.

Frank nodded. "It'll get worse. Get any sleep?"

"Not much. Hard to rest when you're hanging up here by a thread. I'll be glad to get to Camp 4 and off this wall," Greg said, pulling a candy bar out. He unwrapped it and bit off a chunk. "So, us being last in line. Isn't that risky? I mean, what if the window decides to close in on us?"

"To answer your question; yes. But I'm willing to live with it," Frank said, buttoning his pack. "Once you've summited, you want to get down as quick as you can. Being last means not having to fight traffic coming up the mountain. Believe me, you don't need that headache up here."

"Guess I see your point. There's a lot of weekend warriors here as far as I can tell."

"Don't I know it," Frank agreed. "It's why I insist on proof of prior climbing experience."

Greg nodded. "Aldan seemed a bit green to me."

"Well, his application did give me pause, but he had a good resume of free rock climbs, so I made an exception. Won't do it again," Frank said. He crouched down to check his crampons, making sure they were on tight. "You talk to your mother last night?"

"Some."

"How's she doing?" Frank said, looking up at Greg's long, wind-battered face.

The man turned and eyed the blanket of surging clouds shrouding the Western Cwm far below. Popping the rest of his candy bar into his mouth, he said, "Pretty good, I guess." He turned back to Frank. "She asked about you."

"Yeah, meant to radio her, but I got a little distracted last night," Frank said.

Greg frowned. "Damn it!"

"What?"

"My freaking bladder," Greg said. "Been pissing like a race horse the last three hours."

"Happens," Frank said, tightening one of the crampon wires around his boot. "Hey, be careful, all right? I don't like being the bearer of bad news to nervous mothers. Not healthy."

Greg chuckled. "I hear that."

* * *

An hour later, Frank and Sherpa Yang-dzum led Sully and Carlo to the foot of the *Yellow Band.* Now, at 7,600 meters, each step over the thin ice and snow dusting the yellow limestone underfoot was a labored event. Three breaths to every step, and it would get worse, to say nothing about his head feeling like it was about to explode. He adjusted his mask and checked the fixed ropes as the sound of his breath rasped in his ears. To his left and up another 1,250 meters through the cloud cover, reigned the summit with its trademark comet tail of snow blowing off into the rarified air. To the right, Lhotse's knife-edge ridge trailed off into a guess.

He nodded to the Sherpa to drop back with Carlo and then clipped on to the fixed ropes. Leaning into the brutal thirty-knot wind roaring back, he started up the snow-dusted rocky incline. As he did so, the sting of icy pellets pummeled his face and it wasn't long until his goggles fogged over. He pulled them away from his face and wiped the lenses as best he could amidst the swirling dervishes of snow.

A moment later, he was fighting to keep his balance as the fixed lines lashed at the bare rock beneath his crampons. He gripped the fixed line and took a wary step. As his foot came down, he felt his metal spikes slip and slide over the bare rock. Every muscle in his body flexed, and with an iron-will he scuttled forward and regained a tenuous purchase on the slope. Taking a deep breath, he eyed the tiny black dots ahead of him that were moving in fits and spurts. The climbers from the Winslow Camp couldn't have been more than thirty meters away, but they might just as well have been on the moon for all he could tell.

So, it went one arduous step at a time, slipping and sliding headlong into the wind, until finally, Frank stepped off the last of the limestone band into the snow pack. As he did so, he turned his back to the wind and collected himself. Despite the punitive weather, they were making good time. Barring disaster, they'd all be at Camp 4 by mid-day.

All that remained now was the Geneva Spur and the final hike to the South Col. He adjusted his goggles and started back off toward the rocky buttress. Once up and over the steep pitch of the spur, it would be a gentle slope to Camp 4.

In the meantime, it was a slow methodical march slogging through the knee-deep snow. As he went, he fell into an altered state, ignoring the assaulting elements that were waging war on his tired body until at last, he came to a halt. Turning around, he checked on Sully and Carlo's progress. The two men, along with Sherpa Yang-dzum, were veiled in the windswept snow sweeping down the slope. Again, Frank removed his goggles and wiped the fog from the lenses. After a quick drink from his thermos, he put them back on and shoved off ahead.

Thirty minutes later, he was peering up at a deep blue sky. But the wind refused to relent. In fact, it had picked up and was gusting near fifty knots. A hundred meters or so ahead, the Lhotse face rose steeply over the dark rocky buttress. He came to a halt and drew several more breaths. The 40-meter high spur would be the last test of today's climb. After that, it was an hour and a half hike across the snow-laden shoulder to the South Col where they'd hunker down one last time before the summit push.

Frank dug in and slogged toward the buttress, and it wasn't long before he was crawling up the face of the ragged spur. As he jammed his crampons into the icy face, a howling blast of frigid air pushed him backward. Ignoring the plummeting 1,500-meter slide behind him, he swung his ice axe into the glistening face of the black rock. Shoving his jumar ahead on the dubious fixed line, he forced his leaden-weighted legs to take another step upward.

It was one meter at a time, picking a zigzagging course up the side of the icy wall until he finally reached the top where he plopped heavily upon the ground exhausted. As he sat trying to catch his wind, of which there never seemed to be enough, he gazed out over the clouds stretching over the Himalayan range. Poking through them, were the towering spires of Ama Dablam, Nuptse, Lhotse, Makalu, and Kangchenjunga. To his right was the south summit of Everest. He stared at the frozen ridge for some time, where he'd buried Pasang years ago, as he waited for his team to join him.

To this point, Frank had shunned his bottled oxygen, but he wasn't in his forties anymore, nor had he summited in the last eight years; his aching body was now making him well aware of this fact. He wiggled out of his pack straps and let the heavy bundle flop down beside him. As he pulled his bottled oxygen and regulator out, Sully's bright red hood popped up over the edge of the buttress. He glanced up as the Irishman pulled himself over and flopped like a seal onto the crenulated rock surface. If he weren't so exhausted, he would've laughed.

Ten minutes later, Sherpa Yang-dzum, Sully, and Carlo were sitting beside him huffing and puffing as they peered out at the deepening blue sky on the horizon. Frank tapped Sully on the shoulder and pointed east up a gentle slope toward Camp 4. In the distance, a long line of men and women were trudging through the sculpted snow dunes. At last Frank stood, and dragging his pack up over his shoulder, clipped into the fixed rope and started off on the last leg of the day's march.

* * *

By the time the team came to Camp 4, it was after 2:00 PM. Frank eyed the throng of yellow tents scattered over the barren, undulating landscape. Beside each of the tents was a small stack of yellow and orange oxygen bottles. Downslope, men and women of the Winslow and Eckert Camps were putting the finishing touches on their bivouacs. Otherwise, Camp 4 was quiet. But soon, the early arriving expedition teams would be back from their summit attempts. In their absence, several large Gorak ravens were hopping about their tents, scavenging for food. Frank saw a bird snatch a candy wrapper and flit away. Then, to his surprise, he saw John Patterson pop out of a red Andersen tent. Frank blinked. What was he still doing here? Then he noticed the camp wasn't deserted at all. What was going on? Had the weather window suddenly closed, and if so, why hadn't Sangye radioed him before they left Camp 3?

Frank turned his oxygen off and dropped his pack to the ground. As soon as he was done pitching his tent and collecting snow for melting, he'd radio Sangye and find out why everyone was still there. He panned the gentle slopes beyond the blooming yellow and red tents. Real estate was at a premium, so there wasn't a lot of room. Bringing up the rear had its down side, indeed. As Sully and Carlo staggered over beside him, he pointed to a patch of jagged rubble above the Winslow encampment.

An hour later, Ke-tsum's team arrived and shortly afterward Da-wa's. The men unpacked, and before long had their domed, high altitude tents set up beside Frank's. As the nylon skins snapped under a fierce north wind, Frank went around, checking on his clients' health. The men were all haggard, Carlo and Toby especially so, but they seemed to be in good spirits. Greg gave him the thumbs-up. Satisfied, Frank crawled into his tent and radioed down to Sangye. As he waited for the Sherpa to reply, he set up his portable gas burner and started melting snow.

It didn't take long until a crackling burst of static came hissing back at him. Frank picked the radio up. Sangye's tiny voice was on the other end. "Base Camp to team 1, do you read? Over."

"Camp 4, here, over," Frank said, putting his ear close to the receiver. "What is the current weather status? Over."

After a short pause, Sangye said, "Jetstream 30 north, 90 east — wind 245/50 … Over."

The jet stream had suddenly moved back and was almost on top of Everest. *Damn*, Frank thought. He depressed the talk button. "When did it start moving? Over."

The radio crackled and hissed. Finally, Sangye said, "Started late last night. Didn't Chok-pa radio you? Other expeditions are all holding up at Camp 4. Over."

Tell me something I don't know. "No, he didn't. Where is he? Over."

"Don't know. Not see him since last night. Over."

Frank bristled. Chok-pa was already on secret probation with him for a prior dereliction of duty. "Never mind Chok-pa for right now. From now on, I want someone there around the clock. Understood? Over."

"Roger … over."

Suddenly Sarah's voice came crackling through. "I know how to read the forecasts."

Frank smiled despite his foul mood. "Thanks, Sarah. I know you want to help, but no. Sangye, what does tomorrow look like? Over."

"Hold on, over." Another pause, longer this time. "Jetstream 30 north, '90 east — wind 240/60. MS42. Over."

That meant a full day at Camp 4 before taking a shot at the summit, which wasn't so much an issue for Khum Jung Mountaineering as it was for the other expeditions who were already suffering a full day in the rarified air. A second day, oxygen or not, would levy a heavy toll on his climbers' failing bodies. Frank gritted his teeth. "What does Thursday look like? Over."

Several minutes passed, and Frank wondered if he had lost a connection. Finally, the radio hissed. "Jetstream 36 north, '96 east — wind 250/22. MS34. Over."

Much better, but for how long? He thought. "Okay, we'll shoot for Thursday, then. Over."

The radio crackled again. "Hello Frank, Sarah here. How is Greg?"

"He's good. Why? Hasn't he contacted you? Over?"

"Hasn't answered any of my messages."

Frank coughed. "When did you call up to him? Over."

"Last time was a couple hours ago," she said.

"Well, he was very busy right around then. You can try him now. Over."

"Oh, Okay. How are you?"

Frank dug a *Cup-a-Soup* out of his pack. He dropped a water purifier tab in the fresh snowmelt on the gas burner and dumped the contents of the packet in. As he sat back on his heels, he said, "Tired and hungry. And you? Over."

He heard her cough on the other end. "I'm fine."

Liar, he thought. "I'm going to tan your hide if you don't take care of yourself. Look, got to get a bit of rest here. Will talk more later. Over."

"Okay. And — please be careful."

"Roger. Night. Over." He powered the device off and lay back on his bag waiting for dinner to cook.

* * *

The following morning was blistering cold, but the wind had died down to twenty knots. The lull wouldn't last long though, and Frank knew it. He cooked himself a sparse breakfast of oatmeal and topped it off with a hunk of marzipan, then grabbed his small hand shovel and a snow bag. As he went out into the breath-taking air to gather snow for melting, he saw Da-wa and Ke-tsum along with their assistant Sherpas huddling up around their gear.

Da-wa glanced up as Frank approached. "You look like crap," the Sherpa said, and smiled.

Frank stepped beside the man and grumbled. "Dhan'yavāda hru Cheen. So, anything I need to know about?"

Da-wa looked off towards the *Balcony* and the south summit. "Not that I can think of." He got up and pulled Frank aside. "I heard about what happened yesterday down at Base Camp."

"Yeah, Chok-pa took a hike by the sounds of it. Sangye says he hasn't seen him since night before last." Frank said, glancing up at the wide plume of snow being blown off the mountain. He turned his gaze back onto his lead Sherpa. To a degree, he felt bad for the man. Da-wa had vouched for Chok-pa a couple years ago when Frank was looking for some Base Camp tent help.

"You gonna let him go?" Da-wa said.

Frank stared off. "He's not giving me a lot of choice, is he?" He shook his head. "I ... we ... need folks we can depend upon, Da-wa. We'll deal with it when we get back down the mountain. Right now, let's just take care of business, okay?"

The Sherpa nodded. "It's going to be a big rush up the mountain tomorrow. Lot of climbers all at once."

"Yeah, exactly what I'd hoped to avoid," Frank said, eyeing the Andersen encampment. Outside one of the red domed tents, he saw John looking over a small stack of oxygen bottles. Frank pressed his lips together and thought about going over to chat with the man about the present situation. Up until two years ago, Andersen and Khum Jung Mountaineering had shared intel regarding the weather up here. But the way things were between them now, chances were

John wouldn't be receptive to it. Still, when lives depended on it, people did what they had to.

He rolled the snow bag up in his hand and gritting his teeth, handed Da-wa his shovel and bag. "Be right back."

As he approached the Andersen Expedition tents, John turned around and gave Frank the once up and down. "Didn't expect to see your sorry ass up here," he said, putting his hands on hips.

"Thought I'd give it another go," Frank replied, looking back at the smirk on the man's hatchet-like face. "Interested in trading a little info?"

John glanced away and spat. "Sure, why not?"

Frank ran his numbers by him, and said, "What do you have?"

John adjusted his baseball cap as the wind dashed his long hair over his up-turned collar. "Pretty much the same thing." He spat again, and looked around at the gathered array of tents blooming on the windswept saddle. "Gonna be a big fucking traffic jam up there tomorrow morning."

"Yeah, it's an accident waiting to happen. What about your teams?"

John frowned. "What about 'em?"

"They doing okay?"

"Most of them," John said, crossing his arms. He grinned. "By the way, I heard that little siren of yours is manning your tent."

Frank dismissed the innuendo and the leering tone in John's voice. "Not manning it, just helping out. So, what time you thinking on leaving tonight?" Frank said.

"'Round ten-thirty, give or take," John said, turning his back to Frank. He squatted down next to his oxygen bottles, and as he checked their seals, said over his shoulder, "Gotta beat the crowds, ya know. What time you heading out, last as usual?"

"That's the plan."

John chuckled and looked back up at Frank. "You know, one of these days, you're gonna get your ass kicked playing that game. Not that you're gonna be playing it all that much longer."

Frank let the veiled threat pass. "Well, I better get back." He paused then added, "In case we don't see each other again, good luck."

"Luck has nothing to do with it," John muttered, turning back to the oxygen bottles. However, as Frank started away, the man coughed and said, "Hey, quick FYI; they roped the south side of the ridge, so we'll be on the rocks."

Which meant the north side where Frank had laid Pasang and Steve Madden's bodies to rest was snow heavy and ripe for an avalanche. Frank waved back to him. "Thanks."

"Don't mention it," John said, "and by the way, good luck to you, too."

* * *

Frank geared up at midnight and joined Da-wa, Carlo, and Sully outside of their tents under the glittering stars. Low in the northwestern sky was a pale-pink sickle moon that pierced the sable blanket covering the world. A bone chilling northerly wind lashing the South Col was penetrating right through his down jacket and insulated gloves. Frank eyed Toby, Jacob, and Vicq. They were standing a few meters away. The narrow white beams of their head-lanterns were spraying outward into the inky darkness. Beside them, Greg and Lanzo were crouched down and going over their gear one last time.

Frank scanned the desolate field hidden in darkness. Heard the thwapping of the shivering yellow and red tents. The camp just below the *land of the spirits* was empty save for the Khum Jung Mountaineering teams. High above them was a long jagged line of flickering lights crawling up the mountainside. The tail end of it had left the South Col over half an hour ago. The rush to the summit was on. But Frank was in no great hurry. The forecasts Sangye radioed up five hours ago noted the weather window would last well into tomorrow night and maybe even into the next day. Of course a forecast was exactly was it was: a prediction, not a certainty.

He glanced over at Greg as the frigid air bit at his face and entertained switching teams with Da-wa once again. But he'd been leading Sully and Carlo since Camp 2 and the men had come to trust him, just as Greg and Lanzo had come to trust Da-wa. You didn't switch off at the last minute without a powerful reason. It was probably for the best, he tried to convince himself. But down deep, he felt remorse at not doing the right thing back when he'd had the chance. At last, he fixed his oxygen mask to his face, and with Sherpa Yang-dzum, Sully and Carlo in tow, he started off into the night.

Fifty meters later, Frank was climbing a snow packed trail up the steep triangular face of the mountain. With no one in front of him, he set a steady determined pace through the darkness that would put his team at the Balcony in about two and a half hours. He marched ever upward into the endless night, shining his light on the narrow trail cutting through the snow pack. As he went, the ghostly images of Lhotse and Makalu could be seen in the moonlit distance. Two hours later, the punishing wind died down but the bitter cold was unrelenting, robbing his body of strength with every step. He halted only to switch his 'biner and jumar over, which was no easy task in the dark with thick, heavy gloves. Behind him, Sully and Carlo came on with Sherpa Yang-dzum. Frank turned and pointed to a gathering of tiny lights pricking the darkness high above on the mountain. There, on the Balcony, they would swap their oxygen bottles, take a brief rest and eat a meager meal. More importantly, they would replenish their dehydrated bodies with as much hot tea as they could drink.

Frank checked the valve on his regulator, bumped the flow up a notch to three bars and started back off. As he slid the jumar along the fixed line, he melded in with the pristine world around him and became oblivious to his complaining body and the mind-numbing headache that had tortured him over the last two days. It was just him and pure nothingness as he climbed, and what had only felt like mere minutes, suddenly turned into another two hours that left him standing on the rocky shelf 8,400 meters above the world.

Chapter 24

The Balcony — 4:15 AM

Frank sat munching on a stick of salami as Sherpa Yang-dzum came up follow-ing behind Sully and Carlo. Frank eyed the Italian. The man looked spent as he plopped down on the rocks beside him. As Carlo rocked back and forth, huffing and puffing, Frank said, "You gonna make it?"

Carlo looked up, and stared at Frank for a long moment under the bright spray of his head-lantern. Finally, the man pulled his oxygen mask away from his face and shook his head. "I am … nothing left."

Frank nodded. "No shame in stopping now." He pointed to the man's water bottle. "Take a drink and rest. Yang-dzum will take you back down when you're ready." Frank turned to Sully, who had just pulled his oxygen mask off. "How you doing?"

Sully nodded as he shut the valve off on his oxygen, then removed his pack and sat across from Frank with his head between his knees. Sherpa Yang-dzum joined him. No one said anything as they drank from their water bottles and forced their meals down. As they did so, Frank peered down at the bobbing lights of his other two teams that were strung out along the mountainside. They'd be up on the tiny shelf of rock in twenty minutes, give or take, but he and Sully would be long gone by then. He took another gulp of tea and polished off the last of his salami and cheese. Finally, he said to Sully, "We'll take five more, then gear up. How's your hands and feet? Warm enough?"

Sully stretched his arms out and flexed his fingers inside his gloves. "I'm good."

Frank nodded then dug into his pack and pulled out a fresh oxygen bottle. As he switched out tanks, he glanced at Carlo. The man had removed his mask to eat and was struggling to sit upright. Frank tapped him on the arm. "Hey, why don't you start heading back down now?"

Carlo swallowed hard and took a deep breath. Frank shot Sherpa Yang-dzum a knowing glance, and a moment later the Sherpa had Carlo's oxygen bottle switched out. As the guide helped Carlo back into his mask, Frank held up four fingers. The Sherpa nodded and went about setting Carlo's regulator valve to four bars.

The increased oxygen flow perked the Italian up, but it wouldn't last for long nor was it wise to keep the level up that high for any prolonged duration. Frank stood up as Carlo got to his feet. "Have a safe trip down," Frank said, patting the man's shoulder.

Carlo wrapped his hand around Frank's arm, gave it a firm squeeze and drew the sign of the cross over Frank's down jacket. Then returning the pat on the shoulder back to Frank, he turned around and started back down with Sherpa Yang-dzum following close behind.

As Sully geared up, Frank watched the Italian retreat into the cold darkness of Everest. He had been rooting for Carlo to make it to the top, but it wasn't to be. The good thing was, the man knew his limitations, an asset which Frank respected the most in any climber. Finally, Frank turned back to the task ahead. For the next six to eight hours, he and Sully would be tested to the limits of human endurance. Fitting his mask to his face, he turned the valve to three bars and continued his climb up into the breathless domain of the *land of spirits*.

* * *

Base Camp — 6:10 AM

Sarah felt a hand on her shoulder and started out of a restless sleep. She bolted upright in her chair, disoriented and jittery to find Sangye standing beside her. Rubbing her eyes she stretched aching muscles from a long night bent over a table in the command tent with her head buried in her arms. "What time is it?" she said as Sangye set a cup of hot chocolate on the table in front of her.

"Quarter after six," the Sherpa said. "You hungry? I can make you porridge, oatmeal, or perhaps you like an egg?"

Sarah shook her head and coughed several times. "No, the hot chocolate will be fine," she said, dragging the warm mug into her hands. "Any news from Greg or Frank?"

Sangye sat down in front of the base station laptop and booted the computer up. "No news. They okay, don't worry," he said.

Sarah eyed him. As if she could put away her fears just like that. It was like asking her to hold her breath for the next three days until they were all down. She coughed again. "So, where do you think they are right now?" she rasped.

"Hmm … probably nearing south summit now. Maybe passed it. Hard to know. Sure you don't want anything to eat?"

"Quite sure," Sarah answered and drank a gulp of her hot chocolate. "They will radio down once they've reached the summit, right?"

"Ho. Maybe also at the Hillary Step." The Sherpa bent forward toward the open window on the laptop screen and sat back in his chair with a frown.

"What's wrong?" Sarah said.

Sangye didn't answer back though. He grabbed the mike on the base radio. "Base Camp to team 1. Frank you there? Over."

Sarah felt her heart jump as the radio receiver crackled and hissed. "Sangye, what's wrong?" She repeated.

The Sherpa turned back to her. "Jet stream moving back toward summit. Window close a little bit. Nothing serious, though. They still have plenty of time, but Frank need to know all same."

Suddenly, Frank's voice came back. "This is Frank. What's up, Sangye? Over."

"Window update. Jet stream, moving toward summit. What is estimated time back to Camp 4? Over."

There was a long moment of static. Finally, Frank said, "Should be back there around 4:00 PM at the latest. Why? What's happening with the jet stream? Over."

Sangye studied the data on the screen. "Latest forecast say jet stream will be over summit around 1930 hours tonight. Wind will be picking up to 230/45 by 2200 hours. Temp dropping to MS45 at FL270. Over."

"Roger. What is FL260? Over?"

"235/30. MS35. Going to be cold one up there tonight."

"Roger that. Over."

Sarah nibbled her lip. The numbers Sangye reported to Frank meant a blizzard was on the way to the mountaintop. That Frank didn't sound worried was of little comfort to her though. An image of him and her son staggering aimlessly along a narrow ridge through a gale of windblown snow flashed before her. She leaned forward, tapped Sangye on the shoulder and motioned to the mike in his hand. When he handed it to her, she coughed and said, "Frank, Sarah here. You're sure you'll all be back by five? Over."

"Yes, dear, we'll be back. You taking care of that cough? Over."

"Yes. Wearing my mask every night. Don't worry about me. I spoke with Greg earlier. He said he met up with Carlo and Toby. I guess they're heading back down. Over."

There was a moment of static before Frank answered. "That's news to me. Carlo, I knew about, but not Toby and Greg. Over."

Suddenly, Greg's voice came over the radio. "No, just Carlo and Toby are heading down. I'm still here. Over."

"Sorry, meant to say just the two of them," Sarah said. "How are you doing, Greg? Over."

"Doing fine. Can't talk right now though. On my way to south summit. Need to keep moving. Talk later. Over." Greg said.

"Okay. Look forward to hearing from you. Be careful. Over."

The radio hissed and crackled for several minutes. Finally, Frank's voice came back over it. "Sangye, any sign of Chok-pa?"

"No, he never come back. Over," Sangye said taking back the mike from Sarah.

"Okay. Guess you're just going to have to deal with being short-handed down there."

Sarah bent close to Sangye and spoke into the mike. "I'm here. What can I do? Over."

Another moment of static followed. Finally, Frank said, "You're bound and determined to be hired, aren't you? Okay. Keep me posted every thirty minutes from here on out. I want to know what folks are doing up here. Oh, and Sarah, if you think you're on the payroll now, think again. Over."

Despite feeling anxious, Sarah felt a smile come to her face. "No problem. I'm only interested in the bennies." She sensed Frank smiling on the other end. "Be careful. Will radio you back in fifteen. Over."

"Roger that. Over."

* * *

South Summit — 7:05 AM

The sun blazed down on the south summit as Frank picked his steps along the rocky south face of the ridge. A little ways ahead and over the other side was where Pasang and Steve Madden had fallen in the drifting snows of Everest. It seemed like an age ago to him now as he jumared along the fixed line. Coming to a halt, then for several minutes he eyed the jagged ridge that cradled their bodies under a blanket of snow. There, in the buffeting winds, an image of Pasang standing on the summit looking out over the world flashed before him. Though he had never been with the Sherpa on a summit bid, this image was how he preferred to remember him; triumphant and proud. Sully, who was following close behind, tapped him on the shoulder.

"Something wrong?"

Frank shook his head. "No, just taking a breather." He swung his arm out over the panoramic mountain range swimming in a sea of white rippled clouds. "Quite a sight, isn't it?"

Sully nodded. "Magnificent."

Frank turned to him. "How you doing?"

"Good, if you can call having your head squeezed like a grape, good."

Frank smiled. "It'll get worse, but it's worth it in the end. How's your O2?"

Sully checked his gauge and gave Frank the thumbs up. Frank nodded and turning back to the fixed line beside him, switched his carabiner and jumar over to the next link of the rope. As he did so, he checked the piton wedged in between the rocks. It wasn't as secure as he would've liked so he dug into his pack and pulled a hammer out. Giving the spike a couple of firm slugs and driving it deeper into the crack, he continued onward.

An hour later, he came to the foot of the Hillary Step and eyed the line of climbers waiting their turn to jumar up the face of the steep narrow slope of piled boulders. On either side of the step, was a 2,000-meter plummet. At sea level, this bump on the mountain was mere child's play, but up at 8,760 meters it would test his exhausted body suffering from the frigid temps and blustering winds. He checked the time. It was 7:10 AM. With any luck, he'd have Sully standing on top of the world in another hour and change. Ke-tsum's team was an hour behind him and Da-wa's team another thirty minutes behind Ke-tsum. Plenty of time for all to get back before the weather window started to slide shut.

At last, he took a couple of deep breaths and slogged ahead to the last of the weary climbers. As he joined in with the line, he discovered one of them was John Patterson. Frank blinked and looked again, wondering if he was seeing straight. Coming up from the Balcony, he hadn't paid much attention to those he passed going back down, but now that he thought about it, he hadn't seen the Andersen Expedition leader. He watched the man looking up at a struggling climber in the breath-taking cold.

At length, Frank pulled his radio out and switching it to all channels, removed his mask and said, "John, Frank here. Do you copy? Over."

The man turned and looked back at him. As usual, John was climbing without oxygen. He pulled his radio out, fumbled with the dial and brought it to his mouth. "Copy. See you finally arrived. Over."

"You know me. I like to make a statement," Frank said. "Figured you'd be on your way back down by now. Over"

Frank saw John shake his head. "Me, too." He peered up at the struggling climber. "She's a real trooper, but the last 500 meters of the mountain has been a killer for her." He pulled his radio away from his mouth. "Doing great, Darcy, just a few more steps and you'll be there." Bringing the radio back, he continued, "I trust you're not going to push us here? Over."

"No rush. By the way, you heard about the window closing down sooner than expected, right? Over."

"Yeah, just got the news. Shouldn't be an issue. You're it coming up the mountain, right? Over."

Frank coughed. "Far as I know. Have a couple teams following along that should be here in about an hour. Over."

"Roger that. Good luck. Talk later."

The channel went static, so Frank switched back to Khum Jung's frequency. "Frank to Base Camp. Status report, please. Over."

As he waited for Sangye or Sarah to respond, he watched the struggling climber finally reach the top of the step. Once she was clear, a slow procession of climbers moved up after her one at a time. Finally, Sarah's voice came over the radio. "Hi, Frank. Sarah here. Window is still holding as of last report thirty minutes ago. Waiting for update. Where are you right now? Over."

"Hillary Step. Should make the summit in an hour or so. Have you spoken with the other teams? Over."

"Yes. Everyone is doing fine. Over."

"Okay. I want that report as soon as you have it in your hand. Over."

"Will do, dear. Over."

Frank smiled at the endearment. He knew she was trying to keep a lid on her fears. As the line started moving in front of him, he said, "Okay, back at it. Over."

* * *

Base Camp — 7:33 AM

Sarah studied the data on the laptop screen with Sangye. The jet stream was moving toward the summit quicker than anyone could've guessed a day ago. At its present rate, it would be on top of the Monster between 4:30 and 5:30 PM. Another thirty to sixty minutes was being sliced off the window. She knew Greg was forty-five minutes to an hour behind Frank, which meant that if everything went right for her son in his climb, he wouldn't be back to Camp 4 until just before 3:30 PM. Things were getting just a little bit too tight for her comfort, not that she had ever felt comfortable with this whole odyssey to begin with. Her stomach tightened as she looked at Sangye.

"Are you sure they can make it back to Camp 4 in time?" she said.

Sangye glanced at her. "First, let's talk to Frank." He picked up the receiver. "Base Camp to team 1. Over."

The radio hissed a moment before Frank's raspy voice came crackling back. "This is Frank. Over."

"Weather window update. Jet stream will be over summit between 1630 and 1730 hours. Wind steady at 233/35, MS30 at FL270. What you think? Over."

There was a long pause. Finally, Frank said, "Things are definitely tightening up. Let me check with Da-wa and see where he's at. Over."

Sangye sat back and turned a confident expression onto Sarah. "Frank not take chances. If he worried, he'll tell Da-wa to turn things around. But I think if Da-wa near Hillary Step should be no problem."

Suddenly they heard Frank's voice calling to team 3 over the radio. "Da-wa, what's your position? Over."

There was a long pause. Finally, Da-wa's voice broke the static. "Fifteen minutes to Hillary Step. What is traffic like up there? Over."

"Not bad, maybe thirty ahead of us," Frank answered. "Just got a report from Sangye. Window is shutting down quicker than we thought. Need to get back to Camp 4 by 3:30. Can you make it by then? Over."

"Should be no problem. No one on Step right now. Over," Da-wa said.

"Okay, roger that. Over," Frank said then continued, "Sangye, moving ahead for right now. Team 3 should make the summit by 9:30. With no one to fight going down Hillary Step, they should make Camp 4 by 3:30 easy. Over."

Sarah nibbled her lip and taking the receiver from Sangye, coughed and said, "Frank, are you sure? Over."

"Don't worry, Sarah," Frank said. "I won't take chances. As long as the window remains where it is right now, no one should have a problem getting down. Over."

Sarah's voice cracked and her words came out in a hoarse rasp. "Okay, you know best. Over."

"You better have your mask on or I'm gonna paddle your butt when I get back down there," Frank said. "All right, need to move on now. Will call back when we reach the summit. Over."

But Sarah didn't have her mask on. When Sangye shot her a smile, she put her finger up and stared defiantly at him. "Don't even think about tattling on me." She pushed her chair back and forgetting about her ankle, got up. "Oww … Shit, that hurt."

"You okay?" Sangye said hopping up beside her.

Sarah grimaced. "Yeah, I'm fine," she lied. "I need a drink of something hot. Where do you keep that awful stuff you call hot chocolate?"

* * *

Everest Summit — 8:16 AM

Frank trudged beside the snow packed knife-edge gripping the fixed line. For the last hour, it had been a steady steep climb along the bare rock face leading up to the summit. Below him was a world cloaked in ice, snow, and clouds for miles on end out to the distant brown steppes leading up to the Himalayan range. Above was a deep blue sky with a molten sun that was showering the desolate summit. He stepped over a jagged rock caked with snow and switched his 'biner and jumar over onto the last hundred meters of fixed line. Ahead, a tangled array of prayer flags streamed out in the swirling wind strafing the top of the world. He took a couple of deep breaths of his oxygen and checked on Sully who was a couple meters behind. The Irishman had his head down, focused on his next step.

Frank turned back to the summit and slid his jumar along the rope. His last hurdle, which was to pull himself up onto the snow laden northern slope, was directly ahead. He dug his crampons into the precarious rock underfoot, and as he put his weight down, felt his foot lurch to one side for an instant before grabbing hold of solid ground. The final push to the summit along the southern face of the ridge had been like walking on marbles since leaving the Balcony three and a-half hours ago. Catching a stolen breath, he moved on and a moment later was scrambling up and over the serrated edge of the ridge. There he met a trodden path through a smooth, sloping plane of snow that overlooked the Tibetan landscape 4,000 meters below.

Again, he took a deep breath and waited for Sully to join him. Fifty meters or so ahead was a joyous group of tired mountaineers snapping photos of each other and raising their arms in triumph. Frank smiled, slapped Sully on the back and struck off toward them. This brief moment of seeing a client realize a dream was magic for him and he wanted it to last as long as possible so he took his time and slowly marched ahead, counting down the minutes until at last there was nowhere else to go but down.

As he waited a couple meters away for the celebrating group to give up their claim to the summit, Frank pulled his mask off and pointed out the great sister peaks bowing to the king below. Poking up through the clouds a hundred and twenty kilometers to the east stood the gleaming three-sided spike of Annapurna and closer-by, the gray, four-sided pyramid of Makalu. To the west, the jagged white crowns of Nuptse and Lhotse and the bleached bunion of Cho Oyu waded in a silvery mist that flooded the Sagarmatha valleys far below. Everywhere he looked, Frank found the simply purity of what it meant to be alive and breathing in the clean cold air.

Finally, the group at the summit departed, and with them went John and a very happy, if not exhausted client, Darcy. Frank watched them walk away, and saw the hidden goodness in the expedition leader's heart that the conglomerate that owned Andersen Expeditions had yet to touch. But it was getting close and it wouldn't be long until the powerful money machine that ran Andersen would own the mountaineer's heart. But this moment was for Sully, so Frank dashed the thought away and together they claimed the summit.

Frank pulled out his camera and snapped a few pictures of Sully sitting among flapping prayer flags, and a couple more with Nuptse and Cho Oyu in the background. Then, as Sully snapped some photos of his own, Frank radioed down to Base Camp.

"Team 1 to Base Camp. Over."

"This is Base Camp. Over," said Sangye on the other end.

"Base Camp, team 1 has arrived at the summit, and it is beautiful. Over," Frank rasped as his hood fluttered around his face.

"Wonderful!" Sarah said. "Sherpa Dave said he's less than an hour away from you. Over."

"I assume the window is holding stable? Over," Frank said.

There was a short pause. Finally the radio hissed. "So far, yes. Next report is coming in shortly. We'll let you know as soon as we get it. Over."

"Roger that. Okay, heading down in five. Over."

Chapter 25

"Team 3 to Base Camp, over."

Sarah dash-hopped over to the laptop and grabbed the receiver. "Greg! Where are you? Over."

"We're here, and it's fantastic! I can't tell you how awesome it is. I can see forever up here. Over," he said.

"How are you feeling? Over," Sarah said, sitting down.

"Great!" Static filled the silence of the command tent for a moment. "We're the last in line, so have the top all to ourselves for a bit. Lanzo says to say, hi. Over."

Sarah smiled, happy for her son, yet anxious for him to start getting down. "You heard about the window closing sooner than we thought, right? Over."

"Yeah, we heard. Gonna hang up here for a few, then start down. Got to get that Kodak moment! Over."

"Right. But don't stay there too long. Over."

"You worry too much, Mom. But no, we won't linger. Over."

There was a long pause and Sarah wondered if he had signed off. At last, Greg said, "It was weird passing the south summit knowing Dad is up there."

Sarah's heart skipped. She knew what it meant to him to be up where his father had passed away so long ago. Wishing she could be there to put her arms around him, she said, "I know. Over."

There was another long pause. "Anyway, got to start working the camera. Talk soon. Over," Greg said, and once again static filled the command tent.

Sarah sat back in her chair as the faded memories of Steven flooded her thoughts. Her husband's face was but a vague image to her now and she could barely remember what his voice sounded like. Oddly enough, the anger she'd harbored all these years over his leaving her to die needlessly on this mountain wasn't there anymore. She didn't quite understand why she suddenly felt acceptance of what had happened, only that it had something to do with how she felt about Frank. God had brought him into her life, and through him, had opened up a part of her she thought was lost. She would treasure that and all the memories of the last three weeks for the rest of her life. The lock that had held her heart prisoner for so long, was finally open. Frank was right. Living in the moment was the important thing. And right now, that meant dealing with her fears of the impending storm threatening her son and the man she deeply cared about.

* * *

Balcony — 11:03 AM

Frank sat looking out over the vast Himalayan range, feeling good about Sully's success reaching the top. The others would be along soon and he looked forward to hearing about their experiences. For a while, he worried about Greg and his motives for climbing, but it all turned out well. He munched on a power bar as members from other teams sat around him. That John had ended up being one of them was due to his shepherding his female client, Darcy. Frank eyed him as the icy wind tugged the hood of his down jacket.

Suddenly, his radio crackled. "Da-wa to team 1, over."

Frank dug into his pack and took it out. "This is Frank. What's up? Over."

"American acting strange, not paying attention where he walking. Keeps looking over to north side of ridge. Over."

Frank frowned. *I hope you're not thinking what I think you are, Greg.*

Sarah's voice came rushing through the radio. "What's going on, Frank?"

Frank bit his lip. "Greg, come back. Over?"

The radio hissed in the icy wind. "I'm here. What's up? Over."

"I'd ask you the same thing. What's going on? Over." Frank said.

"Nothing. Over."

Really? Frank thought. "Then how come you're dogging it up there?"

"Wasn't aware I was," Greg said.

But Greg's reply seemed distracted to Frank, as if he was concentrating on something other than descending the mountain. "You don't have time to monkey around up there, Greg. Weather window is closing. You need to move along. Over."

"I am moving, don't worry."

"My job is to worry, Greg. I'm responsible for you. Over."

There was a long pause as Frank waited for his response. After several minutes passed, Frank radioed Da-wa. "Da-wa, what's he doing?" Over."

"Nothing. He stop. Looking down at the south summit."

Frank sighed. The one thing that concerned him most since Sarah told him about what Greg had said about his father was coming to pass. He stared up at the pale blue sky, and brought the radio back to his mouth. "Greg, listen to me, I know what you're looking for and you're not going to find it. You need to stop searching for him and come down now. Over."

"Greg, what are you doing?" Sarah's raspy voice cried through the radio. "Listen to Frank. You need to come down."

"I see him," Greg called out.

Frank heard the radio hiss then all of a sudden, Da-wa's voice could be heard calling to Greg. "Hey, what you doing? Don't go over there. Too much snow! You cause avalanche."

"Shit! Greg, listen to Da-wa," Frank said as sharply as he could. His throat burned from breathing in the frigid air and sent him into a coughing fit.

Sully who was sitting a little ways away, moved closer. "What's going on?"

Frank put his finger up to Sully as the static of the radio crackled in his ear. "Da-wa, talk to me! You there? Over."

"Ho. He unclip himself and went out on north ridge. Very bad place. Lots of snow. He crazy!" Da-wa cried.

Sarah's frantic voice wailed through the radio. "Greg! No!"

"Damn it," Frank growled. "Greg, listen to me. You need to come back and get clipped back in. It's not safe up there."

But all that came back was static and hissing. The last thing Frank wanted to do was invoke his cardinal rule; not with Sarah listening in on the other end, but he was running out of options. He gritted his teeth. "Greg, if you don't come back and start down, I'm going to tell Da-wa to leave you there and you will die. Is that what you want?"

"No! No! Frank, you've got to do something!" Sarah cried.

Frank could sense her tears and anguish on the other end. He caught his breath as his chest tightened. "Trying to!" To Greg, he said, "Your father isn't up there."

Sully tapped Frank on the shoulder. His face was ashen. "Jesus, Frank. You can't be serious," he said.

Greg's muffled voice crackled through the radio. "Yes, he is! I see him."

Frank was beside himself. What more could he say? He was running out of reasons. Again, he repeated himself. "Greg, you will die! Come down."

"What's going on?" John said, suddenly beside Frank. Frank looked up at the Andersen Leader who was staring down at him.

"One of our teammates is in trouble," Sully said.

Frank looked off toward the south summit knowing it was a lost cause trying to talk Greg out of searching for his father. If he had led the young man, none of this would be happening. It was his own damned fault. He had let his selfish need to keep Pasang's resting place secret to himself and now it was going to cost him. But he would try one more time. "Greg, this is the last time I'm going to say this. Turn around and come back down or I'm going to tell Da-wa to leave you. Over!"

Sarah's voice was wretched and small on the other end. "Greg, please listen to Frank."

Sully reached over and shouted into Frank's radio, "Greg, come back down. There will be other chances."

"Kid's come unglued, Frank," John said soberly. "Nothing you can do. Poor bastard."

"There's got to be something someone can do. We can't leave him there to die," Sully shouted back.

Frank said, "Da-wa, what's he doing now?"

"He digging in the snow," the Sherpa said.

"How far out on north ridge is he? Over," Frank said as a dark thought reared in his mind.

"Very far. Near north edge. He gonna cause avalanche!"

Frank sighed, suddenly knowing there was no talking Greg down. Whatever he thought he saw, it wasn't his father. Pasang and Steven weren't buried on the north side of the ridge. Frank looked upward and called to Greg one last time. When he didn't reply, Frank braced himself for Sarah's heart wrenching plea. "Da-wa, I want you to come down."

"No, no, no, you can't do that, you can't … please Frank," Sarah cried. "Please don't —"

"You sure?" Da-wa said. "He'll die up here. Over."

"Yes, I know," Frank rasped. "Start down."

A short pause followed. "Okay."

The sound of Sarah sobbing over the radio, pierced Frank's heart and his throat tightened.

"Frank, you just condemned him to die," Sully yelled.

"Don't you think I know that!" Frank growled, shoving the Irishman away.

John grabbed Sully by the shoulder. "There's nothing anyone can do about it, kid,"

"Frank, please, please do something!" Sarah cried. "Oh, my God, oh my God. Frank…"

Frank sat looking out over the world as he battled with his conscience. He had brought this upon himself and now he had to deal with it. *Damn it!* He stiffened his jaw and turned to the Irishman. "Sully, I want you to head down, now!"

The man eyed him defiantly. "No."

Frank bolted up. "I said, now! John, get him the hell down the mountain," Frank roared then went over and shoved another bottle of oxygen into his pack. He turned, looked up toward the south summit and clipped onto the line.

"Hey? What're you doing, Frank?" John Patterson said, marching up from behind.

"Going up to get him," Frank said over his shoulder.

"Frank, it's suicide," he argued. "Even if you find him and convince him to turn around, you'll be walking into a damned blizzard. You'll die right along with him."

"Well then, you'll have me off the mountain then, won't you?" Frank said, spinning around to face the Andersen leader.

John was speechless.

Frank turned back to the jagged ridge leading upward, and as he started up the line, he heard John tramping behind him. He stopped and was about to rip into the Andersen leader when he saw John clip in to the ropes. "What're you doing?"

"Coming with you."

"This isn't your problem, John."

"Maybe not, but I'm coming whether you like it or not. So, stop the grand-standing and let's get on with it!"

* * *

Base Camp — 11:43 PM

Sarah stared at the radio though tears, hardly realizing that Bob and Tashi had come into the command tent. Sangye stood near-by and was looking down pensively. The nightmare she feared was happening all over again, and it was needless. Visions of her son lying frozen in the snow tortured her as Bob squat-ted down next to her. Why was Greg doing this to her? And why wasn't anyone doing anything to stop it? She hated and adored both of the men who were up on the mountain and she didn't know what to do about it. Again, she picked the receiver up and shouted at Greg, begging him to start down before it was too late, but all she heard was hissing and crackling coming back.

Bob took the radio receiver from her. "There's still time, Sarah. I've known Frank for years. Believe me, he doesn't give up easily."

"But they've stopped talking," Sarah cried, although her voice was no more than a hoarse whisper. She coughed and wiped her eyes with the sleeve of her jacket. Her world was crashing around her. Everything she had feared was happening and there wasn't a damn thing she could do about it. She slammed her fist down on the table. "Frank, you bastard! I thought you were different. I thought you had a heart." She got up and stalked out of the tent. Looking up at the streaking gray clouds, she collapsed to her knees. "Dear God, why are you doing this to me? What do you want? Wasn't taking Steven enough? I'll give you whatever you want. Just don't take my son from me," she cried, choking on her words.

A hand settled on her shoulder and she turned to see Tashi standing beside her. The lama gazed down at her compassionately. She expected him to reel off some trite Buddhist parable, but he said nothing. Instead, he sat down beside her and looked off into the bleak horizon as a numbing sensation of losing her only child blanketed her. They sat there for some time, until Bob came out and squatted beside her.

"Sarah, I'm sorry," he said.

The medic's words of comfort were only babble in her ears. She eyed him and as she did so, heard Sangye working the radio inside. "Base Camp to Frank. Over. Frank, you there? Over. Come back Frank. Over." Several minutes passed before he repeated the call. But there was no reply. Finally, the Sherpa, said, "This is Khum Jung Base Camp. Anyone out there, come back."

A moment later, a voice came crackling through. "This is Da-wa. Over."

Sarah's ears pricked.

"Da-wa, what's going on up there? Over." Sangye said.

"Team 1 in trouble. American stuck at south summit. Altitude sickness. Frank go to get him."

Sarah's heart leapt and she jumped to her feet. As she bolted back into the tent, Bob and Tashi followed.

Bob took the mike from Sangye. "When, how long ago? Over,"

"Don't know. Passed him and John Patterson on way down."

Bob blinked. "Say again. John Patterson? Over."

"Ho."

"I'll be damned," Bob muttered.

God had answered her prayer. Frank was a man of heart. How could she ever have doubted him? She felt embarrassed and guilty as hope welled inside her.

Someone behind her said, "I thought they didn't like each other."

"They don't," Bob muttered. "But I guess they put aside their war for the moment.

* * *

South Summit — 1:45 PM

Frank trudged up the steep rocky slope leading to the south summit with John following close behind. They had been climbing up the limestone face for the last hour at a brisk pace. He stopped, gasping for air and looked to the snow-laden ridge. His anger toward Greg he would deal with later. Right now, time was slipping away and he and John still had a solid thirty-minute hike ahead of them. Hopefully, Greg was still in the vicinity where Da-wa had left him and hadn't taken a tumble over the north face of the mountain.

Frank checked the piton that was hammered into the rock face and switched his 'biner and jumar over onto the fixed line. His lungs screamed for air and every muscle in his body ached. But there was no time to rest. Already, he could feel the wind picking up, and in the distance saw clouds gathering in the deep blue sky. He brought his oxygen mask to his weather-beaten face. Turning the valve on, he drew a couple deep breaths before shutting it down to conserve what little remained.

Ten minutes later, Da-wa's voice came crackling through the radio clipped to his harness. After filling him in on the weather at Camp 4, Frank calculated they had a little less than three hours before the brewing tempest hit the mountain. Even under the best scenario of finding Greg right off and convincing him to start moving down the mountain, they would just make the Balcony when the storm hit. Depending on the severity of the weather that meant a three-hour descent through blinding snow and pummeling winds. But he knew that when he started off after Sarah's son. What surprised him was John's tagging along. Even though there was bad blood between them, the man was risking his life for him. It confirmed what he'd always believed about the man. If nothing else, John was a man of integrity when it came down to things that really mattered. Frank would not forget that.

At length, the south summit appeared before him and he climbed up onto the jagged point and scanned the sweeping snow-laden northern slope running down to the distant Tibetan plain. As John stepped beside him, Frank saw a bright orange figure clinging to a small rock near the north face fifty meters down ridge of them.

John pulled his mask away and said, "Holy shit! What the hell … was he thinking? That snow-pack … can give way … any minute. He has HACE … I'm telling ya, Frank. We tried. No one … can blame you. Let him go … and let's get down."

Frank surveyed the situation. He didn't know what to think, but he would not give up until he knew for sure. He strode down the ridge with John following behind until he was adjacent to Greg. The man was fifteen meters away, sitting in knee-deep snow near the edge of the north rim. Stripping his mask off, Frank turned to John. "How long … a line do you have?"

"What?" John said.

Frank huffed. "How long … a line?"

John shrugged. "Twenty-five feet."

Frank had a ten-meter line in his pack. Between the two of them, they had perhaps just enough. He reached into his pack and took out his length of nylon rope. "We'll daisy-chain 'em."

John frowned. "Are you nuts?" He paused; catching his breath, then went on. "If that ridge gives away, no line is gonna save you. Give it up!"

Frank took several deep breaths. "Look, … I never asked you … to come. If you wanna leave, … be my guest, but I'm gonna … gonna give him the benefit of a … of the doubt."

John shook his head, but pulled out his rope and handed it to Frank. As John tied the line off onto the piton holding the fixed lines, Frank braided the two lines together. John said, "You sure … about this?"

Frank eyed the man a moment knowing John was right. It was insane, but going back and leaving Greg to die was not an option. At last, he nodded and slowly stepped out onto the tenuous snow pack. Ten minutes later, he was but five meters away from Greg when a surging crack opened up in the sculpted drift. As it ran several meters in both directions, Frank's heart drummed in his ears. If he made one wrong move, Greg and he would both end up dead, fixed line or not. Frank tugged the rope, checking its grip on the piton John was watching over and said, "Greg, it's Frank … don't move, okay?"

Greg turned and stared back at him. His oxygen mask had been pulled away from his face and there was a vacant look in his eyes. Frank sighed. But then, Greg said, "I thought … it was him. I … really did. I'm … sorry. I fucked up."

"Happens … don't worry about it," Frank lied. He brought his mask to his face and took a couple deep breaths. Pulling it away, he continued, "Right now … only thing … matters is getting … getting you down." Frank drew a couple more breaths of oxygen. "Gonna throw you a line. Want you to clip onto it … and slowly get back up."

"I'm wasted. Got nothing left … leave me," Greg said.

Frank coughed. "No! I will not … let you die. Grab the line when I throw it … damn it." Frank coiled what was left of the rope in his hand and tossed it out. "Grab it!"

Greg stared at the rope, which was centimeters from him and as he did so, Frank could see him turning dark thoughts over in his head.

"Grab … the damn rope!" Frank shouted.

As life hung in the balance between them, Sarah's face flashed before Frank. He closed his eyes willing Greg to take the rope and as he did so, prepared for the worst until at last, he felt the rope grow taut in his hand. He blinked and seeing Greg tying himself on, smiled.

"All right … try and step … into the same footsteps you took getting out here," Frank said. "Real slow."

As Greg stood and took his first step, Frank held his breath and leaned back, bracing himself in the snow-pack. When the ridge held, Frank took a step back and waited for Greg to step ahead. As the men did the slow, methodical dance three meters apart toward the fixed ropes, the cracks in the snow drift grew longer and the gaps wider. Frank's muscles tensed with each step. *Just a few more meters*, he thought. *Don't rush it.*

Suddenly Greg stopped. "The ground's moving," he cried.

"Run, God damn it," John shouted from behind them.

Greg sprang forward as the drift undulated behind him. Suddenly, snow sky-rocketed up into the air. As the ground slid away under their feet, Frank saw John grab the nylon line. The man wrapped a figure-eight loop around his ice axe and plunged the pointed handle of the tool into the ground.

As the drift sloughed away from under him, Frank gripped the line. He didn't know what was up or down or where Greg was. All he could see was a white world until at last everything went still. He looked up, coughed, and saw the blue sky soaring above.

"Frank, you alright?"

As John's face hovered above him, Frank gasped. "Yeah. Greg?"

John nodded. "He's ... okay. That was ... fucking ... close. Jesus!"

Frank grimaced. "Yeah ... Help me up ... and let's ... get the hell out ... of here."

* * *

Base Camp — 1:55 PM

Sarah looked at her watch as she sat next to Bob at the base station radio. It had been almost an hour-and-a-half since the last contact with Frank. Despite Bob saying that they were probably concentrating on getting up the mountain, she couldn't understand why they hadn't called down at least once.

"Shouldn't they be there by now?" she said.

Bob pressed his lips together, and she could feel his reluctance to answer her. Finally, he said, "Or very near it, anyway. Be patient, we don't know what's going on."

Sarah gritted her teeth and coughed. "I've been patient! I'm tired of waiting. I need to know what's going on," she said. She picked up the microphone. "Base Camp to Frank. Over." The radio hissed, filling the indifferent silence in the tent for several minutes. Sarah called again, but there was no reply. She looked upward and as she did so, she felt Bob put his hand over hers and gently pry the microphone out of her hand.

Bob said, "Sarah, you're exhausted. Take a break. I had Sangye bring your pad over. Go lay down."

She snuffed and looked at the tall, dark-haired medic as the weight of the last thirteen hours crushed down on her. Her head felt like it was going to explode and her heart burned in her chest. "I'm alright," she lied.

Suddenly, the radio crackled. Sarah jumped. "Base Camp — do you read? Over," said a faint voice on the other end.

"This is Base Camp," Bob replied. "Who's this? Over."

There was a long hiss until finally, the voice came back. "John Patterson … we found the American … We're on our way down. Over."

"Roger that, John," Bob said. He glanced at Sarah guardedly and continued, "Everyone okay? Over."

Several moments of static followed. Finally, John said, "For the time being … yes. Status … on window, please."

Tears flooded Sarah's eyes and she buried her face in her hands as Sangye brought the laptop over. "Still same," the Sherpa said. "Jet stream directly over mountain at 1630 hours, wind at 245/35, MS20 at FL260. Better hurry."

Bob grabbed the microphone back. "Is Frank there? Over."

"Affirmative," John said.

"Can you put him on? Over," Bob said.

"Hold on."

There was a long pause. Finally, Frank's voice came back. "Yes, Bob."

"How you feeling? Over."

The radio hissed a moment. "Like crap — but okay."

"What's your O2 look like? Over," Bob said.

"Six-hundred … liters," Frank said.

Bob's face darkened. "Six-hundred? You sure about that?"

"Affirmative. Climbed without — to preserve tank … for trip down," Frank said.

Bob looked away, and Sarah got the distinct feeling it was to avoid her seeing his expression. But it didn't matter. She knew exactly what the medic was thinking regarding Frank's shunning of his oxygen. But she could only deal with one thing at a time. She grabbed the microphone from Bob and said, "Frank, is my son alright? Over."

There was a long pause that frightened her until finally, Frank answered, "He's good, Sarah … got to go now. Bob, keep us posted … on the window. Over."

Sarah closed her eyes in relief, then opened them and said, "Frank, can I talk with Greg? Over."

"Hold on." The sound of amplified wind filled the command tent. Finally, Greg's voice came crackling back. "Hi, Mom."

"Are you alright?"

"Yeah, I'm okay. Don't worry 'bout me… all right. Look … Frank says … we gotta get going."

Bob turned back and took the microphone. "Roger that. Tell Frank we'll keep him posted. Over."

"Okay, will do," Greg said.

Bob set the microphone down, sat back in his chair, letting out a long sigh and muttered, "May God be with them."

Sarah studied the medic's face as a new terror grew in her heart. The men's endurance; Greg's especially.

Chapter 26

Frank sat in the snow with his knees drawn up in front of him. Resting his elbows on top of them, he handed John the radio and leaned forward trying to draw breath. He was utterly exhausted and his lungs burned from inhaling the biting air. At last, he gathered his strength and slowly rose to his feet. Behind him, he heard John talking with his Andersen Base Camp team. Greg sat off to the side, his dull blue eyes staring out over the Western Cwm far below.

At length, Frank stood and brushed the snow off his jacket. As he fitted his oxygen mask to his face, he heard the telltale hiss of oxygen rushing out into the buffeting wind. He looked at the regulator and saw a crack in the housing. *Damn it!* With no way to repair it, the bottle would be empty long before he got back down. That left two bottles between the three of them, plus what little Greg had left in his. It was enough to get down, but still.

John stepped up beside Frank. "Problem with your mask?"

"Yeah … the regulator housing's cracked," Frank said. "Must have happened … when I fell."

John inspected it and shook his head. "It's toast." He called over to Greg. "Hey … how much you have left … in your bottle?"

Greg startled and looked back. "What? Oh, hold on." He reached up and detached the bottle from his shoulder strap. "Two-forty."

"That's an hour and change," John said. "I could live with that. Here … take mine. We'll give Greg … the spare we brought up."

Frank shook his head and coughed. "No way. You've done enough … You keep yours. I'll switch with Greg."

"Frank, I'm good … really," John protested.

But Frank waved him off. It was his decision to come back for Greg and he was damned if he was going to put John's life in anymore danger than it already was. He switched out bottles with Greg and stared the young man in the eye. "Now you need to get up ... and show me I didn't make a mistake coming back for you ... you hear?"

Greg nodded and slowly got to his feet.

Ten minutes later they were clipped into the fixed ropes and carefully picking their way along the rocky slope toward the Balcony that was an hour and a half away. As Frank led the way with John bringing up the rear, he glanced upward at a prominent snowy notch on the ridge. In it, below the heavy drift of snow, lay Pasang and Steve Madden. As he switched his carabiner over onto the next fixed line, he debated whether or not he should point it out to Greg, not because he wanted to keep it secret to himself anymore, but because it was both inaccessible and time was running out. Still, what was the point in keeping quiet about it? If they didn't make it back then all of this would come to nothing.

He brought his mask to his face and waved Greg up behind him. Pointing upward to a pair of egg-shaped rocks, he said, "Up there ... behind the boulder on the right ... is your father. I'll give you five ... then we need to get moving again."

John came tramping up and joined them. Removing his mask, he said, "What's up?"

Frank said, "His father lies up there. Just giving him a minute here."

John eyed Frank dubiously as Greg stared upward and Frank knew the reason. That someone had died on it and had not yet been discovered would be implausible to the Andersen Expedition leader. But it wasn't important whether John believed it or not so he remained quiet as Greg removed his mask and contemplated what he'd risked his life for. Could Frank say he would not have done the same? He eyed Sarah Madden's son who was staring longingly up at the ridge where his father, Steven, was buried in the snow and ice. It wasn't that many years ago that Frank had come upon Pasang and Steve lying frozen in the snow. The image of the ill-fated American climber lying across the lap of his Sherpa had been burned into Frank's mind and would never leave him. Finally, he tapped Greg on the arm. "Time to move on."

Greg nodded and an hour later they were within eyeshot of the Balcony, which was still an hour and a half away give or take. Frank eyed the fading blue sky and coughed. The wind was picking up and the temps were dropping.

Every step down the mountain was getting harder for him and his vision was clouding over. He raised his mask and took another short breath from Greg's oxygen bottle, which he'd taken for himself and turned the regulator valve back to one bar.

Focus, he thought. *One step at a time. Pay attention.* He flexed his fingers inside his gloves, and fumbling with his carabiner and jumar, switched them over onto the next fixed rope. Below him, thick clouds were gathering around the rocky and snow-laden slopes. Scattered snowflakes were dancing in the air, swirling and bobbing erratically in the eddying currents. Frank gritted his teeth, forcing his stiff and tired limbs to move and started back off down the treacherous slope with dogged determination. He knew the only way he was going to make it down to Camp 4 was to get mad-dog mean. But the over-riding purpose was in getting Greg down, otherwise the breaking of his cardinal rule would end up pointless.

By the time the three weary men trudged onto the Balcony the wind was gusting nearly to thirty knots and blowing gritty snow into their faces. John scavenged through the discarded oxygen bottles, searching for one that might have something left in it while Frank sat coughing and gasping. Greg removed his mask and tapped Frank on the arm.

"Here, take a few blows," he said.

Frank saw the look of guilt and fear in the man's eyes over what he was putting them through. *Good,* Frank thought as he nodded and put the mask to his face. *Next time, he'll think twice before he does something stupid.* Right now, though, Frank needed air so he inhaled the precious oxygen into his aching lungs and fought to keep his wits about him. As he shut his eyes, John grabbed him by the shoulder.

"Frank! Stay with me!" John shouted.

Frank jerked his head and shook away the insidious fog that was clouding his thoughts. As he did so, he saw John unstrapping his oxygen bottle from his jacket holster. A moment later, Frank's spent bottle was replaced and air was rushing into his oxygen-starved lungs. He stared up in wonder at the Andersen Expedition leader, who'd just given up his last bottle for him. Reaching out, he grabbed the man's arm. But John just smiled and said, "Don't waste it old man … I ain't dragging your sorry ass … all the way down the mountain."

If Frank could have laughed, he would've, but he didn't have the energy to. He forced himself up, and clipping back onto the fixed lines, started down into the blowing snow and the bleak unknown of the approaching storm.

* * *

Two hours later the climbers were in a blinding white world fighting howling winds with snow so thick they could barely see five meters ahead of them. At length, Frank came to a halt and wiped the snow from his mask and frozen beard. Despite having set his oxygen rate at four bars, he just couldn't get enough air. More than that, he could barely feel his legs and feet. If he fell, he knew he would not be able to get up. But the deadly thought of lying down for just a few minutes was so tempting.

He shook his head, banishing the thought and looked down at the fixed rope that was doubling and tripling itself before him. As it writhed back and forth over the snow-packed slope, Frank felt his body prickle. Suddenly, the piton the line was attached to was moving around of its own accord. He took a breath and blinked, then reached down to grab the line. After a couple of misses, he snatched hold of it and switched his 'biner onto the next line. As he fumbled to attach his jumar, a dark thought in back of his mind whispered, HAPE.

Ignoring it, he turned around to check on Greg and John. Their wraith-like figures plodding through the lashing, gritty snow were barely discernable. Frank waited for them to catch up and turned back to the line running into the oblivion of the white world in front of them. How far away from Camp 4 they all were was a guess, but at the rate they had been descending he figured they had at least another two hour trek ahead if not more.

John said, "I think … we should build … a snow shelter. Weather the storm … here."

Frank eyed the Andersen Expedition leader, knowing the man was right. The only problem was, it would most likely cost Frank his life. He considered their dwindling options and nodded.

* * *

Base Camp 6:15 PM

Sarah had not moved from the radio since her last contact with Greg just after 3:00 PM. She sat back in her chair at her wits' end and chewed her nails as Bob and Sangye studied the latest data coming in on the Met from the UK. Behind her, in the far corner of the tent, sat Tashi, who had come down hours ago after hearing about the situation unfolding on the mountain. She huffed and said, "It's been three freaking hours. Why haven't they called yet?

Bob looked up and turned to her. As he put his hand on her shoulder, he said, "I'm sure they'll call as soon as they can. My guess is they're pretty busy up there right now."

Sarah stared back at the medic, wanting desperately to believe him. "I know you're probably right, but not even a simple radio call?"

"Nothing's simple up there, Sarah," Bob said. "They'll be alright."

She coughed several times and nodded grudgingly. "How bad do you think it is up there?"

Sangye backed away from the laptop and for the first time, Sarah saw outright concern on his round ruddy face. He pressed his lips together and said, "Very bad, I think. When storm hit mountain, very hard to see far and they are very high up. Need to be extra careful coming down."

Bob picked her heat-exchanging mask up off the table and handed it to her. "Put it on," he said firmly.

But all she heard was Sangye's warning and with it came terrifying visions of her son and Frank falling unfathomable heights.

"Sarah!" Bob shoved the mask into her hands. "The mask; put it on."

Dazed, she looked up and mindlessly obeyed the medic's order. After she pulled the mask over her head, Bob took her hands in his and soothingly said, "Sarah, one huge thing your son has in his favor is that he's with the two best mountaineers anywhere around. Have faith in that."

"I know. It's just hard. Every time I close my eyes, I see them falling or staggering aimlessly in the snow." She looked at Bob hard then and forced herself to ask the question that had been tormenting her for the last hour. "How long can they last in the death zone?"

Bob was thoughtful for a moment then said, "There is one extreme case I know of being nearly 48 hours, but I would say no more than 24 hours before things started going downhill quick."

Sarah did the math. Greg had been in the zone for close to 18 hours. Time was running out.

Bob picked the microphone up. "Base Camp to Da-wa, come back. Over."

A long silence ensued until a faint voice on the other end said, "This is Da-wa. Over."

"What are the conditions at Camp 4? Over," Bob said.

The radio crackled and sputtered. Finally, Da-wa answered, "We in full-blown blizzard. Any word — from Frank? Over."

"None," Bob said. "Last we heard from him, was around 3:00 PM at the south summit. He found Greg and they're on their way down. Over."

Another long pause followed before Da-wa said, "Then they should've — Balcony by now. Over"

"Hopefully," Bob said as Tashi came beside them. Bob glanced at Sarah. "Otherwise ... otherwise they're in trouble."

But Sarah knew what he meant to say; that her son, Frank, and John were probably dead or near to it. She put her hand to her mouth to muffle the cry that was straining to be released.

Bob went on. "Da-wa, as soon as things clear up, would you go up and see if you can find them? Over."

"Will do," Da-wa said. He added something else, but his voice crumbed in the static.

* * *

Snow Shelter — 6:30 PM

The wretched climbers worked as fast as they could under the harsh conditions and culled out a narrow trench in the snow just large enough to fit the three of them in. Fortunately, John had a tarp rolled up in his pack for just the occasion, which they used as a roof to shelter themselves from the ravaging storm. Thirty minutes later, the men crawled breathlessly into the makeshift shelter and huddled together in the dark frigid cold.

As the tarp above them snapped and rattled from the ferocious winds strafing the mountain, John pulled his head lantern out and turned it on. "Let's hope ... this isn't ... our tomb," he rasped.

Frank nodded, and as he drew breath from his mask he stared at his companions who were gasping for each breath as if it were their last. John's face and bristled beard, which was covered in snow, was barely discernable and his hood and gloves were coated in ice. Greg was bent forward with his arms crossed over his chest. As he rocked back and forth, Frank glanced down at his regulator gauge. There was perhaps two hours left in the bottle before he was on his own. By the looks of what was going on outside, they were going be pinned down a lot longer than that. Essentially, he was screwed, and he knew it. His body was breaking down and there was no way he could see himself making it back to Camp 4 alive.

Karma was staring him in the face. He had made his choice in sending Greg up with Da-wa and now it was time to own up to the consequences. He looked off toward the ragged opening that was being slowly sealed in by the blowing snow outside, and thought of Pasang, remembering how the two of them used to talk about all the mountains they were going to climb when they had their own expedition company. And then there was the school in Khum Jung and Tashi and Tembe and Cho and Lotti and all the mountain folk who'd been woven into his life. Yes, he had lived a rich life; one few people in the world could ever hope for. That karma in all its grand design had brought him to this moment was absolute poetry.

He glanced back at John. The tall, uncompromising blond had been a thorn in his side for the last five years, but here he was, risking his life for him. And wasn't that what it was all about; doing the right thing when it mattered most? Last of all, was Sarah. He never thought he'd fall in love with anyone, much less the widow of Steve Madden. If there was one thing he hated leaving undone, it was not seeing her again. But karma had made its decision, so he reached down and shut the flow of oxygen off to his mask. There wasn't a lot left in it, but what there was might give John a fighting chance of making it down if the weather broke.

* * *

Base Camp — 11:30 PM

Sarah stared at the radio under the bright stark light of the LED lantern hanging from the nylon line above her head. She hadn't strayed from it since noon except to use the latrine. Her heat exchanging mask and plate of garlic seasoned potatoes and rice sat on the table beside the radio. A cup of tea was cold and untouched. Tashi sat next to her, silent and watchful. Bob and Sangye spoke in hushed tones over in the corner. Hope was quickly draining away from the Base Camp crew, and as it fled into the cold night outside of the command tent, it left an all-consuming apathy behind.

Sarah looked up as one of the Winslow crewmembers came in. The other teams on the mountain had been regularly checking in to hear if there was any news. A few of them had brought food for the Khum Jung Base Camp team. Sarah heard the men whisper something to Bob.

"Nothing yet," she heard Bob mutter.

Tashi stirred beside her. "Sarah, you need to drink. You will become dehydrated. Then you no good to anyone."

She turned to the lama, bleary eyed. "You think they're still alive?"

Tashi studied her with his dark penetrating eyes. "It not matter what I think; only what you think."

"I don't know what to think," Sarah rasped. "There hasn't been a word from them in eight hours." She picked her tea mug up and tried to take a sip but couldn't. She set it down and burst into tears. "God, it feels like a funeral home in here," she cried and buried her face in her hands. "Why haven't they called, damn it?"

Suddenly, she felt a pair of arms around her and heard Bob's voice whisper in her ear. "Don't give up."

"I'm not! I'm just not sure how much more of this I can take," she said and broke into a coughing fit.

Bob pulled her up and led her over to a sleeping bag that had been brought into the tent. Handing her the mask, he gently but firmly said, "Here, lay down and get some rest. If anything comes through, you'll be the first to know."

Too tired to fight, Sarah bent down and curled up in the bag. A moment later she fell into a restless sleep.

* * *

Snow Shelter — 2:05 AM — the following day

Frank felt an all-consuming chill enter his body as he drifted mindlessly in a boundless empty darkness. Something was tugging at him, but he didn't know what it was. Suddenly he felt a thud and then a sharp stinging sensation radiating through him. A moment later, a muffled voice entered his mind. He felt another tug and a thud then all at once, the voice amplified.

"Frank, wake up, God damn it!"

Another stinging sharp pain ran through him and as it did so, a bright light pierced the utter darkness. He stared up uncomprehendingly at a fierce bearded face looking down at him then felt his body heave.

"Breathe, you fucker," the voice roared in his ears.

Frank coughed and felt his chest contract. But the air his lungs were desperately trying to suck in was but a trickle.

"Greg, put his ... mask back on. Turn the valve ... all the way ... to five bars. God damn it ... where's my dexy? Frank, you bastard! You ... better not die ... on me."

Frank felt something cover his mouth and with it a rush of air. But breathing was like sucking breath through a straw. He jolted forward and coughed again.

"There you are! Strip ... his jacket off ... so I can ... inject him."

Frank felt a sudden chill as hands tugged the warmth of his jacket away. A moment later, he felt a pinprick in his arm.

"Greg ... see if you ... can raise Base Camp."

"I've been trying ... for the last four hours."

"Try again ... asshole!" There was a pause and Frank could feel the warmth return. "Hey Frank ... just juiced you up ... with a shot of dexy. Stay with me ... guy."

Frank sucked another breath of air and stared at John's blurred face wishing the man had let him go. Though he wasn't bent on dying, he couldn't see the point in taking someone else with him. As Greg worked the radio nearby, he felt his body reacting to the drug. A moment later things came into focus. But drawing breath was near impossible. It was as if his chest had been frozen into a block of ice.

Then out of the silence, a garbled voice came back on the radio. He listened to the broken words filling their tiny shelter. It sounded like Bob on the other end. John snatched the radio from Greg and spoke in a halting, hoarse voice, telling Bob about their situation.

"He's in real ... bad shape," John said. "Can't breathe ... Gave him a shot of dexy ... But he needs to get down. Any ... suggestions?"

There was a long period of static before Bob answered. "Can you sit him up?"

"Not very easily," John replied. "Have limited room here. Hold on ... will try."

Frank felt John's hands grab him by the shoulders and pull him forward. Sitting upright with his feet splayed out before him brought a rush of air into his lungs, but it also launched him into a succession of deep suffocating coughs. Reaching up, he tore the mask away from his face, but it didn't help the violent demands of his oxygen-starved body. As he fought to draw air into his battered lungs, John got back on the radio.

"He's choking ... What do I do now? ... God damn it!"

Bob's voice came back. "You know how to do the Heimlich maneuver?"

"Yeah, I know it."

"Then do it," Bob said.

"Seriously?"

"Yes, do it!"

John set the radio down and said to Greg, "Help me … get his jacket off." The dim light of John's head lantern flickered in the dark, tight quarters. A minute later, hands were wrestling Frank's jacket over his listless, hacking body.

"Move out … of the way," John barked to Greg.

"Where?" Greg said.

"Outside," John barked. "Hurry, damn it."

As Greg clumsily crawled past John and pawed through the snow banking up to the shelter's opening, John maneuvered around behind Frank. The Andersen leader wrapped his powerful arms around him, and with a sudden jolt, the man thrust his fist upward. Frank's lungs heaved. Something dislodged in his chest. Another thrust, brought up a small chunk of frozen phlegm.

The grip relaxed around Frank's gut, and with it, a steady stream of air flowed into his lungs. John scrambled for the radio. "He brought something up."

"Good," Bob's crackled voice came back on the other end. "Give him a few more shots and see if there's anything more."

"Right," John said.

Again, John tightened his grip around Frank and thrust upward. Five jolts later, Frank coughed up another chunk. As John backed off, Frank reached up and brought his mask to his face, devouring the rush of air coming through the regulator.

Bob's voice came back on the radio. "Any more?"

"Some," John said. "He's pretty weak … needs to get down. But we're pinned … up here. Don't know … if he'll make it … too much longer."

"We got help coming up to you once the storm breaks. Looks like you'll be through the worst of it in another hour or so. Can you hold on that long?"

"Hope so."

There was a long pause. Finally, Frank heard Bob say, "What's your location?"

"Two, maybe three hours … from Camp 4," John answered.

"Hi John, this is Sarah. Please don't give up."

Frank smiled as John answered her back, "Not planning on it."

Bob cut back in. "Good. Keep Frank upright as much as possible. It'll help him breathe. If things get hard for him again, give him a few more Heimlichs. By the way, how are you, John?"

"Been better. Hey, battery is … running low here … I'll check in later."

"Roger, that. God speed."

As John set the radio down, Greg poked his head in through the opening. "It's beginning … to let up out here."

Chapter 27

Base Camp — 5:20 AM

Sarah huddled in her jacket as she sat in the corner of the command tent. It had been nearly two hours since the storm had let up on the mountain, allowing Da-wa and a small crew of Sherpas to strike off to find Greg, Frank, and the Andersen Expeditions leader. Tashi sat beside her silently reading from his prayer cards as the Command Tent skin snapped and rattled from the wind outside. The old lama and Bob had been her source of encouragement and strength over the last twelve hours. But right now there wasn't any amount of encouragement or reassuring that would calm her thundering heart. They had to be alive. There was no other option, not after all she'd gone through.

She chewed her nails or rather, what there was left of them and took a pull from her water bottle as crew from other camps came and went; some bringing hot tea and food, others to get the latest news. Sangye pulled a weather report out of the printer and studied it with Bob. Then finally, Da-wa's voice came clattering out of the radio.

"Da-wa to Base Camp, come back."

Sarah sprang to her feet and Bob rushed to the microphone. "Base Camp here, over," Bob said.

Sarah held her breath along with everyone else in the tent waiting for Da-wa to reply. The radio hissed a moment. "We found 'em. Everyone alive, but Frank … he in bad shape. Coming down soon as we get him taken care of. Over."

Sarah closed her eyes thanking God the men were still alive. But it was a long way from being over for Frank and she knew it. She watched Bob glance down at the weather report in his hand, thinking about what Frank had done to save her son. Knowing how he felt about people who didn't listen to common sense on the mountain, his going up to get Greg meant the world to her.

"Roger that Da-wa," Bob replied. "Just checked weather forecast for next 24 hours. You have more snow heading your way, but nothing major with little or no wind. Looks like things are in your favor. Can you get Frank down to Camp 2 before then, over?"

"Believe so. Better have chopper ready when we get back to Base Camp," Da-wa said.

Bob put his hand over the microphone. "Sangye, get on the horn. Tell the fly-boys to have a chopper stand by for a pick-up at Camp 2." To Da-wa, he said, "Roger that, we'll meet you at Camp 2 instead."

"Okay. Will call down when we get near. Out."

Bob set the microphone on the table and let out a long exhale into the crisp cold morning air. He turned to Sarah and Tashi. "We're not out of the woods yet, but at least there's a fighting chance for Frank now. Keep your fingers crossed."

* * *

Sarah went to her tent. Over the last 24 hours she had been an emotional wreck worrying about her son. But now that she knew he was alright, her thoughts turned to Frank. He had risked his life for her son and she knew it was because of her that he did. She would never forget that and it only made her care for him all the more. But right now there was nothing left to do but wait and hope Frank would make it down the mountain alive.

She gazed out the open flap of her tent at the mountains as she sat on her sleeping bag. Digging her rosary beads out of her pocket, she wished she could comfort the enigmatic man who had come into her life. He just couldn't die, not after all he'd done; not before she could tell him what he meant to her. She closed her eyes and prayed God would bring him back to her. It didn't matter that her visa was running out and that she had a plane to catch to go back home. Visas could be extended and plane reservations canceled and re-done.

* * *

Sarah woke from a fitful dream and pulled her mask off. Her body felt like it had been beaten up and the persistent headache she'd had over the last couple of weeks pulsed in her temples. She coughed as she rolled out of her sleeping bag. Outside, she heard people milling about the camp as a stiff wind rattled the sides of her tent. The scent of garlic-fried potatoes was in the air. She glanced at her watch. It was a little after 4:00 PM. Grabbing a comb and mirror, she went about putting herself together. Staring at her reflection, she saw a woman she barely recognized. It was as if she had aged a lifetime in the last four weeks. In fact, she could barely remember the woman who had come to the Himalayas.

She set the mirror down and pulled back the tent flap. The signature blue sky of the Himalayans was peeking through the scudding clouds. She wasn't hungry, but figured she should try to eat something. She coughed again and as she did so, grimaced. Her throat was raw and her chest ached. She dragged her boot and ankle brace over and pulled them on. Her ankle, though still tender, was getting stronger. She wiggled her toes and felt the familiar twinge reminding her to have a care putting her weight on her foot, then rolled a thick woolen sock over the brace.

Ten minutes later she hobbled back into the command tent and poured herself a cup of tea. Behind her, she heard Sangye talking on his cell phone in Lhasa. In the far corner, Bob had crashed on the sleeping pad that had been brought into the tent.

Sangye finished his phone conversation and said, "You hungry?"

Sarah shrugged. "Sure." She handed him her plate and watched him pile a large spoonful of potatoes, onions, and rice on her plate. "Any further news from Da-wa?"

The Sherpa shook his head. "Not yet. Everything be okay, you see."

Sarah forced a smile, was quiet a moment then said, "I'm sure it will be. I'll just be glad when they're all down." She sipped her tea as Sangye set her plate down next to the base station. Her glance strayed over to Bob. "How long have Bob and Frank known each other?"

Sangye came back and took her tea. As he set it next to her lunch, he said, "Don't know, long time. Why?"

Sarah hopped over and took a seat next to her lunch. "Just wondered." She stabbed a potato with her fork and mused on the climbing community surrounding her. They were like most families with their share of combative and territorial personalities, yet they came together when it mattered. She wished she could say the same for those who were her educational family back home.

She wondered what life would be like if she remained in Nepal with Frank. There wouldn't be any more fancy dinners out or spending time on the California beaches, no more running down to the local café shops for her lattes or heading across town to the gym, and forget about keeping her hair dyed and primped. So many things that she took for granted back home would be gone, yet did she really need them? Did she need her wide screen TV, her fancy Bose stereo system, and a closet full of designer clothes? She couldn't honestly say that she did. What she needed was to feel fulfilled and happy. But what did that look like? And more important, could she find it here in the mountains with Frank?

It was all fantasy though. She knew she couldn't bear to be half a world away from her son and all the people back home who were her extended family. At least that was what she was telling herself when the radio came alive.

"Da-wa to Base Camp, over."

Sarah set her fork down, and as she grabbed the microphone, Bob popped up from his sleeping mat.

"This is Base Camp, over."

"We at Camp 3," Da-wa said. "Gonna spend night here and head down to Camp 2 in the morning. Should be there by noon at the latest, so have chopper waiting, over."

"Will do. How is Frank, over?" Sarah said as Bob joined her.

"He very weak, but breathing better. John give him another shot of dexy an hour ago."

Bob took the microphone from her and said, "Keep a watch on him overnight and don't let him lie down. He needs to be sitting upright so his lungs don't fill up. Has he been able to drink at all? Over."

"Some, not very much, over."

"Get as much into him as you can. And keep an eye peeled for hypothermia. His body in its weakened state is susceptible to it. Over."

"Will do. John Patterson wants to talk to you. Hold on."

John's raspy voice was nothing more than a whisper coming back. "Bob, you there?"

"I'm here. How're you doing, big guy?"

A string of loud coughs came through the radio. Finally, John said, "Been better. Need a favor."

"Sure. What?"

"I'm gonna need a chopper, too."

Bob's face darkened. "What's going on with ya, John?"

There was a long silence. Finally, John said, "Haven't felt my feet for the last few hours."

Bob pressed his lips together. "Roger that."

Sarah felt her throat tighten, knowing what it probably meant. The price of her son's poor decision had become too costly. Suddenly, she felt guilty and responsible. How could she look at the Andersen Expedition leader again knowing that her son's actions might mean the loss of his foot or worse yet, his leg? She resisted the urge to ask about her son. Greg was alright or else Da-wa would have said so otherwise. Getting up, she slipped out of the command tent and headed out onto the barren moraine to be alone.

* * *

Base Camp — 12:15 PM — the next day

Sarah washed up outside of the latrine. It had been a long night in the command tent and a longer morning waiting to hear from the men on the mountain. She glanced upward, taking in the snow-covered peaks that were basking under the noontime sun. One more day and this would all be over and done with and then life would return back to ... what? She wasn't sure what 'normal' meant anymore. She squeezed a dollop of sanitizer on her hand and was about to head back when she saw Bob pop out of the command tent and head toward her.

"They're back at Camp 2," he said.

Sarah felt her breath catch and she wiped her hands. "And?"

"So far, so good. Choppers are on the way for 'em," Bob said, coming beside her.

"Thank God," Sarah answered, looking up. Suddenly all the angst and worrying she had balled up inside her came tumbling out in tears. She put her hands to her face and as she did so, felt Bob's arms wrap around her.

He held her for several minutes until she regained control of herself, then pulled back and said, "I told 'em to stop here on their way back to Namche to pick up another passenger."

Sarah wiped her eyes and stared back at him puzzled. "For who?"

"You, Miss Lightfoot," Bob said and smiled warmly. "You're not going too far on that bum ankle of yours, so might as well hop a ride with Frank, unless you'd rather wait and go alone."

"No," Sarah answered, "But what about Greg and John?"

"Greg is doing okay from what I'm told. John will be flown down separately." He pressed his lips together. "I know he's your son, but I think he needs to spend some time alone with what happened up there."

Sarah knew he was right. Her son had needlessly jeopardized his life and those who had saved him. Even so, she was anxious to see him. At last she nodded. "I'll get my things packed."

* * *

The chopper arrived at Base Camp, kicking up a thick cloud of dust forty minutes later. Sarah took Bob's hand and ducking her head, followed him out under the thwapping blades slicing through the crisp mountain air. As they neared the fuselage the bay door slid back and a medical technician hopped out. The man grabbed her pack and tossed it inside as she hugged Bob.

"Thank you," she rasped into the medic's ear. He patted her back and flashing her a thumbs up, helped her inside. A moment later, the technician was inside with her and sliding the bay door shut. As the man did so, she turned and saw Frank lying on a stretcher. He was wrapped with a heavy wool blanket and an oxygen mask covered his gaunt, bearded face. Her eyes widened. *Oh my God, he's lost so much weight.* She scooted over next to him and took his hand. "Hi, stranger. Mind if I share a cab with you?"

He shook his head and squeezed her hand as the technician handed her a pair of headphones to dull the roar of the engines thrumming through the craft. Putting them on, she felt tears come to her eyes all over again. She bent her head down close to him, and putting her hand to his face, softly said, "I'm going to take care of you, don't you worry."

* * *

The Namche Hospital that was located on the rim above the village was more of a clinic than it was a hospital. The modest two story stone structure housing only the bare necessities and an emergency bay was at the front lines of the wild Sagarmatha frontier. Sarah sat off to the side in the cluttered stucco finished room with a vaulted ceiling and hardwood floors. It was a far cry from the emergency rooms in the States. Wooden cabinets and bookshelves crammed with books and medical supplies lined the room and a laptop sat on an old wooden desk in the corner.

She sipped a hot drink of mango juice that one of the clinicians brought to her and looked on as the doctors examined Frank and John, who had been stripped down to their thermals and were covered in woolen blankets. Although both men had gotten their color back, they still looked as if they had just been rescued from a concentration camp.

As the doctors ministered to them, Sarah's glance strayed to John's battered feet that were being wrapped in dressings. Both of them had deep blue toes and a purple and sallow sheen went up to the ankle. She had never seen frostbite before, and she was quite sure she never wanted to see it again. When she looked back up, she found herself in the clutches of the Andersen leader's icy blue eyes.

"Pretty ugly, isn't it?" John rasped, from where he sat on the exam table.

Sarah didn't know what to say. Sorry didn't seem to cut it. "Does it hurt?"

John shrugged. "Not right now, but it will in a while." He paused. "So that was your husband up there?"

Sarah nodded.

Frank coughed and said, "John, let it go, please."

"Right … Anyway, it's over with." He glanced over at Frank. "How're you doing over there, old man?"

"Better, and thanks," Frank said as the clinician got him up. "Well, looks like they're taking me in for an x-ray now. Behave yourself."

"Don't you worry about me," John said.

After Frank left the room, Sarah got up and came next to John. For the life of her, she couldn't figure the man out. She eyed him for a moment and said, "I want to thank you for saving my son."

John shook his head. "Your son had nothing to do with my decision. I went for Frank, that's all."

"But you don't like him," Sarah said, puzzled.

"That's right, I don't." John replied. He coughed and cleared his throat. "But it was the right thing to do. Besides, he'd do the same for me."

"So, it's some sort of code?" Sarah said.

"Something like that," John answered and averted his gaze toward the window at the end of the room.

Sarah was quiet a moment, wondering if she should ask the question that had been on her mind off and on since she met the man. "Why do you dislike Frank?"

John turned back to her with a furrowed brow. "He screwed with my team. You don't do that. It's wrong."

"What do you mean, 'screwed'?" Sarah said, trying to reconcile the character of the man she adored with the accusation coming back at her.

John's piecing blue eyes dug into her. "Like Frank said; let's just drop it, okay? Your son is down and life goes on."

Sarah nodded and backed off. Her son was safe and so was Frank. But the ordeal was far from over for all of them. She thought of Greg. She knew her son pretty well when it came to certain things, and in this case she was certain he was beating himself up pretty hard for what he'd done. Bob had said Greg needed time alone to deal with the decisions he'd made on the mountain, and the medic was right. Would Greg ever be the same again after leaving the mountain? Probably not, but that was part of making mistakes. You learned and went on from them. The question was, would he let his mistakes rule his life going forward? She hoped not, but it was out of her hands. And for the first time, she realized she needed to let go of her son and let him live his own life.

That left her to consider hers. She adored Frank and the thought of never seeing him again after she left to go back to the States weighed heavily on her heart. Could she give up everything to be with him? She battled with that thought, knowing that time was running out for them and very soon a decision would have to be made.

* * *

Later that night, Sarah helped Frank down to one of the local teahouses where they took a room for the next week until Frank had the strength to travel back home to Khum Jung. As they lay cocooned in each other's arms under a heavy blanket in the tiny room, she couldn't help feeling a distance between them. He hadn't said much since they were reunited in the chopper, which in all honesty could be understood. He was exhausted from the ordeal. But there was something else bothering him. She draped her leg over his thigh, wrapped her arm around his waist and laid her head on his chest. At last, she said, "Do you think they're all down yet?"

"Not yet. Probably day after tomorrow," he muttered.

Sarah lifted her head up and stared at him through the gloom. "What's wrong, Frank?"

276

"Nothing. I ... I'm just tired." He didn't say anything for a long time. "I'll be alright."

Sarah sighed. *Please talk to me Frank. Don't shut me out. Not now.* "So, I'm going to see Khum Jung. I'm looking forward to it."

"Me too," he answered. "'Night."

Sarah lay with that a minute, turning anxious thoughts over in her mind. In all the time she'd known him, he had never been this ambivalent towards her except maybe in the beginning. At last she said, "Are you angry with me?"

"No, why?"

"Well, Greg's my son, so —"

"Stop, Sarah. You're not responsible for his decisions," Frank said. He coughed and rolled onto his side. "Just let it go, okay?"

"There seems to be a lot of letting go of things lately," Sarah persisted. "Frank, problems don't solve themselves by avoiding them."

Frank turned back toward her. "I'm not avoiding anything, Sarah," he said pointedly. He eyed her pleadingly then and sighed. "I'm just tired, is all. Please believe me."

But she didn't believe him. If it had nothing to do with her, then something had happened up on the mountain. But it would have to come out when he was ready to talk about it. For the time being, all she could do was to be here for him, so she lay back down beside him and spooned up next to him.

* * *

Frank slept most of the following day and throughout the night. While he got his strength back over the next four days, Sarah went about town and picked up some new clothing, underwear especially. What she had with her was going in the trash along with all her socks and thermals. Along with her shopping spree was a trip to a local salon for a trim. It wasn't her usual feathered cut, but it did just fine. But it was the showers she relished most, and she spent a good twenty minutes every morning under the hot pulsing spray, rinsing away the crud of five long weeks of living in her clothes.

Friday morning, Sarah found herself waking up alone in their room. She sat up wondering where Frank had taken off to and gazed out the window at the deep blue sky soaring overhead. As she got out of bed, the door to her room opened and Frank came in with a couple mugs of tea.

Offering her one of his trademark winks, he said, "Namaste, Lightfoot."

Sarah eyed him in surprise. He had shaved and his long gray hair had been trimmed back to the top of his shoulders. "Morning, Mountain Man. You're up early."

"What's that look for?" he said.

She stepped up to him, took her mug of tea and said, "What look?"

"The look that says, don't rush things," he answered. He sipped his tea. "I'm quite alright now, I assure you."

"You're a lousy liar, but I forgive you," she said, then turned her head and coughed.

Frank snickered. "You don't give up, do you?"

Sarah took a drink and set her mug down. As she dug her brush out of her pack and started running it through her hair, she said, "Not easily. Raising a child requires persistence. But I can wait."

"Gonna be waiting a long time," Frank said, and smiled. "Anyway, breakfast is being served in half an hour and I'm starved. Think you can get yourself around by then?"

"I'll give it a shot. I must say it's nice to feel hungry again."

Frank went to the window and stared out over the terraced landscape fleeing to the Dudh Kosi River gorge below. In the bright sunlight flowing in around him, his emaciated body looked like a wraith to her. Over his shoulder, he said, "And headache free?"

"That, too," she answered, grabbing a towel and toiletries from her pack.

* * *

Thirty minutes later, Sarah sat across the breakfast table from Frank. As she ate, she listened to the local chatter around them. The chief topic was what had happened up on the mountain. John Patterson had become an overnight sensation of sorts for his herculean efforts in rescuing an American and his guide on the south summit. When Frank glanced up from stuffing his mouth with fried potatoes, she gave him a knowing glance, which he returned.

"Seems John's reputation is getting quite a shot," she said.

"That it is," Frank answered. "But I don't begrudge it one bit. He saved my life up there."

Sarah popped a slice of apple in her mouth. "Do you think he'll be alright? His feet looked pretty bad to me," she said.

Frank pursed his lips. "I'm hoping so. I have a proposition for him."

"Oh, what's that?"

"Going to ask him to take over Khum Jung Expeditions," Frank said, matter-of-factly. His glance drifted off into space and he was quiet for a moment. Finally, he said, "I believe I'm done climbing."

Sarah sat back astonished. Frank's expedition company was the lifeblood of his charity work, or so he had said. That he would suddenly give it up didn't make sense. "Really? Why?" she said.

Frank shivered then came to himself. He said, "He deserves a shot at being his own boss up there without a corporate bigwig looking over his shoulder every minute."

"You didn't answer my question," Sarah said, pointedly.

Frank stared at her puzzled. "Oh, that," he said. He set his fork down and paused. At last he went on, "You're probably going to think I'm batty, but when we were waiting out the storm on Everest, wondering if we were going to make it through the night, I heard a voice in the wind. At first I thought I was in a dream, and maybe it was, I don't know. But it was there and it was telling me, 'it's time to move on'."

"I see," Sarah said warily. Having experienced a presence near her during difficult times, she could easily sympathize with him. But she always took the experience with a grain of salt. That Frank was making such a radical decision based on a voice 'telling him to move on' alarmed her. Yet, what Frank did with his company was none of her business, except it was part of who he was and that in turn made her worry for him. She sipped her tea and said, "You think John'll take it? He doesn't exactly like you."

Frank sucked down the rest of his tea and picking up his fork, stabbed a piece of potato. "Don't know. But I'm going to offer it anyway."

"What are you going to do?" she said.

"What do you mean?"

"Well, don't you need the money from your expedition company to support your charity work?"

"Oh! I'm not walking away from it," Frank said. "I'll still be handling the books and lining up clients."

"And if he doesn't take it?" Sarah countered, popping another piece of apple in her mouth.

"Then I'll find someone else, I suppose. I have a feeling he'll take it though. John was born to climb. It's in his blood. Speaking of climbing," Frank pulled out his cell phone, "let me give Sangye a call and see where they are." As he waited for his Sherpa to answer, he eyed her plate. "You gonna eat your toast?"

"Umm … why?"

"Well, if you don't want it, I'm in town."

Sarah laughed. It was good to see Frank getting his spark back. But she wasn't fooled by it either. The way he stared off into space when he thought she wasn't watching warned her he was still troubled about something.

Chapter 28

Sarah stepped out of their teahouse into another bright and crisp Himalayan morning as Frank checked them out of their room. As she stood there by the front door, she scanned the deep divide to the snow-covered ridge to the south. It was only five weeks ago that the two of them were standing on the narrow stone passage in front of her, trying to figure each other out. It felt like a lifetime ago. She smiled as a vision of Frank shaking out his long gray hair flashed before her.

"Ready, Ms. Lightfoot?" he said, coming beside her.

"Good to go," she answered, putting on her sunglasses. She was just about to step ahead when his hand fell on her shoulder.

"Not quite," he said. He turned her around, adjusted the height of the daypack riding on her back and checked the water supply in her camelback. He patted her shoulder. "Now you're ready."

Sarah looked back at him. "You're being a fuss-budget you know, but thank you."

"That's because you have a fair march ahead of you on a sore ankle. Last thing I need is to have to carry you pig-a-back all over the countryside."

"I'll be fine," Sarah protested. She grabbed her crutch the clinic had given her and hobbled down the front stairs onto the stone terrace with Frank trailing behind. Ten minutes later, they were turning onto the terraced alleyway that bisected the bustling Namche marketplace. As she climbed the stone-laid steps with Frank at her side, she tried to ignore the ominous farewell that was coming all too soon. It was more than likely Frank did as well. Yet, the moments of disquiet in him over the last week lingered in her mind.

But he was bright and affable this morning as he led the way up through the maze of alleyways snaking into the brown hillside that overlooked the red, blue, and green roofs of Namche. Sarah was grateful for that. She reached out and took his hand as they wended their way around the brambles and thickets crowding the zigzagging trail.

As he intertwined his fingers with hers, she said, "So, we're meeting up with Greg and rest of the team in Khum Jung?"

"That's the plan," Frank said.

"Are you angry with my son?"

"More angry with myself," Frank answered. "I should've led him and Lanzo. If I had, none of it would've happened."

"So, why didn't you lead them?"

Frank stopped and looked at her with a pained expression. At last, he said, "I was selfish. I wanted to keep the place where Pasang and your husband fell to myself. I'm not proud of what I did, Sarah. I just thought he'd see the futility of searching for his father up there and forget trying to find him. But I was wrong and it nearly killed all of us."

"Is that why you went back for him?"

"Part of it," he said. He squeezed her hand. "Come, we'll talk about it later. Right now, it's a beautiful day and I don't want to ruin it by talking about such things." He paused and studying her tenderly, said, "Do you know the song, Country Roads?"

The question caught Sarah quite by surprise. She stared at him wondering where it came from, and said, "You mean the one by John Denver?"

"I think so. It goes like this." He cleared his throat and sang, "Country roads ... take me home ... to a place ... I belong ... West Virginia ... Mountain Mama ..."

"That's it!" Sarah said, both astonished that he would know it and delighting in his rendition. "Didn't know you were a country music man."

"Don't know about that. Just heard it a few times and liked it," he said. "Anyway, figured you might know it, being it's an American song." He grinned. "So ... I like to sing while I walk sometimes. Makes the trip go faster. Want to join me?"

Sarah smiled and a moment later they were walking and gleefully belting out the country ditty under the vast blue dome overhead.

* * *

They arrived at the saddle that overlooked the village of Khum Jung shortly after 2:00 PM. As she stood at the top of the sweeping sandstone stairway leading down into town, Sarah gazed at the mass of simple, single-story stone buildings with dark green roofs running up into the hills beyond. Frank pointed to a long stone lined passageway below that cut across the rolling dun landscape. At the end of it, she saw a monumental white Stupa flanking the fenced-in grounds of the Khum Jung campus, which was comprised of five buildings. One of them had an annex that was under construction.

"So, that's your addition," Sarah said.

"That's it," Frank said. He went quiet then and when she looked back at him, she sensed he was a million miles away. She resisted the urge to press him about what he was thinking and found a seat on one of the large sandstone boulders beside them. At last, he turned to her. "How's the ankle?"

"It's there," she answered, feeling a twinge. She wondered if she'd overdone it hiking to the village without taking more rest stops. But she was anxious to see her son again, and up until now, her foot hadn't complained. Her armpit did though. The crutch had seemingly dug a burning hole into it.

Frank stepped over beside her and sat. Grabbing the tube leading out of his camelback, he put it to his mouth and sucked a drink of water. As he did so, she pulled out a bag of trail mix and opened it. "Want some?" she asked, holding it up to him.

He reached down and grabbed a handful. As he popped some in his mouth, he kicked his leg against the stone.

Sarah helped herself to a handful as well, folded up the bag and set it between them. Sitting there next to him, she felt like a kid again. "It seems like I've been here forever."

"Me, too," Frank said, dashing the rest of his trail mix into his mouth. He shot her a playful grin then eyed her meaningfully. "You miss your home back in the States?"

Sarah shrugged. "Yeah, I do a bit. But your being here makes it easy to forget about it most of the time."

Frank smiled and put his arm around her. "I'm going to miss you, Lightfoot."

She studied the soft gray eyes gazing back at her from his thin sculpted face and said, "Stop. Let's not let the future steal away the time we have left."

"Using my words against me, huh? I better watch myself going forward, who knows what else I'll get nailed with." He winked, and staring out over the windswept grasses tumbling down the hillside toward Khum Jung, pointed to a prominent structure on the far side of the village. "See that big red roof over there by those trees hugging the hillside? That's the monastery where Master Tashi lives. I live —" He pointed to a small green roof enclosed by a wall of stone to the left of it. " — right there. It's not much, but I call it home."

"Was that your parent's home when they were alive?" Sarah said.

Frank nodded. "That it was. You need a few more minutes or you ready to go?"

Sarah wiggled her toes in her boot. A little twinge came back, but nothing serious. "I think I'm good. So, where's the team staying in town?" she said, getting to her feet.

He pointed to a broad, dirt field in back of the school campus. On the other side of it was a sprawling single story whitewashed building with green shutters and trim. "Right there. Will you want to stay there with your son?"

She paused suddenly realizing she hadn't given much thought to it until now. Were she back home in the States, the answer would be easy. But here, no one really knew her except her son, of course, and he was no prude. Still, she was torn. She felt she should probably stay with Greg, but what she really wanted was to stay with Frank. And then, there was the way Frank had just asked her where she wanted to stay. Was he trying to avoid being presumptuous or did he want to be alone?

At last, she said, "Umm … Can I think about it?"

"Sure. Well, we'd better start heading down," he said, getting up. He held his hand out to her and helped her to her feet. As they started down the earthen stairway to the Khum Jung valley ahead, he added, "By the way, if you're interested, I could arrange a guided tour of the campus later on."

Sarah smiled and squeezed his hand. "I'd love it."

As the gentle breezes tugged at their collars, the two of them ambled down the winding stair, and fifteen minutes later they were shuffling along the broad by-way striking through the tiny campus. As they walked side-by-side, passing the playground toward the front gate, a bell rang out. Suddenly, children of all ages poured out of the simple stone buildings. When the youngest ones saw Frank, they came running over.

Sarah stood back and watched Frank drop to his knees as they surrounded him. For a man who had no children of his own, he certainly was a natural when it came to interacting with them. *You would've been a great father*, she mused as the youngsters peppered him with questions while pawing at his backpack. After he shooed them back off to their next class, she said, "They certainly love you."

"That, and they also love what's in my pack," he said getting to his feet and dusting himself off.

"You mean the chocolate bars you picked up in Namche," Sarah said. "By the way, what was that name they were calling you; Ang Tar-chin?"

"Oh, it's just a term of endearment." He put his hand on the small of her back. "Come, let's go find your son."

Frank led her out through the front gate of the campus then and as they crossed the wide dirt field toward the teahouse, she saw the front door of the hostel open. Out of it, stepped her son. He stood in the shade of the front porch roof and stared at her then came marching out. As he walked toward her, Sarah felt her throat tighten. She dropped her pack and crutch beside Frank and tottered ahead, wiping tears away from her eyes.

When they came together, she wrapped her arms around her son, kissed him all over and buried her head in his shoulder. "Are you alright? You're a bag of bones," she said, pulling away and looking up at his thin, bearded face.

He shot her a lop-sided smile. "I'm good, Mom." He studied her with his deep blue eyes and as he did so, they glassed over. "I'm sorry I put you through all that. I'm so sorry, really I am."

Sarah nodded. "The only thing that matters right now is you're alive and in my arms." She tightened her grip around him. "But if you ever do anything like that again, I'll personally come up there and kick your ass!"

"Don't worry, I won't." He looked past her toward Frank. "Does he hate me?"

Sarah opened her mouth, then paused and re-considered her answer. She knew how Frank felt about what had happened on the mountain. Letting go of her son, she pursed her lips. "Why don't you go find out for yourself?"

* * *

That evening, Sarah returned with Frank back to his home on the far side of the village. Opening the front gate, he let her into the yard that surrounded the stone built house. Not unlike many of the homesteads she'd seen when hiking up the Sagarmatha trails, it was cluttered with sacks of feed, baled grasses, and farm implements she had no name for. As Frank closed the gate behind them,

Sarah noticed a pen with a chestnut coated horse. The animal looked up from nibbling at a clump of montane grass under a large flowering rhododendron.

"You didn't tell me you had a horse," Sarah said.

Frank straightened a pile of junipers boughs stacked beside the stone laid fence. "Actually, she's a mare and she's my bread and butter in the off-season. Name's Me-to. It's Tibetan; means 'flower'. She carries my building materials up and down the mountain."

"Who takes care of her when you're gone?" Sarah said, heading toward the wooden fence penning the mare in.

Frank reached down in a wooden bin beside the stone fence and took an apple out. Following Sarah over, he said, "One of the boys down the road." He whistled and called the mare over.

As he offered Me-to the apple, Sarah ran her hand over the mare's neck. "She's beautiful."

"I like to think so," Frank said. He was quiet a moment. "So, shall we go in?"

He led Sarah around front of the simple, cruciform shaped house. Entering in, Sarah caught the telltale whiff of mildew and stood to the side while Frank went about lighting a couple of oil lamps. As the room brightened under their saffron glow, she saw a stone fireplace to her left that doubled as a stove with wood cabinets on one side and a place for split logs on the other. A stone mantle hung above it bearing hooks that held wrought iron pokers.

Frank set a lamp on a small wooden table with two chairs in front of a curtained window and went about starting a fire. "It's not much. Take a look around and make yourself comfortable. Bathroom's at the end of the hall over there if you need it," he said pointing over his shoulder toward the back of the room.

Sarah set her pack down beside her and took her jacket off. As she hung it on a hook beside the front door, she scanned the large open room that doubled as a kitchen and living area. To her right, was a cordoned off area he was using as an office of sorts. In it was an old wooden desk stacked with files. A tattered, leather upholstered chair on casters was pushed up to it. She went over to the window beside it, and opened the sash to let some fresh air in. As she did so, she perused a tall open cabinet to her right whose shelves were stuffed with books, pictures, and an assortment of porcelain Buddha statues.

"I trust you have toilet paper," Sarah said, heading for the bathroom.

"What's that?" Frank said with a lilt in his voice.

Sarah groaned. "You better have," she said, passing the open door to his bedroom. She peeked inside. It was bare save for the unmade double bed and a small dresser with no mirror. A small oil lamp sat on one side of the dresser. On the far side of the bedroom was a window that peered out over the back yard.

She opened the bathroom door and was greeted by an eastern style toilet on a concrete floor. An archaic looking showerhead hung on the wall beside it with a flexible water hose hanging down the wall. A bare light bulb with a pull chain hung from the wooden ceiling above a tiny lavatory. An eight by ten wood framed mirror that had seen much use and a roll of toilet paper hung from nails tacked to the wall.

Maybe I should've stayed back with Greg," she mused. But the truth was, she didn't want to be anywhere Frank wasn't right now. She pulled the chain on the light and shut the door, praying there weren't any spiders lurking around to terrorize her.

An hour later, the tiny house was warmed up and the bed stripped and remade. Sarah dug out a couple of blankets and used one as a tablecloth to give some kind of ambience to the stark dining area in front of the fireplace. If nothing else, the window needed some fresh curtains and a nice carpet to cover the splintered and faded surface of the wood plank floor underfoot.

"I'm taking you shopping tomorrow to spruce this place up," she said, sipping a mug of ginger tea at the table. She shot him a smile. "And to get something else in this house to drink besides this damned tea. Don't you ever get tired of it?"

"Don't you ever tire of coffee?" Frank replied.

Sarah shrugged. "Guess you have a point, but still." She paused, thinking about the dinner they shared with the team back at the teahouse. "It was good seeing the guys tonight and they were especially kind to Greg. I didn't expect that."

"You thought they'd ignore him?" Frank said.

"Something like that. But they didn't. I know Greg felt humbled. He's really beating himself up," she said.

Frank looked off toward the window. "No one is infallible up there, and those men know it now. Climbing Everest is much more than a physical endurance test. It strips away your ego and reveals the real person underneath. Attempting a summit reminds us that folks who live in glass houses shouldn't throw stones. It could've happened to any one of them."

Sarah reached across the table and took his hand in hers. The memory of losing all hope when she believed Frank abandoned her son to die flooded her thoughts. She had never felt so empty in her entire life. And then she heard Da-wa say that Frank was going up to get him and her faith was restored. But what price had it exacted from the man sitting in front of her? The one thing God had hammered home to her during those terrible moments was that life was more than just about her needs and wants.

She kneaded his bony fingers and squeezed his hand. "Something happened up there, Frank. Won't you tell me about it?"

He was quiet a long time and she could see him struggling with whatever it was that had happened. Finally, he turned back and eyed her with a pained expression. "I gave up and I'm not proud of it."

"What do you mean?" Sarah said.

Frank shrugged and she saw him swallow. "We were in the snow shelter and I was fighting for every breath. I looked at my oxygen supply and then at the blizzard going on outside. There was no way I could see myself making it down alive, so I turned my bottle off and gave in, thinking maybe whatever I had left might save either your son or John." He pressed his lips together and his body shook. Suddenly tears came to his eyes. "But John wouldn't let me die."

Sarah got up and went around to Frank. Pulling him into her arms, she held him while he wept. Finally, she pulled back and wiped his tears away. "We all need to be saved sometimes. You saved me, do you know that?"

"From what?" Frank said, looking up at her puzzled.

"From myself," Sarah said. "I've been carrying this anger over Steven abandoning me and Greg around for more than twenty years and you took it away by showing me how to live in the moment — most of the time anyways. And you gave me back my son."

"I owed you that," Frank muttered.

"No, you don't understand. Before we came here, Greg and I were at each other's throats half the time. I didn't know him anymore. He was a stranger to me and I'd thought I lost him. I didn't know it was me that was lost. I was too busy telling him what he should and shouldn't be doing. And then he tells me he wants to climb Everest. It was like punching me right in the stomach, and he didn't care. How could he do that, I said to myself. I never knew why he wanted to climb because I was too bent on stopping him.

"But he came and so did I — kicking and screaming. I had no idea God was giving me a chance to find him again. And then I met you and you showed me a world I never knew existed and made me look beyond myself, and because of that, I have my son back." She smiled then and cradled his face in her hands. "Do you have any idea what you mean to me, you dear man? No matter where I am from now on you will always be in my heart."

Frank nodded as his tragic gaze searched her. "And you will always be in mine. I —"

But Sarah put her finger to his lips. "I know, and so do I." She bent down and tenderly kissed him. "Now, I have five days left here, and I don't want to waste one moment thinking about the future or the past. I want to know all about your home here and I want to meet all the people you love and care for. Show me everything. I want to see this land through your eyes."

She pulled him back into her arms and held him fiercely for a long time until at last she drew back and cradled his face in her hands. Gazing at him, she drank in his suffering soul and the haunted years of drifting aimlessly, looking for answers no one could give. Though they were worlds apart, they were the same in so many ways, both afflicted by the same wounds, tortured by the same memories.

She bent forward, softly touching her lips to his, drew back and kissed him again. Felt his hands slide up her back. Her breath caught in her throat. Breaking away, she looked back and held his gaze as she slowly unbuttoned his shirt, revealing his haggard and weather beaten body little by little. Her hands drifted lightly over his chest and moved downward, tugging his shirt tails out then went back up and dragged the garment off his shoulders and let it fall to the floor.

As he stood there in the flickering firelight, fixing his dark gray eyes upon her, she moved around him, trailing a soft caress over his arm. Leaning close she inhaled his sandalwood essence, traced petal soft kisses over his neck and undid the leather thong around his ponytail. As she did so, she heard him draw breath and her body tingled. Closing her eyes, she slid her hands over his back, felt the warmth of his skin radiate up her arms. She was going to love him like no other tonight; take him away from the world to a safe place and give him peace. Softly, she wrapped her arms around him and leaned in, pressing tight to his back and dribbled butterfly kisses over his shoulder. As her hands drifted down him, he reached back and ran his fingers through her hair. A soft murmur left his lips as her hand glided over his abdomen.

He shivered as she explored him and she buried her face in his long, gray hair, while her hand roamed over his chest, down his side and into his open palm. As their fingers intertwined, he brought her hand to his mouth and kissed it, then turned his head searching for her lips.

"Not yet," she whispered into his ear as her hand softly stroked him. Slowly, she dropped to her knees behind him, drawing his pants down over his knees. As he stepped out of them, she planted a kiss on the small of his back and turned him around. "Sit," she said, nudging him back into his chair. She unbuttoned her blouse and tossed it to the side then bent forward and sprinkled tiny kisses up his thighs as his hands dallied in her hair. Looking up at him, she held his languorous gaze for a breathtaking moment. Everything was for him tonight and there would be no part of him left untouched or unloved. Locking her eyes onto him with an unbreakable bond, she reached up and took his hands in hers then removed her pants and straddled him on the chair. As he slid into her, she kissed him passionately while the crackling pine scented fire flickered behind them. She had always heard about the feeling of 'one beating heart', but until tonight she had never believed in it. But now, she knew it was true. She looked down at him, felt the eternal bond of two lost souls finding each other solidify. She just never believed it would ever happen, especially not here, the last place in the world she ever wanted to be in; the land of Everest.

Chapter 29

The following morning, they woke late and enjoyed a quiet breakfast together before heading out down to the school. As Sarah strolled leisurely beside Frank, hand-in-hand along the shaded lanes that were hemmed in by fieldstone fences, she thought about the night before. Even now, she could feel the intensity of loving him flow through her veins. She smiled as the remembered tucking Frank into bed and lying beside him.

Frank cleared his throat. "What's funny?"

"Nothing," she said. "Just thinking. The village is busy this morning."

"Yes, it is. Many of them I've known for years, some of them since I arrived here in Khum Jung."

Sarah saw an old woman waving to Frank as they approached. "Who's she?" she said taking in the short and very round woman.

"That is Nuri," Frank replied. "Come, I'll introduce you." He led her over to the old Sherpa woman, whose bright inquisitive eyes were pinned on Sarah and Frank's interlocked hands. After looking Sarah up and down she poked Frank in the arm and said something that made him laugh.

Frank turned to Sarah and said, "She thinks you're a bit young for me. Anyway," he turned to Nuri and said something in Lhasa, then turned back to Sarah. "Sarah, Nuri."

The woman bowed politely and said something more back to Frank. Frank said, "She wants to know if you made it to the summit."

Sarah smiled and gave Frank a knowing glance. "Tell her I did. You can also let her know I'm just helping an old man along."

Frank cocked his brow and translated back to the old woman, which brought about a toothy smile. They spoke a bit longer in Lhasa until at last Frank reached out and took the woman's hand in his and gave it a gentle squeeze. It was the first time Sarah had seen Frank touch one of the Sherpa women in all the time she had been with him.

As the woman and Frank parted company, Sarah said, "She must be someone special."

"She is," Frank said, eyeing her sidelong. "She's Pasang's mother."

Sarah glanced over her shoulder at Nuri, who had gone back to sweeping off her flagstone porch and then back to Frank. She didn't know what to say, so she buttoned her lips and took his hand. A hundred or so feet ahead, the lane divided. They bore to the left, following the serpentine route through the congested maze of homesteads until at last they came out next to the teahouse where her son bunked with the rest of the team. Frank stopped and shot a knowing glance back toward the front entry.

"He's welcome to join us on the tour if he wants," Frank said.

Sarah thought about it a moment, and just as she was about to answer, Greg came out with Sully, Lanzo, and the rest of the team trailing behind.

"Hey," Greg said.

"Hey, yourself," Sarah replied, going up and giving him a hug. After they all exchanged morning greetings, she said, "We were just heading over to the school. Frank's going to show me around. You guys interested in joining us?"

"Love to, but we have other plans," Greg said. "See you tonight for the farewell party, though."

Sarah patted his shoulder and as she stood back, sensed her son and the boys were planning something. What it was, she had no idea, but if Toby and Jakob were involved, it was bound to involve copious amounts of beer. She eyed the two Austrians and said to them, "Don't you get him in trouble."

"Wouldn't dream of it," Toby said with a leering grin.

Sarah shook her head, and waving them good-bye, turned and joined back up with Frank. As they walked across the dirt field to the campus' front gate, she said, "They're up to no good, you know that, right?"

"Oh, absolutely," Frank replied. "But I have a few surprises of my own."

"Oh, really? What, pray tell?"

"Ahhh, now they wouldn't be surprises if I told you," Frank said, and winked.

"You're impossible."

"And you ask too many questions," Frank volleyed back as they entered in under the painted blue and white wooden banner leading to the campus grounds.

Twenty minutes later, Sarah was sitting in the back of an eighth grade class-room listening to the kids give their science reports. As she listened to them reading their papers, a boy sitting kitty-corner from her turned and beamed back a broad smile. For a moment the boy and she were locked in a search-ing gaze, until at last, the teacher in the front of the room spoke up and drew his attention away from her. Suddenly, Sarah felt something click inside her and she slipped back to the days when she stood in front of twenty-something students waiting to be challenged. She missed that time more than she knew, and though there had been bad days, the good times always outweighed them. She nibbled her lip as she considered a thought that had just popped into her head. It would mean a change of lifestyle when she returned home, but the bottom line would be happiness in doing something she wanted to do, instead of doing what everyone else wanted. She sat with that a moment with Frank at her side. Glancing over at him, she remembered what he said back in Namche about bringing John on board and giving up climbing to spend more time doing his charity work. Why not give up her position to go back into the classroom as well?

The next stop on the tour was the addition. Frank showed her around the project and introduced her to the masons and carpenters who were busy putting the building together. The addition was a simple rectangular building that would house two new classrooms and a small shared toilet room.

"Most of it's finished," he said, "with the exception of a bit of roofing, throw-ing in a couple lavatories and adding a front entrance stair." Punch list items, he called them. Then, last of all, he took her to the main high school to meet the schoolmaster who was a fortyish, square jawed man with dark laughing eyes and a broad white smile. His name was Sonam and his greeting was warm and enthusiastic, which grew in intensity once he found out she was an educator back in the States.

She could see Frank out of the corner of her eye watching Sonam ply her with questions. A minute later, she started to get the feeling she was being interviewed. If she didn't know better, she would have thought Frank put the Sherpa up to it. But Frank had never left her side since they arrived in Khum Jung. Besides, Frank wasn't the type to go around trying to manipulate things. Finally, Frank came to her rescue and the two of them headed into the market place. He had some items to pick up for the evening as well.

* * *

Sarah put on a cream colored silk blouse that Frank called a *raatuk* and stood back to look at herself in the tiny mirror she'd stolen off the bathroom wall and had set on his dresser. On the bed, lay a full length green dyed woolen dress called a *tongkok*. Frank had picked it out for her along with the blouse during their shopping expedition in the village. Being the stinker that he was, he had insisted on paying for it. *Well, you might have won the battle, Mountain Man, but I will win the day.* She mused on the gift she had gotten him when he was busy taking care of last minute *Party Details* then pulled the dress off the bed and slipped it on. Smoothing the creases running down the side of it, she molded it to her body, then reached for the brown Yak bone necklace on the dresser. She smiled to herself as she clasped it around her neck. *He's trying to turn me into a Sherpa woman. And by the looks of me, he's doing a good job of it. I wonder what the people at the office back home will think when I wear this into work? There's sure to be some raised brows.*

"Are you almost ready?" Frank said coming to the bedroom doorway. He crossed his arms and took her countenance in. "Oh, my!"

"You like?" Sarah said, turning around and giving him the full picture. He smiled as he stood watching her. She quite liked the crisp beige tunic she'd picked out for him. With his hair tied back over the upturned collar it gave him a rustic, earthy appearance.

"Very much," he said, and stepped into the room. "You'll be the star of the party."

Sarah pursed her lips as he put his hands to her waist and pulled her toward him for a kiss. "Behave yourself," she said, wiggling out of his grasp and gently pushing him away. "There'll be time for that when we get home."

"Hmm … yes, I suppose you're right," he said, lingering on her words. "Well, we ought to get going." He made way for her and followed her out of the room.

As he collected his satchel by the front door and ushered her outside, she said, "Oh, look at that moon."

"Yes, we have a full one tonight," Frank said coming to her side.

They studied the amber tinted orb drifting low above the eastern horizon a moment then strode off down the lane toward the teahouse. As they walked, Sarah said, "Will you be coming with us when we drop down to Lukla?"

"Yes. You still think you can manage it?"

"I think so," Sarah said. "The ankle's still a bit tender, but if I take my time and not rush, I should be alright. Besides I have a ride waiting for me when I get down the ridge. Is our flight locked in?"

Frank nodded. "I had Sangye confirm it today. What about your flight to the States?"

"Greg checked with the airline and we're good. We have a red-eye to Hong Kong on Saturday. Leaves at 11:00 PM."

"Make sure you get to the airport three hours in advance," Frank warned. "It's a bit of a hassle getting through all the paperwork and security."

"Will do," Sarah answered. She took his hand and squeezed it. "So, what surprises do you have cooked up for tonight?"

Frank eyed her sidelong. "Haven't we already had this conversation?"

"Can't blame a gal for trying," Sarah said.

"Right," Frank answered as they turned down the lane cutting through the village. When they came to Nuri's house, he stopped. "Wait here."

Sarah watched him push the front gate open and walk up to Nuri's door, wondering what was up. When Nuri answered Frank's knock, Sarah saw that the old woman was wearing in a handsome cream-colored dress he called a chhuba. Frank took a bag from her and carried it as Nuri trudged out onto the lane to join Sarah. The woman offered Sarah a friendly smile as Frank pulled the gate shut behind them.

"Nuri is going to be joining us tonight," Frank announced as they started back off.

Nuri looked at Frank and said something in Lhasa.

Frank said, "She thinks you look very nice." Just then, Nuri added something more and tapped Frank's arm. "Oh, and she thinks you are doing more than just helping an old man along."

Sarah felt herself blush under Nuri's narrow gaze, which quite surprised her. She eyed Frank wistfully, drinking in his shining face and said, "Tell her, that's because I love this old man."

Frank held Sarah in a longing gaze for a moment then spoke at length to Nuri. The old woman listened, and after he was done, reached out and took Sarah's hand and patted it. She turned to Frank and motioned to the bag he was carrying for her. When Frank offered it to her, she reached in and pulled out a long saffron silken scarf.

Holding it in her old mottled hands, she broke into a short speech and waited for Frank to translate. Frank turned to Sarah and said, "She has a gift for you. She says, 'it was supposed to be for later on, but she thinks it would be better for you to have it now.'"

Sarah dipped her head as Nuri placed the ceremonial scarf around her neck and drew it together with a loose knot. Unlike the *khata* the men had received during the *Puja* ceremony, this one had been embroidered on the ends with green and red Lhasan script, which she recognized as the 'Om mani padme hum' mantra.

Sarah bowed to the old matriarch. "Dhan'yavāda."

Nuri bowed back. They all started back off then and ten minutes later came to the teahouse just as the stars started to prick the darkened skies. Inside, they were met by Da-wa and Sangye. They followed the Sherpas into the large dining area where the team all sat at tables that were lined up around the perimeter of the room. When the men saw them, they stopped chatting with each other and got up to greet them.

Carlo was first to reach out and he gave her a hug. The Italian had a bristled gray beard on his round, luminous face. "You look absolutely radiant tonight," the man said, pulling back.

"And you are looking very dapper in that beard," Sarah said. She turned then to see Greg standing beside Lanzo and Sully.

Greg stepped up and gazed at her with wonder. He took in her dress and *khata* then wrapped his arms around her. As he held her tight, he whispered in her ear, "You look beautiful, Mom."

Sarah melted into him and whispered back, "I love you." She let go of him and went back to greeting the rest of the men. Then to her delight and surprise, Bob and Tembe came in with the old lama, who was dressed in his red robes.

She gave the medic a hug and bowed to Tembe, then greeted Tashi. The lama's shining face broke into a broad smile. "Namaste, Sarah. Have you been enjoying your time in Khum Jung?"

"Very much, thank you. I love this village. It's like an old shoe." When the lama looked at her quizzically, she added, "Comfortable."

"Ahhh … yes, comfortable. I hope you are hungry," he said, nodding toward a long table that was set up to one side. On it, were several covered dishes and baskets of *roti* and another bread she had no name for.

Frank joined her and bowed to Tashi. "Namaste, Master. I trust your trip back from Base Camp went well."

"Oh, yes. It was good to get out of the Monastery and see the Mountain again. How you feel?"

"Much better, thank you," Frank replied.

Just then, the host came out and announced it was time to eat. Everybody drifted back to their tables. Sarah followed Frank, Bob, Nuri, and Tashi to a table near the front of the room. As she took her seat, she scanned the room that was decorated with rice paper paintings of the surrounding Sagarmatha landscapes. On the windowsills were several colorful Buddha statues alongside porcelain vases of white and red rhododendron flowers. A large banner hung on the far wall ahead with the words, 'Khum Jung Expeditions, 2013' that was strung across a photo of Everest in the background. Below the words were small inset photos of the team members.

Da-wa went to the center of the room. "Namaste. Tonight we feast and celebrate. Chomolungma has been merciful to us this year and has brought us all back home. First, I want to thank our kind host; Sherpa Harka, his wife, Lhakpa, and daughter, Lhamu for opening up their home to us." Da-wa waited as the hosts joined him. "They have prepared some traditional dishes for you tonight, which I hope you will like."

Everyone clapped.

"Before we begin," Da-wa said, "I have gift for Frank from whole team." The Sherpa reached into his back pocket and pulled out an envelope. "This is for your charity work to the Khum Jung School." He walked up to their table and gave it to Frank. Sarah watched Frank as he took the envelope and saw him swallow hard.

"I don't know what to say," Frank said, standing up. He set the envelope down on the table and went around the table to the Sherpa and embraced the man. To the team he said, "You have all touched me deeply. What you have given here means so much to the people I call my family. I also want to say, that everyone here has summited a mountain in the last few weeks. Climbing any mountain, whether it's Chomolungma or Annapurna, is about stretching ourselves, not to see what we are made of, but to know what we are capable of. So, I say to you; 'Walk away from this experience knowing you have glimpsed but a tip of what you are all capable of'. I am proud to have climbed with all of you."

Sarah felt her throat tighten as Frank came back and took his seat next to her. She reached out and put her hand over his bony fingers and felt the torrent of emotions that were brimming inside him. "That was beautiful."

He turned to her and as he did so, she saw glassy eyes. "I meant every word of it."

"I know," Sarah answered, as the sound of the covers being taken off the dishes clattered in the background.

Da-wa said, "I don't know about you all, but I'm hungry!"

Everyone rose and got in line, helping themselves to the prepared food.

After they returned to the table, Frank said something to Sangye and a moment later the Sherpa returned with a mug and set in front of Sarah. She stared at the hot dark liquid in the mug. It smelled like coffee and looked like coffee, but was it coffee? She glanced at Frank, who smiled then shoveled a forkful of rice into his mouth.

"Don't mess with me, Mountain Man. Is this what I think it is?"

Frank winked. "Try it and find out."

Sarah put the mug to her lips and took a sip. *Oh my God. It is coffee.* "Have you been holding out on me?"

"Nope. Bob brought some on his way up."

Sarah stared down the table at Bob, who had just sat down. "Anything else you brought up that you'd care to share with me?"

Bob grinned. "Nope. Frank radioed down shortly before I left Kathmandu. Told me to bring a couple cans up for a coffee deprived client. How is it?"

"Wonderful," Sarah answered although it was a far cry from what she was used to. She dug into her dinner as the noisy chatter died to quiet conversations between the dinner guests. As she ate, it suddenly occurred to her that she was next to a man who could perform a wedding and also that she was sitting at a head table next to a man she loved along with a group of men that included her son. If that wasn't enough, there was a pile of gifts that were set on a table in the far corner of the room. Add a cake, which she hadn't seen yet and you had the makings of a — . She set her fork down, suspicious of what Frank's surprise might be and leaning toward him, said, "Feels like a wedding reception in here."

"Really?"

"Yeah. Anything I need to know about?"

"Not that I can think of."

"Hmm …" *But it wouldn't be possible anyway. Besides, we're at dinner. That happens afterward and we'd have to have gotten a license and — wait a minute! We're not in the States! How do I know how they do things here? He wouldn't, would he?* "Just checking."

Twenty minutes later, the dinner plates were all removed and Frank was standing in the middle of the room with his satchel and several large canvas bags by his feet. He cleared his throat and took a drink of water. "Okay folks, my favorite part of the evening is here. This is where I get the chance to give back a little to each of you for spending time here on the mountain with me. First of all, I have certificates of your amazing accomplishments that have been logged into the record books here for you."

He opened his satchel, and took them out. As the men came up to receive them, he reached down into the canvas bags and gave them each a Sherpa jacket with a Khum Jung Mountaineers logo stitched onto the upper left side. Then he called Da-wa up. As he dug out a silky brown fox fur hat, he said, "For you, my dear friend, a new *Washa* to keep those ears from freezing. Tembe, come on over here. For you I have a dozen new aprons and a nice shiny *kyetig* to hold them onto that shrinking waistline of yours."

Tembe walked up to Frank, eyed his withered body over pretty good, and said, "Maybe I give back to you … hmmm? You look like you need *kyetig* more than me." Which brought a raucous laughter all around the room.

Frank held the belt up, and with a measuring gaze at it, said, "It's a bit large for me, I think." Another round of laughter followed. Finally, he called San-gye up. "And to my trusted all around friend and organizer," Frank said, putting his arm around the Sherpa's shoulder, "A top of the line iPod to hold all that music you have."

Sangye smiled and as he ogled it, bowed. "Speaking of music, we dance now," Sangye said. He set the iPod on the table and ran over to get the drums that were in the corner of the room. A moment later, he was hitting a lively beat that got the Sherpas' feet moving.

Sarah sat clapping as Frank, Da-wa, and Tembe hopped around the room to the rhythm of the drum. As mugs of millet beer went around, someone dug out an old cassette player and threw a tape in adding what sounded like guitars and flutes to the festive dance, and not long after, everyone was up and moving along with them. As for Sarah, she sat back swaying in her chair, wanting to join them as the festivities carried into the night.

When things began to die down, Tashi got up and came to her. "So, it is time for me to go and for us to part company at long last," Tashi said. "I wish you well. You have been more a teacher to Frank than I have in all these years I've known him. You, Sarah, were the lesson Frank needed that I could never give."

"And he was mine."

"Ah, so right," Tashi said, eyeing her pointedly. "I think sometime we will meet again."

Sarah gazed back at the old wizened lama and smiled. "I think you're right."

Tashi dipped his head slightly. "Namaste." Then he turned and quietly shuffled out the front door without anyone noticing but her.

* * *

That night in bed, Sarah asked Frank to just hold her. It would be the last time they would share a bed together and she wanted to remember it as a night of sharing stories before the wings of flight took her home eight thousand miles away. She breathed in the man lying by her side, committing his musky scent to memory, listened to every word he uttered, imprinting his voice on her heart. But more than that was what she learned from Sangye tonight when she asked the Sherpa about the name, 'Ang Tar-chin', that she'd heard the children call Frank at the school yesterday. *Beloved Giver.* She smiled. That was who Frank was, and that was what had drawn her to him, and what would keep him in her thoughts as she went forward with her life.

Tomorrow, she and her son, Greg, would travel to Namche with Frank. Once down the steep sloping ridge into the Dudh Kosi River gorge, they would meet up with a Sherpa who would take them by horseback the rest of the way to Lukla. The rest of the team would follow the next day with Da-wa leading. As Sarah peered out the window by the bedside toward the obsidian sky beyond, she thought of all that had happened and how her life had been shaken and turned upside down by this man and the people and land that he loved. Yes, she was going back home, but instead of returning to an uncertain life and continuing to fight against things she couldn't control, she could now let go and allow the things that made her happy enter into her world. And she had gotten her son back.

She thought of the fight Greg and she had had on the plane coming into Kathmandu. *Neither one of us were listening to each other, were we, Greg? How far we've come. You're no longer distant and I'm no longer trying to organize your life. Tashi was right. My fears were stealing away precious moments. I don't know if I can overcome all of them, but now, at least I'm aware of the insanity of worrying about things I can't control.*

Yes, someday I'm coming back, Frank. I don't know when it'll be. I have to get my life in order first, take care of me for a while, do the things I want to do, see some more of the world. I know you can understand that. Soon as I get back home, I'm writing a letter of resignation to the Board of Education and I'm getting back in the classroom with the kids where I belong. That's where I'm happiest. That's where I need to be; not pushing papers.

Sarah closed her eyes feeling more alive than she had in years. She nuzzled her head into Frank's shoulder. Miles away, the ground rumbled under her tiny prayer tower. The rocks she had carefully stacked trembled then suddenly they toppled down onto the deserted moraine.

Bibliography

This novel was conceived whilst I was in the Sagarmatha National Park in Nepal on my way to the Everest Base Camp, and much of the land and the people that I saw and experienced are expressed within this novel. But there is much more to this beautiful land and its people that can be conveyed in so short a writing. Nepal is a land rich in culture and steeped in colorful history. In this land you will discover a world unlike any place on the planet.

While the Himalayas, with their abundance of eight thousand-meter peaks dominate the mind, there is much more that hides at the feet before their steppes. Kathmandu is a vibrant city dating back over two thousand years and it is populated with all manner of shrines and temples. It is not unusual to see cattle walking down its narrow city streets among the rickshaws, motor-bikes, and compact cars. Hindu and Buddhist festivals occur almost daily in some part of the city.

Chitwan National Park — *Heart of the Jungle* — used to be a favorite hunting ground for Nepal's ruling class during the cool winter seasons. Until the 1950s, the journey from Kathmandu to Nepal's south could only be reached by foot and took several weeks. However, that all changed shortly after 1950. Seventy percent of Chitwan's forest and grasslands that extended over more than 2,600 square kilometers was cleared and the population of about 800 was reduced to just 95. The dramatic decline of the rhino population and the extent of poaching prompted the government to institute the *Gaida Gasti* — a rhino reconnaissance patrol of 130 armed men and a network of guard posts all over Chitwan. The park has made a comeback thanks in part to tourism dollars and stewardship.

Pokhara lies on an important old trading route between China and India. In the 17th century it was part of the Kingdom of Kaski, which was one of the Chaubise Rajya (24 Kingdoms of Nepal) ruled by a branch of the Shah Dynasty. ˆ+ˆ+ Many of the hills around Pokhara still have medieval ruins from this time. In 1786 Pokhara was added into the kingdom. It had by then become an important trading place on the routes from Kathmandu to Jumla and from India to Tibet.

From 1959 to 1962 approximately 300,000 exiles entered Nepal from neighboring Tibet following its annexation by China. Approximately 2500 Tibetans cross the border into Nepal each year, ˆ+ˆ+ many of whom arrive in Pokhara; typically as a transit to Tibetan exile communities in India. About 50,000 - 60,000 Tibetan exiles reside in Nepal. Tibetan settlements in Pokhara are well built, each with a Buddhist monastery with its particular architecture. Until the end of the 1960s the town was only accessible by foot and it was considered even more a mystical place than Kathmandu.

These locations I've listed above are but two of the many fabulous places in this wondrous country. For further reading, I've compiled a list of websites and books below that encompass mountaineering, people and historical locations. Enjoy!

Mountaineering Sites
http://www.mounteverest.net/expguide/dream.htm
http://www.climb8850.com/Everest_South_Col_Route.html
http://www.eliasaikaly.com/2013/05/into-the-death-zone/
http://www.alpineascents.com/everest-faq.asp

The Tibetan Sherpa People
Sherpa Culure:
http://www.sherpakyidug.org/sherpa/sherpa_names.asp
Sherpa people on the mountain:
http://www.learnnc.org/lp/editions/mount-everest/5259

The Land
Sacred Sites:
http://www.chriswalkeronline.com/files/sacred-sites-brochure.pdf
Chitwan National Park: http://chitwannationalpark.net/
Lumbini: http://whc.unesco.org/en/list/666

Bhakatpur: http://www.go2kathmandu.com/plaza/bhaktapur.htm
Other Various Locations: http://www.himalayasguide.com/changu-narayana-temple.php

Further Reading:
Into Thin Air *by John Krakauer*
Body and Emotion *by Robert R. Desjarlais*
Paradise Lost *by Ali Riaz and Subho Basu*
A History of Nepal *by John Whelpton*

And Finally:
For those who might be interested in considering a trek to Everest Base Camp, may I suggest ***Active Adventures*** out of New Zealand? They were fabulous — well organized and attentive to the trekker's needs. You can find them at: http://activeadventures.com/himalayas

Loving Neil

Chapter 1

December 5, 1979 —

A blast of frigid air ripped through the parking lot whipping Janet's long, dark hair. She gripped the front of her coat, pulled it tight around her, and ran for the entry door of the banquet hall. Shaking her head to sluff the snow out of her hair, she opened the door and stepped inside to the warmth of the lobby. There, she removed her gloves, shoved them in her pockets and made her way through the lounge to the reception hall.

She was an hour late and most of the one hundred or so guests for her brother's wedding were already there. Her gaze swept over the sea of white linen-covered tables, and searched for her father. When she saw him, she took a deep breath and headed in his direction.

"Where've you been?" he said, getting up to greet her. He pulled her into a practiced hug as if they saw each other every day. But the fact was, he hadn't seen her in over six months.

"Traffic," she said, not entirely lying. She flashed a smile toward his wife, Christine, who was barely older than she was. You certainly like 'em young, Dad. To Christine, she said, "Sorry I missed you at church. Love the gown." She took in Christine's long, black, strapless formal and the necklace of gold winking at her, wondering how much they set her father back.

"Thanks. How've you been?" Christine replied.

"Not bad. Nice place."

"Nothing but the best for your brother," her father piped up. He introduced her around. "This is John and Sarah Barrett, friends of Christine's. They're loaning their beachfront house to Craig for his honeymoon. Isn't that nice of them?"

"Yes, very," Janet said.

"So, you're Craig's sister! The picture on your father's mantel doesn't do you justice," Sarah said.

Janet took the compliment in stride, trying to figure out just what picture that might be. Hopefully, it wasn't her senior high portrait, which she hated.

"My daughter here is a free lance photographer for one of those nature magazines out west," Janet's father said. "Is that what they call them these days?"

"Close enough, Dad."

"Sounds exciting," Sarah said. "I bet you travel a lot."

"Not really. Most of what I do is within a couple days."

"Ah, there's my boy," Janet's father said, cutting in. His graveled voice stormed across the room. "Hey, Craig, come over here and tell your sister about that new job of yours." To Janet, he winked and said, "Got him hooked up with a firm down in West Palm Beach."

Craig looked up from talking with the D.J. and started for them. "Hey, Janny," he said, giving her a brotherly hug. "Damned weather. Sorry we missed you at the church. How was the flight?"

"It was."

"Yeah, I know, shitty," Craig said. "But you're here and that's all that counts."

"So, Dad tells me you have a new job."

"Yeah, and I'm gonna need it 'cause Belinda wants a boatload of kids. Say look, I gotta get back to her. Catch ya later?"

Janet gave him the thumbs-up.

The snow continued to fall throughout dinner, and with each glance out the window, Janet grew more wary of the drive back to her hotel. She nibbled at her dessert as the chatter flowed around the table, much of it about people she didn't know — high society friends of Christine's and their various exploits.

As she pulled her black sweater cape off the back of her chair and wrapped it around her shoulders, her father leaned toward her, and said, "So, how's things with June's estate?"

"It's in probate right now. Shouldn't be much longer, next month maybe," Janet said.

"Any idea what you're going to do with another house and a rental cottage?"

"I haven't thought about it, to tell you the truth."

Her father finished the last of his cake and wiped his mouth with a napkin. "Well, you'd better start. The sooner you get them on the market, the better."

Janet frowned. "I'm not sure I want to sell."

"Well, what are you gonna do with all that property?" her father asked, eying her pointedly.

Janet didn't want to talk about it. It had only been five months since her beloved aunt passed away, and she missed her terribly. "Dad, can we change the subject please?"

"Yeah, sure." He was quiet a moment then nodded toward the window. "Wow, it's coming down pretty hard out there. You're welcome to crash at our place."

"Thanks, but no."

Now it was his turn to frown. "What is it with you, Janny? Do you hate Christine that much?"

Janet set her fork down. "I don't hate her, Dad. I just don't like everything I do being judged."

"Judged?"

"Yes." Janet sighed. "I'm sorry, but it's the way she makes me feel."

"I see." He turned and started for the bar.

Janet rose, collected her purse and followed him. When she caught up next to him, she said, "Dad, I love you, you know that, right?"

Her father shot her a tight smile. "Right. Don't worry about it, Skeeter, it's okay." He glanced toward the windows. "You'd better get a move on. Don't forget to say good-bye to your brother."

Why does it always end like this? Though, in truth, she knew the reason. It was her always slapping away his helping hand. But then, it was a little late for his helping hand. Where was he when she needed him? "Yeah, right. I'll call you later. Maybe we can do something tomorrow."

"Sure," he said. "Sounds like a plan."

Janet looked off, biting back the urge to say, 'forget it', then reached up and pecked him on the cheek. "I'm gonna go find Craig. Love you."

He studied her a moment, as if he were trying to decide whether she meant it, then nodded. "Me, too."

Deep ruts scarring the plowed snow-packed highway set Janet's nerves on end. The car skated back and forth, drifting dangerously close to the snow packed shoulder of the road. She backed the wipers off as the exit ramp from I-80 neared. On it was a semi moving at a fair clip. As it merged onto county route 82, she moved into the passing lane.

"Just what I need," she growled. Her heart raced as she braced her hand on the wheel. The truck sprayed slush at her windshield. The road suddenly disappeared. Thunk! The wheel jerked loose in her hand and the car dove, knifing into the darkness until it jolted to a halt.

Janet sat shaking for several minutes. Her throat burned, and the taste of bile swam in her mouth. She swallowed, forced it down and gulped a deep breath. The sound of her heart thumped in her ears. Her head ached. Am I Okay? Gingerly, she moved her legs and then her arms. Nothing hurt. That was good. She pulled the key out of the ignition. Sat back. Tried to make sense of what had just happened.

Truck — slush — windshield — can't see — steering wheel — ouch. Her wrist. It hurt. She rubbed it. The car? Shit! Was there a huge gash on the front end? A tire turned under like a broken ankle? She brought her hands to her head. Kneaded her aching neck.

She looked out the driver's side window. Snow was up to the rear-view mirror. Getting out that way was impossible. She crawled across to the passenger side and peered out, put her shoulder to the door and pushed it open.

Outside, the wind whipped across the median, and icy grit slapped her face. She burrowed her head into the lapel of her coat and trudged through the knee-deep snow. Think, Janet, think. But the only thing that came to mind was to walk. But to where?

She ground her hands into her pockets and kicked at a chunk of hard packed snow. Tears collected in her eyes and slipped over her cheeks. "What am I gonna do? I'm so screwed," she muttered, plopping back against the rear of the car.

Just then, a pair of bright headlights came over the crest of the road. As they headed toward her, she stepped away from her car. A moment later, a large pickup slowed down and pulled up behind her. The driver's side window slid down.

"You okay?" said a voice from inside.

She nodded as the door opened and a man got out. He was big, towering over her. In the dark of night, he looked like a monster out of a B-Budget movie. She backed up keeping her distance.

He put up his hand. "It's okay. I'm here to help. You look like you're freezing. Why don't you get in my truck while I call a wrecker?"

"No, I'm okay, really."

He trudged closer and she saw a ruddy hard-bitten face. Myterious, dark eyes stared back. A bushy mustache spilled out under a broad nose. A mop of short, curly hair tickled his ears. Add a beard and a red suit and she could easily imagine him being Santa Claus. But he wasn't Santa Claus, and he was there with her on a dark road in the middle of the night. There was nothing between them except the wind and her long distance running legs, which were one step away from being jelly.

"Alright," he said. "At least let me get you a blanket." He went back to his truck and brought her a thick woolen wrap reeking of smoke. He handed it to her with an outstretched hand. "So what happened?"

"I was run off the road by a semi," she said, pulling the blanket around her shoulders.

The man shook his head. "Damn cowboys." He eyed her then the car, then back at her again. "You sure you're alright?"

"Yeah, I'm okay." She backed up a step and turned around, sizing up the damage to her car. It didn't look like there were any dents or creases. It was just buried. If I could just get it out, no one would ever have to know. But doing it will need his help. That means … She chewed her lip. "You think we could pull it out of there?"

"The car?"

"Yeah."

"Not without chains."

"You wouldn't happen to have any would you?"

The man's brow wrinkled. "I do, but I don't know. You're buried in there pretty good. I think it's best to call a wrecker."

"'Cept it's a rental," Janet said.

He drummed his fingers on the hood of his truck. At last, he said, "We can try it, but I can't guarantee anything." He waded out into the snowy median and surveyed the car. After a once around, he came back. "I really think it's better to call a wrecker. I could end up doing more harm than good."

She looked up at the blackened sky and closed her eyes.

After a relenting sigh, she heard him say, "Okay, you go around and climb in while I see what I can do." He stepped over to the back of his truck as she got in her rental, and two minutes later she heard him pawing around underneath her car. It seemed like he was under there forever before he finally knocked on her window.

She rolled it down.

"Okay," he said. "When you hear me hit the horn, you give her the gas, alright? Don't stop until you feel the wheels grip the road."

She nodded and watched him trudge back through the snow. When she heard the horn honk and felt a jerk from behind, she stepped on the pedal, pushing it to the floor. The car lurched backward as the tires spun, screaming into the night.

Suddenly, the tension between the two vehicles eased. The pickup's lights flashed, and shortly afterward he was at her window again. "We made a little headway, but I just don't have enough traction. One last time and if you're not out, we call a wrecker."

She nodded. Please, please. Just once, give me a break. The truck's horn honked, and her foot slammed on the accelerator. The car shimmied and moved back inch-by-inch. She gripped the wheel, as if doing so would make the car try harder. Don't stop, please don't stop! The acrid smell of burning rubber drifted through the open window as the rear of the car shifted and came to a grinding halt.

The man got out of his truck and trudged back to her window. "You're half way out," he said, "but that's as far as you're gonna get."

"Just one more time … please?" she muttered.

He wiped his brow with the back of his hand. "Okay, one last time."

He grabbed his shovel, dug more snow out around her tires and got back into his truck. The horn honked, and a moment later Janet's rental car lurched back, breaking free of the deep snow. Relieved, she sighed and got out as the man pulled his tow chain free.

"I don't know how to thank you," she said.

"Forget it. I have a daughter your age. I'd hope someone would do the same for her if she were in your shoes." He bent down and started clearing her snow-packed wheel wells. "You live around here?"

"I'm heading into the city."

"Alright. When I'm through, I'll follow you in. Make sure you get where you're going."

"That's alright, I'll be fine." She dug into her purse. Pulled out a ten-dollar bill. "Here."

He looked up and frowned. "Put it away."

Great, now I've insulted him. "Are you sure?"

"Positive." He stood up and dusted the snow off his jeans.

"Thanks. I'm Janet."

He put his shovel in the back of his truck. "Neil, Neil Porter."

About the Author

Ron is a practicing architect living in upstate New York. An avid hiker and photographer, he has traveled to Nepal, New Zealand and throughout the United States, Alaska and Hawaii collecting ideas for character driven stories of romance and adventure. Look for Beyond the Veil, situated in the dense rainforest of the South American Amazon Basin, and Losing Neil, situated on the beautiful Oregon coast, both out on Amazon for Kindle, and on Barnes and Noble for Nook.

Connect with Ron via Facebook at R.J. Bagliere or on the World Wide Web at: www.rjbagliere.com

Look for more exciting books soon from the fabulous author.

If you would like to be notified by email when new books are released from Next Chapter Publishing by this author or other authors, send an email to https://www.nextchapter.pub/ with SUBSCRIBE in the subject line.

Lightning Source UK Ltd.
Milton Keynes UK
UKHW042010250121
377669UK00009B/831/J